KRESLEY COLE

THE PRICE
of
PLEASURE

POCKET BOOKS

New York   London   Toronto   Sydney

This book is a work of fiction. Names, characters, places and incidents are products of the author's imagination or are used fictitiously. Any resemblance to actual events or locales or persons, living or dead, is entirely coincidental.

An *Original* Publication of POCKET BOOKS

POCKET BOOKS, a division of Simon & Schuster, Inc.
1230 Avenue of the Americas, New York, NY 10020

ISBN -13: 978-0-7434-6650-9
ISBN -10:   0-7434-6650-0

First Pocket Books printing July 2004

10 9 8 7 6 5

POCKET and colophon are registered trademarks of
Simon & Schuster, Inc.

Cover illustration by Franco Accornero

Manufactured in the United States of America

For information regarding special discounts for bulk purchases,
please contact Simon & Schuster Special Sales at 1-800-456-6798
or business@simonandschuster.com.

To Mom & Dad—
Dad for encouraging me to be a writer,
and Mom for showing me how.

Acknowledgments

My heartfelt thanks go out to three wonderful friends and authors. To Beth Kendrick, another newly published writer: Thank you for stumbling along the road to publication with me and for letting me know I'm not the only clueless one out there! To Caroline Carson: Many, many thanks for your midnight line edit. You'll sell your book by the time this one comes out, so I'll be able to return the favor in kind. And to Sally Fairchild: Thank you so much for all your help. Because of you, I stumble a lot less.

Every man has his secret sorrows, which the world knows not; and oftentimes we call a man cold when he is only sad.

—Henry Wadsworth Longfellow

In nature there are neither rewards nor punishments; there are consequences.

—Robert Green Ingersoll

Prologue

A journal by Victoria Anne Dearbourne, 1850

January 17

Today is the third day of our time here. Mother, Miss Scott, and I survived the wreck of the *Serendipity* and drifted in a leaky lifeboat to a deserted isle somewhere in south Oceania. Becalmed for weeks, we'd been unable to escape the approaching typhoon season. Mother said it was as though we'd been held in place for the storm.

When the timbers began to break, the sailors scurried—like rats, all of them—to abandon the ship and every one of us. One crashed into Mother—he didn't even hesitate when she fell into the lifeboat from the height of the deck. Her back was separated and her arm was shattered as well. But she is strong, and I am convinced if we find help, she will recover.

We have not yet found Father. I looked up through the rain and foam and spied him atop the deck, a child in his arms. With the next crack of lightning, the deck was gone. Is it wrong for me to wish he'd left the children screaming down below and escaped? The vile crew did. It doesn't matter what I wish—he never would have left them.

It was this morning that we received a windfall of supplies from the sea. Mother whispered to me that it is the hand of Fate that brought us these gifts, though Miss Scott says it's only a repeating current—the same that brought us here (Mother has said that though Camellia Scott is only in her twenties, she is very wise, and so I don't know which version I wish to accept).

Miss Scott and I hauled ashore several trunks, a cask of much needed water, a paddle, and other various goods. Among the trunks, we found the captain's footlocker, and inside was an empty log and a bottle of ink. Miss Scott bade me record our time here.

She probably believes if I am occupied so, I won't be able to see the misery that has befallen us. But I have, and even as I cared for Mother and wrote, I still saw the two bodies that floated in with our bounty. The sea had done awful, awful things to them.

I know Miss Scott dragged them to the edge of the jungle and buried them, because I see the tracks in the sand and her palms blistered from the paddle handle. Miss Scott has only been with us for a short time, and I know she wants to spare us any harshness. But I hope she would tell me if one of the deceased was Father.

January 18

Last night was the first night Mother cried. She tried to be strong, but the pain was too great. Rain began to drizzle and the wind gusted. Miss Scott found flints in the lifeboat and tried time after time to light a fire. It was hopeless, but I think it took her mind from the situation. By the time she'd given up and fallen asleep where she knelt, her hands were sliced and ragged.

Mother told me I must help Miss Scott because "she is so very young for such an important charge."

January 19

I see how much I've written and worry that one log will not be enough, but Miss Scott predicted we will be rescued well before I run out of paper.

Later in the day, she found a map in one of the trunks and tried to determine our location, sending me to look for firewood on the beach despite the fact that we have no fire. When I returned, both she and Mother seemed resigned to staying here for some time. We must be far away from civilization. Though Miss Scott and I beg her, Mother has stopped taking her share of what little water we have left.

January 20

Last night I dreamt of Father, of him laughing with Mother and me, of him patiently teaching me to fish or tie knots. Father's laugh is wonderful, hearty because of his barrel chest, and he's quick to it. He loves Mother so much he looks to burst with it. With each new land we explored, the two would search for creatures, some little beastie never seen before. He always marveled when Mother sketched its exact image, though she'd done it again and again for the articles they published. Then he'd set down her drawing and twirl her around, grab me up under his arm, and proclaim that the three of us were the best team in this hemisphere, at least. And then Miss Scott joined us too, to teach me deportment and sums, and to become Mother's boon companion. Everything had seemed so perfect.

Luckily, I rose before Mother and Miss Scott because I woke up crying miserably. I dried my eyes, but all throughout the day when I thought of him, I felt just on the verge of tears, my lip trembling and face turning hot, just like the babies I played with on the ship.

Both Miss Scott and Mother tell me each day to be brave, but today they seemed even more insistent. Yet in the afternoon, Mother woke to find me with my head in my hands crying like a little child though I am thirteen!

I told her I didn't know if I was strong enough to do everything that needed to be done on the island. I know we need to build a shelter. I try to remember everything I've learned from our travels, but she and Papa always did the hardest things while I played with whatever children we came upon.

Mother told me that I am indeed strong enough to survive here. She said, "Remember, Tori, diamonds are born of pressure."

January 21
The deep cuts on Miss Scott's hands are not healing and are so swollen she can't close her fingers. I know how dangerous this is in this climate. I did not know I could worry even more than I had been. There's still no sign of Father, but I have to believe he survived and is even now standing on the bow of some grand ship (bigger than that hateful *Serendipity*) searching for us.

January 22

I am always dreaming about food and water now that we have so little of both. It drives me to think of ways to get them. Miss Scott wants to go inland to search for a spring or some fruit but fears leaving us alone on the beach or taking me with her into that dark jungle. The sounds at night tell us it's packed with creatures that we mightn't want to see.

This afternoon, Mother made me sit beside her. In a solemn voice, she told me that Father might not have lived. Hearing her say that was like a hit to my chest. It wasn't real until she voiced it. When my tears finally died down, she looked me in the eyes and told me that no matter what, my grandfather would find us. She swore that he wouldn't stop searching until he brought us home. But I know that he's too old to journey so far. Mother vowed he will send someone in his stead.

January 22, Afternoon

We have decided that I will go with Miss Scott. The hungrier I get, the less the jungle frightens me. But I have a sense I can't shake—a heavy feeling that something is happening. I know it, and the back of my neck feels like it's covered in ants. Something's about to go wrong.

I almost laugh at the words above. About to go wrong. How much more wrong could our circumstances be?

I glanced over at Mother and saw her urgently whispering to Miss Scott. My mother, who's always been so sensitive to others' feelings, was unaware she was squeezing Miss Scott's ruined hands. Miss Scott winced as she listened, but said nothing.

Am I to lose my father and my mother as well?

Sometimes I feel as if all my fears and sadness are held in check with something as thin as lace. And sometimes I'm tempted to rip the threads open, to tear at my hair and scream so long and loud that I become frightful. That the things I fear will fear me instead.

We leave for the jungle at daybreak.

One

*T*he short relay from the *Keveral* to the inscrutable island before him reminded Captain Grant Sutherland of the whole bloody voyage: Dooley, his first mate, working tirelessly, his restless eyes darting around even in this small rowboat to find a crisis to forestall. Grant's crew—wary around their captain, obeying orders quickly out of their fear of him. His cousin, Ian Traywick, reeking of spirits and still—after all the miles and islands they'd covered— drunkenly optimistic of success.

"I have a good feeling about this island." Ian slapped Grant on the shoulder, then swiped a hand over his bristly face, attempting to smooth the bed linen indentions that still pinkened his skin. Throughout the voyage, Ian had provided what he called "shipboard levity" for a crew commanded by "one cold bastard." "Mark my slurred words, it's going to be this one. And as much as you think it won't be, surely it must."

Grant scowled at Ian. Reason dictated that Grant begin accepting his failure—this island marked the end of an exhaustive search and was the last in the Solais archipelago. After four months of sailing just to reach the Pacific, they'd spent another three futilely scouring every island in the chain for the Dearbourne family, lost at sea eight years ago.

"And if we find them today," Dooley added, clapping his weathered hands for emphasis, "we can make a run and dodge us some typhoons." The old salt was as kind as he was capable and would never rebuke Grant, but Grant knew he'd kept the ship in this region far too long—weeks into the peak storm season.

Both Dooley and Ian were still hopeful that they'd find the Dearbournes. Grant thought hope at this point was an indulgence.

And Grant Sutherland *never* indulged.

As the boat neared the island and the smell of damp earth and seaweed smothered the brine, Grant's thoughts turned inward. He scarcely registered the mountain, cloaked in foliage, or the emerald bay guarded by reef. They'd rowed out to search countless times before today, and variations of paradise had greeted them each time.

"Cap'n, what do you think about the north end of the shore?" Dooley asked, pointing out a beach cupped between rock outcroppings.

Grant studied the salt-white beach and, noting the channel through the reefs in front of it, waved them on.

Back into the lulling pattern of inching forward, then pausing after each stroke, Grant peered down through the crystal water. A massive bull shark prowled beneath them.

Not surprising—sharks were legion in this area. He hoped that wasn't how the family had met their end.

Perhaps they had made it to one of these islands only to die of exposure. Little better, that. Grant knew exposure took lives as a cat kills a downed bird, playing with it, never quite extinguishing hope until the last. Yet both scenarios assumed the young family had escaped their foundering ship. Most likely, they'd been pressed against their cabin wall as they watched the water eclipse them.

As the last of eight search parties, Grant's mission was either to find them or confirm their deaths. He dreaded the inevitable time when he would have to deliver the news—

"*Cap'n?*" Dooley cried in a strangled voice.

Grant's head jerked up. "What is it?" Before his eyes, Dooley's craggy face swelled crimson.

"You ain't—you just ain't gonna believe this. *Over there!* South-southwest."

Grant trained his eyes in the direction of the man's periscope. And shot to his feet so hastily that several hands slapped wood to clutch the pitching boat. Speech refused to come.

Finally, somehow, he managed, "*I'll—be—damned.*"

A woman ran across the beach, seeming to light over the sand.

"Is it the daughter?" Ian demanded, as he stood as well. He clamped Grant's shoulder from behind him. "Tell me that isn't her!"

Grant shook him off. "I . . . can't say for certain." He turned to the oarsmen and barked, "Put your backs into it, men. Come on, then!"

He was just about to shove the smaller sailor away from the starboard oar and take it himself when he spotted something that defied belief. Hair spilled out from under her broad-brimmed hat and swayed down her back. Hair so blond it was white, just like the girl's in the daguerreo-type Victoria Dearbourne's grandfather had given him.

The closer they got to the beach, the more certain he became. He could more clearly make out her appearance—long legs stretching out as she picked up speed, one slender arm raised and bent to keep the hat atop her head. A tiny bared waist. Grant frowned. Plainly bared.

Victoria Dearbourne. It had to be. Grant's mind could hardly wrap around the idea of finally finding her. By God, he was going to bring her back to England alive and obviously hale.

They were closing in on the breakers when she caught sight of them. She stopped so suddenly, sand kicked up at her feet and caught on the breeze. Her arm went limp and her hat, forgotten, cartwheeled away.

The boat was close enough now for Grant to see an expression of total bewilderment on her face. He felt the like. In the wind, wild hair blew to her side, or curled around her ear and streamed across her neck like a collar. Thoughts bombarded his head. She'd been a pretty child, but now . . .

Exceptional. So alive.

She was drawing back.

"Stay there, girl!" Ian called. "Stay put!"

But she continued backing away—*getting away*—igniting in Grant a frustration like he'd never known. "She can't hear you over the breakers," he snapped.

Then Grant witnessed something he knew would be branded forever into his mind. Never slowing, she spun forward with startling agility to sprint from them. He'd never seen a woman run like that.

She ran . . . *fast as hell.*

Then she was gone as though the jungle sucked her inside.

"My God," Ian cried. "Tell me I'm not seeing this."

Grant wanted to speak, but no words came. After a muted chorus of swearing, the astonished crew looked up at him expectantly.

Never taking his eyes off the spot he'd last seen her, Grant said, "I'll just go retrieve Victoria now." And then he was swinging out of the boat and charging through the waves. When he reached the shore, he ran faster, not even pausing at the looming mesh of trees and vines. Grant matched her entrance and followed her to a well-worn path. He caught glimpses of her but couldn't gain.

Then, she was just before him—holding something to her side—eyes intent. When he got over his shock, he drew a ragged breath to speak. "I'm . . . Captain . . . Gr—" The slim muscles in her arms relaxed; Grant heard a whoosh. A branch whipped into his chest, toppling him to the ground. He bellowed in pain, his anger hot and blinding as he pushed himself up. He swung his head around, but couldn't spot her. Continuing on the trail, he loped with the pain, then picked up speed. All he could hear was his heart pounding in time with his shallow breaths.

He ignored everything as though wearing blinders, seeing only shadows of her as he gained, nearly able to reach her. Just when she came into view and he was about to lunge forward, she put her hand flat on a tree, using it to swing around. Now they were on opposite sides of the thick trunk. He ran to his right, she to hers. He reversed directions; her eyes narrowed in challenge. Then she feinted right, only to go left and hedge around him. He reached out at the last moment to grab her.

Got her. He wanted to howl his triumph.

Until he stared in disbelief as the skirt he clenched in his fist stayed there while she tripped forward. The sound of ripping cloth and her cursing him melded together over his own heavy breaths. He gaped as the worn fabric ripped a swath straight up the side of her thigh to her waist before tearing free. And then she was gone once more. Bloody hell. *Bloody, bloody hell!*

Anger gave way to frustrated fury. He tore off faster. *Catch her. Explain who I am. Put her on the ship. Damn it, just catch her!* As he plunged deeper into the jungle, the air grew cloudy with mist. The leaves that slapped at his chest were slick.

A waterfall of mythic size roared into view, the driving water deafening on the black rocks below. Out of the corner of his eye, he spied her white clothing amid the green.

Amid the green, *across* the rushing river.

"Victoria," he bellowed. Amazingly, she slowed. "I'm here to rescue you."

She turned and marched into a clearing. Putting her hands to her mouth, she yelled back at him. The words were incomprehensible over the water. "Bloody hell!" She'd have had no better luck hearing him.

Seeing no way around it, he ran to the bank and dove in, swimming furiously across the sweeping currents. Choking water, scarcely able to breatne, he hauled his big frame onto the opposite shore and staggered forward. He spotted her ahead, but as he returned to an agonizing run, he knew there was no way to catch her, no way to gain. Then he saw it, a chance.

She was following the path—he could cut through the brush separating them and intercept her. He veered left, hurtling a lazy palm, gaining already.

Then, strangely, he saw his feet—above his head. Right before he felt the first punch of earth as he plummeted down a ravine.

Even as he dropped, helpless to stop himself, he knew she'd led him here on purpose. When he caught her . . . He tumbled one last time and landed on his back so hard, the impact knocked the air from his lungs.

Before he could focus his eyes, she stood over him, prodding his hip with a stick, sunlight through the canopy haloing her hair. She tilted her head. "Why were you trying to catch me?"

He fought for breath, fought to speak, but only managed wheezing sounds. He could see her blond brows knit and her lips part to demand "Why?" once more, but she heard his men crashing toward them. She looked back at him, running her eyes over him, thoroughly, slowly, until she leaned in closer to taunt, "Next time you try to run me down, Sailor, I'll drop you off a cliff."

She turned to stride away. He lunged over onto his front and sucked in a roar of air, breathing in the moisture from the plants enmeshing him. Coughing violently, he reached out a hand, wanting to stop her.

But she didn't look back. An iguana scuttled in her path, hissed at her, and deepened its stripes aggressively. She hissed back and disappeared into a black-green wall of brush.

Though she was loath to show it, Tori Dearbourne's heart hurt from fear as she plunged, arms raised above her, through foliage so thick it was like wading through water. She could hear the band of sailors, hear them hooting and laughing, slashing through the undergrowth behind her. She shuddered. Just like the last batch to land here.

No, at least they'd acted like friends, even saviors, before their heinous attack. Now, this towering giant, with his fierce eyes, hadn't even waited for the boat to reach shore before he charged like a lion after her, then pawed and ripped at her clothing.

Her fear beckoned worry as well. She just couldn't afford fear, and Lord knew she should be immune to it by now. Fate had tossed her about so much that that part of her simply should have withered away.

At least she hadn't appeared as terrified as she was; no, she'd just coldly made sure that if he attempted to cut her off, he'd take a spill for his troubles. She'd yelled a warning. For the tenth time, she told herself he'd chosen his own path.

All she'd planned for this morning was to check a trap in the shallows. A simple, routine chore. She'd been intent on reaching the waterline and rushing back to the canopy, avoiding the burning sun as one would run in from the rain, and hadn't exactly expected company after so many years. . . .

A rebounding branch slapped at her thigh, startling her with its force, the pain cutting through her thoughts. She looked down to see blood streaming from the slash, staining what was left of the white lawn skirt she wore. Curse it! She might've mended it, but she didn't think the fabric could take another scrubbing before disintegrating.

Forcing herself to slow, she looked back in her wake. She knew better than to leave such a trail—splintered branches and now blood on a broad leaf. After a deep, calming breath, she returned to her task of picking through spiny palm fronds until she reached the trail to their camp. Ten minutes of sprinting up the hillside brought her to the arch of banana leaves serving as an entryway to their home.

"Men!" Tori gasped as she lurched into the clearing. "Men and a ship!" She bent over, sucking in air, then sank down, her thighs tight against her mud-speckled calves. No one answered. "Cammy?" she called. Nothing. Their hut, supported high in an ancient banyan, was silent. So help her, Cammy had better be in there. How many times had Tori ordered her to remain in the camp?

And Cammy would've been able to remember if she hadn't begun losing her wits at a spectacular rate.

Rushing to the ladder, she took two bamboo rungs at a time, then hurried to the door flap made of old sail. She yanked open the cloth to peer inside. Empty. Tori looked away and back as if she hadn't seen correctly. What if Cammy wandered all the way down to the beach this time?

There were two trails to their little shelf of land on the hillside, one hidden and one more hidden. She'd already run the length of the former, so she dashed over to the latter. Halfway down she found Cammy sitting back against a tree, breaths shallow, face waxy, her lips chapped and cracked.

Tori shook her shoulder, and after a few seconds Cammy opened her eyes, blinking against the light. "Where is your hat, Tori? Have you been in the sun?"

Relief soughed through Tori's body like a breeze. Cammy scolding was much better than Cammy sleeping like the dead.

"With your fair skin, it's just common sense . . ." She trailed off when she saw Tori's bloodied leg and wet, tattered skirt. "What has happened now?"

"Men and a ship. After a giant chased me and ripped my clothes, I lost track of the hat."

Cammy gave her a smile that didn't quite reach her distracted hazel eyes. "We can't be too careful about our complexions, now, can we?" she asked vaguely.

Vague. That was the best way to describe Cammy now. Before, she'd been a vibrant woman, as vibrant as her fiery red hair, with a crisp, lively intelligence. Now she seemed wilted, and her clarity of mind faded in and out with no discernible pattern.

Tori mentally counted to five. Sometimes, when Cammy got that unfocused look about her, Tori wanted to shake her. "Did you hear what I said? We're not alone."

Just when Tori decided she wouldn't understand what was happening, Cammy asked, "What were they like?"

"The one that came after me had the coldest, most piercing eyes I've ever seen. I had to put him in the ravine to stop him."

"The ravine?" she asked. "Oh, how I wish I could've seen that."

Tori frowned at the fresh memory and said almost to herself, "It really is true about the bigger you are, the harder you fall." She shook her head. "The rest of them were slashing at the foliage, getting ready to enter."

"Sailors combing the brush." Cammy shivered. "History's repeating itself. . . ."

Both froze when the birds nearby fell silent. "We've got to get to the camp," Tori whispered.

"I'm going to slow you down. You go and I'll follow."

"Why, yes, that's just what I'll do," Tori said while wedging a shoulder under Cammy's arm and lifting her. After painfully slow moments, they clambered up the trail. As their home came into view, Tori surveyed it, trying to see it from a stranger's eyes. How odd it would be to have men in their camp, gazing at the shelter, walking past the rock-ringed fire pit. For outsiders to see the workmanship, or workwomanship, more precisely, that was a testament of their dogged survival. Tori knew it was terrible of her, but she was almost eager for someone to marvel at their work. Her pride would be her downfall, Cammy would say.

Tori didn't believe in downfalls. It would have happened by now. Nature and Fate united to mete out challenge after challenge, and she and Cammy had beat the odds every time. They lived and lived, and would some more. No, there'd be no downfalls. Tori frowned at her thoughts. Cammy had told her she was proud, but Tori feared that she was arrogant as well.

But then, arrogant had always served her better than afraid.

"What direction did they set off in?" Cammy asked.

"It doesn't matter." Tori's smile was cold. "It will always be the wrong one."

Two

Grant limped to meet his crew at the canopy line near the beach, teeth gritted in pain, one arm across his chest, hand clutching his opposite shoulder. Water dripped from his hair and mixed with the sweat on his forehead to trickle into his eyes.

Blindsided. That's what he'd just been. Thoughts racketed in his head. Why would she run in the first place? More important, why the hell had he chased her like a dog after a carriage, and about as mindlessly? Why, if he had to do it over, would he run after her again?

"Grant, you look like you tussled with the wrong feral girl," Ian drawled. "Round one to Victoria. Or maybe not," he said, with a pointed glance at the soaked cloth still bunched in Grant's free hand. Grant felt his skin flush before he could grab his pack from Dooley and stuff it in.

"Congratulations, Cap'n, you've found a survivor!"

Dooley cried, his face creased in a baggy smile. "I knew you would."

Where Dooley's unwavering confidence in Grant came from, Grant had no idea.

Ian slanted a look at Grant. "Ah, but wasn't finding her supposed to be the hard part?"

Grant swung a lowering look at his cousin, then barked to the crew, "Get some more supplies. Just enough for one night. And scavenge as much food as we can hold for the trip back."

Though Dooley appeared delighted to have a chore, for the first time his sailors hesitated at their orders. They looked up at Grant with the ever-constant fear, but now he saw confusion as well. Their emotionless captain, who worshipped logic, had bolted like an animal after a girl.

Grant decided to reassure them. "Move," he said in a tone lacking feeling or inflection of any kind. "Now."

He almost had to laugh when they spun around and fled in various directions. Most of his crew were more afraid of his controlled demeanor than of his brother Derek's infamous rants. A boisterous, lusty lot, they couldn't understand someone who behaved as he did. They reasoned that sooner or later a man as cold as Grant would simply . . . snap. *Still waters run deep*, he'd heard them whisper to each other in warning.

Ian snorted. "One day they'll realize you won't slit their throats in the night. Then where will you be?"

"Retired." Grant yanked off his sopping boots and ruined shirt, then snatched dry clothing out of his pack. After he changed, he found Ian gathering a machete and canteen from the pile of equipment. "You're gearing up as if you're going in with me. Let me make this clear—this is a jungle. There will be no revelry, no drink, and no women of your . . . distinct caliber."

"Understood, *Cap'n*." Ian shouldered the canteen. "But I'd still like to go. If, of course, my shore dress is acceptable to you," he said, a jibe no doubt referring to the time Grant had sent a sailor back to tar the ship because his shirt had been untucked.

"*Nothing* about you is acceptable to me."

Ian's face split into a satisfied smile before he turned to the nearest opening in the jungle wall.

Grant shouldered his own canteen and machete, then exhaled a long breath, drawing on some deep inner well of patience. As he followed, he reminded himself that though Ian was twenty-six, he was a young twenty-six. Then he wondered what would happen when the well went dry.

"So, what are we looking for?" Ian asked.

"A trail, footprints, a campsite. Anything," Grant answered curtly, hoping to stem a conversation with Ian. He didn't want to talk—he wanted to think about what had just occurred and sort through the last unbelievable hour of his life. He shook his head, still unable to grasp that he'd found her. Or that she'd turned into a wildcat.

Blindsided. Tricked, misled—literally—and attacked. By a girl.

He didn't like surprises, mainly because he'd always reacted so poorly to them. He let out a pent-up breath. *Concentrate on the task at hand, Grant.* And the task really was very simple when he boiled it down: Get the *girl* into the *boat*.

"Do you think the island was deserted before?"

Grant exhaled. "I have no idea. This one's bigger than the others. There could be a bloody metropolis here for all we know."

Ian slowed and turned, assuming a thoughtful expression. "Grant. You know I would never criticize you in front of the crew—"

"Yes, you would."

Ian waved an unconcerned hand. "In any case, what got into you back there? I've *never* seen you behave like that. It was as if you'd been possessed."

He scowled, though Ian was right. Grant did nothing without careful consideration, never acted without plodding examination. "I've waited a long time for that moment." His explanation sounded weak to his own ears. He had *felt* possessed. Impulses had fired in him and for the first time in memory, he'd obeyed them without question. "I wouldn't have chased if she hadn't run."

Ian eyed him shrewdly. "Maybe you're more like your brothers than you think."

Grant's whole body tensed. "I am *not* like my brothers. I'm staid, respectable—"

"I know, I know," Ian interrupted. "You've mastered yourself. You have limitless control and restraint." He tilted his head. "Or perhaps it's like the crew says—you've carved any lust for life from yourself until you're like a stone."

Grant slowed. "They say I'm like a stone?"

"They say worse, but that's all I'll divulge."

"Then just shut up, Ian." He marched faster.

"But you weren't like a stone today, that's for sure." Ian caught up and confessed, "I'm glad you chased her."

Grant gave him a long-suffering look. "For what possible reason?"

"You showed you're still human. For once, you weren't ruled by cold logic. And maybe the woman brought it out in you."

"My reward for finding her brought it out in me. The fact that she's a woman is incidental."

"And the fact that she's a beauty?" He raised his eyebrows. "Well, I'm sure you've scared the hell out of her. You're not a small man. Yes, she's probably huddled somewhere crying right about now." He made a tsking sound. "That's one thing you did not inherit with your Sutherland blood—a way with the ladies."

Grant willed the irritation from his face. As usual, his cousin baited him. As usual, Grant restrained himself from reaction. Ian's impulsive, volatile personality ran as opposite to his own as possible, and if Grant had been less guarded, they would have been at each other's throats for seven months now.

An uninvited passenger, Ian had run aboard minutes before they cast off in London. For the hundredth time, Grant regretted taking on his ne'er-do-well, rakehell cousin. He swore under his breath and surveyed Ian squinting up at birds, happily snagging and eating a banana. Ian, for all his faults, for his uncanny ability to irritate, for his laziness, for his— Grant stanched that interminable train of thought, admitting to himself that for all his faults, Ian was like a brother. If Grant had to do it over, he knew he'd repeat the mistake of taking him on.

During his harried race down the docks to the *Keveral*'s berth, Ian had been looking over his shoulder, eyes wide.

He was quelling the temptation to remind Ian of his nonpaying and nonworking status on board when Ian snapped his fingers. "Just thought of something—this means Victoria's grandfather isn't mad."

"Some of us never thought he was." That was a disingenuous answer at best. Grant *had* wondered about the sanity of Victoria's grandfather. Edward Dearbourne, the old earl of Belmont, was considered insane among polite society and by all connected with London shipping. What else could you call a lonely old man who longed for his lost family so fiercely that he imagined them alive and unfound for all these years? Even after he'd commissioned failed search after search throughout the South Pacific, impoverishing himself?

Grant knew what to call him. *Right.*

At least about Victoria. Grant remembered his first meeting with the earl. Tears had tracked from Belmont's filmy eyes as he'd explained the history of his lost family. Uncomfortable with the emotional display, Grant had offered him platitudes. *The three are gone. Best to accept it and move on. They're in a better place.*

Yet against all reason, the man had continued to believe. Grant frowned. Against all logic.

He gave a sharp shake of his head. The earl's intuition or "gut feeling" that his family lived wasn't what gave him hope. Grant knew the man had hope because the alternative was unendurable. . . .

"Imagine the look on his face when we bring her back. Hell, the look on everyone's face." Ian's normally languid eyes were snapping with excitement. "And here I thought we were the fools accepting a fool's errand."

"We?"

Ian looked affronted. "I believe it is you and I out here, hence the *we.*"

Grant glared and passed him. For the next three hours, he made good headway until another blister gave way beneath the sweat-dampened handle of his machete. He hissed in a breath through clenched teeth. When Ian trailed farther behind, Grant stopped, put a mud-coated, bloody hand against a tree, and leaned in, fatigued to his bones.

The inner island was like an oven—gone were the soothing breeze and powdery sand. Here mud and fallen plants congealed into a pulpy floor, hungry with suction and grueling to slog through. He drank water, fighting not to guzzle, and took note of himself. Lacerations criss-crossed his skin and blisters the size of crowns pocked his hands; a reddening band spanned his upper chest.

"Grant, this isn't a race." Ian wheezed as he reeled forward. "Are you trying to cover the entire island this afternoon?"

Grant had no pity for his cousin. "I warned you."

"I didn't imagine it could be this . . ." He trailed off, eyes widening. "I can't feel my feet. Bloody hell! I can't feel my feet!"

Leaving Ian to stumble around and ascertain that he was still bipedal, Grant ignored the stinging of his own abused body and pushed on.

"Slow down, Grant," Ian pleaded.

He faced his cousin. "You fall behind, you get left behind. I hope you've kept track of where you are."

Ian peered around him at the tangle of trees and vines with what could be called a cool panic. "I didn't because I knew you would."

Such was the way of their relationship.

"Then you'd best keep up." Grant sustained such an unrelenting pace for more reasons than one. He'd found Victoria and, yes, he was one step closer to realizing his goal, but he also wanted to make sure she was safe. He considered her under his protection now. Yet at this moment she was alone, a young, slight woman—albeit a fierce one—somewhere on an untamed island that was shaming strong men.

Throughout the day, his anger over her tricks had given way to guilt when he thought about chasing her down; yet after seven months—*seven months*—she'd been at his fingertips. Even now, his fingers curled at the thought. But then her face appeared in his mind. The look in her eyes, the confusion. He hadn't wanted to scare her, but he'd done just that.

She'd been through enough—years without comforts or civilization, and both parents possibly dead. Of course she'd be afraid. He could almost understand why she'd put him into that fall and nearly beheaded him with the sapling. He couldn't quite reconcile her poking him with a stick and taunting him, but perhaps she was putting on a brave front.

They searched until a three-quarter moon rose in the sky, then limped their way back to the camp. At his crew's curious looks, Grant said, "We'll find her tomorrow." His tone was authoritative, but he wasn't nearly as convinced as he had been.

When Dooley bustled over to hand him a tin cup of coffee, Grant sank onto a horizontal palm, stupefied, drinking without thought. Finally, even that became too arduous. Too weary to drink, he threw the rest of his coffee into the sand, then mustered the energy to grab his pallet.

He unrolled it under a break in the canopy, and even after the others slept, he lay looking up at the too-bright stars, thinking about the turn his life had just taken. He had actually earned Belmont's payment for the search, the last thing the man had to offer: his home. When the earl died, Grant would assume ownership of the sizable but declining Belmont Court. He would finally have his own home, his own people.

Yet this mission had always been more than that.

Victoria's grandfather, with his sad eyes and palpable lone-liness, had somehow convinced him that his family might yet live.

Grant had never felt particularly heroic, but if they were out here, he had wanted to save them. Now he was so close to bringing at least Victoria back. She'd managed to stay alive. To thrive somehow. But she couldn't go on indefi-nitely. She needed to be saved even if she didn't have the sense to realize it.

"Have you come up with any ideas?" Cammy asked. She took her second bite of banana, patted her sunken belly as though full, and considered breakfast over. No wonder she continued to lose weight, Tori thought. The bones of her wrists and her collarbone jutted beneath her skin, and her cheekbones were sharp in her face.

Resolving to make her eat more, Tori paced the small hut. The floor of banded planks beneath her feet creaked but didn't give. "Lots of ideas. Just none that are feasible. I simply can't see us sailing away in their ship while they stay on shore scratching their heads."

"What a perfect solution!"

Tori raised an eyebrow at Cammy. Luckily, Cammy was joking. "We need more information about them."

"Yes, what if the rest of them are good? What if the man chasing you was a . . . a drunk?"

Tori shook her head. "No, he was dead sober."

"A lunatic, then?"

She opened her lips to say "no," but then remembered his eyes. Though focused and ice-blue cold, they had looked a bit . . . savage. "Then why would they send him in an advance party?"

"They were sick of him on the ship? Or in the process of

marooning him?" Cammy mused. "You may have helped them!"

Tori sank down cross-legged on her straw-filled mattress. "I suppose anything's possible."

"So how do we walk this line once more? Play the risk of them leaving us against the possibility that they'll kidnap us for villainous reasons?"

Tori felt her neck and shoulders tensing. *What a critical walk. One misstep . . .* "If I saw a woman on deck, or a child even, I'd feel better about approaching them."

"Or perhaps even a chaplain."

Tori nodded. "I'll just have to get a better look. Maybe sneak down to the beach."

"Why don't you stay up here and use that?" She pointed to the spyglass standing in the corner of the hut—standing because it could no longer telescope *in*.

Tori's gaze flickered over it. "That artifact? The end glass is cracked down the middle."

Cammy pursed her lips. "Well, you won't see any worse—you'll just see two of everything."

"Right now, they'll never find us up here, but if I use that, the glass might reflect," she countered. "And if I can see them, they can see me."

"Wait for a cloud and hide under the brush." In Cammy's mind, the subject was closed. "Tori, do be careful."

Tori sighed. "Cammy, do stay here."

And so minutes later, Tori was crawling on her stomach, digging her elbows into the dirt, lugging a rusting, broken spyglass with her and cursing Cammy for being lucid for once.

She brought the glass around, setting up her view, chin on the back of her flat hand, then waited what seemed like hours for a passing cloud. It moved shyly, as if someone just out of her eyesight beckoned with a crooked finger. With the sun finally cloaked, Tori swung the spyglass down, prepared to divide everything she spotted by two.

In the lengthy space of cloud cover, she saw no women with their skirts billowing on the deck of the ship, no children playing among them—no black-robed chaplain— just a pack of common sailors.

Her heart sank. She knew all about sailors.

Tori scuttled backward, then returned to camp, her mind a knot of ideas. She found Cammy lolling in her hammock outside the hut, nearly rocked to sleep by the sea breezes.

"Good afternoon, Tori," Cammy said with a yawn. "Did you catch any fish?"

One, two, three, four, five . . . "I went to reconnoiter the ship, remember?"

Cammy's eyes widened, but she covered her surprise. "Of course!" She moved to a sitting position with practiced movements. "I was jesting."

Tori narrowed her eyes. "Is the forgetfulness getting worse?"

She sighed. "How would I know? If I made a determination, I'd just forget it."

Cammy had once described her episodes of vagueness, saying they were like when one first wakes up in the morning, disoriented. And often as easy to shake off. At times, she attributed them to some spoiled food, other times to an underlying sickness.

"Tori, don't keep me in suspense. . . ."

"There was nothing there that we'd hoped to see. I don't understand it. Captains and first mates often sail with families."

"They could be inside."

Tori shook her head. "The cabins would be like a furnace on a day like today. Anyone able would be on deck beneath the tarpaulin."

"What flag did they raise?"

"The Union Jack." Their nationality wasn't reassuring. The last crew had flown the same flag. And Britain impressed just as many convict crews as any other country. Tori sat on a driftwood log. "I was thinking about our 'the rest of them are good' theory."

"Doesn't that mean we have to counter with a 'the rest of them are bad' theory as well?"

Tori nodded. "I'm worried that we want a rescue so badly that we're making excuses for them. I was chased and pawed. Fact. There are only sailors aboard. Fact. I didn't hear them chastise the one that came after me. No, they seemed overjoyed. And he wasn't sent back to the ship."

Cammy's tight expression clearly evinced her decision about the men. "Haven't we learned the hard way? I think we've learned the hard way *enough*."

"But they might have medicine."

"And what do you think they'd want in exchange for it?" Cammy rubbed her perspiring forehead. "Forgive me, Tori. This illness colors my moods. But these men could very well be like the sailors before." Her face became a mask of disgust. "Or like the ones from the *Serendipity* reeking of the urine they washed their clothes in. At least now you're safe and unharmed." Her voice grew quieter when she said, "And what help could I be? I just don't know that I am strong enough to . . . to do what might be necessary." She wrapped her thin arms around herself.

Tori dropped her gaze. She could never expect such a sacrifice from Cammy again. Lord knew, she hadn't expected it the first time. When Tori glanced up, she tried to appear impassive. And failed.

"Oh, Tori, your eyes are so revealing, it's as if I can see your mind working. I know you want—you need—a battle plan."

Tori leaned forward. "The way I see it, we need to find out what kind of men they are. Suppose they're good? Maybe they like to think of themselves as British gentlemen? Well, a man of honor would never leave a lady stranded. No matter what *circumstances* befell them."

Cammy arched her red brows in interest. "But a crew of cutthroats might be persuaded to leave. I like this. If we can make them leave, then they weren't the sort we wanted here in the first place." When Tori nodded, Cammy asked, "Can you be certain they won't catch you?"

"No one can catch me," she scoffed.

"We've been wrong in that thinking before."

Tori put her shoulders back. "I'm older. Faster."

"What do you have in mind?"

"Do you remember that plant that made us throw up for days?" Tori tapped her cheek. "I think I'm going to spice their food."

Cammy unconsciously clutched her stomach. "Now, that I shall never forget. For the better part of a week, I begged to die."

Tori jerked upright, gasping as she woke, the sound of the *Serendipity* breaking apart still thundering in her mind.

Her hands fluttered up to her face as she just stopped herself from covering her ears. She didn't think she could ever forget the whine and vibration of boards splitting. Never stop imagining the force it would take to break thick lumber. She moved her hands to her eyes, wiping the tears there. Luckily, Cammy slumbered on, since it wasn't yet dawn.

Though she hadn't had the nightmare in years, this was the second morning in a row it had plagued Tori. She'd always tried to hide her abject fear of ships from Cammy, but knew she hadn't been successful. When they realized they'd never be rescued, Cammy had said, "Look on the bright side. At least we'll never be in a shipwreck again." Tori had thought it was a quip, but Cammy's face had been grave.

Yet now another ship tossed in the bay. Tori shivered and burrowed down farther under her patchwork quilt, then cracked open her eyes. She had a job to do.

Even after she dressed and descended to the sailors' beach camp, the early morning fog stood thick and made it easy for her to slip in while they slept. Silently, she checked container after container until she worked open their supply of oats. She poured a gourd of discolored mush inside, digging down to stir with her hands. She returned the lid and brushed off her hands, tossing away the gourd and slipping back into the brush. As she watched, the men woke and began preparing for the day, stoking embers, cooking. She smirked to see several men spooning the slop into their bowls.

The giant rose with the others, though he slept away from them. Seeing him up close and standing confirmed her earlier impression—he was the tallest man she'd ever seen. With those shoulders and deep chest, he was the biggest as well.

She'd wondered before if he was a drunk, a lunatic, or, Lord forbid, even their captain. Now she knew. He had the look of a leader stamped over every inch of him—shoulders back, his squared chin lifted a bit higher than the other men's. He looked as if everyone was on the verge of some error, and he was on the verge of a terrible anger. The sailors, in turn, were wary around him and behaved as if he might launch a fist at any time.

Instead of drinking or eating with the others, he said something to a squat, nervous man, then scooped up a leather roll-up case and a machete and strode in the direction of the smaller falls. She used that trail daily to get to the pool and bathe, easily walking under the banana leaves, but he had to slash at them with his machete just to get his upper body through.

Why isn't he eating? She frowned, then silently followed him to one of her favorite places on the island. The scene was Edenic with a clear pool, dark from the shade and the smoky-colored rocks enfolding it. Two trickling falls fed it with bracing water.

Her eyes widened. He was unbuttoning his shirt. To bathe? Sweet God, he was going . . . to bathe. She bit her lip, tempted to stay. Why not? This was her island. *I can see his chest!* He was the one trespassing. *One boot off.* Besides, she needed—desperately needed—more excitement. Before they'd come, life for her had turned into a routine of work, work, work, avoid death, work. *Hmmm. He really is lean, even with his size.*

Her lips curled into a smile when she concluded she deserved to look at the naked man! Yet by the time he'd gotten down to just his trousers, he'd turned and she only saw his backside. Only? It was enough to quicken her heartbeat. His shoulders and upper back were broad, defined as though sculpted, tapering to this muscular part of him. She caught herself nearly pouting when he dived in.

While she gawked, he swam back and forth as though trying to loosen up his soreness. Finally, he waded to the shallows and stood, shaking water from his hair. *Any sec-*

ond now, he'll be out of the water, the big naked man. When he did step out, she darted her gaze to his face, avoiding any sight of that part of him.

He was just so big. And so, so . . . naked.

Just when she realized she was being ridiculous, that she was allowed to look, he grasped a large drying cloth, effectively covering his lower body.

Her jaw went slack when she saw him rub the cloth over his chest, more lightly over the glaringly bruised strip she'd provided, and then run it lower over his torso. His stomach was flat and rigid. She swallowed, noting that the muscles there bunched as he moved. *Fascinating.* A trail of black hair started below his navel and trailed down—she wanted to see to where, curse it—but the cloth covered him. She'd never been so curious or frustrated. Her hands clenched the water reeds around her. *Move the cloth. Drop it, now. Drop . . . it!*

Then he did.

Her mouth opened wordlessly and grew dry. Her chest and neck flushed with heat. She'd seen men without clothing before—many of the tribes her family had come upon weren't particularly shy—but she'd been young and reduced to giggles each time. Now, seeing him, all of him, startled her into stillness and enlivened her at the same time.

Power, strength, and grace fused together. *Perfect.* How right she'd been to label him . . . *big.* She could no more look away than she could quit breathing. The thought made her realize she *wasn't* breathing. When she did, she sighed, embarrassing herself.

He looked up sharply in her direction. Though he couldn't have heard or seen her, her heart drummed in her chest. She leapt to her feet, her skin on fire, then ran through the jungle as though wild.

Three

Grant had a sinking suspicion that he'd been watched bathing.

Yes, the weeds suddenly bobbing near the falls could have been caused by an animal, but he suspected not. When he returned to the camp and saw his men scrambling toward the bushes to lose their breakfasts, he was certain. Ian woke, looked up from his pallet at the scene, and through a yawn decreed, "Round two, Victoria."

Grant concluded the same. She'd done this. He ground his teeth. If she wanted to turn this into a battle of wills, he'd oblige.

What a way to start the day—annoyed, exhausted, his body pained and recently ogled by a young woman. And what he wouldn't give to have that situation reversed, he thought, then flushed.

Ian rose, inching up in stages. "There's something on my body that *doesn't* hurt," he croaked. "Can't say what it is just now. It'll come to me."

Grant understood. Even after his swim, his head pounded in waves. And his back—he was certain someone had grabbed his shoulders and shoved a knee into his spine during the night.

Ian hobbled around camp. "Dooley, you have any food you'd trust?"

"No, Master Ian, not yet. I just don't understand. It must've been bad water. Or maybe a dirty cask." Dooley looked so pained when he said the last that Grant was tempted to tell him what he suspected. Then he remembered his sister-in-law describing her time aboard Derek's ship. Two dozen men had blamed her for a poisoning and clamored hourly for their first female keelhauling. For Victoria's sake, he'd have to let Dooley take this one on the chin.

Ian announced, "Grant, I'm going with you."

Grant simply looked at him.

"Why? Because I'm starving and wouldn't chance anything here. Since you ordered the crew to remain in camp, my best bet's to go with you."

Grant shouldered his pack and couldn't hide a wince. How had the damn thing gotten so heavy since last night? "If you complain like you did yesterday, I won't be responsible for my actions."

"Understood. I won't complain like yesterday," Ian promised as they started off. "I'll either complain a little less or a bit more."

As noon approached and the sun stabbed the canopy from directly above, Grant concluded he would not have better luck with Victoria than on the previous day. In fact, he had the impression she mocked him—staying close but just out of reach, sending them on punishing trails to marshes, seep holes, boulder-blocked paths.

When a fly lighted on Ian's face, he slapped his cheek hard enough to leave a handprint. "That one had *bulk*, forgodsakes," he mumbled. "You know how explorers are always writing in their journals about the jungle, comparing it to a woman? A woman indifferent to your suffering? I believe it! This jungle's a rutting bitch."

Grant didn't agree. No, indifference would be preferred. The jungle toyed with them, suffocating them, protecting them from the sun, yet collecting its heat to weaken them. Grant wasn't an explorer by nature. His philosophy was to expend all that energy making home so satisfying you'd never want to leave. He'd be happy to be tied to one land, if it was the right one, his entire life. Wasn't that the purpose of this trip? To claim Belmont Court?

He froze in the trail, coming face-to-face with an immense spider. Bigger than his hand, it sprawled eerily among the geometric patterns knitted in its web. He bent beneath it and tossed a loose warning back to Ian. Seconds later, Ian bellowed a curse.

Grant hurried back to see Ian's head entangled in the web, the dusty brown spider attached. Ian scrabbled backward, the web and spider wafting after him. Yelling, batting, retreating, he barreled through a copse of low trees directly into more webs, a cluster of them glinting in the sun. He gave a harsh cry, arms flailing like a windmill, harvesting each one as though on purpose. Finally, he toppled over, covered in web, swatting spasmodically. Grant reached him and brushed the spiders free.

"Christ, Grant," he said, sounding baffled. "Why didn't you tell me there was a spider?"

"It was over half a foot long—I didn't think you could miss it. Besides, you've made it past everything else in the trail."

"Everything else? *I didn't see anything else!*" Lips thinned, Ian clutched the earth at his sides. "I've had it with this ante-diluvian muddle! I tell you right now. I'm done and you can go to—"

Grant slid his machete free and raised it high. Ian's eyes grew wide. "I take it back! I'm not complaining!" But Grant had already swung the blade, slicing through a leaf near Ian's hip.

There, on the ground, just beside Ian's splayed fingers, was a footprint.

"How'd the morning go?" Cammy asked when Tori strolled in. Strips of spiky palm fronds littered the floor around her. One green sliver had caught in her hair and protruded upright.

"The sailors got a taste of island life," Tori said with a grin. It faded when she saw Cammy was weaving a broad-brimmed hat, most likely for her. She hid a grimace at the bright feathers scattered all over the floor, soon to be hat plumage. Cammy was enjoying herself, but a milliner she was not.

"And the big one? How'd he react?"

"Sadly, we'll never know. He didn't eat."

"A lunatic drunk who doesn't eat?"

Tori chuckled. "I think he's actually the captain. He left to go bathe."

One red eyebrow cocked. "Bathe?"

Curse it! Sorting the feathers by color grew very impor-tant. "He left in that direction," she said airily.

"Uh-huh."

"Oh, very well," Tori said, lifting her face. "I followed him to the falls and watched him."

Cammy's eyes grew bright. "Did he undress completely?"

Tori folded her lips in and nodded, blushing anew.

Cammy sighed, resting her chin in her palm. "Was he handsome?"

Tori paused, wondering how to convey how heart-stopping she'd found his huge, rugged body. "The most handsome man I've seen in years."

"In years? Well, aren't you the amusing one today?" Cammy stabbed a bright yellow feather into the finished hat. "Spying on naked men agrees with you."

Tori flashed her a quelling look, then crossed to the fire pit. She dug up an ember and added tinder she'd gathered during the day. Kneeling, she blew against the twigs, feeding in larger branches, and soon a fire crackled to life. "Are you hungry?"

Cammy laid the hat aside and sat down on a driftwood log near the fire. "Unceasingly, no," she said, anxiously stretching to the warmth. "Am I ever? I've forgotten everything about *appetite* except how to spell it." She frowned. "And that might be gone as well." Biting her lip, she reached down to draw letters in the dirt.

Tori pasted on an excited smile. "Well, you're going to want to eat tonight. I've found a good supply of taro."

Cammy looked up with a grimace. "Taro. Delightful."

Tori sighed as she placed a halved taro and a butterflied fish on their makeshift grill, forcing her mind away from visions of tarts, milk, shepherd's pie, and rain-wet apples straight from the tree.

The footprint led them to a previously hidden trail winding up a steep grade. When they climbed it to a clearing on a small projection of land, Grant's breath whistled out. Her camp, her shelter was here. He turned in a circle taking in every detail.

Two handwoven hammocks stretched between palms and swayed in the breeze. A fire hearth dotted the middle of the clearing, with rocks and driftwood logs bordering it. The structure was strategically wedged into the aerial roots of an extensive banyan tree, with walls made of sail connected to a reinforced bamboo frame. A square of densely woven palm made up the aslant roof, and a porch with rails coiled in jasmine fronted it. This was permanent. A home.

"Look at that," Ian breathed. "We can be sure some men made it off the ship."

"For once, I agree with you." Grant slid his pack to the ground on his way to the ladder. "Guard the trail," he ordered, leveling a finger at him. "Don't let anyone get past you."

"Anything for the cause," Ian answered, and promptly sank into one of the hammocks.

Grant climbed tentatively on the hollow bamboo rungs, but they held. He pulled back the canvas door flap and leaned over to enter. . . .

"Did you hear something?" Tori asked, glancing around in every direction.

"No, but then your ears are better than mine." Cammy tried on the hat and looked in their one fragment of mirror.

"I thought I heard footsteps."

"I don't see how. No one could ever slip up on us here."

Tori relaxed and lay back on her pallet, using her bent arm as a pillow. "You're right. We've taken every precaution."

"But did we have to take this one?" Cammy grumbled.

Tori picked up a feather and idly ran the tip up and down her nose. "A fox continually moves her den."

Cammy pursed her lips at the moist cave walls looming around them. "I thought there'd be more satisfaction in outfoxing him."

Empty.

She was gone again, elusive as ever. Grant shut his eyes for a long moment, getting his irritation under control, then opened them to find books littering the room, stacked in every corner, and all well read. He flipped open one that was decaying slower than the others. Many of the pages were marked, and copious notes filled the margins.

A pearlescent comb atop a rough-hewn table caught his attention. He crossed, noticing the floor had no give, even under his weight. When he picked up the carved comb and ran his finger over its smoothness, he noticed a single strand of hair. It glowed white and gold in the flickering sunlight.

A basket of folded linens occupied one corner, a stolid trunk another. He bent to the trunk's lid and opened it, the rusting hinges resisting. Inside were more books, and among them he found a weighty journal bound with a strip of linen.

A journal by Victoria Anne Dearbourne, 1850

Though it was the worst invasion of privacy, Grant gently opened it, hoping to garner some insight into who had survived and how. As he read the beginning pages, he strove for detachment—he had a job to do—but for once in his life, he wasn't successful. He scrubbed a hand over his face, recoiling from the knowledge of what had happened to this family. It was worse than he'd imagined. Grant had had only one real tragedy in his life, and yet this young girl had borne one after another. When she questioned if she was to lose two parents, something in his chest tightened.

The journal also confirmed his suspicion that her father hadn't made it off the ship. Dearbourne not only had been a renowned scholar, he'd had a reputation as a man of honor. That he'd stay behind was no surprise. So no men had made it here? He skimmed through and read about Victoria planning the shelter. She'd done this?

He flipped back to near the beginning.

When we returned from the brush with water and fruit, laughing, celebrating our find, we found Mother lying as though asleep. But for the first time since we'd come here, the features on her beautiful face weren't tightened with pain.

"Victoria, your mother's passed on," Miss Scott told me. Mother was at rest where nothing could ever frighten her or hurt her again. Though I could never tell Miss Scott, on that day, I longed to go with her.

He closed the pages softly, flushing as though he'd been spying on someone. Yet that feeling didn't stop him from tucking the journal into the back of his trouser waist before climbing down the ladder.

Victoria wasn't here alone. Unless Miss Scott had died too, there were two women on this island.

When Ian noticed Grant was back on the ground, he asked, "What's it like inside?"

Grant didn't want to admit it was damned impressive. Seeing the shelter anew, he marveled that Victoria had designed it. He studied how the banyan's roots enveloped the structure and had begun absorbing the platform, making it that much more sturdy. He noted old knife scars on the wood around the joists and realized she'd cut wedges out to fit the baseboards.

Amazing. She'd known exactly how much to cut without killing the root. It was an ingenious idea—letting nature do her work. The attention to detail was remarkable.

"It's durable," Grant answered, and didn't elaborate. He snatched up his bag and stowed the brittle journal inside.

"Are we staying here from now on?" Ian rocked in the hammock.

"We'll go back to the beach."

"It's going to rain soon, and that hut looks watertight."

Grant shook his head. "No, we go back."

Ian flashed him an impatient look that turned defiant, then leapt up to untie and steal the hammock. Grant let it go and followed him, pausing only to glance back one last time. After reading the journal, he recognized that Victoria had compiled the notes in those books. He'd wondered if she could still read, but now knew she'd made a study of all of those texts. Her intelligence continued to impress. Except when she used it against him.

When they dragged into camp, Dooley greeted them with coffee and stew. After being assured of the food, Grant ate, not tasting. The pain from his muscles grew more intense now that he'd slowed from the day's pace. He reached for his pallet, unrolled and followed it, every inch of him protesting as he eased down. Though he could scarcely keep his eyes open, he lit a lantern and pulled out the journal.

Victoria as a child of thirteen had written with a clarity belying her young age. The words describing her mother's burial weren't maudlin. In fact, Grant got the feeling that as she wrote of her mother's death, she didn't accept it. There was an underlying tone that read like someone recording a bizarre dream they'd had the night before.

A drizzly misting of rain began, dousing the fire in a series of hisses, and splattering on the fragile journal pages. He and his crew were ill prepared for camping on land. He could order the tarpaulin brought to shore, but that would be admitting he might be here longer than one more night.

Not likely. He yanked his jacket off his back and shielded the journal.

> . . . at the first glimpse of sail, we hurriedly dressed in our best and ran to the water. The sailors were unsettled to find us, but seemed polite, their captain acting the gentleman. That night around the fire on the beach, the crew drank spirits, became boisterous.

Grant turned the page, perplexed to find his ship wasn't the first to land here.

> The first mate sat beside Cammy—close—and put his arm around her. She stiffened but appeared not to know what to do. When the man reached to touch her chest, Cammy slapped him. The entire group grew silent.
>
> I was almost between them when he slapped her back, so hard her teeth snapped together and her lip split. I helped her up and forced myself to be calm. I told him we were tired and that we would see them in the morning, then bade him good night. We turned and slowly walked away. As soon as we entered the brush, a loud cry broke out. They yelled and laughed, and we could hear them readying for the chase and making claims on Cammy and the "young one."

Grant tensed when a bolt of lightning flashed nearby, punctuating the words. The drizzle persisted, and the lantern flickered. He thought more insects had settled on the glass, until the light completely guttered out. He lifted the lantern, brows drawn. *Bloody hell.*

Out of oil.

He could read by the fire. He jerked his glance over, but the embers were wet. Rigid with irritation, he folded the journal into an oilskin pouch. He pulled on his jacket and turned up the collar, attempting to sleep. A futile gesture. Victoria had lived, but what had she lived through?

No wonder she'd been so frightened when he chased her. He rubbed a hand over his face, flinching from his actions. He wanted to find her and assure her that he was there to help. He wanted to comfort her as best as someone like him was able.

He wanted to read on so badly, the pouch seemed to burn.

"So, how's the campaign?" Cammy asked from beside the popping fire. Though it was wet and gusting outside, they were relatively snug in their hideaway.

Tori leaned back and placed her hands behind her head. "Today he'll get a delightful view of the twin seep holes on the west side. And for tomorrow, I planted a trail through the mangrove thicket that won't wash away." She hoped she appeared utterly confident, but the truth was, she had no idea if she was proceeding in the right direction. They showed no signs of leaving, nor staying for that matter.

"What else have you planned?"

"Now, just hear me out before you say anything." Tori leaned in and lowered her voice, as if what she was about to impart would be disturbing. "I was thinking that I could—" She broke off. "Why are you looking at me like that? I haven't even told you—" The look of horror on Cammy's face made her freeze. "Something's directly behind me?"

Cammy slowly nodded, gasping. Tori spun around, placing Cammy behind her.

Only to come face-to-face with a thick, black-mottled snake, so close that her breath fanned it and would have made it blink, if scaly serpents had eyelids.

When its tongue slid out close enough to touch her cheek, Tori, in turn, piped out her lip to blow a curl from her eyes. "This is the *last* time, snake. The cave is *our* dry place, not yours." She hefted up the weighty boa and began to lug it out into the rain.

"Tori?" Cammy said in a squeak. Tori turned, the snake still casually looped over one shoulder. "Do you think you could take it farther away this time, so it won't slither right back?"

"All right, but I don't know where to put . . ." She trailed off as an idea came to her. Absently patting the snake's plump torso, she said, "I know just who would appreciate your company."

An hour after dawn the next day, Grant still hadn't set out, but continued to read, engrossed.

"Put the bloody book down," Ian hollered from his hammock. As he had for the last two outbursts, Grant ignored him.

> . . . I'd never been so frightened. Not even the night of the wreck. But we knew the island better and escaped. I'd found a jut of land with hidden accesses, like a lip plateau against the bare rock wall, and took

Cammy there. We left our soft sand camp and moved within the roots of the banyan, among the night bats and creatures. I felt safe within the grand old tree, but we were running out of food. We fought like spitting cats over who would leave, each wanting to protect the other. In the end, I planned to wait until she slept, then creep out before dawn. When I woke Cammy was gone. . . .

"Are you going to read or are you going to search?"

Grant reluctantly glanced up and found Ian standing over him, readied for another day. "I thought you'd had it."

"Walking until my feet rot off actually beats staying here—"

"So, we're out of liquor?"

Ian didn't even have the grace to look shamefaced. "Quite so. And bloody boring without it. Besides, when I found the shelter, it whetted the explorer appetite in me."

"*You* found the shelter?"

"Would you have found it without me?"

Grant scowled before looking down at the words covetously.

"Don't you feel guilty reading her journal?"

Yes, he struggled with it at every page. "I might be able to find a reference to another hiding place."

"You might put the journal down and find her sitting in her hut."

"She's too smart for that."

"So, now you know her?"

He knew she was courageous and wily and loyal. He held up the journal. "I know her."

Four

Just after midnight, Tori padded into their camp, her footsteps silenced by the sand. She dragged her woven sack with difficulty and crept closer to the shadowy form of the captain, an imposing form even at rest.

When she stood directly over him, she knew she should hurry away, but she was curiously content to watch him by the light of the dying fire and the waxing moon. His brows knitted in sleep, and a lock of hair teased his eyes. If she were objective, she'd admit that he was a particularly good-looking man, with his strong chin and chiseled features.

After several moments, the contentment faded as the curious urge to touch him surfaced. What would his skin feel like? She'd wondered since she'd seen him in the pool. And the faint beginnings of his beard? Would his face be rough where hers was smooth? Captivated, she inched closer.

And promptly kicked over a lantern.

She tensed to run. He mumbled something in his sleep, his voice a deep rumble, and rolled over, but he didn't wake. Relaxing somewhat, she noticed a book tucked by his side. Setting down her roiling sack, she leaned forward, wondering what a man like him would read.

My journal. The bastard was reading it. She pulled it free, heart hammering as he muttered again. The pages opened to where he'd placed a mark, and she read, the journal trembling in her hands. As though it'd been the morning before, she remembered finding the captain of that other ship attacking Cammy, remembered the rage she'd felt that he would dare try to hurt her. Tori had been blind with it.

Yet at the end of that harrowing trial, Tori had known she and Cammy could do whatever it took to stay alive. That realization had made her strong. The same knowledge seemed to frighten and weaken Cammy. . . .

Tori shook her head hard. Reminded of why she was here, she gathered up her prize once more and guided it from the sack. When it coiled under his blanket, she sprinted away, hearing the captain bellowing in the distance. After another five minutes of racing away, she wondered if she could slow a bit.

Until loud footfalls crunched the ground behind her.

The blood left her face, making it cool. Her run returned to a sprint as she pumped her arms for speed. He couldn't catch her. All she had to do was make it to the line of downed trees. He was too tall, too lumbering to run beneath them. The horizontal trunks were too high to scale. To the trees. Seconds more. She had them in sight.

Everything went black.

The air shot from her lungs as a crushing weight

pressed down. Her eyes opened in slits to find the big man straddling her.

"Don't move another inch," he said, then frowned. "Ah, hell, girl, your breath will come back—"

It did. She screamed.

He looked so confounded by her shrieks that she thought she could hit him and roll away.

She might as well have hit a rock.

He grabbed her fisted hands and thrust them over her head, pinning her arms down as she bucked beneath him.

"Damn it! I want to help you." He was breathing as heavily as she was as he held her down. "I'm here to rescue you."

She glared at him. "I don't need rescuing, except from the likes of you."

He gaped as though the idea of him as a villain affronted him. It was only then that he moved his gaze from her face to take in their position—him riding her hips and leaning forward over her to keep her hands restrained. Transferring both her wrists to one hand, he lifted the opposite shoulder to stare down at her heaving chest. His breath hissed out of him. He swore and dragged her to her feet, his huge hand clenched around her arm, and peered down at her in an unnerving way.

All sound from her evaporated. She'd never looked up at anyone as large as he. She'd been a fool not to run faster.

His face was tight, as though he struggled to control his anger. "Cover yourself."

She pulled at the collar of her blouse, trying to shimmy back in, but that only seemed to make him angrier.

"Leave it," he commanded. "I have proper clothing for you back on the ship."

Proper clothing? . . . "I'm not going back to your ship. I don't know who you are."

"I'm Captain Grant Sutherland. I've been sent by your grandfather to return you to England." He paused to gauge her reaction and found her raising her eyebrows at him. "You don't believe me? I know your name is Victoria Dearbourne. I know your parents' names."

"That proves nothing." She added in a nasty voice, "Except that you can read."

"Yes, I've read your journal," he grated, "but that doesn't change the fact that I've been sent here for you."

"Why did you chase me?"

"Because you tossed a snake in bed with me," he snapped.

"No, the first time."

He opened his mouth to speak, then closed it, looking genuinely perplexed. "I don't know why. You've been missing for nearly a decade, and you were within reach. I didn't want to let you out of my sight."

"If you've read my journal, then you know why I have a hard time believing you."

His brows drew together. "Yes, I do. And I wish I could take the time necessary to explain things to you, but we don't have that luxury. We'll talk on the ship."

His words seemed pulled from him. She got the impression this man didn't have to explain himself or his actions very often. "*I* have nothing but time."

"If I don't get my ship out of this area before a storm strikes, we'll all need rescuing." He caught her gaze. "Where's Miss Scott?"

"You don't really expect me to tell you that?"

"You'll simply speed up the inevitable. Because if she's on this island, I will find her and get both of you back to England." He pulled her toward his camp again. She allowed it, giving him time to relax his guard. When something scampered across the trail, catching his attention, she lifted the arm he held and brought his hand to her mouth to take a bite.

His hand shot down. "Do not," he said in a menacing voice, "even entertain that idea. I advise you not to anger me more than you already have."

Anger him? She was the grubby one, banged up and bewildered. "Or what?" she dared to ask.

"Or I'll turn you over my knee," he said with an absolute lack of emotion before pressing on.

Dear Lord, he would. She'd bragged that he'd never be able to catch her, yet here he was dragging her along. She needed a plan. *Think.* They were about to pass the pool.

"Captain? Sir? I've been hurt." She stopped and pointed at her thigh. "I need to clean the cuts on my leg."

His eyes widened. He grasped the back of her knee and lifted her leg so high she had to hop around on her other foot. He bunched up the skirt enough to see the beginnings of the scratch, then higher still. Tori began shaking slightly as though chilled, but she was far from cold. Her skin felt hot and sensitive to the calloused pads of his fingers.

Abruptly he lowered the skirt. "You are cut," he said in a voice different from before. Now his words rumbled from him.

She was indeed. From days ago, not that he could see that from mere moonlight. She could swear he felt guilty. She blinked up at him and said softly, "It really stings. I need some water." When he hesitated, she pressed. "If you're truly my rescuer, this is a good start."

"Of course." He coughed, and then said in a sterner voice, "Tell me which way to go."

"Past the great breadfruit tree, take the path to the left."

Moments later: "There is no path."

"That's not a breadfruit tree."

"Very well, you lead." He propelled her in front of him. "But don't try anything."

She walked on, guided them left until they came upon the pool he'd bathed in before.

He seemed at a loss, but finally he put both her wrists in one of his hands. "I, uh, don't have a cloth to wash the cut."

The giant did feel guilty. Perhaps he wasn't that frightening. "I'm filthy all over. From where *you* tackled me," she reminded him. "I'm getting in."

"I think not," he snapped. "Now wash the leg."

When she looked down at her hands, he abruptly released her.

Victoria sat at the edge of the water, pulling her skirt up and cupping water to her scratch. Grant swallowed hard. The water, he knew, was chilled and she shivered, sighing out a breath. The sound teased something deep in him and made him grow hard as steel.

He was a gentleman, damn it. But first he was a man, and now in some forsaken jungle, he was alone with a lithe, young beauty garbed in clothing like gauze. "That's enough."

She twined around to frown at him, and her skirt pulled farther up her slightly spread legs. She had long legs, defined, going on forever. A man could get ideas. It had been so long since he'd seen the smooth skin of a woman's thigh. . . .

By dint of will, he turned away. A glance at his hands showed them shaking.

He heard her slip into the water and twisted around. "Get out of the water. *Now.*"

Swimming as though she'd been born to it, she glided out farther.

"I said to get out of the bloody water!" He couldn't remember ever being so angry. So why did he still have an unbearable erection?

"Looks as though you'll have to come get me," she taunted.

Little witch. In seconds, Grant had his boots and shirt yanked off. *"Come here."* He tensed against the cool water when he waded in. Told himself he wouldn't throttle her. "I said, come here," he grated.

She smirked and waved at him then, fingers to the heel of her hand, the exaggerated way a child waves good-bye. He *would* throttle her. *Slowly.* Then she sank below the surface. What the devil?

He swam out to where she'd been. Even with the moon and the clarity of the water, he couldn't spot her. When a minute passed, he dove under, reaching out blindly. Another minute gone. His head began to throb in beat with his thundering heart. Again and again, he sucked in another breath and went down.

He broke the surface once more, was inhaling a gulp of air when he heard, "If you are who you say, then prove it. If you're not here for a rescue, then it's best if you give up early in this game, Captain Sutherland."

Grant jerked his head to the shore. "What," he demanded with a seething calm, "are you doing with my clothes?"

"I," she replied in a tone mimicking his, "am picking them up."

"Drop my bloody clothes."

"With pleasure!"

He barely had an instant to wonder at her words before she'd run away.

"Bloody hell!" He raked the hair from his eyes. "Bloody, bloody hell!"

From somewhere high above him, she said, "Oh, and, Captain, I'm keeping your shirt. And one boot."

He twisted in the direction of her voice, saw her on a cliff jutting out over the pool. Alarm clawed back up his spine, and he began to sweat even in the water. She was up too high. If she lost her footing . . .

He had only a second to think before his boot landed with a splash, inches from his head.

Five

"One bloody boot."

Grant slashed out at the growth around his knees with a gnarled stick. "What the hell does she want with one boot?" he asked himself yet again as he leveled the unfortunate bushes around him. Perhaps marking his path would prevent him from unevenly ambling in the same circle he'd made countless times already. His brilliant idea to track her from the pool last night had only resulted in his being lost.

Again, Victoria had eluded him. She'd definitely gotten the better of him. But that was about to change. He needed to get the girl on his ship, so he would be one step closer to getting her out of his life. Unfortunately, she'd turned out to be tempting. Even for a man with his control. Even when he wanted to throttle her.

She had the softest skin he'd ever felt. And when he'd stood next to her, he could smell the clean scent of her hair.

But if his thoughts hadn't centered on how incredible she smelled or the sensual feel of her skin, she might not have escaped him last night.

He entered the camp after dawn, shirtless, one foot cut to shreds, his damp trousers clinging to his legs. The men all had the same reaction. Shock.

Ian got over it first, and laughed uncontrollably. "I take it you caught her!" *Laughter.* Then, in a voice imitating Grant's own, Ian said, "Sailor, your shirt's not tucked in." He feigned a face of realization. "Oh. You're not wearing a shirt!" *Laughter.* "One boot, and it looks like your trousers are wet! To boot!" He howled at his pun.

With watering eyes, Dooley at least struggled to contain his mirth. "Sir, the snake wasn't poisonous."

"I realize that. *Now.*" He made an effort to calm himself. "Dooley, row to the ship and get me some more clothes and another pair of boots." He let out a breath and said with disgust, "And prepare to be here a few days longer."

While Grant waited for Dooley, Ian's laughter died down, only to rise again. He repeated this cycle for several minutes before finally lounging back in the purloined hammock—his adopted favorite place—a strand of reed lazily perched between his lips.

When Dooley returned, Grant gathered up his clothes and changed, impatient to get out of his wet trousers.

"So. Did you talk to her?" Ian asked as soon as Dooley and the crew were working out of earshot.

Grant took his older pair of boots and collected his polishing kit, determined to ignore his cousin.

"Hah! You did." Ian scrambled to sit up and straddle the hammock. "What'd she say? What was she like?"

"It's none of your concern," Grant snapped. "Just go away, Ian. Go back to the ship."

"Oh no, Cousin. Things are just getting interesting." Ian tucked the reed into the corner of his mouth and gave Grant a too-easy smile. "You want her, don't you?"

"That's enough." Grant swiped at his boot with the polish brush, missed much of the leather, and blackened his hand.

Ian slapped his knee and cackled. "Why am I asking? It's obvious she's got you tied up in knots."

"I won't say this again. Leave me the hell alone."

"So you caught her and she escaped. The nerve of the little minx, absconding with your boot and shirt! She's clever, I take it."

She was clever, all right. In the newly declared war between them, she was winning all the battles—or, as Ian had sniped under his breath, *Round three to Victoria.*

"You know, this whole experience could be good for you. Loosen you up a bit."

Grant glowered at him. "I do not want to be loosened up."

"Wound up too tight—that's your problem."

Grant faced down his younger cousin. "Do you really want to discuss our respective problems? Solve the number of them you have yourself before you focus on me."

"I can't do anything until I return." Ian raised his hands in the air. "And I can't return because you sailed to the bloody other side of the world!"

Grant was unprovoked. "You ran aboard my ship."

"Better your ship than the pack of thugs chasing me," Ian blustered. "Or so I believed. I thought you were sailing to the Continent. Or even America. Not *Oceania.*"

"That's the thing about thugs," Grant began as though imparting a secret. "Generally, they don't chase you if you don't owe them money."

Ian's face fell. "I thought I was paid up. I really did."

"You thought?"

"Some of us aren't financial wizards." Ian shot him a pointed glare, but Grant refused to apologize for his one true talent.

"If you actually are paid up, then it has to be about a woman," Grant reasoned. There wasn't a man in the kingdom more cosseted by ladies, and Ian lapped it up. "Some cuckolded husband probably got sick of sharing." Besides gambling, drink, and debt, Ian had a reputation for midnight leaps from his married lovers' windows.

"At least I take what's offered to me," Ian snapped.

Grant stomped into his boots. No, he didn't toss up the skirts of every society woman who offered. He had his reasons. None of which were Traywick's business.

When he snatched up his pack, Ian said, "Wait for me."

Grant turned, raising one finger. The look on his face stopped Ian.

"Perhaps I'll let you go at it alone today." With wary eyes, Ian sank into the hammock.

Later, Grant was glad to be alone as he labored up a root-strewn trail, again replaying the sparse minutes with Victoria and his own unusual reaction. If she were the society lady lifting her skirt, would he be able to resist? He feared not.

In less than half an hour, he'd been enlivened by the chase, then angered, then aroused. The cold water had had no impact on his erection—he wondered if anything would have—until she went under. Alarm had gripped him before fury overwhelmed again.

He checked his disappointment as the setting sun closed yet another day. She might return in the night. When she came back to add company to his pallet, he'd grab her.

She didn't return that night.

He knew he'd catch her, so why did he feel like he needed to see her *at that moment?* Where was his hard-won patience? His brother would be alternately amused and encouraged if he could see his notoriously unemotional sibling now.

Grant looked up at the stars. His image of Victoria Dearbourne as a helpless, sweet girl had certainly been shattered. She'd grown into a spirited young woman, but she was still a small thing, hardly above five and a half feet—well, small compared to him at least, and thin. Though he'd sensed a latent strength in her, he still was uneasy thinking about her out there in the night. Out there alone. He wanted to protect her, damn it.

And every hour of the day, he pictured how the concise, neat script in her journal had grown wild and erratic as she described that captain's assault. Grant remembered the blood that had splattered down to the page as she'd recorded the event.

The man had discovered Miss Scott and attacked, but before he could truly harm her, Victoria launched herself onto his back, trying desperately to strangle him. While reading the words, Grant had cheered her.

The cutthroat had flung her off and turned once more to Miss Scott, but Victoria had run at him again scratching and kicking. When he read how the bastard had back-handed her, Grant had held the journal so tightly his fingers made permanent indentions in the moist cover.

He'd been proud when Victoria spat a mouthful of blood on the man's boots, even while dreading his reaction. But then Miss Scott had been behind him, bringing down a rock. . . .

Grant wasn't an emotional man, so the blinding rage he'd felt toward that bastard had staggered him.

As did his fear.

He'd felt desire for Victoria, and couldn't help comparing himself to that captain.

Christ, he wasn't anything like him. It was inconceivable to Grant how a man could hurt a woman or touch a girl.

Damn it, Victoria was no girl at nearly twenty-two. She was strong—able to hold her own. But another part of him argued that though she was older, she was still woefully naïve. She *was* strong, but still in an incredibly vulnerable position.

It wasn't until the moon had set that he slept.

Finally, he slept.

As Tori waited at the edge of the camp, she watched the captain contemplating the stars, his face in a pattern of scowling, relaxing, and scowling again. She'd wondered the other morning why he unrolled his pallet directly under the one break in the canopy of limbs above and decided he wanted to prevent anything, or anything living, from falling on him. Now she knew he lay so he could look to the sky.

The thought was incongruous with her idea of him as the forbidding, stern captain, but then she was rethinking him anyway. Though she had no experience, no touchstone or guide stick to determine a man's duplicity, she'd begun to believe he was telling the truth. He'd come for them.

Now to get Cammy to believe. This morning, when Tori related her exchange with Captain Sutherland, Cammy had said she feared he'd taken the information from her journal. Tori admitted that she was torn, with half of her thinking Sutherland told the truth, but Cammy had seemed more concerned about any possible journal mention of the cave.

When Sutherland's eyes finally slid closed and the rise and fall of his chest grew deep and even, the wind had picked up to sieve the palms and curl waves ashore, as though in tune with Tori's unsettled feelings. She wrapped her arms around herself. Why had the sight of him gazing up at the stars softened something in her?

Lost in thought, Tori trudged back to the cave and was surprised to find Cammy waking.

"You've made a decision," Cammy said, stretching her arms over her head. "It's written on your face. So, do you think your grandfather sent him?"

Tori scratched her ear. "Yes."

"Eight years after the fact?" Cammy sat up and brought her knees to her chest.

Tori sat on her own pallet and considered the question as if she hadn't already done so fifty times. "I know I shouldn't, but I think he came for us."

"Are you trusting him because he's handsome?"

Tori flushed and stared at her toes. He *did* easily fit her idea of a rescuing knight with his tall frame packed with muscle, his expression intense and resolute, but he also exuded a sheer force of will that she had never reckoned with. He wanted her on that ship. "No, because he's determined. I got the feeling he's been fighting to find us for some time."

"I might not trust him, but I do trust you. If you think he's taking us back to England, then that's good enough for me." Cammy pulled her blanket closer around her. "Imagine going back after all this time. I have no family left there—that's part of the reason why I signed on with your parents—but how I've missed things! English tea, soft sunlight, *tea*, seasons other than wet and dry, *tea*." She grinned, but then her face turned serious. "I miss riding a horse across green fields more than I can bear sometimes. I'd hoped for it for so long. Then, after the . . . incident, I stopped thinking of it."

Tori knew exactly how she felt. After the second year here, the idea of a rescue seemed as far-fetched as flying. "If this Sutherland is telling the truth, then we have a lengthy voyage to look forward to."

Cammy pulled her braid over her shoulder and smoothed it down. "But you'll be able to see your grandfather and your true home. I know your parents always planned to live there after they'd finished their studies. They would have wanted you to return to where your roots are."

Tori's memories of her grandfather were mere sequences in her mind. She remembered him chuckling and swooping her up on his shoulders. She vaguely recalled that they'd stolen a batch of muffins from the cook and eaten them in the tree house he'd had built for her. "Cammy, if you agree with me, I'll approach him tomorrow. But I will say this—when we sail from here, it will be on our terms. I'm going to demand that we break up the voyage and get you to a doctor." Tori's fierce words were garbled by a yawn she failed to stifle. She wouldn't have thought sleep could be compatible with this new idea of rescue, but her eyelids grew heavy.

"Get some rest," Cammy advised. "We'll talk later."

Tori gladly slipped under her quilt, dozing off immediately. She only slept for a couple of hours until dawn, but it was time enough for her dream of the wreck to plague her. She rose, cheeks wet, relieved Cammy wasn't inside. A shudder ripped through her. Would she ever be shed of that night?

She ambled out to lean against the cave entrance and found Cammy in the clearing blithely cutting a mango for breakfast. Tori lifted her gaze to the red sunrise. She noted the amplified colors of the sun hitting clouds and inhaled deeply. The air was heavier, cloying even, and the water was warm enough to kill fish. But then, the ocean storm season was always palpable even before it fully manifested. She wondered if those men, sitting on a ship that was like food for these reefs, knew what was about to befall them.

She paused. If she was right about Sutherland, it would befall all of them.

The rain came again that day in frenzied bursts, dotting the towering waves in the bay. A hot wind tore through the trees. They were running out of time—the air was stifling, the water too. The region was primed for a typhoon.

If Grant didn't sail soon, they'd be floating in the middle of a cauldron.

He returned his attention to a rough map he'd sketched of the island. He flattened it across a crate, trying to add information, but the wind made it impossible.

He looked up in frustration. Ian was in his hammock, rocking wildly. "Ian," he yelled, "come hold this down."

Ian rose, pulled his oilskin tight, and shuffled over.

"I need you to hold the corners."

Ian placed his palms on two edges. "What is this?"

"This is how I'm going to find Victoria."

When Ian scratched his temple and the map flew up before he pinned it once more, Grant reluctantly explained, "We know she's been leading us where she wants us to go. Which means that she's leading us away from something. I've drawn a map of the island and marked each definite sign of her we've found—a net, a spear, obvious footprints—then weighted each item to calculate a mathematical probability of where she'll be."

Ian looked at Grant as if he'd spoken in tongues. "I thought you were only good with math that involved pound signs. Well, where is she then?"

Grant pointed at an elevation on the parchment. "She's hiding high in the mountain." He glanced up at the cloud-draped peak. "I hadn't thought she'd climb up so far."

"It makes sense. And it's about the only place we haven't covered." Ian's gaze followed Grant's. "Can we make it up there today?"

Grant turned to his ship, noting how she tugged at her anchor, then to the beach. "We have to. You see the row-boat?"

Ian blinked against the rain. "The sea's gone down about ten feet from it since morning."

Grant couldn't hide his look of surprise.

"Yes, Grant, even I notice things."

"Did you happen to notice it's supposed to be high tide?"

Ian's cocky grin vanished. "Storm's coming?"

"Big one."

Ian rapped a knuckle on the map. "Then let's go."

An hour later, they picked up a trail of footprints in the mix of sand and earth and followed it to a clearing. A cave, more a small crack in the foot of the peak, came into view.

Making his way inside, Grant lit a lantern, lifting it like a shield against the dark. Instead of the wet and mold he expected, he smelled a fire. Moments later, he could hear wood crackling. Triumph filled him and anticipation ran up his spine like a woman's nail lighting up his back. One more corner . . .

A body lay inside as though dead.

Six

*I*s she alive?" Ian whispered.

Grant nodded as they stepped closer. "I think she's breathing." The woman's face was impossibly pale, her breaths shallow through cracked lips. Her clothes bagged on her frail body. Yet her hair was a fiery mass of red, looking anomalous with the rest of her.

"Miss Scott?" Grant said, as Ian bent down and tapped her shoulder.

She rose slowly, as though she ached, then rubbed her eyes and squinted. She didn't seem surprised to find two strange men in front of her. In fact, she patted her disheveled ginger hair, coquettishly trying to neaten it.

"Miss Scott, I've been sent here by Lord Belmont to find the Dearbourne family."

"There's only one of them left. Who are you?"

"I'm Captain Grant Sutherland from England."

She tilted her head at him. "I'm Camellia Scott. Lately from somewhere in Oceania."

Ian chuckled. When Grant leveled a glare at him, he covered his mouth with a fist and coughed. "This is my cousin, Ian Traywick."

She looked him over, blushed, then gave him a girlish wiggly-fingered wave.

What was it about Ian and women? "Can you tell us where Victoria is?"

"Haven't a clue," she said with a casual sweep of her hand. His eyes followed it, noticing the pitted scars covering her fingers and palms.

"You don't appear very excited to be rescued."

She shrugged. "I couldn't muster excitement if the queen herself came to this island." She stared at the ground, getting lost in some memory. "I saw her once in a procession. She had this plumed hat and green riding habit that I would have given my right hand for—"

"Miss Scott," he interrupted.

She looked up. "We still have a queen?"

Impatience flared through Grant with each crack of lightning. A feral girl had kept him from getting his men to safety and now an addled nanny was thwarting him as well. "Miss Scott—"

Ian leaned in to whisper, "Grant, she's lived away from people for nearly a decade. A soft touch might work on this one."

Grant waved his cousin away and said, "The queen is alive and well." The woman gave him a blank look as if she didn't know what he was talking about. "Now, about Victoria. We need to find her and convince her we're here to rescue you both."

"I'm sure a rescue was the last thing we would have thought. More likely pirates or some kind of military operation." She gave him an arch look, then said crisply, "Plus, you are abysmally late."

Grant felt apologetic, as though he were somehow tardy. "I'm leading the eighth voyage that Victoria's grandfather, the earl of Belmont, commissioned. Obviously none ventured this far out."

"So we're no longer dead to the world. Astonishing," she said in voice that sounded not the least astonished. Her eyes narrowed. "If Belmont sent you, then describe his home."

He shook his head, then reluctantly began, "The manor house is an old graystone, shaped like a squared figure eight with two courts inside. The land is vast and filled with downlands, parklands, rolling hills dotted with sheep." He exhaled. "Now that my facts match up—"

"Oh, I don't know about that. Never been there myself," she said airily. "I just wanted to know what kind of place I'll be traveling to."

He gnashed his teeth in frustration. Ian laughed. The winds outside strengthened. "We leave today," Grant snapped. "Tell me where I can find her."

"I couldn't tell you even if I wanted to. She's been known to range over the entire island in one day. All I know is that she was looking for the handsome captain."

Damn it, it was no use with this woman. *Wait . . . Handsome? Did Victoria say that?* Grant stifled an unwelcome flush of pleasure. "Ian, take Miss Scott to the ship. Tell Dooley to use his best judgment with the storm."

She shrank back. "My first time back on a ship is going to be during a storm." Her face was expressionless. "Can't wait."

"It won't be so bad," Ian said, as he gently took her hand.

She swung her gaze back to Grant. "I don't suppose I have a choice in the matter?"

"I can be more certain of your safety on the ship."

"If Tori returns to find me gone, you'll have hell to pay."

He straightened. "Thank you, but I think I can handle a slip of a girl."

She gave him a pitying look. "That would be your first mistake."

"Cammy, you'll never believe the weather—" Victoria froze when she saw Grant sitting by the fire. A visible tension thrummed through her. "*Where is she?*"

"She's with my cousin and the crew aboard the *Keveral*," Grant answered slowly.

Swooping down, she snatched up a bamboo cane. Her voice was shaking with fury. "Why did you take her?"

He rose by degrees, standing low, trying not to appear threatening. "I meant what I said before. I was sent here to rescue you. We need to get you both on the ship and out of the area."

She shook her head, refusing his answer, and asked again, "Why did you take her?"

"Because I know you'll follow."

Her face tightened. She wanted to strike him—he could feel her anger, raw and radiating from her. Her fingers whitened on the cane. Just when he was convinced she might, she dashed from the cave.

He snatched his pack and shot to his feet to follow her outside, immediately raising his hand to shield his eyes. The rain fell, not merely spilling from the clouds, but pitched down to beat the earth. Broad leaves of the multitude of banana trees thundered from the force. He almost longed for the puling rain of England instead of this assault.

Lightning split the sky, relentless, one bolt erupting just as another touched down. Flashes illuminated Victoria as she ran before him, her hands grasping vines overhead or trees beside her, her whole body in league to propel her forward. She moved over rocks and downed trees with an ease, and a recklessness, born of practice. Grant followed, running sideways, one foot over the other as they descended sliding hillocks toward her home.

She stumbled past her hut out to the edge of the shelf, flat hand to forehead, straining through the wet curtain for a glimpse of the ship. Grant saw her sway on her feet, thought he heard her breath whistle out.

Unbroken darkness covered the water.

The ship was gone.

Seven

"*Where's the ship?*" Victoria rushed to him and shoved her palms into his chest. "*Where's the bloody ship?*"

He grabbed her hands. "My first mate has standing orders to preserve the *Keveral*. They'll sail to open sea, away from the reefs, in preparation for the storm. I waited here for you."

She twisted her wrists free. "She's sick. This is her first time back at sea and you take her out in a squall?" A bolt lit the stricken expression on her face.

"I think they beat it out," Grant shouted over the wind. "My cousin will take care of her." He laid his hand on her shoulder.

She staggered back as if shocked senseless, her eyes bleak. "Don't you touch me," she hissed. "Don't you dare." He raised his hands, palms out, so she could see them.

"Victoria, just trust me—" Lightning struck so near that

his ears popped, the light blinding him. A ripping scream pierced the drum of pounding rain. Grant ran toward the sound, scraping his sleeve over his eyes, blinking furiously.

Victoria had disappeared.

"You're nicer than the other one," Cammy said as the young man pulled the covers up to her chin.

"I get that a lot." Traywick grinned, an easy, charming curl of his lips. "If you're comfortable, I'll just let you sleep."

Wind howled over the ship, and she gave him an impatient look. "Not likely."

"Dooley is more than capable of getting us clear," he rushed to assure her. "I don't want you to be frightened."

"I'm not that afraid. I'm the sick one—Tori's the one afraid of ships. I just don't expect to sleep when we're being jostled about like this."

"We could talk," he said eagerly, then added in a more subdued tone, "If it wouldn't bother you."

She scooted up in bed. "That would be nice."

"I'll be right back." At the door he asked, "Can I get you something? Some tea or something to eat?"

"T-Tea, you say?" The one thing she talked about each night by the fire, dreamed about during the day.

He smiled. Enunciating every word, he said, "As much as you can possibly drink."

"Can you make it in a storm?" she asked, her heart in her throat.

Traywick glanced out the port window and said, "This is nothing. Wait until the ocean *really* gets going." He left with a wink and then minutes later, shuffled in carrying a tray laden with a steaming pot, a plate of small cookies, a bottle of spirits, and two teacups.

He handed her a cup of tea and the plate of cookies,

then poured himself a drink in his own cup. She sipped and nearly gasped. Piping hot, doused liberally with sugar—just how she liked it. Her eyes rolled.

He chuckled. "Miss that, did you?"

"Like nothing else. Besides maybe horses. So what shall we talk about?"

"Whatever you like. You're the guest."

"Let's talk about your captain. Tell me who he is and why he's searching for the Dearbournes."

Traywick moved over to the opposite bunk and slumped to a sitting position. "For your questions: *Who?* Grant Sutherland, of the rich Surrey Sutherlands and captain of this pretty boat. Most notably, he is cousin to *me*." He lifted his cup and flashed her an impudent grin over the rim before drinking. "*Why?* Because Victoria's grandfather hired him to undertake this mission."

"Is Sutherland a good man?" She bit into a cookie. It might've been stale; she didn't care. It tasted like ambrosia.

"Yes. Unequivocally yes. He'll protect her with his life." His voice was without doubt.

Cammy relaxed somewhat. Comforted on that point, she absently munched cookies and studied her grantor of tea and consequently her new best friend. Lord, but he was a handsome devil. He had chiseled masculine features, black hair with streaks the color of coffee, and the most vivid amber eyes she'd ever seen. He must have left a score of broken hearts back in England.

The captain was very handsome, in an intense, almost savage way, but this Traywick was perfect. And the ease with which he'd settled in with her indicated that he liked women as much as they surely liked him. She glanced at his unscarred hands. He wasn't a sailor by any means. "What are you doing aboard this ship?"

He took another deep drink. "Funny story, that. I needed to leave town in a hurry and ran aboard, thinking Grant was sailing a short voyage. I've been trapped ever since."

"How awful." He told the story in an amused tone, but she saw that his eyes were shadowed. "Did you leave someone behind?"

He looked up sharply. After a moment, he answered, "I did."

"You must miss her very much."

Traywick stared into his cup as though embarrassed, but replied in a low tone, "I didn't know you could miss a person this much."

Cammy got the feeling she was seeing only the tip of the iceberg, that this young man was hurting more terribly than she could imagine.

"She must be very special."

"Yes." He refilled his cup and changed the subject. "So, you think Victoria won't react well to sailing again?"

Cammy sipped, then said, "Not at all."

"She must've been young when you wrecked."

"Thirteen. She saw the *Serendipity* break open with her father on deck. A sailor pushed her mother over the railing and she broke her back. Tori lost both parents in a matter of days."

"My God, that must've been hard on her." He leaned forward, putting his elbows on his knees. "On both of you."

He looked so sincere, so genuinely sympathetic, that she found herself asking, "Are you to be our friend?"

When the ship pitched, he reached over to lift the safety rails on her bunk. "Yes, I'd like that."

"Good. I feel like we'll need an ally in the coming days." She finished her tea and set the cup on a bedside stand.

"Tori's a beautiful girl. Are you sure Sutherland can be trusted alone with her?"

He hesitated. "Ah, normally, there would be no question. He feels responsible for her—protective of her. And he's known throughout England as a man of honor."

"Normally?" Her heart dropped.

"I've just never seen him behave like he has with her. I've never seen him—" He paused as though searching for the right word. "—I've never seen him *long*."

"Oh, dear."

Traywick took another swig and glanced at the ceiling as if debating whether to tell her something. "Out with it, now," Cammy said.

"It gets worse. Those Sutherland brothers—well, the two older ones, when they each found their woman, they got a little crazed."

"So what happened?"

"One's happily married. The other one's dead."

Grant sprinted to the edge, breath knocked from him as he saw nothing but her small hands clawing at the earth, at slimy roots, frantic for a hold. He dove for her at the brink where the ground beneath her had given way, shooting his arm out and snagging her wrist. Her skin slipped inch by inch from his hand.

"Hang on, Victoria! Grab my arms!" He reached for her elbow, praying all the while that his own position wouldn't give way.

"I can't . . . get a grip." Her eyes were wide in her face, beseeching. "Don't let go. Please . . ."

In that instant, when his eyes locked with hers, he knew he'd follow her down before he'd ever let go.

"*I won't.*" He redoubled his efforts to grab her under her

arms. The closer he came, the more earth fell below him—by flashes of lightning, he could see large clumps exploding on the rocks hundreds of feet below. He nearly had her. . . . Seconds before she fell . . .

"I've got you," he roared, hands clamping behind her elbows. He hiked a leg up to plant a boot higher, pushing against his foothold to raise them to firmer ground. Again, another boot farther back. He dragged her until he could finally scramble back to safety, pulling her on top of him.

She clung to him for many moments, with her hands bunched in his shirt. He reached up to brush the rain from her face and felt warm tears streaming down.

She nearly died. When she pulled away, his hand shot out to cradle the back of her head, tangling in her hair. *She'd almost . . .* Through the rain, he studied her face, so pale, and her stark eyes as though memorizing them, before his hands gathered her face to bring her lips beneath his.

He tasted her, drawing her nearer, laying her back in his arms as he squeezed her to him. Her lips were so soft, trembling. Her mouth . . . sweet and lush. . . .

When she laid her hands flat against his chest, then brushed them higher to clasp his shoulders, he groaned against her and deepened the kiss, taking her with his tongue, savagely slanting his lips over hers again and again.

Distantly, he sensed her breaking away, and forced himself to let her. He cursed himself for frightening her, for clutching her so hard to his chest and kissing her so urgently. Her brows were drawn in confusion as her gaze flickered over his face. Never taking his eyes from hers, he watched as her confusion turned to anger. She bolted to her feet to back away.

But it was too late. That kiss—he'd never experienced

anything like it. He lay back, stunned, while she dabbed her tongue at her plump bottom lip as if she couldn't believe he'd just taken her mouth so fiercely. He cursed and ran a hand down his face, determined to master himself, but in the end, it didn't matter.

The seal had been broken. His control had been pierced, if only for moments.

And he liked it.

Heaven help them both.

Eight

*T*ori shook so hard her teeth clattered. Little wonder. Her best friend had been kidnapped, she'd just been saved from falling to her death, she'd received her first kiss, and the man responsible for all of it was trying to undress her.

After her fall, she'd hurried to the ladder, determined to get warm. When she slipped yet again on the slick rungs, Sutherland was behind her, helping her up. She was exhausted, her body weak, and she let him. Inside, he'd turned his back while she struggled to dry and change, but her arms felt stretched from their sockets. The mattress beckoned, and she buckled to a heap.

He turned around immediately, kneeling beside her. "Oh, no, Victoria, not until you're dry. Come here," he ordered gently as he grasped her shoulder and made her sit up. He took the tail of his shirt and wiped at a smudge on her face.

Still holding her shoulder, he leaned over to the pile of

linens in the corner and found the most absorbent material there. He took the cloth and lightly twisted her hair with it, wringing out the water. How could such a big man handle her with such care?

"You've got to get changed. I won't look if you let me help you." His voice was low, soothing, and deep. Lulled, she let him remove her top, in the back of her mind conscious that he did indeed keep his eyes above her chest. But she tensed when he unfastened her skirt.

"Can you do this by yourself?"

Her arms were dead blocks on the sides of her body. Loath to do it, but knowing how dangerous it was to have wet clothes on in this climate, she shook her head. His eyes never wavered from hers as he tugged down her sodden skirt and briskly wiped down her legs, arms, and belly. Leaving the cloth to cover her, he pulled a large shirt over her. She wondered if he realized it had once been his.

He hadn't ogled her, but behaved like a gentleman. Now. Yet earlier when he'd kissed her . . .

She shook harder at the memory, and he grasped her chin and made her look at him. She couldn't get her eyes to focus. Did his own eyes show worry? Was his face haggard with fatigue?

He laid her down and pulled a sheet over her. Just before her lids closed for good, a gust buffeted the hut. Thinking of Cammy trapped aboard a ship made her feel like crying—or striking him. "You shouldn't have separated us," she rasped. "Not when she's so sick."

"We'll talk about this when you've rested."

Dimly, she heard herself say, "She better be safe. For your sake . . ."

What felt like hours later, she stirred. Cracking open her eyes, she was surprised to see light, then realized he'd brought in a flickering lantern. She peeked at him through the hair that had fallen in her face. He sat with one long leg stretched out, the other bent with a thick arm resting over it. He never took his eyes from her.

Disconcerted, she sat up, pushing her hair back to tuck it behind her ears. His gaze followed her every movement.

"How are you feeling?"

"Fine," she answered curtly, frowning at her hoarse voice.

"I imagine you have quite a few questions."

She moved to sit on her knees, facing him, the lantern shining between them. "I want to be absolutely sure you were sent by my grandfather."

"How?"

"Describe Belmont Court to me."

He eyed her suspiciously and asked in an impatient voice, "Have you even been there?"

"Well, of course."

He exhaled and related, "The estate manager's name is Huckabee. There's a stream running through the property that's full of trout. There's a walled rose garden adjacent to the south side of the manor."

"So he did send you," she said in resignation. "Why did it take so long?"

"I'm heading the eighth mission. The others must not have journeyed so far out."

"Why you?"

Her question obviously took him aback. "Belmont chose me because he trusts me. I'm known as a man of my word."

He said the last reluctantly, as if he despised talking about himself. But he'd neglected mentioning one thing she was *very* interested in. "A man of your word? That's nice." She skewered him with a look. "But what I want to know is *if you can sail.*"

Sitting straighter, he ground out, "I've never had any complaints." Then seeming to curb his irritation, he said, "I'm more than capable of getting you home. My older brother is also a captain and I learned a lot from him. For the four years before this voyage I oversaw his estate, but before then I sailed routinely."

She chewed her bottom lip, waiting for more information, but he didn't elaborate. Reading him was like reading a rock.

He must have misconstrued her silence, because he said in a severe tone, "I will protect you with my life."

She leaned forward, her gaze catching his. "That's what the captain of the *Serendipity* said . . . and he did!"

He had no answer for that.

"What are you to protect me from?"

"Perhaps from falling." When she flushed, he added, "Belmont entrusted me as your guardian in the event your parents had passed on."

"Is that why you feel you can order me about?" Tori asked.

"I was given that duty, yes. You're my ward now."

"What's your incentive for bringing me back?"

"Belmont is . . . compensating me in his will."

He'd hesitated. Was he lying about the will? *Will?* "Is he sick?" she demanded.

"No, no," he assured her. "Not that I could see."

She sighed in relief. Strange to feel such an instant, biting fear for a man she hadn't seen in almost a decade, even if he was her last blood relative. When she saw he scrutinized her reaction, she hastily asked, "How long is the trip to England?"

"It all depends on the trade winds. We made it to Oceania in four months, but the return will take longer."

"Four months . . . Cammy won't make it four weeks."

"Once I explained who I was, Miss Scott was glad to go, relieved that you'd finally be rescued."

When the enormity of the situation hit her, she felt dazed. "Putting her on a ship for the first time in a storm." She looked at him in confusion. "Why would you do that?"

"I wanted her where I could be assured of her safety." He leaned forward. "I'm going to be putting you aboard as soon as they return."

She narrowed her eyes. "We're at cross-purposes, Captain. I refuse to travel farther than New Zealand until Cammy's better."

Obviously struggling with anger, he snapped, "I'm not some *hack* to deliver you wherever you deign to go—"

A limb cracked nearby and tumbled against the roof, startling her. She couldn't imagine what Cammy must be going through. Though to be honest, Cammy had never voiced a fear of ships. Still . . . "You're a cold-blooded bastard for doing this to her."

His eyes grew dark and forbidding. His voice was brutal when he said, "You're not the first to call me that and you won't be the last. Regardless, it's logical. If I get her on the ship, I know you'll follow. And I have a responsibility to get my crew out of here."

"Cold-blooded."

"Shrewd," he grated.

"Go to hell, Captain Sutherland." She lay down and turned from him in a huff.

"Fine thanks for someone who just saved your life."

Over her shoulder, she said, "You can't imagine what I'd have said if you hadn't."

For the entire night, the storm lashed the shelter, but the hut kept out the elements flawlessly. Grant struggled to stay awake, reasoning that he wasn't *sleeping* alone with his ward in her room. He was *guarding* her, as was his duty.

At dawn, the rain abated, and Grant blearily stumbled down the ladder to check for the ship. When he found the bay empty, he scuffed to a rain trough on the side of the hut and set up to shave. Just as he finished, she walked by, changed from his stolen shirt. Her face was still pink with sleep, and the morning breeze toyed with the tips of her hair and the ragged fringe of her clothes.

"The ship hasn't returned." Her voice was raw.

"No, not yet."

"Why? It's fair weather."

"The storm might have blown them farther out. Don't be worried—this sometimes happens." Remembering the way she'd felt in his arms last night after the fall, he couldn't draw his gaze away. Even when she looked at him with disgust.

"Don't be worried? Are you jesting? I don't even know you, much less your ship or your crew. I don't know that they are good men. I don't know that they aren't sinking somewhere as we speak. Every minute that ship is missing"—her lips thinned—"is a minute I despise you more." She snagged a covered basket hanging from the platform and a broad-brimmed hat, then swished by him.

"Where are you going?" he asked.

"How can you think that's any of your business?" she tossed back.

"I'll simply follow you if you don't tell me."

She slowed and turned. "We've established that you've got a one in two chance of catching me." As he approached, she openly scrutinized him, as if sizing him up and finding him lacking. "I feel good about making it one in three."

Without warning, he snared her handwoven basket. His brows drew together as he recognized the leather from his boot.

To be honest, it did make a fine handle.

"Give it back!"

Holding the basket so she couldn't reach, he opened the lid to find a knife, bone hooks, some type of thin, fibrous line. "Fishing? If I were inclined to let you out of my sight—which I'm not—I would go fish and leave you here to do more ladylike things."

She hopped up and snatched it back. "Such as?"

"Perhaps mending some of the more unfortunately placed holes in your attire." He gave her blouse, where a tear gaped from the shoulder toward her chest, a pointed look.

"If I were inclined to let you out of my sight—which I've been from day one—I would leave you here and go fish since I'm much better at it than you."

He shook his head. "How do you know that? I could be a master fisherman."

Her chin shot up. "Because I'm the best ever. So no one could be better."

"Victoria, you'll learn in England that young ladies aren't usually so arrogant." He frowned, then added, "Well, they might be, but they hide it better."

"Hide arrogance." She tapped the side of her head. "There. Noted. Now, good day."

"Wait." He put his hand on her arm. "It seems to me that you'd want to keep me in sight."

She gave his hand a withering glance. "Why? If you're truly the gentleman you brag to be, then you'd never leave without me."

Damn it, he hadn't bragged. His mind cast about for some kind of leverage over her. "Listen, you want things from me—"

Her eyes widened. "I want *nothing* from you."

"Don't you? It's possible I could be persuaded to stop at Cape Town to break up the journey for your friend and find a doctor."

"If I did what? Let you kiss me again?"

He felt himself flush. "That . . . that was a mistake. It won't happen again."

"You don't know how right you are about that," she said vehemently.

Was it so terrible for her to be kissed by me? "I was thinking more along the lines of cooperating with me, and staying close by." She was an easy read. Her emotions warred on her face. He knew the instant she determined to go along with him, because her face fell.

"You must swear we'll stop at Cape Town."

"I swear it."

"I'll agree to it, but"—she put her weight on one leg and cocked her hip in a saucy stance—"if you get in the way of my fishing, I will leave you. And it's not to be held against me."

His lips curled. "Don't worry yourself on that score, Victoria."

"We'll see," she scoffed, then whirled around to rush down a steep path—Grant following close behind her—until they came upon an inlet draped in shade. Grant had traversed this section of the island before and remembered the mangrove trees that littered the water's edge. Now he noticed the thick fish darting among their roots and the din from hungry terns racketing above the canopy.

Seeming oblivious to his presence, Victoria dropped her

basket, then grabbed a spear from within a rotting tree trunk. When she walked to the bank, she stopped only to ruck up the ends of her skirt and tuck them into the waist.

He battled an urge to look around and make sure no one saw her like this. Most of her legs—her thighs—were bare. "I don't understand you at all," he said in exasperation. "You think nothing of decorum but won't be caught dead without a hat."

She shrugged as though he had it exactly.

"Aren't you embarrassed to be seen like this, or in your transparent blouses?"

She arched her eyebrows. "Noticed them, did you?"

He flushed and said gruffly, "Answer the question."

"Well, now, there's the crux of it. All my clothes are like this or worse, so would it embarrass me more for you to continue seeing what you've already seen, or for you to see me blushing and stammering when I can do nothing about it?"

"Why don't you borrow Miss Scott's, then?" he asked reasonably.

"And ruin hers as well when I have to work?"

He scowled because she had a point.

She'd already begun scanning the water, and within seconds, she lofted her spear and stabbed it down with incredible speed, then kicked it on its opposite end to display a plump fish. "I didn't sign on as your provider, Captain," she said while levering the fish off. She took a line tied to a nearby root and looped it through the fish's gills. "If you want to eat, you better get to work."

When he snagged another spear from the trunk, she faced him, raising her chin in challenge.

Grant was reminded of two duelers meeting at dawn. But with her gauzy clothing hugging her body and her hair shining all around her face, he was terrifically outgunned.

"Ready, master fisherman?" she said, smirking.

So she wants to lay down the gauntlet? "Always."

Tori had studied the captain and determined that though he was brave, he was obviously miserable on the island as it worked against his straitlaced manner, his impossibly crisp shirts and shined boots. He appeared as stiff-necked as Tori was carefree. No, the captain wasn't easy; he wasn't amenable. He would not be a man who reacted well to losing. All the better when she handed him this defeat on a platter.

Though her arms were like slabs attached to her shoulders, she refused to rest. He took his first fish, and then another. She spiked two more.

Irritation stamped his face and settled in tight lines. The madder he appeared, the more of his clothes were yanked off. First, his broad hat, so he wouldn't have to remove it to wipe at the sweat on his forehead. Then his shirt. Then his boots, so he could wade deeper. She wondered for a moment if he was trying to distract her—it was effective—but seeing how intent he was on his catch, she discounted the idea.

Tori brushed her hair out of her eyes with the back of her hand and surreptitiously surveyed him, noting how his lean body flexed, then stilled just before he launched his spear. Her gaze followed his long arms raised above him as he stretched afterward. When he leaned back to dunk his head underwater, the muscles in his bronzed torso tightened, and her lips parted.

Tori frowned. She hadn't ever wondered if she could acclimate to society—she'd just assumed she could do anything necessary of her—but now she felt a pause. She was beginning to see that there was a yawning gap in her knowledge, that there were questions she couldn't begin to divine answers for. Like how was it possible to detest a man and yet get more pleasure from simply looking at him than she'd ever known? What she felt when she watched him move—was it attraction? Or even lust, when she wanted to put her hands on him? Why had she momentarily enjoyed his kiss when she hated him? *Mysteries all,* she thought with a sigh.

When he caught another fish, Tori impatiently marshaled her thoughts, determined to win. They were tied when her arms finally gave out completely. Yet he continued, spear raised, waiting, waiting. The fish must be huge for him to take so much time with it. She shrugged. Though she'd have one fewer overall hers were still larger. She took pleasure in knowing they were competing by total pounds, not quantity. Even if he wasn't aware of that fact.

She waded farther up the inlet where the shaded water was fresher, and undressed. She washed her body, scrubbed her clothing and wrung the water from it, then dressed and finger-combed her hair until it was nearly dry.

When she returned, she saw him still poised over the fish, following at a glacial speed. She perched on a palm, drumming her cleaned nails on its trunk, piping her lip out to blow a strand of hair from her face.

Enough of this. She scooped up a rock on her way to the water, and tossed it right in front of him.

Nine

Will. That's what would defeat this monster of a fish. Every time Grant tensed to launch his spear, the thing uncannily moved. But he was a patient man and could wait out the prey for hours if necessary. His arm ached from holding the spear aloft for so long, but he was dogged. And it would be worth—

Water splashed up to his face and the fish darted away, both in recoil to the huge rock sinking before his feet. Teeth clenched, he looked to the edge of the shade, where Victoria gave him a triumphant smirk. With a growl, he hurled the spear like a javelin at the waterline, where it plunged upright, then strode toward her. With every step he took, her chin notched up higher. When he stood directly in front of her and gave her a look that had cowed convict sailors, she didn't even flinch. She wasn't afraid of him or intimidated by him. Perhaps she should be.

Without a word, he clasped her in his arms and started for the water.

"No! Sutherland," she cried. "I'm warm and dry! Don't!"

Nothing could stop him from dumping her in. Except at the last second, she went from beating on his chest to a stranglehold behind his neck. Just as he hoisted her away, she pulled him down with her.

He shot past the surface, coughing water, close to laughing.

She was sputtering, pushing hair from her face. "You bastard! You'll regret that. . . ." She trailed off as she looked down at her chest, no doubt following his gaze. Her shirt was twisted and half torn off her shoulder, revealing the top of one breast. The sandy fabric clung to the other. She plucked the shirt from her chest, but it insistently molded back to display her hardened nipples. The sight of them, the thought of touching her, his mouth on her . . . Explosive want burned inside him.

His hands clenched as he sorted through the thoughts and impulses wracking him. All morning he'd watched her, eyes locked on her long legs or her nearly bare breasts. The taut flare of her backside had nearly brought him to his knees. He would've given his life, he was sure of it, to hold her there, to heft the curves and fit his fingers around her flesh. He'd worked himself to a frenzy in an effort to quell the near constant erection he battled.

Now she stood before him as though unclothed. He wondered if he affected her as she did him. Her breaths were shallow and her eyes were wide, raking over his chest and lower, boldly, appraisingly.

He thought, in this brief sliver of time, that she might welcome his kiss, might let him brush her shirt from her shoulders and run his hands over her breasts. *Victoria, unclothed, in the water with me.*

He made some rough noise in his throat, then hauled himself to the bank. Never slowing, he snatched up his boots and shirt and stormed away. He paced furiously up and down the glaring white beach, only stopping to fling a shell or imagine his ship at anchor. Before he'd found her, he'd been in no particular hurry to return home. Now Grant saw it as his only salvation. Victoria would lose her appeal in his world. She was too outspoken, too bold.

He stared at the sinking sun, struck by the violent searing of color across the sky. Only here would he see such a scene—bloodred battled orange, magenta, and the night's coming blue, the fierce colors mirroring his own crazed feelings. Grant was about control, and if she destroyed his control, she destroyed him. She stirred his emotions to a startling degree. A dangerous degree.

No woman had ever made him . . . *want.* Made him desire more than he could or would have.

When he returned to the inlet, she was gone, so he trudged to the camp. Halfway up the trail, he smelled cooking. Nothing could smell that good. The scent became more intense and, like an animal's, his mouth watered.

He found her preparing their catch in the open-fire hearth, and concluded he'd never been more hungry in his life. After sweeping a glance around the clearing, he asked, "What do we eat with?"

She laughed without humor. "You're assuming you get to eat?"

"Utensils?" he grated.

She gave him a long-suffering sigh. "You're looking in vain. Be glad for the plate."

He peered down at the wooden disk she called a plate,

piled high with flaky white fish. Eating fish with his hands?

Victoria had already begun and her savoring sounds didn't help his resistance. Finally, even manners were tossed aside, and he scooped the meat into his mouth. He closed his eyes before he could stop himself. It nearly melted. The taste, the texture, the smell registered with him as no food had before. He caught her observing him and flushed.

They devoured everything. Grant struggled to eat like a civilized person, but in the end, he wasn't particularly successful. He'd shoveled every bit of food into his mouth like a beast and was looking for more. Victoria had to yank twice at his plate to take it to clean. The island was beginning to get to him. He wouldn't—couldn't—let it. He was stronger than the pull here.

"What are you doing?" he asked when he saw her squeezing juice from some type of fruit onto her fingers. She didn't answer, just tossed him the other half. The scent was tart and obliterated the smell of fish on his hands.

"You got along fairly well without the utensils," she mused as she fell sinuously into the remaining hammock.

"I don't see why you haven't made some. I saw you'd carved hooks out of bone. I know you're capable."

"Why would I waste my knife—my *one* knife—carving a fork when I have fingers and opposable thumbs?"

He sat on a log before the fire. "Because you'd have some semblance of civilization? You're going to have a lot to learn when you return."

"What if I haven't forgotten?" she asked. "Perhaps I've chosen to disregard certain things."

"Such as?"

She dropped a leg outside the hammock and used her toe to rock herself. "Such as what doesn't fit out here.

Dressing like a lady, for instance. Putting myself in three hundred pounds of petticoats—even if I had them— would be suicidal. You have to adapt or you'll die."

"That's not the civilized mind-set." Taking a branch from a pile of tinder, he stirred the embers. With the fire banked, he could clearly see her face. "It doesn't matter where you are—you can't lose your manners, your dress. Otherwise, you lose your identity."

"And why would I want to keep my identity?" She tensed and eyed him. "Understand this, Captain. For eight years, we thought we were dead to the world. There's a freedom in that." She relaxed again. "And whether you know it or not, you're adapting just as I did."

"What do you mean?"

"Taking off your shirt, your boots—"

"Noticed that, did you?" he asked with raised eyebrows, and she crossed her arms over her chest. "I understand why your clothes are like"—he waved a hand at the colored scarf she had tied around her chest—"that. But still, maybe a blush from you? You were old enough to know propriety when you landed here."

"*Propriety?*" she spat. "Shall I call you Saint Captain or Captain Saint?"

Grant worked to hide his exasperation.

"Yes, I was old enough to have learned that. *If* I'd been taught what was proper. When I was younger, my mother used to say that nothing limited the human spirit like propriety. She would've called you a sanctimonious killjoy."

"I am not a killjoy," he protested before he could stop himself. "I adhere to propriety because it's the backbone of Britain. It's what separates our society from every other one on earth." He raked a hand through his hair and tried to reason. Of all the things for her to misunderstand or be ignorant of—this should not be one of them. "The rules for propriety didn't simply spring up in a vacuum. They were formed by layers of time and are upheld for a reason."

She looked at him thoughtfully. "Yes, that's what I'll call you. Captain Killjoy."

He glared at her. She hadn't listened to a bloody word he'd said. "If identity and propriety mean nothing to you, I wonder if you even want to leave."

"Just because I didn't run down to the beach to meet you doesn't mean I don't want to leave. You've been reading too many castaway stories. And trust me, they have it wrong. When should women—whom no one would miss because they're believed dead—ever run out and greet sailors who'd been out to sea for months?"

"Actually, I believe you were right to be cautious." He stared into the fire, thinking of the journal, wondering what had become of the captain. "You never wrote about that captain after Miss Scott hit him."

Her toe braked her swaying. She sat up, her body rigid. "That's because his story was over. He died and we left him there. After a day, when the crew couldn't find him, they spooked and sailed." Her bearing dared him to criticize her.

"Do you regret anything about it?" He hoped not, but how could a woman *not* be plagued with nightmarish memories and misgivings? *He had her, he was hurting her*, she'd written. *I wanted to protect her—I wanted to hurt him. It was as though I lost my mind.*

"Regrets? Certainly. I wish we could've avoided the entire situation. If not, I wish I'd brought down the rock instead of Cammy and spared her that."

Grant barely prevented his eyes from widening, not believing her words. Any woman he'd ever been with would have wrung her hands, waiting for help in the same situation. Not one of them would have launched herself onto a fiend's back and tried her damnedest to strangle him.

Now, years later, Victoria wished she'd dealt the final blow. Grant stared at her, at her steady, clear gaze, and for a moment, he was awed by her. He understood and wouldn't want to change her actions, but it was still disconcerting to be around a woman so different from any he'd known. He coughed and said, "I appreciate your caution. You were right to be wary. The pranks, however, I could've done without."

She shrugged and sank back. "They felt right at the time."

He was glad the topic had changed "Felt? I suppose you would choose instinct over logic."

"You get the same end, only instinct's quicker." Her rocking resumed.

Had been glad. Now he wanted to shake her. "How can instinct help you when you want to plan your life, or strive for something more than the most basic needs?"

She looked at him as if he'd just bayed at the moon. "My only plan is staying alive. And I think it's a noble one."

Grant couldn't understand her. He had the rest of his life planned out. In detail. He would return Victoria. Earn the Court. When the old man passed, he'd assume the estate and restore it to its former glory. After he'd achieved that, he'd begin the search for a wife, the way he did all things—thoroughly, without emotion. With an estate like that, Grant thought he could attract the type of woman he wanted—a placid English bride of impeccable manner and lineage. . . .

"What's your cause, Captain Killjoy?"

He gave her a black look. "To bring you back, and then make a home for myself."

"You disapprove of me for not having my life planned out," she commented with a sigh. "But how can I? I have no idea what my life's to be like when I return. For instance, how will I live in England?"

"Your grandfather will care for you until you wed."

"What will happen to Cammy? She has no family."

"I'm sure Belmont would allow her to stay with you until you married," he pointed out reasonably.

"Then what?"

"You ask a lot of questions, Victoria."

"I'm *planning*. Besides, this is my new life—I'd rather not go into it blind."

He couldn't argue with that. "Fine. Perhaps your husband would let Miss Scott stay on as a companion for you or a governess to your children."

"Perhaps?"

"If not, she could marry."

"Is that the solution to everything? Marriage? It's a wonder there are even any unmarried people to choose from."

When he gave her an unamused look, she exhaled as though overwhelmed. There *was* much for her to think of, and sympathy arose in him.

"Plan on this, Victoria. You'll marry well. You'll have children," he said with absolute certainty. "You will have friends and family."

She appeared momentarily dazed. Then her face softened. He'd wager she'd once loved children. Deep in thought, she murmured, "Those things could be." He couldn't take his eyes from her. When a breeze capped the fire and blew tendrils of her hair, she roused, then absently said, "Good night." For the first time, she didn't seem to regard him with fear or disgust. She strode from the hammock to the shelter, lost in thought.

That mysterious look seized his thoughts. He'd concluded that she was an easy read, but now he didn't know. He unrolled his pallet, looking for a break in the canopy, then stilled. Had she meant what she said about being dead to the world? Could she truly have given up all hope of ever leaving? And if so, how had she lived with the knowledge of all the things she'd never have?

The idea troubled him. But it shouldn't now. She *was* returning. She *would* have children, a family, friends. Though she was ensconced in her hut, he called out to her, "Victoria, I *will* return you safely home so you can have all those things."

After a moment, she called back in a grudging tone, "Move to the right if you want to see the stars."

Ten

Grant woke when the first fat drop of rain slogged his forehead. He swore when it was followed by another and another, until he was pitched into a tropical storm. He'd slept in drizzle out here before, he told himself—he just needed to accept the situation. *That night wasn't nearly like this though,* a part of him argued. He glanced up at the hut, knowing it was dry inside.

Share with her or remain outside. He rose but didn't approach, determined to stay away. He settled under a leaf, pulling up his collar. This wasn't so terrible. . . .

When he began to breathe rain, he swore violently and grabbed his pack, making his way up the ladder. He sluiced off the worst of the water and entered to find her snug and relaxed. Seemingly unconcerned at his entrance, she didn't even sit up.

He took off his pack, knelt, and delved into it. All of his clothes were soaked. He sank back on his heels.

"I'm going to enjoy watching your skin rot because of your beloved propriety."

He stopped scratching his arm and glowered at her in the dark.

"There's no light." Her tone was exasperated, as though she dealt with a difficult child. "Your modesty will be preserved."

"My modesty is not the issue." Sleeping with his ward in her room. Without his clothes on. This was just bloody brilliant.

"What is the issue then?"

"*Your* modesty. Just turn so I can get out of these clothes."

With a long-suffering sigh, she rolled away from him. "Take Cammy's bed."

He stared at the ceiling while he stripped down, then felt his way to the homemade mattress of grass.

The exertion from the day caught up with him as soon as he placed his head on his forearm. His eyelids grew too heavy to fight. He had a last hazy thought: *Isn't so bad sleeping here with her . . . situation like this, sometimes you have to bend the rules. . . .*

Grant was rewarded with the most amazing dream of his life. Victoria was curled next to him under her quilt, her breast soft in his hand. He cupped the other and, to his amazement, he felt her fingers on his torso, trailing lower.

His breaths grew ragged. His hand closed around her breast—the warmth, the unbelievable softness of her skin, could he possibly have dreamed this perfection? He cracked his eyes open, just as her lashes fluttered up. Vulnerable and soft with sleep, she was irresistible. He probably was still dreaming. . . . Leaning in close and slanting his lips over hers, he brushed his thumb across her nipple. She gasped and her hips rolled forward.

As he continued kissing her, outlining her lips with his tongue, her hand traveled down to explore his erection. He shuddered when the pad of a curious finger brushed the slick head, and groaned as a smooth nail trailed up the base. If she continued touching and squeezing him like that, he would spend. He wanted to. It had been so long. . . .

A shock of light flooded the room. Grant froze. Victoria's whole body tensed.

"And to believe I scoffed at the idea of using you as an example of a proper British gentleman," Ian boomed from the doorway. "Let me tell you, I am now ready to carry the torch!"

Ian was leaning into the hut, flashing Grant a proud grin.

What the bloody hell? Under the cover, Grant's hand still was wrapped around Victoria's breast, and her hand grasped him. Her lips thinned, while his teeth clenched. They both jerked away from each other. She was quicker than he, and when she moved, half her blouse caught at his wrist. She yanked it closed, but it remained an open V down to her flat belly.

"Aww, look at you two lovebirds."

My God, the humiliation is complete. "Go to hell, Ian." Grant threw his boot at the entrance, flushing to remember all the lectures he'd given Ian. He'd believed everything he'd told him, but one week on this island had undermined a lifetime of care. Had he really just had his hand on his ward's breast?

"Hell? Already been there," Ian informed them. "That storm was a monster—"

"Where's Cammy?" Victoria interrupted. "Has she worsened?"

"She suffered a little mal de mer, but we got through it fine," Ian said. "When I left, Cammy was in her cabin reading as voraciously as she's hit our tea supply."

"*Cammy?*" Grant mocked his use of the woman's nickname.

"That's what she asked me to call her." Turning to Victoria, he said, "Lady Victoria, I'm Ian Traywick, cousin to the ogre just here."

Victoria surveyed Ian in an appraising manner. "Thank you for caring for her. I can't tell you how much I've worried." She glared at Grant.

"It's my pleasure. Cammy's a wonderful lady."

"She is, indeed." Victoria smiled then, beaming at Ian as if he were some hero of old.

Grant's breath whistled out. He'd seen her smirks and sneers, but her smile . . . Her teeth were perfect and white, her eyes lit up, and God help him, she had a beguiling dimple in her cheek. Even Ian seemed taken aback and looked to Grant for direction. Now, with her cheeks rosy from sleep, her hair curling in thick white and golden strands all about her shoulders, the dip between her breasts bare—he had no defense against this. . . .

Would Ian?

Her shirt was open. He pinned a flat hand over her chest.

She gave him a fierce look, slapped at him, then tumbled away.

Ian was struggling not to laugh.

Grant snapped, "We'll be in the camp shortly. Since Miss Scott's on board, have her choose some clothes for Victoria from the trunk I brought."

"I live to serve." Ian flashed one last grin and turned to go.

"Ian?" Grant called. "I can trust you won't say anything about this?"

Ian turned and placed a hand over his heart. "You wound me. Would I betray a confidence?" He ambled away, snickering.

They were ruined.

Scrubbing a hand over his face, he cast about for something to say. "You moved to my bed last night."

She gave him a nasty look. "No, you moved to mine!"

He had. Christ, this was awkward.

She was looking away, bundled in her cover, knees to her chest. He grasped his forehead with one hand. "I apologize for this. It should never have happened. It *won't* happen again."

She waved his words away. "You keep saying that, and yet you keep touching me and kissing me."

His shame turned to anger. "I believe you were touching me quite enthusiastically as well."

"I was half asleep!"

He'd let her have her lie. "I need to get dressed."

This time instead of making a derisive comment about propriety, she grabbed her clothes and dashed from the room.

When he descended, he found her dressed, staring at the *Keveral*.

"We're leaving today?" she questioned softly as though she didn't believe it.

"With the next tide."

"And you will stop in Cape Town?"

He hesitated, tempted to remind her that she was in no position to make demands, but finally answered, "Just long enough for Miss Scott to see a doctor."

"Leaving today," she mumbled again, her face pale.

Never taking her eyes from the ship, she said, "I have to get some things before I go."

"Then you've got the rest of the morning. I'll accompany you."

"No." She shook her head. "I want to be alone."

Unfortunately, Grant knew her request was reasonable, but he didn't want to let her out of his sight. "Very well." She'd *think* she was alone.

He gave her a head start, then followed, sure that she would have sensed him behind her if she hadn't been so distressed. Just when he'd decided that she did know he'd trailed her and was purposely dawdling, doing nothing, probably talking to flowers, she entered a clearing.

He found her kneeling by a makeshift cross, marking what was obviously her mother's grave. He remained hidden, watching her tearfully whispering, wincing when her small shoulders shook.

The realization of what Grant was taking Victoria away from hit him hard. She was leaving more than just the island, or even a way of life.

He'd begun thinking of her as a prize, a goal, a *means to an end*. Now he saw her as a young woman who hurt. Someone who was under his care, but was afraid.

She opened an old wooden box placed by the grave, and from inside she took a length of twine with something on the end, like an amulet. When she placed it around her neck, he knew that she would indeed leave with him, and so he crept away, truly allowing her privacy.

Two hours later, Victoria returned with a box of mementos and a motley collection of seashells. He found her at the edge of the beach, regarding him and the men packing up the camp with uneasy eyes. He gathered up the clothes sent from the ship and met her there.

She stared at the bundle he pressed on her as if it were incomprehensible.

"Do you remember—?"

"I remember," she whispered.

"I'll stay here in case you need help."

Mechanically, gaze forward, she began undressing.

He twisted around. "And I'll turn to give you privacy."

"I'm done," she said minutes later, her voice flat.

He faced her, unnerved by what he saw.

This morning, he'd encountered her first smile. Later, he'd realized he'd never wondered how *she* felt about all this. Now, another blow—garbed in a light-blue day-dress, she looked like such a lady, such a *young* lady, that his shame deepened. This morning, the way he'd touched her ... It seemed inconceivable as he considered her in that dress.

He frowned. She fidgeted with it, though it fit her slim form well, with straight narrow sleeves and a tightly gathered waist. A large, fussy bow sat on the neckline and clearly irritated her. She ripped it off, leaving a smooth, clean bodice, and looked at him, daring him to say something, but he thought it much better. She needed no embellishments.

Victoria glanced out at the ship and her face tightened. Something about her, with her fire banked and her considerable pride tempered, touched him. He'd finally figured out that he was attracted to her strength. And now to her vulnerability as well? When was he *not* attracted to her?

Even when her body trembled, she raised her chin. And he'd be damned if he wasn't proud of her.

Tori stared at her home, overcome that she would never see this place again. She felt as hollow as the island seemed, though not much had changed here. They weren't, after all, *packing up*, but it was lifeless just the same. Haunting, even.

"Victoria, it's time," Sutherland said, his tone emotionless.

Unable to move away, she was startled when he picked her up, until she recalled that women were always conveyed over the water. Sutherland was ever the gentleman, carrying her with a detached politeness that belied his passion just hours before.

He handed her into the boat to the small man, Dooley, as though she were fragile china. She stiffened and scrambled to her seat. Some of the sailors regarded her with curiosity, some smiled. She thought Sutherland glowered at anyone who looked at her, but she could have imagined that.

Being around his crew made her uneasy, but that feeling was blunted by the numbness of leaving. When they pushed off and the oars sliced into the water, the overwhelming scent of jasmine was lost to her for the first time in years. Her island grew smaller. She could see flocks of birds like dots, suspended over the trees, and cascades like silver threads fluttering to the ground. For all the dangers and hardships they'd faced there, her home still looked like heaven.

Too quickly, they reached the ship. Sutherland took her hand, helping her up to stand below the ladder as they bobbed with the waves. When her feet rested on the first rung, she turned back to him. He climbed up as well, standing next to her, steadying her.

"It's nothing to be afraid of," he said for her ears only.

"*I'm not afraid*," she whispered to him. But she didn't move. She craned her neck up to see the ladder crawling on and on up the side of the ship. If a person should fall from that height . . .

He patted her shoulder awkwardly. "Come, now, Victoria. We need to be off."

Anger drowned the worst of her fear. His detached politeness for the crew—so they wouldn't suspect he'd been fondling her throughout the night—riled her.

She climbed easily, even in her godforsaken dress, with him just down and to the side of her the entire way. She'd resolved not to look down, and finally made it to the deck, clutching the rail like a lifeline. While the others stepped aboard and raised and stowed the boat, Grant gave out orders.

She paused, moved with the ship, then sank down miserably in a heap of skirts. Tori smelled the moist sails and hempen ropes, and memories crept over her mind like a film. She remembered the old captain of the *Serendipity* had told her once that from the minute a ship met water it began decaying, dying.

"Weigh the anchor." Sutherland's voice was toneless. Dead.

Not yet. Not yet! As they made sail and lurched forward, she clambered up to see her island, sitting so serene and sure.

The movement of the ship, sliding under her like a slick embankment, made her stomach twist. She retched but didn't shame herself. Tears blinded her eyes. No control. Tori almost laughed in her panic—*tossed about like a ship at sea . . .*

All her anger and fear rose in her, threatening to strangle her. She remembered the horror when she and Cammy had looked about them on the island on that first night.

No idea where to find water. No idea where to search for food. A dawning comprehension of doom when Mother finally succumbed to the pain—the low, stifled cries. Seeing

Cammy bloody herself on those damn flints to make a fire for Mother. Seeing something in Cammy fade when she failed that wet, gusty night and darken altogether, nearly a year later, when she dropped the bloodied rock next to the captain's limp body.

Tori's hand shot to the string around her neck, fingers digging in her dress to yank out her mother's wedding ring. *Cammy took it from her dead finger because Mother told her to.*

All of the memories welled in her like a long-capped fountain ready to explode.

Tori had had a life-or-death situation thrust onto her, and she'd adapted. She turned narrowed eyes on Grant. Here this man was using her to further himself, and in doing so was snatching her from one life and shoving her headlong into another.

When would she have some control over her fate? Fear warred with a fury so hot it scalded inside. So loud, she heard nothing but her pumping heart.

The ship bucked as the wind snapped the sails taut, making her insides feel wrenched, and the island grew hazier in the distance. She stood, tottered forward, and grabbed at the wheelhouse.

"Victoria, Miss Scott will show you to your cabin," Sutherland said from behind her. When she turned to him, he frowned at her. "Camellia's just here."

She vaguely heard him. In her mind, his mouth moved slowly—really no words came out. Her eyelids grew heavy and then she was spinning, able to see the sun straight above her. A loud thud sounded somewhere near her. She heard Cammy screech, and noticed the side of her head ached unbearably. She wanted to cry. The captain spoke again, only this time his words came from just beside her, not commanding but asking. "Victoria, please open your eyes."

When she struggled to open them, she saw that his face was tight.

"Keep your eyes open, sweet."

The ship bucked again, making her moan. When her eyelids fluttered, he scooped her into his arms. Vaguely, she felt Cammy slapping at the captain to get to her, and him squeezing her tighter into his chest. *Then take her to the cabin*—Cammy snapped—*"if you won't let her go."*

Eleven

The nightmare came with a vengeance. This time the sounds of the groaning ship boomed in her ears. Her stomach tumbled with the jagged rise and fall of the bow. Tori opened her eyes, waking into her nightmare, not out of it.

Cammy peered down at her, a feigned smile pasted on her green face. Tori scrambled up in bed, unable to mask her alarm over her appearance. *Green around the gills?* She'd never really understood the saying until now.

Tori sat up too fast. Her head felt light but for an insistent throbbing on the side of her skull. "Cammy?" she muttered. "What's happened?"

"You fainted and hit your head."

Fainted? Her? "I meant, what's happened with you."

"Seasickness." She gave a harsh laugh. "Ill on the island, sick on the ship."

"Don't say things like that. It'll pass." Her optimistic

words did not match her thoughts. Cammy clearly felt wretched and needed to be in bed. Though the ship vaulted up a wave, Tori rose and went to the washstand.

"What are you doing?"

"Trying to wake up." When they plunged into a trough, water sloshed from the bowl. *Ignore that thundering sound. Ignore the way the boards shake beneath your feet.*

"You need to rest!" Cammy said sharply.

"I was just about to say the same to you."

"But you've been hurt. . . ." The last words were snuffed behind Cammy's tightened lips. Against her obvious efforts, she flew to a bucket and retched. Tori petted her hair, resisting the near overwhelming urge to join her. Fighting it was a grueling ordeal. Sweat drenched her, her breaths became gasps, and she had to lock her jaw. Tori knew that once you gave in to seasickness, you didn't stop until you hadn't the energy to move, a condition sailors called the special kind of hell.

Grant held out as long as he could. He didn't miss the looks Miss Scott gave him each time he came by the cabin. And his excuse that as a captain it was his duty to check on passengers? She waved it away.

At the door, he heard two voices. Finally, Victoria had awakened. He knocked and heard Miss Scott say waspishly, "If that man comes by one more time . . ." To him, she called, "Go away! She's fine. She's awake."

Damn it, woman. He hadn't wanted Victoria to know how often he'd been by. Just when he was about to leave, Miss Scott apparently changed her mind and called him in.

He greeted each with a cool nod.

"I need to talk to you, Captain," Miss Scott said.

Victoria frowned at her.

"You've got to get Tori out of this cabin. She's going to be sick like me if she stays."

Her eyes went wide. "I'm not leaving—"

"*You are,*" Miss Scott said with a fierceness Grant would've thought impossible the day before.

"This is a cargo ship," he said. "There isn't a free cabin."

"Then move me somewhere. In the hold—I don't care."

"Victoria, come with me," Grant commanded.

"I said I'm not leaving!"

Miss Scott rose, her face pinched as she prepared to say something.

Grant grabbed Victoria's arm. "You're only going to upset her more. She doesn't need this from you."

"Indeed," the woman bit out before sinking back down.

Ian strolled by at that moment. "What's all the commotion?"

"They want me to leave Cammy," Victoria said, the words like an accusation.

"So she won't get sick," Grant added.

Ian swung his head in to survey the situation. "I was planning on entertaining Cammy today anyway—you know, regale her with all my engrossing tales."

Victoria scrutinized Ian for several tense moments.

"Listen to him, Tori," Miss Scott ordered. "He's got a stomach made of lead. You can return when you get yourself settled."

"Victoria, we'll be fine," Ian assured her. "I took care of her before you came aboard. And if you don't stay well, I'll be nursing two of you."

Seeming to make a decision about him, Victoria reluctantly nodded, and Ian entered. "Cammy, where were we?"

Miss Scott muttered, "You were about to tell me one of your exaggerated stories and I was about to lose my breakfast."

"Ah, just so."

When Grant drew Victoria from the cabin, he propelled her forward so he could shut the door. She stumbled back. Looking down at the considerable drop to the water made her eyes go wild. Grant swore under his breath and placed himself between her and the rail as he guided her to his cabin.

Once inside, she appeared to relax somewhat and openly studied the room. He wondered what she thought of it. Nothing superfluous cluttered the Spartan interior. It was tasteful but not colorful, and every piece had a purpose. "This appears to be straight seasickness with Miss Scott. Ian will make sure she's comfortable," he said.

"I believe that he will." She added in a mumble, "Otherwise, I never would have left." When she turned to his bookshelf, she sucked in a breath and hurried over. "Beautiful," she sighed. "And intact." She pulled out the first book, *Robinson Crusoe,* and raised her eyebrows. "Research?"

He stood straighter. "I've got to get back to work. I'll have some food sent in when you feel better."

She replaced the book and nodded, but he made no move to leave. "You gave us quite a scare," he found himself saying. Luckily, his tone was casual. He hoped he didn't look as exhausted as he felt.

She sat at the edge of his bed, the first woman ever to be in his cabin. "Were you worried about me?"

So much that I didn't sleep. "You took quite a hit."

When she ran her fingers over the bed linens, images flashed into his mind of her flushed with pleasure and tumbled from sex. Realizing he liked her in his bed far too much, he excused himself, and attempted to run the ship.

Near dusk, the seas got lively. Grant returned to get his oilskin and found her sitting ramrod straight, fists bunched in the sheets, eyes wide and fixed directly ahead.

"Victoria, I should let you know there's a squall headed for us."

She swung her gaze to him. "I never would have figured that out all by myself." In a huff, she stood and paced.

"There's nothing to be afraid of. I'm going to keep you safe." She never stopped, never even acknowledged what he'd said. Did she not believe him? Did she not think he could? The idea rankled. "You need to buck up. This is the first squall, but it won't be the last, nor the fiercest. You're just going to have to be strong."

"Be strong? So if I tell myself to be strong, it will just happen? Self, be better with arithmetic." She held up her hands. "Nothing there either." When he scowled at her, she said, "The truth is, I don't *want* to be strong."

The room canted up and to the right, and she stumbled into the bed, latching on to it. When they landed with a teeth-clattering thud, she moaned. He noted with alarm that tears spilled down her cheeks. "I'm sick of being strong! What I am now is scared to death!"

In the past, if a disgruntled woman cried, he'd always said, "I'll leave you to compose yourself." But now he couldn't stand the idea of her hurting.

Grant wasn't completely without feeling, no matter what people said. Hadn't he just yesterday battled the urge to bundle her in his arms on the deck? And lost? Though he was needed on the bridge, he said, "I'll sit with you awhile, if you don't want to be alone."

She hesitated, then weakly held out her hand, the simple movement beckoning him to sit by her. He did, and she sidled closer, looking up at him with such gratitude, her eyes were brimming with it.

In a low, soothing voice, he explained every song, yell, and knotted vibration. "That snap is the sail grabbing a gust. . . . That knock just there is a loose pulley someone really should tighten. . . . No, no, when the timbers groan, that's good. It means they're bending as they should."

In a particularly rough dive, she grasped his hand in one of hers and tucked them both against her chest. Moments later, her head fell against his shoulder and rested there. How long they stayed like this, he didn't know. But when her breathing grew soft and steady in sleep, he lowered her and drew a cover over her, then went to battle the storm, muttering to himself about promises to keep.

Tori rose, altered from the night before. Yet another storm had failed to harm her. And last night, the captain had shown that, at heart, he was a good man. She'd felt, for the first time in so long and in the middle of a tempest, safe. He was so big and strong and utterly confident in his ability to protect her that even she had begun to believe it.

Attacks, falls, storms—these calamities continued to happen to her, and she kept walking away with her life, lending proof to her suspicion that she was invincible. This time she walked away with a fresh resolve. She sank down before her new sea trunk and pulled the string from her neck. She kissed the ring, saying good-bye once more, then folded it in linen and tucked it deep into a corner, treating it like the treasure it was. Though her mother had wanted her to have the ring, it wasn't Tori's to wear.

She was about to rise when her teary gaze caught on the

journal Sutherland had brought aboard and put with her things. It looked heavy—laden with memories.

When something weighed you down, it was best to cast it aside.

She plucked one of the prettier dresses out of the trunk, washed and dressed hurriedly, then set out to find the captain, journal under her arm. Though she was uneasy with the ship, she refused to be afraid. She climbed up to the bridge, and found Sutherland speaking with Traywick. "Captain," she said to his back.

He turned, obviously surprised to see her. "I didn't think you'd be up, much less out on deck."

"I wanted to thank you for last night."

He opened his mouth, then closed it. "You're . . . I . . ."

"That's all I wanted to say," she interrupted. "Just thank you."

She left them, with Traywick making some dig and the captain telling him to go to hell.

Her next stop was the side rail, where she stared at the white foam churning beside them, thinking about the incredible turn her life had taken. She'd been given a clean slate, to fill as she chose. When she returned to England, she could be anyone. She could be a terrified girl, cowed by the tragedies of her past, or she could be a dauntless woman, who'd taken everything thrown at her and was taunting Fate. Her lips curled up. Decision rendered.

With a lift of her chin, she scanned farther out. Last night, the ocean had boiled to fury. Today, smooth water stretched unbroken. And she stood unharmed. She smirked at the flaccid sea. "Was that *all* you could muster?" In one motion, she flung the journal to it.

Cammy's cabin was next. Her unsure walk became a march down the boards. Tori daringly skimmed her finger down the rail. At the cabin, she knocked, swung the door wide for air, and used one of her new, pinching shoes to wedge it there. "Good morning."

Cammy cracked open bleary eyes. She frowned and craned her neck to see behind Tori.

"You came alone?" At Tori's nod, she asked, "You walked here by yourself?"

Tori stood on the opposite bunk and opened a ceiling vent. "Uh-huh."

Cammy gaped. "So now you're roaming about the ship? I take it you feel better about things?"

Tori shrugged and sat. "I trust Sutherland to get us back. And I figure if I was meant to die in a shipwreck, the first one surely would've been it." She surveyed Cammy and found her looking less . . . green. "How're you feeling this morning?"

"I drank some tea and had some crackers. I feel better." With effort, she sat up in bed. "So you're not still angry at the captain for putting me aboard? You seemed to bridle around him."

She flushed, remembering how he'd held her hand the night before. He had such calloused and rough hands, but he'd touched her tenderly. "I thought it heartless at the time, but he had his reasons." She knew what it was like to see something you wanted and use every means at your disposal to get it. "I understand him better now."

"I want you to know he was very polite to me." Cammy's brow furrowed. "Well, except for yesterday, when he wouldn't cease coming by here. I've never seen a man more worried."

"Of course he's worried. If something happened to me, he wouldn't get paid."

"That's not it. Traywick's told me he's a very decent

man." Cammy lowered her voice and said, "Sutherland has feelings for you."

"For me?" Tori asked warily. "What do you mean?"

Cammy smiled. "I saw him react to your faint on the deck. He's smitten." Over Tori's protests, she asked, "You haven't seen it yourself?"

He'd kissed her on the island. Kissed her with a desperation she'd never imagined, and touched her . . . as though reveling in her. She suppressed a shiver. "Most of the time, he's cold and distant to me."

"Traywick thinks the two of you would suit."

Changing the subject, Tori said, "You and Traywick seem to have gotten quite chummy." She gave Cammy a piqued eyebrow. "Quite chummy."

"We are friends. Yes, he is glorious to look at and utterly charming, but he's young." In a conspiratorial tone, she added, "I've always had a tendre for the older ones, truth be told." She smoothed the cover over her lap. "Besides, his heart's taken. Completely."

Tori leaned back against the paneled wall. "So, when can I return and stay here?"

Cammy eyed her as if she had to reveal a hard truth. "Well, this cabin is so very small. Small for two people, much less two women." She added in a rush, "And Traywick sits on your bunk when he reads to me."

Unbelievable. "I'm ousted by the tea peddler?"

As though they'd conjured him, Traywick appeared at the doorway. He smiled at Tori and kindly let the comment pass. "You certainly look better than yesterday."

"Tori adapts," Cammy said proudly. "It's her gift." She glanced at the book he held. "Were you going to read?"

When he nodded, Tori stood to leave, but Traywick said, "I wouldn't hear of it, Victoria. Please stay."

She shuffled her feet, then perched on the far edge of the bunk. As though sensing she was skittish, he sat at the foot. "So what were you two talking about?"

"Before we talked about you, we discussed Captain Sutherland's infatuation with Tori."

It was Tori's turn to gape. Cammy shrugged.

He leaned back and plopped his feet on Cammy's bunk. "A favorite subject of mine as well." He smiled at Tori. "You've got him not knowing up from down anymore."

"Why are you discussing him with us? He's your relative," Tori said in a disapproving tone, then added, "You should have more loyalty."

"Perhaps I'm not just idly gossiping," he said. "What if had a purpose?"

"And what would that be?"

He hesitated, then said, "When Grant chased you—that was the first impulsive thing I've seen him do since he was a boy. It made no sense, it wasn't logical, yet I don't think anything could have stopped him." He boldly looked her over. "You would be good for him."

Embarrassed, she rushed to ask, "Why are you so concerned with this?"

His expression of casual indifference slipped. "Grant, my dear, is dying inside. He's already a cold man, and unless something changes, he's either going to snuff out whatever fire is left in him or he's going to snap." His eyes bored into hers. "I don't want to be shipbound with him for either."

He opened the book and cleared his throat to read, as if he hadn't just told her something that shook her to her very bones. Against their protests, she absently excused herself, her mind focused on Sutherland. Tori believed Traywick was exactly right. Simmering—that's what Sutherland was, like a volcano.

She thought about the night he'd kissed her, remembering the way his lips had seared hers, the way he'd clutched her shoulders, the savage promise in his eyes when she'd broken away. *What* did they promise?

She allowed herself to imagine what would have happened if she hadn't pulled away then, or if Traywick hadn't interrupted them that morning in the hut. She'd lied when she'd said she half slept through touching him then. She'd been wide-awake, heart fluttering with each new touch, stifling gasps at each new texture, his kisses making her body ache. . . .

Back in his cabin, Tori snooped through his belongings, craving more knowledge about him. Her nosiness was his fault, she reasoned. If he'd ever volunteered the tiniest detail about himself, she wouldn't be forced to take this action. Plus, he'd read her journal—turnabout was fair play.

For hours, she leisurely searched through his desk, scanning boring shipping documents, and reading from a cache of old letters stowed haphazardly in one drawer. One from his mother expressed her utter confidence in Grant on this voyage: *"If they are alive, you above all men will find them and bring them safely back."* Another one from his brother, Derek, provided an overview of the *Keveral,* detailing every quirk and distinct trait of the ship, with a closing that again conveyed a perfect confidence in his brother.

Did the man ever make mistakes? His family didn't think so.

She found notes and notes of indecipherable mathematical calculations, and turned them sideways, trying to read them. Each outcome was fixed with a pound symbol. Money. He was probably in dire straits to think about it so much. *Wonder if his mother knows that?*

She picked up his obligatory copy of *Robinson Crusoe,*

and read through Crusoe's first days, when he lived like a parasite off that wrecked ship, hauling tool after tool, goods, and seeds for days. Would've been nice.

She set it back on the shelf, and the next book caught her attention. *The Physical Geography of the Sea*, by Matthew Fontaine Maury. Inside was a dedication: *Godspeed, Grant. Love, Nicole.*

Love? Who was this woman?

And why was Tori bristling? Because he had some woman at home, yet he'd kissed her and . . . touched her, that's why! Her stomach tightened. What if he was engaged?

Traywick would know. She heard him laughing with a sailor on deck. *On deck among the sailors.* Swallowing her disquiet, she marched across the sea-swept boards to where he sat and dumped the book on his bolted-down table. "Who is this?" She stabbed the name with her nail.

"You'll have to move your finger. Oh, that's just . . ." He trailed off and instead asked, "Why do you want to know?"

"I just find the idea that he has someone waiting at home surprising."

His amber eyes were fixed on her. "Don't you find it the least bit disappointing?"

"Don't be ridiculous. I'm outraged that he'd . . . he'd . . . Well, you were there! That he'd take liberties with me when he is in love with someone else."

"That's Nicole Sutherland—"

She gasped. "He's married!"

"—his brother Derek's wife. They're friends because he helped her and Derek reconcile."

Tori slumped in a chair beside him. Another mystery to solve—how could she be jealous? Because Sutherland was angering her less and fascinating her more?

She looked up to find the captain watching her and Traywick with sharp eyes. She darted her face away and was still flushed when Dooley tromped by. "Lady Victoria, I'm glad to see you about. Can I get you anything?"

Tori stiffened and sniffed, "That won't be necessary."

"We're fine, Dooley," Traywick added. "Thank you."

Dooley rushed off again like a dog who'd forgotten he'd just been kicked.

Traywick's face hardened. "You might want to give Grant's sailors a chance. I don't know what made you so wary, but his men are different."

"How so?" she asked disbelievingly.

"Working for Peregrine is a coveted position. They hire only the best men. No sailors are bought from the jail or lured by a doxy and then crimped."

"What's crimped?"

"It's when a gang of men trick or force some poor bastard aboard a ship to serve a term at sea. Grant goes out of his way to hire family men."

"All these men have families?"

"Except for Dooley—he's a widower—and maybe one or two more, yes. It's important to Grant and it's a lifesaver for some."

While Tori was reeling from the information, Traywick said, "Don't get me wrong—they're still boisterous and like their rum, but you should see the forecastle. It's wallpapered with old letters from wives and likenesses of their kids."

Tori's eyes followed Dooley bounding around deck, helping everyone, and guilt gripped her. A widower. She'd treated him like the worst sort of criminal. She sighed, deciding she'd be kinder to him. In fact, she stared around at all the men as though with new eyes. She'd always perceived they were surprisingly clean, both in language and clothing, but now she noticed they were generally pleased, not surly like the other sailors she'd known.

"Amazing." She turned to Sutherland, seeing him anew as well. The wind blew a lock of hair over his forehead. Why did that make her want to smile? He raked it back irritably.

"Now that you've made it out here, we might as well play cards," Traywick said to her back.

She didn't turn. "Yes, perhaps."

She was so busy staring at the captain, she barely heard Traywick say, "Round four to Grant."

Twelve

Grant might have been able to deny his attraction to Victoria when she was wary, arrogant, and angry, but self-sure and charming would make short work of him. Each day at sea, she became more accustomed to the ship, and her confidence rebounded to a staggering degree. It was as if she'd emerged from a shell, shucking off her old life and its fears like a skin. Apparently, she'd even gotten over her pique with him, and would thank or compliment him after each storm.

By the second week, she looked as though she'd been born on a ship. When Miss Scott slept, which was for most of the day, Victoria learned sea chanteys from Dooley and helped him mend damaged sails. When they fished, she'd go wild over all the new species.

"You never know what you'll pull up," she'd said to Dooley in breathless excitement.

She'd gotten used to her new clothes, making alterations when necessary, and she laughed often as Miss Scott showed improvement, flashing her smile unreservedly at the competing antics of the sailors. The crew adored her.

But while she flourished, Grant suffered from lack of sleep—he'd commandeered Ian's cramped cabin since his cousin usually passed out on deck anyway—and suffered more from the lack of . . . her.

He would give his right arm to be able to touch her again.

And yet she spent most of each day with *Ian*.

This morning, as they played cards on deck, Grant struggled with jealousy, an emotion he'd never given much credence to. Now he envied his young cousin spending time with her, envied him telling her old jokes she'd never heard.

Jealousy was a cuckold's emotion. Not at home in the heart of a detached man.

Grant scrutinized them, watching like one bent on finding something. Though they were near in age, and most women inexplicably found Ian irresistible, Grant could not detect the barest hint of attraction between the two. In fact, he often caught Victoria watching him on the bridge.

Yet it drove him mad to hear her laugh because of something Ian said.

"I don't want you spending any more time with her," he warned Ian when Tori strolled to the bow.

"It's either me or the crew. And I must confess, her language is colorful as it is . . ." At Grant's scowl, Ian added, "It's not like you think. Even if I weren't preoccupied with another woman, Tori reminds me of my *sister.*"

"Which one?" Grant asked with suspicion. Ian had three sisters, none of whom reminded Grant of Victoria.

"Emma."

"Emma?" Grant scoffed. "She's just out of the school-room—"

"She's eighteen."

"Just stay away from Victoria," Grant ordered, his voice low. When Ian flashed him a devilish grin, Grant rose to his full height and moved to a menacing position in front of his chair. "She's the granddaughter of an earl. Surely even you would know better than to trifle with a peer's granddaughter."

Smiling to himself, he said, "I didn't know better than to trifle with a peer's *daughter.*" Ian leaned forward and low-ered his voice. "Besides, that's the great thing about these out-of-country affairs—no one would ever know."

Grant yanked Ian from his seat with one hand, barely keeping his other fist from smashing his cousin's face.

"Don't look at me like that, Cuz. I'm not going to touch her." Ian tsked. "Just testing the waters."

Grant released him and exhaled loudly. "Do you think that's why I told you to leave her alone? Because I want her?"

"The point is—she's all yours. I feel protective of her. Like a brother. I don't want her that way."

Grant ran a hand down his face. "As if I do?" His tone sounded bewildered even to himself.

"Damn it, man. Open your eyes. I've never seen you like this." Ian slapped him on the back and turned to walk away. He faced Grant once more. "Why do you fight it?"

"Why?" His short laugh held no humor. "Because I don't want to be *like this.*"

Dooley walked by then and found Grant's eyes locked on Victoria.

"That one, she's learning her charms and what she can do with them," Dooley said. "She's got the crew wrapped 'round her finger—all with a smile."

Grant muttered, "God help the men in England."

Ian gave him a pitying smile. "Cousin, pray for yourself first."

Throughout the previous night, Grant had labored against a weak but persistent squall. When it finally abated, he conducted himself as he did every morning—adjust the course, inspect the ship, toss out orders, and watch Victoria—and not necessarily in that order. She was pacing, scowling at Ian, who read instead of entertaining her. Boredom emanated from her.

Though clear, the day was chilled, so he returned to his cabin to change from his wet clothes. Inside, he hung his coat and was struggling to peel out of his drenched shirt as he turned to shut the door. But Victoria waltzed in right after him.

"What do you think you're doing?" he snapped. "If you want to thank me about the storm last night, there's no need. It's my job." She didn't respond, just studied his chest, making him uncomfortable. The look in her eyes said she wanted to touch what she stared at. "Get out of here," he commanded, his voice unaccountably rough.

"But I'm so bored. You said you'd protect me—well, I'm about to repeatedly butt my head against a wall."

He checked a grin. "I need to change."

"There's nothing I haven't seen before."

Saucy little— *Wait . . .* "You watched me at the falls, didn't you?"

As she did whenever she didn't want to answer a question, she ignored him, flopping onto his bunk and facing the wall. "All right, I won't look."

He hesitated, then rushed through washing and dressing. When he stomped into his boots, she rose, grabbed his captain's log, and sank back into the bunk.

"I didn't give you permission to read that."

She continued flipping through. "Your entries are so precise, so meticulous in the beginning. But after the island, they're less"—she stared at the ceiling, obviously thinking of the word—"exacting! Yes, less exacting and less thorough." Her brows drawn together, she turned the log clockwise. "In fact, some of these entries don't even make sense."

He snatched it from her hands, then tossed it atop a set of high cabinets where she couldn't reach it.

When he turned back, she sat in front of his trunk, her hand diving down among the organized layers of his clothes. Investigating, always investigating. "Are you having difficulty concentrating?" she questioned without turning. "It's because of me, isn't it?"

Arrogant chit. "It's because I'm still bloody exhausted."

Finally, she faced him. "You could be exhausted. That's true. But I like the idea of you unable to stop thinking of me to attend anything else."

She has the right of it. She pulled out a folded shirt, then flipped it over her shoulder, preparing to take it. At least now he knew where they'd been going.

"Just go, Victoria. And leave the shirt."

Her eyes narrowed as she stood. "I'm going to make you like me. That's what I'm going to do. Like me so much you can't bear it." With that, she sashayed out the door, shirt over her shoulder—a picture of perfect assurance, readying for a battle she'd already won.

What is happening to me? Tori wondered, unnerved by her feelings. Just now, the urge to press her cheek to Sutherland's wet chest, to turn her lips to him, had been nearly overwhelming. How could he have become even more attractive to her? Tori hadn't thought there was room for escalation there. Though the captain was arrogant and infuriating, she'd ached to touch him. She wanted to know why he was so grave, so somber. She wanted to smooth the line between his brows.

She shook her head sharply, then found her accustomed seat on deck, sitting dazed for several moments. When he'd looked at her this morning, when his eyes met hers, she'd seen something more in him. Certainly she saw want. Even she could recognize that. But he'd also looked lost. . . .

A sharp snap of fingers an inch from her forehead yanked her from her thoughts. Apparently, Ian was finally joining her.

He opened a deck of cards for a game of German whist for two. "I take it you and my cousin are getting on well?" he commented dryly.

She felt her skin flush. *What* was happening to her?

As he dealt their hands, she changed the subject. "Cammy told me a few days ago that your heart's taken. So why aren't you with her?"

He exhaled loudly as he fanned and sorted his hand. "I needed to get out of town in a hurry, and thought Grant was only going to America or something. Not the bloody South Pacific."

"You're not serious! You've been trapped on this ship?"

He nodded. "But maybe all this is for the best," he said, more to himself. "I'm only twenty-six—I didn't need to settle down so soon."

Tori folded her cards and clapped happily. "You were thinking of getting married?"

"Well, when you meet the one—"

"What does Grant think about this?" Tori wondered.

"He doesn't know. Not a lot of people do. He'd lecture me on how unfit I am to be a husband and take on the responsibility of a family."

"What's her name?"

"Erica," he murmured with a wistful smile.

Tori chuckled at his obvious infatuation. "Do you think she'll have sent word to you? Perhaps when we stop in port, you could see if she's written. I bet she was heartbroken that you had to leave so fast."

He shrugged.

"Is she waiting for you in London?"

He drew a card and strove to say nonchalantly, "I don't know that she'd wait this long."

"Oh, Ian, you underestimate yourself—"

"I'm not entirely sure she knows what happened to me," he admitted, his face tight. "If she hasn't gotten my letters, then she most likely will think I disappeared. Or worse."

"Or worse?"

Raw pain flashed in his eyes. "That I left her."

Tori sucked in a breath. "She might not know? She'll be sick with worry."

"Worry? Or would any woman who knew my reputation just assume I'd run off?"

He had a point, but he looked so stricken that she

said, "When you get home, you'll have to make it up to her."

Ian nodded absently. "I just want to be with her. Do you understand what I mean?" He looked out at the ocean. "I just want to be near her."

As it did a thousand times a day, Tori's gaze rested on the captain.

Thirteen

Since the beginning of the voyage, Grant had extended invitations to dinner to his passengers, as was his duty as captain. Victoria and Miss Scott always declined. Ian never missed a dinner. Today, Victoria was the only one who accepted.

Grant waited for Victoria to visit Miss Scott, then approached Ian on the deck. "Any reason you're not attending?"

"I would like to—hate to miss it—but I'm exhausted."

"From what?" Grant asked incredulously.

"Entertaining," he said smoothly. When Grant stalked off, Ian called, "And by the way, I heard Victoria say she would dearly love a bath."

Without turning, Grant held up his hand, indicating that Ian should shut up. Yet when the seas calmed by midafternoon, Grant called Dooley to the bridge and, like a fool, said, "Will you set up a bath for Lady Victoria?"

"A hip bath?" Dooley asked.

Grant resisted the urge to run his hand over the back of his neck. "No. Full."

Dooley raised his brows. "With fresh water, sir?"

When he nodded, Dooley rushed to fill the order. Grant almost called him back. Why was he giving her an extravagance? *Because she wants it,* was his alarming answer.

Oddly nervous throughout the day, Grant was relieved when the hour finally arrived. He stood when she appeared at the table, and his breath whistled out. She was exquisite. A vision dressed in jade silk with her shiny hair braided atop her head. She smiled up at him when he seated her. Christ, he liked it when she smiled at him like that.

When they began dinner, he was surprised to see she knew exactly which utensil to use and when. But the way she used them . . . The tines clanged loudly against the china with each attempt. She would knife much too hard against butter as though she'd forgotten its consistency.

She could have learned everything, but without the tools to practice, the knowledge diminished. She adjusted to soften the sounds, but then the food would slide off the fork. He frowned, thinking of how much could be forgotten. It was like knowing archery, but being out of practice shooting an arrow. Targets were bound to be missed.

When she glanced up and found him watching her, she colored and pushed her plate away, though she was obviously very hungry. She was always hungry, especially for new foods, yet tonight she drank copious amounts of wine instead.

After a crewman cleared the dishes away, and pained silence stretched between them, Victoria said, "Your crew is wonderful."

He nodded, knowing he had a choice crew.

"Some of them I have to avoid, but only because they'll talk my ear off about their children."

When he nodded again, but added nothing, she tried several times to start a conversation to fill the quiet: "What's your favorite season in England?" "Do you have a dog?" "Do you like to play cards?" "What's your favorite number?"

Yet he'd never been good at idle conversation. He answered, "Never thought about it," "No," "Occasionally," and "I have no favorite number."

"Oh," she said, disappointment lacing her tone. But then she rallied. "My favorite number's fifteen. I believe I'll share it with you."

"Why fifteen?" he found himself asking.

"That's how old I was when I finally got the hut to hold together in storms. I never had to rebuild since." She sighed and ran her fingertip along the rim of her glass. "Fifteen was a good age."

Here he was thinking about himself, concerned over his future in the face of such temptation as Victoria leaning back in her chair, smiling over at him with wine-red lips. Now he was reminded of all that she'd missed. At fifteen, she should have been celebrating grown-up dresses or her first peck on the cheek. Instead, she'd been content because their home wouldn't crash down around them.

"What were you like when you were fifteen?" Her voice sounded languorous.

Now he wanted to respond, but he'd been a prankster, bent on terrorizing everyone around him with his tricks. "I was staid and grim, just as I am now. I followed my hellion older brothers around and learned how *not* to behave."

When she chuckled, Grant's brow furrowed. How could

she think he was amusing in any sense of the word? He was steady and serious. To avoid the risk of becoming anything else, he supposed he'd taken those attributes to the extreme and become, well, dull. Amusing he was not, yet at that moment, he wanted to be the kind of man Victoria would like.

She took another sip of wine. "What's your favorite color?"

"Green. Green's my favorite color."

"Oh, mine too," she cooed, and leaned forward, setting the glass down and perching her elbows on the table. Her bodice gaped and displayed the tops of her breasts. He scrubbed a hand over his mouth and chin. Was it just his imagination, or had they gotten larger? She appeared fuller, softer all over, and for a man already struggling every hour to keep from touching her, the change was not welcome.

She innocently licked a drop of wine from her plump bottom lip, and need fired in him. *Take her on the table. That's what I should do. Of course.*

He was on his feet as though burned by the chair. "I'll walk you back."

She blinked in surprise, then stood. "Do you dislike me?" When he gave her a confounded look, she added, "You don't care to be around me. Even now, it seems as though you can't wait to be off."

He raked his fingers through his hair. "It's complicated. . . ."

"You don't think someone like me would understand?" She sounded dejected.

"No, that's not it," he hurriedly said. "I might like you in an . . . an inappropriate way."

The fingers she'd been twining fretfully paused. "Oh."

No, she wouldn't understand. How could she, when even he didn't? He took her arm and escorted her across the slick deck. The wind blew mist over them, but he welcomed it, hoping the brisk water would cool him. At her cabin door, she gazed up at him through wet, spiky lashes as though deciding something. Or awaiting something.

Get away from her. Get her out of reach—and out of temptation's way. "Good night, then."

"Yes, thank you for dinner."

He drew himself up. "Sleep well, Victoria." He closed the door behind her but didn't walk away, instead leaning against the wall as though stunned. She couldn't be more alluring to him, and he wanted her with a ferocity that alarmed him.

He didn't fantasize about laying her down and making love to her. He fantasized about devouring her, making her come beneath his lips before he pinned her hands over her head and rode her furiously. If he ever gave in to it, he worried that he'd hurt her in his desperation. He fought to ignore his erection, sensitive against the fabric of his clothing, and shook his head to clear thoughts of her naked and writhing beneath him.

Aside from his fear, he knew he couldn't have her unless he married her. He attempted to list all the ways they would disappoint each other if they were to wed. Lengthy lists, to be sure. When he had promised Belmont to find Victoria, he'd had no idea he'd be facilitating his own ruin. And hers as well.

Grant looked up at the stars. Their placement in the sky was all wrong.

Tori had been so sure he was about to kiss her. Even now, her heart drummed in her chest. Though disappointed that he hadn't, she couldn't be upset. For one thing, the wine was making her giddy. For another, she realized he did at least *want* to kiss her.

As though in a dream, she pulled her nightgown from the trunk and stepped out of her slippers. Everyday actions seemed trivial compared to the power of feeling she'd just experienced. Her fingers went to her dress to remove it— *where* were the buttons? Curse it! In the back. Maybe Cammy was still awake. She opened the door to find the captain leaning back against the wall, eyes closed.

"Captain?"

He opened them in a flash. "Where were you going?"

"I just realized I can't get out of this." She waved a hand to indicate her dress. "I was going to ask Cammy to help."

"She's abed by now."

"Then Ian."

In a heartbeat, he had her back in the cabin, kicking the door closed behind him. "You are not going to get my cousin to help you undress." His voice was brutal.

Was he jealous? Or was this another breach of propriety? "Then it must be you."

He spun her around and unbuttoned, quickly at first, then slower, as if he began enjoying it. The dress was soon loose, and she had to hold the bodice to her breasts, but he didn't move for several moments.

Just when she was about to say something, she heard him mutter a curse. Then she felt the backs of his fingers skim down her neck. Her eyes slid closed, and she nearly swayed from the small touch. Her head fell to the side to offer him more. When he pressed his warm lips on her skin, she trembled.

"So fair," he whispered as he brushed his lips down to

her shoulders. "Your skin's like porcelain." She moaned softly from his words and leaned back into him. Her free hand trailed up to curl around his neck. As if invited, his hand slid into her loosened bodice to cup her. "Yes," she gasped in delight. Was he finally going to show her more?

He hefted the weight of her breast, molding the flesh. It felt swollen and heavy beneath the heat of his rough palm. When he drew her other arm up around his neck, the dress floated to the ground, leaving her in just a filmy shift. With another sweep of his lips, he ran both hands down her sides, squeezing her hips, then back over both her breasts, pausing at her nipples to pinch gently. Her eyes were heavy-lidded as she watched his fingers kneading her in the soft lantern light.

Her whole body shook when his fingers trailed over her belly and down to her inner thighs, and she feared her legs wouldn't hold her much longer. She wanted desperately to touch him. Even now, her fingers were twining wildly in his hair.

He put his lips to her ear, and she felt a shock of pleasure, making her boneless. She twisted around and glanced up at his eyes, at his lips.

"Victoria, I can't do this to you," he ground out, the words sounding as though they cost him much. Yet he reached out to grasp her around the waist and slowly draw her near. She didn't wait—she pushed herself forward, falling into him, lacing her arms around his neck to pull herself even closer.

He kissed her fiercely, taking her with his tongue, as if hoping to frighten her away. During their kisses on the island, she'd been overcome and passive. Now she boldly met his tongue with her own. He groaned against her lips.

"Please," she whispered, but didn't know for what she begged. "Grant . . ."

He froze, then stepped away, looking as though he came out of a daze.

Grant. It was the first time she'd used his name. How many times had he imagined her saying it? Imagined hearing it on her lips when he drove inside her? It was intimate, too intimate between this girl and himself. He had to remember that.

No. "*No.*" He struggled to catch his breath, struggled not to see her obvious longing.

He had nearly . . . he had nearly made love to Victoria Dearbourne. To Lady Victoria, who faced him now with her eyes dilated and her lips swollen from his kiss.

He still wanted to.

Grant tore away from her. *Consequences. Honor. Trust.* His mind repeated the words until he managed to get his breathing and his aching erection under control. When he turned to her, she stood in her shift, trembling.

"Grant, why?"

Grant knew she was asking "Why not?" In seconds, he would call her to him, and she would come walking to their doom, willingly. "Because I swore to protect you— not ruin you. You are under my protection and I need to start remembering that!" He still was fighting the urge to take her.

He needed to get her out of his sight—and his reach. He stormed out the door and down the deck, steps thundering. He'd vowed to protect her. As if his vows meant anything anymore. Damn it, he was a man noted for his

integrity and honor. But when he was confronted with
his desire for Victoria, both vanished as if never there.

What does that say about me?

"You look like you've grown used to being shipboard,
milady," Dooley said as he lugged away the sail Tori had
mended. He folded it, stowed it, then brushed his hands
together to scan the ship, no doubt for more work. He settled on harvesting fresh water from the rain barrels filled
by this morning's storm. Hell for Dooley would be uninterrupted leisure.

She smiled as she glanced over the busy scene. She had
adjusted to life at sea, having come to trust the captain
implicitly.

When Dooley marched off, Tori's gaze was drawn to
Sutherland. He appeared so solemn as he stood on the
bridge, staring out at the water. His men saw his outward
shell of decorum, strength, and control. Tori had seen his
inner self of want, power, and need. She could scarcely
believe the upstanding captain was the same man who'd
kissed and touched her in his cabin just a week ago.

Since that night, he'd been curt with her, but she'd
become even more captivated by him. Never taking her
eyes from him, she envisioned his barely harnessed aggres-
sion, the way his rugged muscles had tightened around her.
When he'd broken away, she'd realized they were at a critical point. Tori sensed that should she move near him,
touch him in the tiniest way, his resolve would crumble. Yet
she was beginning to know he would feel wretched afterward. She was beginning to care enough that it mattered.

But she'd known that body intimately, had seen every
inch of it, and would again. If it killed her. Tori had a plan,
and if all went by it, she'd have him. She thought that per-

haps the man should be doing the pursuing, that that was what traditionally happened. But she was used to seeing something she wanted and then working to get it. Cammy had called her a problem solver. And not having Grant was a problem.

When she knew he was on the bridge and couldn't easily leave, she would join him. She'd bring him coffee if he looked tired or water on the warmer days.

And if she ever faltered, doubted that she could get him to kiss her again, then the hours spent in his bed spurred her on. That first night she'd crushed his pillow to her breasts, yearning for him, his scent making her wild, and after that, not one night went by that she didn't relive what they'd done, how she'd touched him, what she wished she had another chance to do. Each hour, she felt enveloped by him. Something had to give. . . .

Grant's voice broke her reverie as he tossed out orders to take advantage of the fresh wind. As usual, the crew responded with alacrity and precision. Grant didn't smile, but she knew he was pleased, like one who'd tilled and sowed and saw a field of sighing corn.

It was exciting but rough, so she checked on Cammy and found her awake.

Tori hopped on the free bunk, and said, "I thought I'd come in and read you something, since Ian's working."

Cammy chuckled. "No, really. Where is Ian?"

"I'm serious. He said now that we were better, he was going to apply his 'considerable genius' to learning the ship."

Cammy raised her eyebrows, then said, "And Sutherland. How is he?"

Tori looked down and smoothed a crease in her skirt. "Miffed with me as usual, I suppose," she mumbled.

"What do you mean?" Cammy asked slowly.

"I don't mean to anger him, but he's such a stuffed shirt, it's as if I *must* tease him. Provoking that choked-up look and making him sputter is all I look forward to these days."

Cammy gave her a censorious look. "And how do you go about that?"

Tori chuckled. "Yesterday I realized I could finally fill out the bust of a few of the dresses. So I bounded up to him to tell him the good news."

"Tori!"

"You sound like him. But really, he's the one who could appreciate the change since I catch him looking there all the time. I reasoned this out for him, but he just stared at my bodice, then scowled at me, until finally he called Dooley to the bridge to relieve him."

"You mustn't do that," Cammy scolded. "He's not your husband. And it's just not proper."

She debated telling Cammy the real reason she teased Grant, that she thought she might be falling for him, then decided against it. Not until she could sort through her muddled feelings. "You said before that you thought he felt something for me. Do you really believe so?"

"If I had to bet, then yes. But I don't know if this is a good turn. He's honorable, yes. But every man has his limits." Cammy wrung her hands. "Remember when we had the talk about what goes on between men and women? Well, he might try something like that with you."

Had they been leading up to making love in the cabin? Tori certainly hadn't wanted to stop. When he'd left her, an empty longing had suffused her. She understood that she wanted to know passion with Sutherland. She'd boiled the situation down to the facts. She wanted him; he did not want her.

Now Cammy believed he might.

"You think he wants to"—she looked around, then said in a lower voice—"make love to me?"

Cammy pursed her lips. "Don't sound so excited! You have to be married to do that."

Tori thought she might gladly pay that price . . . if only he would *finish what they'd started.*

"Just be careful, Tori. And remember—there's a difference between lust and love. It would be disastrous if you and Sutherland confuse them."

Fourteen

*L*ike an amphitheater of rock, Table Mountain loomed behind Cape Town.

As the *Keveral* glided into the busy harbor and Grant gave out orders for their arrival, Victoria sidled up to him, her eyes snapping with excitement. When he finished, she said, "I thought you were a harsh taskmaster, but now I see why."

He knew she saw the other ships' crews looking haggard, their clothes slovenly. Grant's men carried themselves with pride.

"Ian said working for Peregrine Shipping is a coveted position."

Ian bloody said. "That's true. Even with a harsh taskmaster like me."

She smiled, choosing to think he teased with her. Hell, maybe he did.

"Your ship is the most impressive here. Against these hulks, it's like an . . . an imagined ideal."

He liked that she'd noticed; he hated that she noticed.

She sighed, turning her attention to the seals playing among the whitecaps and on the mammoth boulders circling the harbor. "It's breathtaking here, the way the mountain cradles the city. Do you think we should wake Cammy?"

"No more than we should wake Ian, I suppose. Camellia needs her sleep and I need time away from Ian."

She smiled and play-tapped his arm. "I want to buy candy while I'm here. Enough to stuff myself every day of the week."

Grant checked a grin.

She grabbed a rope overhead and used it to pirouette directly in front of him. "And while you're here, you can buy me flowers."

His amusement faded. "Victoria, there won't be any flowers," he promised, anger coloring his tone. "Whatever happened the other night was a mistake."

Still holding the rope, she skipped back a few steps. "I don't feel like it was a mistake."

He simply glared at her.

"Yes, one day you'll bring me flowers, and you'll tell me you think I'm pretty."

He would *never* call her pretty. He might not admit many things to himself, but there was no denying she was an exceedingly beautiful woman. He let out a breath. "Victoria, you are an odd, odd creature."

She smiled at him and let go of the rope. But under her breath, she assured him, "One day, Captain."

The nerve.

Yet as they closed in on the port, he saw her first look of uncertainty in over a month. The sights of civilization must be overwhelming for her. Surely everything was hard, jarring, and loud compared to the soft ease of her island, the colors faded. When they docked, the confusion registered more clearly on her face, as sounds and scents began to manifest.

He and his men were inured to the smells of the quay, but the odors must affect her so much more. The scent of pungent Malay cooking wafted over them, mixed with the smell of low tide and coffee. But as he should have predicted, Victoria's look of bewilderment soon turned to one of curiosity. He could feel how badly she wanted off the ship to explore her new surroundings, and as he needed to deal with the port master, he decided to let her shop in some of the nearby waterfront food stalls.

"You can go visit one of the first rows of the shops. But don't go far. Here's some money—"

She was fidgeting in her excitement, not even looking at him, no doubt trying to decide where to go first. Then his words sank in. "Oh, I can't take anything from you. You've done enough."

"Here," he insisted, grabbing her hand and forcing the money into it. "Your grandfather sent you this."

Her face lit up. "In that case . . . Do you know how long it's been since I *bought* something?" She looked around at all the stalls full of colorful wares. "I want to buy everything!" Turning back to him, she said, "But I don't remember money so well. How much is this?"

"I defy you to spend it all." She laughed and reached over to squeeze his hand, thinking he was jesting with her, when he'd said it in all seriousness.

Later when he met up with her, he noticed she was lugging a weighty bag of something very sweet and very sticky. She insisted he try some, and wouldn't budge until he did. He relented and choked back a laugh. It was a mix of sugared hard candy, crystallized ginger, and horehound drops. She must have cleaned out a shop's confectionary jar. At the rate Victoria was enjoying them, she'd be very sorry indeed.

Once she'd woken Camellia and helped her to get ready to move to lodging on firm land, the three took a hansom cab down the dusty streets toward a hotel Grant remembered from a past visit.

Without taking her eyes off the sights, Camellia asked, "So, you've been here before?"

"Yes, several times," Grant answered politely, stiffly.

Victoria said, "You look like you don't like Cape Town."

"I don't. There's no order."

"Then I suspect I'll love it." He scowled at Victoria, which only seemed to delight her more.

"Oh, I like that hotel," Camellia said, pointing out a quaint Dutch Cape–style hotel with wildflowers growing all around. Whitewashed buildings were prevalent on the Cape, but English neoclassical structures were peppered among them.

"No, we'll go on."

"Why?" Victoria asked. "Not *staunch* enough for you?"

She and Camellia tittered, and he glowered at them. As if to make up for their teasing, Victoria solemnly handed him more candy. She'd already determined his favorite.

He settled them in an imposing, Regency-style hotel. Not as quaint, certainly lacking the atmosphere, but safer. He had to admit that "safe" was a relative term in Cape Town, especially after dark. The city wasn't known as the "tavern of the seas" for nothing. It could be an unruly, dangerous town, no matter how many proper Regency town homes dotted it.

As expected, Camellia didn't feel well enough to venture

out, but insisted Victoria go see the city. Grant wanted to come up with some excuse not to spend the day with her, but knew he would end up looking like an ass denying a sick woman.

So he took Victoria to the city center and all along the foreshore, but noticed that her dress cut differed from those of other women her age and station. No wonder—the clothes he'd bought for her were a year old, and apparently fashion had leapfrogged them in the meantime. She needed new things, and he supposed it fell to him to provide them. Victoria was delighted to go shopping, dazzled by the exclusive boutiques, especially since he falsely assured her he would bill her grandfather for anything she purchased.

Later he would blame his spending on her. She wore everything well, and as he'd already determined, she was a woman who made her clothes instead of the clothes making her. Different fabrics, bold colors—she looked stunning in them all. She must have caught his look of appreciation as she modeled a low-cut evening dress, because she cocked a hip out, and said sarcastically, "I bet you can forget I was nearing savagehood when you found me."

His lips quirked into a grin that was wiped off his face when the shopkeeper related she'd just received from France the latest fashions in *unmentionables*. Just what he needed to be thinking about—Victoria in nothing but wisps of cloth. He'd already seen that and barely survived.

He could hear their conversation from the dressing room as the clothier helped Victoria into the "new Parisian delectables." Victoria's questions of "So I strap this across there and then under here?" and "You don't think that's too tight?" already had him sweating, but when she said, "You can see right through that!" his fingers went white on the chair arm.

The coup de grâce came when Victoria worried that she wouldn't be able to get out of the lingerie. The shopkeeper said archly, "When you wear this one, it shouldn't be up to you." Grant suspected she said the last louder for his benefit.

Finally, Victoria emerged in a royal blue walking dress with a white woven hat. With a delighted smile, she closed her eyes and shimmied in the dress, as though getting used to what was under it. He shot from his chair to pay.

Day and evening dresses, kid gloves, warm cloaks for the trip north, hats, cashmere scarves, slippers, and copious boxes of things he couldn't remember were lined up for delivery. He arranged to have what she needed for the next day sent to the hotel and the rest, including tailored dresses, delivered to the ship within another two. He also arranged for a seamstress to visit Camellia the next day.

Victoria couldn't stop touching the intricately beaded bag he'd bought for her or opening and closing the painted linen fan, until the shopkeeper tugged them out of her hands. He was sorry to see that she was afraid to let them go. *If this is how she reacts to Cape Town, she'll expire when I take her shopping in London.* He frowned.

He wouldn't be seeing her, or taking her shopping, when they reached home. Strange how he felt so certain about that, when only moments ago he'd decided with perfect clarity that he was going to carry her to a hotel and rip off the "delectables" with his teeth.

When he returned her to the hotel, she said, "So this concludes my first venture into civilization. How'd I do?"

He leaned against the entrance. "You know very well how you did, and I'm not one to feed your startlingly high opinion of yourself."

She laughed and his lips crooked up, but the conversation soon turned uneasy. No, *he* was uneasy with her. He hurried through a good-bye, gave his best to Camellia, and returned to the ship.

That night, he endeavored to sleep in his cramped bunk in Ian's old cabin. He hadn't wanted to reclaim his own, knowing it would remind him of her, and he was having enough trouble keeping his hands off her as it was. But he couldn't sleep. If he had to say, he'd swear he missed the chit. When the bells chimed for the next watch, Grant moved into his own cabin.

A bad idea.

As soon as he sank into the bed, he smelled her soft, lingering scent on the sheets and instantly became aroused, pulsing and heavy. There'd be no sleep.

What did she dream of when here in his bed? With a woman as fiery as Victoria, she probably tossed and turned, dreaming of passion and fighting desire.

Or perhaps she didn't fight it. . . .

He jumped from the bed as though burned. *Victoria pleasuring herself.* He shuddered at the image his mind conjured up, and his cock pulsed hungrily. What was he thinking? This was why he needed to be away from her. Because he'd already started imagining another wickedness that ought to stay trapped in his fantasies.

Moving to the washstand, he splashed water on his face, but when he looked in the mirror, he hardly recognized the man staring back at him. His hair was too long. His face was too tanned. And for the first time in nearly a decade, he hadn't shaved the entire day.

He needed a woman. The second the thought occurred, he shook it away. If he entertained that idea, he would charge over to Victoria's hotel and pull her away with him. Even a man starving to death wouldn't eat sand after he'd tasted the finest delicacy. He could fight it. He sat in a bolted-down chair to sleep, figuring he had as good a chance there as anywhere. After an endless span, he dozed off.

Early the next morning, a shout awakened him. "A message for Master Ian Traywick on HMS *Keveral!*"

"That's me," he heard Ian reply in a bleary tone.

Grant stomped into his boots to determine who was sending messages to Ian and found him just as he was penning a reply. Ian gave it to the messenger boy, but had to ask Grant for the coin to have it delivered.

"Let me see the letter." Grant snatched the missive he'd received and scanned it.

The doctor Sutherland arranged for is coming tomorrow and I don't want Tori here when I see him. Please come get her for the day. Camellia.

"What did you reply?"

"I wrote to tell Tori to arrange for a picnic."

"The hell you did." He crumpled the paper. "Don't you have some brothel to be in?"

"I've made it this long, I can wait until we return." He leaned forward and patted his chest proudly. "Saving it for a special lady."

Ian had been dropping hints about this mystery woman throughout the voyage. Grant sensed Ian wanted to speak about her, but he didn't pursue it. What help could Grant be? He was the *last* man who should give advice on women.

The thought of Ian and Victoria spending the day together made Grant's stomach twist. He could find something for Ian to do, but he knew why Camellia had a wish for privacy—so she could decide how best to break to Victoria whatever diagnosis the doctor gave.

Bloody hell. "I'll pick her up in the morning."

"Whatever you say. I'd promised to take her to the beach. You have to leave early."

The next morning when Grant arrived at the hotel, Victoria was just descending. She looked taking in the forest green dress he'd bought for her, with her blond hair piled above her head and capped by a jaunty matching hat.

He didn't know what he would do if she appeared disappointed that he'd showed up instead of Ian. Luckily, she didn't. She seemed to light up.

"Grant! Are you to take me out today?"

"I, uh, was supposed to tell you that Ian wasn't coming."

"But you'll take me out?"

He would feel like a bastard if he turned her down. He reminded himself that she probably missed the beach. "I'm to escort you, yes. To the beach."

She gave a little squeal and then settled on his arm. "Wonderful," she breathed.

He tried not to stiffen to her, not to enjoy her touch. She smelled delicious, like the scent that surrounded him in bed.

They walked to the stable where he'd secured two horses, and though Victoria did nothing consciously to draw attention, every male eye stayed on her as though taking a bead. She wasn't aware of it, but her sultry laugh and the sinuous movements of her body exuded sensuality. Victoria unwittingly gave men the impression that she was a woman who wanted to be made love to. And they responded to her.

Grant responded to her.

Victoria unleashed in London? He couldn't imagine the consequences.

Shaking away that thought, Grant untethered her horse, then moved to assist her into the saddle.

"I can do it myself," she said archly, as she snagged the reins from his hand to lead her horse to the mounting block.

He hesitated, but when she made a shooing motion with her hand, he mounted a strapping chestnut gelding. She did no more than stare at her horse. Hell, he should have thought of this. "You weren't taught to ride?"

"Of course I was!"

He gave her a disbelieving look.

She batted hair out of her face. "I just thought the horse would be smaller. With nicer eyes than this one."

Grant wanted to groan. "How are her eyes not—? Forget it. I don't want to know. If you can't ride, we can't get to the beach."

A panicked expression crossed her features. "No! I-I'll remember."

She soothed the horse and, after several attempts, made it into the saddle—leaning precariously to one side, with her skirt caught in something and bunching around one knee, but in the saddle. Her hands clenched on the reins, she shimmied into position, but the horse got edgy before going out of control altogether. The mare gave a half-jump, then advanced to the closest pole to scrape Victoria off.

"Grant!" she yelped in a broken voice.

He couldn't tell if she was laughing or crying. He reined his mount around to her. Her horse plowed sideways into his. Both horses shrieked at each other in warning.

"Oh, for God's sake." He reached over and, gripping her under the arms, plucked her off her horse and into his lap in one sweeping motion. He snagged her dangling reins and whistled for the stable boy to retrieve her horse. Her body shook with laughter.

"Oh, my Lord. Did you see me? Was that not the funniest—?"

"Get down."

Her face fell and she laid her hands on his chest. "Let me try again. Please!"

Grant exhaled loudly. "Get down, and I'll help you up behind me."

And just like that, her face grew bright again. She slid down, immediately raising her arms to be lifted. He hid a smile, grabbed an arm, and helped her behind him. "Hold on to me."

She squeezed her arms around his torso and rested her head against him. He was certain he felt her smiling against his back.

Fifteen

Grant leaned back on a blanket, letting the late afternoon sun warm his face. He was full from their lunch of cold turkey, cheeses, and apples—though they'd skipped the two bottles of wine that had managed to find their way into the basket, no doubt under Ian's direction.

He was content to observe Victoria exploring the beach, running in the sand, fleeing from approaching waves or studiously examining shells. In fact, time had passed too quickly today. He hated to tear her away, but they needed to get back. He stood, stretched, and collected their blanket. A wind was whipping up and had driven all the locals back to the city. He looked down the strip both ways. Deserted.

"Put on your shoes and pack your things," he called. "We need to get back."

When she waved and ignored him, concentrating on something in the water at her feet, he muttered a curse, then started for the horse to pack up.

The basket clattered to the ground. *There was no horse.*

After rushing both ways up and down the beach, searching, he realized their transportation was gone, and—he'd wager—not coming back. Stifling a vicious curse, he returned to meet Victoria.

"Where is he?" she asked. She had her hand to her forehead and was scanning the shore.

He ran a hand through his hair. "Stolen? I don't know."

"What are we going to do?"

"We can walk back."

"If you think that's best." She seemed less than thrilled at the prospect. It had taken them two hours over rocky terrain to get here. She glanced down at the shoes in her hand. She was having trouble getting used to them again.

They'd also be walking through a patch of Cape Town he'd rather not venture into after dark. Escorting a beauty with no weapon. He swore under his breath. *Just the way to protect her.*

Yet when faced with his other choice—staying alone with Victoria until some people from town returned in the morning—he actually was considering it. She might be safer chancing the docks than a night with Grant.

"There are some bathing huts in the next cove. We'll stay there until someone returns."

Victoria exhaled in relief. "Thank you! I wasn't looking forward to blistering my feet." Her tone was animated. In fact, she appeared so excited about the situation, he wondered if she'd untied their only transportation. He narrowed his eyes. Would she do that?

He gathered up their basket, then led her past the wall of rock separating the two beaches. Since the tide had risen, they had to wade past, and the waves crested up to her hips, but she slogged through.

Grant found the first three shelters in the row of brightly colored huts locked, but on the fourth, the door eased open. When he ushered her in, she tripped on her sodden skirts.

"Are you all right?"

"There's a reason women shouldn't wear all this," she said in a bright tone, though she was shivering.

"You need to get out of that." He noted he sounded less than pleased with that proposition.

"Sutherland?" she said in a small voice.

He exhaled loudly. "Turn around and I'll undo the buttons." She twisted around and lifted her hair. Each button revealed more creamy skin, lightly dewed with water. His hands were unsteady by the time he was finished. "Done." His voice was low.

She stood and slipped the dress down her body. This time he didn't turn away. He acted as any other man on earth would when confronted with an enticing woman disrobing, admiring her, wanting her. When she wore no more than a shift, he forced his eyes away to look for something warm she could wear. The best he could find was a pile of folded towels. He handed a couple to her. "Dry off."

She nodded and took the offered cloths, drying her legs and stomach. He never took his eyes from her intimate task as he forced off his boots, throwing them into the corner, and stripped off his soaked shirt to dry his chest. Though uncomfortable, he decided to leave the trousers on. Grant sat on the small floor space, resting his arm on an upright knee, and tried not to think of the fact that he was alone with a nearly unclothed Victoria.

She wrapped a cloth over her shoulders, spread their blanket on the ground, and then sank back down next to him. She rooted through their basket and brought out one of the bottles of wine.

He cast her a chiding look, but when she couldn't open it, he helped and even shared it with her. They sat shoulder to shoulder, passing the bottle back and forth, behaving like the very people he sought to avoid by staying here.

After turning it up a last time, she stowed the bottle, then ducked down and butted her head under his arm. He raised it, wondering what the hell she was doing, and as soon as he did, she settled in under it.

He stiffened, but let his arm rest around her. She laid her head on his chest. And it felt natural. Right.

"I love listening to your heart. It's so strong and calm. Wait, it sped up." She looked up and smiled.

A kind of fatalism crept over him. They were in a cabin, separated from the rest of the world. Fate, destiny, *or Victoria* had conspired to situate them together here in this isolated place. Grant was tired, so tired of fighting what now struck him as inevitable.

"Will you kiss me?" she whispered against him.

What man on earth would fight this? Why try? Ian had asked him that. Grant had given him an answer, but right now, with Victoria's soft breath fanning across his chest, he'd be damned if he could remember it.

She moved to her knees before him and caught his gaze with her own. Before he'd consciously decided to, he reached out and stroked the curve of her cheek, and from his tiniest touch, the merest whisper of contact, her lips parted and her eyes slid closed. She trembled and her breasts pouted just before him, with her nipples tight against her damp shift.

He groaned low in his throat and ran his thumb over

her lips. They felt so moist and soft, he knelt in front of her and replaced his touch with his own lips. She sighed against his mouth, the sound making his erection jerk below them in a sudden flood of heat. Her belly teased him, pressed against the steel of his arousal.

Then Grant had his hands on the back of her head, his tongue sweeping in, urgently, wanting to punish her for making him want her so badly. Without thought, he palmed one nipple through the cloth, and she moaned softly. He brushed the straps from her shoulders, baring her, and when he took both her breasts in his hands, she lapped her tongue against his. She moaned again, and her fingers lighted on his chest, scratching their way down his torso. "Teach me," she whispered against his lips as she dipped down into his trousers to find his swollen flesh, and grasped him.

Now. Now he remembered . . . deep down, he'd never truly wanted to fight it.

Something—locked away in him—snapped. With a defeated, brutal groan, he pulled her eager hand away and laid her down, pulling her legs to him, spreading them.

"Grant?"

"You want me to teach you? I'll show you something I think you'll like."

He inched her shift up her legs, kneading her thighs and bending down to her.

"I don't know—"

He growled against her inner thigh, "*I know.*" But he sensed her continued hesitation. "Do you trust me?"

"But I thought you would—" She cut herself off. "Yes," she whispered. "I do."

His voice was raw. *"Then let me kiss you."*

Her hands went from holding his face at bay, to threading her fingers through his hair. He groaned again, and then, as he'd fantasized for weeks, he kissed her blond curls, slowly tasting her, merely outlining her sex. She cried out in pleasure, then panted.

Her taste drove him to a thoughtless state of desire, but he fought the need to set upon her like some starved beast. Using his thumbs to part her to his greedy mouth, he ran his tongue against her, stiffening it in her.

He dimly noticed her pulling him closer to her as he licked and savored, growling against her in frustration because she still wasn't open enough to him. He shoved her shift to her waist and held her legs wider. She gasped. "Grant!"

"Trust me," he grated as he clutched her thigh, placing it on his shoulder. There'd be no barriers between him and the taste of her on his tongue. With more force, he seized the flare of her backside to lift her. He'd dreamed about her curves, taut yet lush, and now they melded perfectly into his splayed, gripping fingers.

She grasped his shoulders, his hair, cupped his face and grew wetter beneath his lips. Her body began quivering, her legs clenching around him as she neared her climax.

"Oh, God," she bit out as she panted. "Grant, don't stop. *Please*—" As she cried that word, the pleasure took her, with a swift, pulsing power that awed him. Her back arched and her hips undulated, pushing her sex to his lips. Greedier still, he wrung her until she went boneless, lying dazed on the blanket beneath them.

He dared to move, and nearly spilled his seed when his cock pushed against his trousers. He must have groaned in pain because she was on her knees before him, naked and still quivering, bringing her breasts back against his chest and her hands on him. He was so close.

She undid his trousers with quick fingers. Then without hesitation she took him in her palm, her fingers tightening around him. He bucked against her grasp and almost came instantly. There he was in their makeshift bed, on his knees, barely freed from his trousers.

"*Don't touch me.* This was only supposed to be for you."

"Do you think I could actually stop myself," she whispered, "from feeling you as you are now?"

He groaned. "You don't understand—"

"So hard, so heavy." She stared at him as though spellbound. "All I want in the world is to touch you."

She stroked his length. The need for release became a maddening pressure. There was no stopping this. No control . . .

"Don't look, Victoria," he bit out. As though it would be less wicked if she didn't see him. Would the sight of his seed spilling out of him frighten her? "Don't watch me. . . ."

No, she was bold. The question no longer mattered.

Vulnerable. She was about to see him at his weakest. She mastered him with just her fingers working over his throbbing skin.

She pulled him and put her lips against his neck. Her tongue flicked out, and she breathed against his skin. His hands shot to her breasts, grasping them, cupping her, and it was she who moaned as he felt the beginning tremors.

When his release rushed through him, he shouted out from the force of it. Violent. Pumping out into the space between them as he ground his hips into her hand. He wasn't weak. She made him feel like a god.

In seconds, they lay together, her head cradled on his chest. Though the moon had risen, impossibly bright, and bands of white flooded in through cracks, he was asleep in an instant.

Sixteen

After waking, Grant lay with closed eyes, feeling more contented than he could remember. His body was pleasantly warmed, every muscle relaxed more than in years. His eyes slid open. He wasn't dressed? No, he lay naked under the morning sun trickling in, with Victoria resting her head on his chest.

He tensed as memories flooded his mind, exciting slivers of what they'd done. He'd never experienced more pleasure with another woman. Never imagined it could be like last night. And he hadn't even made love to her.

His brows drew together. No, he hadn't made love to her, not like she deserved, with pretty words and lingering kisses. He threw an arm over his face. Instead, he'd let her masturbate him until he spent. Disgust crept over him. Disgust for himself. For his actions. For hurting Victoria even if she didn't realize it.

His behavior with her was deplorable, and all he could

think of was the next time he could taste her. He'd been right about himself. Once he crossed the line, it would be over for him. He was not the same man anymore, and he wondered if he could ever reclaim all that he'd worked so hard to garner.

He thought of his brothers, how they'd lost control. After one night with Victoria, he knew two things. He'd lost his restraint. And he didn't think he regretted it enough.

She obviously didn't either, because when she woke, she sighed happily against him. When he didn't move, she sat up and the towel bunched around her hips. Her hair was a wild tangle and her cheeks were pinkened. In fact, she was lovelier than he'd ever seen her. Being thoroughly touched suited her. She stretched her arms above her head like a cat in the sun, lifting her small, perfect breasts with the movement.

Wait . . . "You're bruised."

She looked down to see the faint smudges marring her breasts. She shrugged and then looked over his body, all of his body, with a satisfied grin on her face. Only then she didn't look satisfied at all.

"Victoria, I've hurt you." As clinically as he could, he touched her breast. "I can see where my fingers were. This doesn't hurt?"

She scrunched up her lips and shook her head. "Not in the least. And I kind of like it . . . a map of where your fingers have been." It was as if she purred the last.

Could this get worse? He was already ashamed of his treatment of her. He'd let her fondle him to release on the ground. He'd pleasured her with his mouth. He'd done things with her that he'd never even done with a courtesan.

She tugged at the corner of the blanket covering his lap,

and God help him, he grew harder. When she leaned forward, he turned to meet her halfway, knowing the futility of fighting something he still craved so badly. No matter how much shame he struggled with. He was about to start the madness again. . . .

They both froze at the sound of children splashing in the water nearby. Victoria's eyes went wide, and she clambered to her feet to dress in her wet, sandy clothes. He followed, then straightened the little shelter, wadding up his seed-stained blanket. Though it was summer, they exited the hut without notice. No one saw Grant toss away the blanket into a rubbish bin.

They found the tide was low, and easily walked to the neighboring cove. Immediately, Victoria cried, "Oh, look, Grant!" She pointed out their horse and clapped happily.

The moment Grant spotted the local man leading the horse, looking for the owner, he had a flash impression in his mind. *Himself, with the reins, leading the horse to a driftwood log. Victoria, excited about the beach, bending over in front of him to remove her shoes, then turning to beckon him down to the water with a saucy smile and her arms wide. Him, dropping the reins, following like a stallion after a mare.* . . .

He cursed his stupidity the entire way back to the hotel, ignoring Victoria's happy chatter and fighting not to react to the scent of her hair as the wind blew it forward over his shoulder. At least on the horse, he didn't have to look at how wanton she appeared. But when they dismounted in front of the hotel, he saw her face was flushed and her lips lush.

Men loitering on the steps outside stared at her with a palpable hunger. Victoria was blithely unaware. One of the men whistled, and she turned with a confused smile. His whistle roughened into a hiss of breath between his teeth.

Grant shot him a look that said he'd kill if the man came closer.

He responded, "Hell, guv. No need to want our blood fer lookin' ."

Another added, "I'd say the man don't know how to share. Should we teach him how?"

Grant's voice was low with scarcely controlled fury. *"I don't share what's mine."* The men backed off as though he'd just bared his teeth at them.

The thought of another man's hands on her, the rage that boiled in him at the thought . . . Where was his notorious detachment? He felt everything so sharply now. She'd brought him more pleasure than he could possibly have dreamed, and he'd lost control. Completely. If he lost his restraint, here, now, what then? Everything would slip, everything he worked so hard to manage would come crumbling down.

He was exactly what he'd abhorred all these years: a man who couldn't control his vices. And she was a vice he'd grown addicted to. He realized that now. Grown men didn't miss a woman after mere hours. A man like him shouldn't get a sick, twisted feeling in his gut from the thought of her with another.

The situation didn't help. He'd compromised her— not fully, but, Christ, it was enough—and he would have to marry her. She was a lady—the granddaughter of an earl. He should have had more restraint. He was sure he would have if he'd never placed his hands on her.

Retrogressing, following the call of his blood. The call that had nearly destroyed one brother. And had killed the other.

•   •   •

Grant looked miserable, but Tori couldn't despair. She felt too heavenly, replaying visions of him kneading her body and kissing her skin. Surely nights like the last didn't happen between just anyone. And now he'd escorted her directly up to her room. She teased herself that it wasn't the men outside they'd just passed but his unwillingness to leave her that prompted it.

She put the key into the lock. Without opening it, she turned back to him. "Don't you want to kiss me good-bye?"

The anguished look was back. This wouldn't do. She wanted him to look at her as he did when he was levered above her. As though he'd lost reason in his need to kiss her, in his desperation to put his lips on her skin.

"You need to change, and get dry." He reached past her and opened the door.

Inside, Cammy was up. Tori flushed. Was what she'd just enjoyed written all over her face?

"Where have you been?" Cammy cried. "I was about to fetch the constable."

"You won't believe what happened," Tori said quickly. "The horse wandered away and we were stuck on the beach." That wasn't exactly a lie.

When Cammy raised her eyebrows at them, Grant asked, "How was your day yesterday, Miss Scott?"

Tori looked from one to the other and thought there was more to the question.

"My day went favorably well. In fact, I have great news. Tori, I saw the doctor."

"But I thought he wouldn't be back for a couple of days," Tori sputtered. "Why didn't you tell me?"

"We didn't tell you because I was afraid of what the prognosis would be. The physician asked me scores of questions and did hours of tests." She paused and said, "I know what's been wrong."

Tori sank down. "Well . . ."

Cammy picked up a piece of paper and read from it. "Patient has persistent fluid depletion—that's a fancy way of saying I don't drink enough water and that makes me forgetful and erratic—and a chronic pathological reaction to ingesting fish of any kind."

Fish? Tori was horrified. "B-But that's all we ever ate."

"Quite."

Every time she'd brought them fish, she'd been unwittingly poisoning her friend. "So you drink water and don't eat fish and you'll be well?"

"It's a bit more complicated that that. I have to get minerals in my blood and build up my strength. And this illness has taught my body to reject food. So I'll be forcing down broth for a few more weeks. But the lingering forgetfulness should fade promptly."

"So you *can* get well."

She nodded. "The return trip will set me back a bit because of the seasickness, but after that, I can make myself well again."

Tori leapt up to hug Cammy. All of the years of worry, of not knowing. Now they had an enemy they could see to fight. And if Camellia Scott was anything, she was a fighter.

Tori thought of this excellent news and of her time with Grant and sighed, "This is the best day of my entire life."

Grant stared into his cup of black coffee, not even glancing up as Ian stomped into the ship's salon and dropped to a chair.

"If you're just going to look at it . . . ," Ian said as he

slid Grant's cup over and drank deeply. "I saw you come aboard this morning."

"So?"

"So, you and Tori . . . Shouldn't you have been whistling?"

"How do you know I wasn't in a brothel?" He might as well have asked, "How do you know I wasn't on the moon?" Ian's unmoved, knowing look was the same.

Grant snapped his fingers. "Wait, I know. Because you would have seen me there."

Ian shook his head, his good mood unaffected by Grant's surly tone. "My companions were my brandy and cheroots. We had a sublime evening lounging on deck." When Grant said nothing, Ian asked, "Can you really say you regret it?"

For him to even ask . . . "Of course I can," he answered, his voice low.

Ian snorted. "If that's what you tell yourself."

Grant raked his fingers through his hair. "You don't understand."

"Then explain it," Ian said, propping his boots up on another chair.

"A year ago, I promised a frail old man that should I find his granddaughter, I would protect her with my life. I told him to rest easy on that score. And should her parents be gone, I swore I'd be her guardian until I delivered her back to him. And he believed me, knowing I've never broken my word."

"But what's done is done—"

"And did you know that if he passes away before we return, I'm to be her permanent guardian? That was how much he trusted me."

Ian looked snared. "So you bungled that—"

"And there was no reason for him not to trust me. I built my reputation. Worked on it. Denied myself to solidify it."

Ian shook his head forcefully. "Life is too short not to take happiness where you can find it. Especially when no one gets hurt. Marry her and be done with all this agonizing. You know you have to. You could even now be a proud papa-to-be."

Grant ran a hand over the back of his neck. "There's no chance of that."

Ian frowned, then flashed a grin of realization. "You sly devil! Grant, you truly have depth."

"If you keep this under wraps, we can avoid marriage."

Ian raised his eyebrows. "I still don't understand why you would want to."

"Did you ever think I wouldn't be the earl's first choice for her husband? Their title is without money, but it's still ancient. I have no land of my own. I'm a decade older—"

"Inconsequential when compared to the fact that you're *her* choice. She chose you."

Grant shot to his feet. "There wasn't a *choice*. She didn't prefer me out of a pool of suitors. She was cheated out of parents, out of a childhood, and now I've cheated her out of something else she should have expected. Courting, beaus, a season. Being young and narrowing her decision down to the right man. And look at her— there will still be courting and beaus, only it'll be after I marry her."

"I don't think you give her enough credit."

Grant stalked the room. It seemed much smaller than usual, hemming him in. "You give her too much."

Ian exhaled in impatience. "I'm going to see her today. Anything you'd like me to tell her? Any flowers to deliver?"

"Tell her I'll be busy this week."

"Does idiocy run in our family, or did it only strike you?" At Grant's lowering look, Ian finished Grant's coffee and strolled away.

Grant slammed his fist against the table. He wanted to forget everything about yesterday, forget that he'd ignored propriety and honor, and forget the things he'd done with a virginal girl in a *shed*. He feared he'd treated her like a whore, bruising her and showing her things no proper lady would ever dream of. And that worry tore at him. He wasn't right when he was around her, and the sooner they parted, the better.

After an incredibly miserable day, he lay in bed, aroused as usual and wondering why he didn't go take what she offered. Technically, they didn't have to marry. But if he was a true gentleman, he'd offer for her. And if he offered for her, then he could have her. All of her . . .

He heard a light tap, and was instantly on his feet, stabbing his legs into his trousers and yanking open the door. Victoria stood, almost shyly, just outside with the wind molding her skirts to her legs. Did she wear nothing beneath? He grabbed her arm and pulled her in.

"How in the hell did you get down here?"

"I walked."

"You could have been killed. You—"

"Well, actually, I bought this map and then had the hotel owner mark all the particularly bad spots." She showed him the map. "See my course? I had to zigzag a bit, but—"

"Where are your damned underskirts?"

"I didn't want to wake Cammy getting those petticoats out." The bubbly excitement left her voice, and she admitted softly, "I missed you. You never came around."

He grasped his forehead with one hand. "We have a problem, you and I. What we did at the beach was wrong. And it can't happen again."

She crossed her arms over her chest. "It had to. And it has to happen again." Catching his gaze, she whispered, "I feel like I'll lose my mind. All I can think about is you and your hands on me." She brought his hand up and laid it on her breast.

He groaned. "Why do you do these things?"

"Because it feels so wonderful."

"So all you're doing with me is obeying impulse?" he asked in a low, cruel voice as he yanked his hand away.

"What's wrong with impulse?"

"Everything." He ran a hand over his face. "What if you have these impulses with another man?"

"But I won't. I only feel this way for you."

"How can you know that?"

"I know that when my mother first met my father, she fell for him, never thinking of another man for the rest of her life. I feel that way about you."

He'd sucked in a sharp breath during her admission, then let it out slowly. "If anything else had happened, you'd be forced to marry me."

"Anything else? So we're not going to have to marry just from what we did?"

"We don't have to marry for that."

"Then the way I see it, we can do just those things again."

"That's not how it works." Did he sound like he regretted that fact? "Things might . . . get out of hand." He set her away. "And then, did you ever think that I might get you with child?"

Her eyes rounded.

"Obviously not," he said, his tone sardonic. "You see—this is not a game, this is your future—"

"Oh, but, Grant, I would love to have a child."

He stilled. Why did her words affect him to such a degree? Was it the delighted sound of her voice? The wide, easy smile accompanying her words? "There can be no children."

"You just told me there might—"

"We're not married. You have to be married."

"Then let's get married." Her tone made it sound as though this was a foregone conclusion. One plus two equals three. "You said I needed to marry. Why not you?"

He shook his head forcefully. "Victoria, I think you are understandably curious about men, but that's all it is. Curiosity. And it's centered on me because I'm the first man you've been around since you became a woman. Surely you don't want to settle on me for the rest of your life. Don't you even want to meet other men? Or be courted?"

She ignored his question, stood on her toes, and kissed his neck. Such a gentle touch, a sweet touch, and already his blood was firing, driving him to do things to her body that weren't *sweet*.

This mission would conclude far differently than he'd planned. He could envision it now: Victoria would step onto England's shores as a girl stripped of her prospects and innocence, married, most likely with a child got upon her—by a lecherous older man who was her *guardian*. He'd robbed her of ever having a choice.

The bastards at the club would slap his back and tell him slyly, "Well done."

She sat on the bed and slowly tugged the silky ribbon at her bodice. The material gaped, and she drew it lower.

He growled low in his throat. In a heartbeat, he had his fingers curled around the material against her breasts.

To yank it up.

As soon as he removed his hands, she gave him a challenging lift of her eyebrows and pulled it down. He snatched it up again. *Down. Up.* She tugged it down once more. "Stop!" she cried, when he seized the material out of her fingers and up again. "*You're going to rip my bodice!*"

"I'm not going to rip your bodice—unless you don't let it go," he added with a growl. "We *are not* doing this."

"Yes, we *are*. And if you rip my new dress, you can say farewell to your trousers."

"Promise?" he grated, then felt appalled with himself.

"Hah! You want this too." She took her eyes off his face and regarded his jutting erection inches from her. She leaned farther down his torso to where, God help him, he could feel her breath at the line of his trousers. She kissed him, a sweeping touch of her lips over his skin. "Can I touch you?" she whispered.

Trust that she truly knows what she wants. Give her credit. Trust her.

He was lost. "Do as you will, Victoria."

Seventeen

$\mathcal{T}$ori ran her hand down the front of his trousers and up again, feeling him hard, straining against the fabric. She'd seen him twice before, but when she freed the trousers and he sprang forth, she gasped, enthralled all over again.

Knowing she could never get used to feeling him like this, she wrapped her fingers around him, stroking, not as she had in the past, but lovingly, slowly exploring every nuance of his flesh. She wanted to experience everything and sensed he was on the verge of finally capitulating.

Everything.

"Grant, yesterday when you kissed me . . . privately?"

"Yes?" he hissed as her palm rubbed the head of his erection.

"Can I kiss you privately?"

"You play at things you don't understand." His voice was raw.

"Then teach me." She knew he was at the precipice, one foot over the abyss. The slightest push . . . Tonight, she would show him no mercy. "Show me how to give you pleasure."

"Victoria, you don't know what you ask." He looked anguished. Torn.

But he hadn't said no. Tentatively, before she lost her nerve, she placed her lips on his skin.

He groaned, hands clutching her shoulders, grating her name. "You don't know what you're doing to me."

She looked up and found him staring down at her kissing him. His breathing was ragged, the muscles in his torso and chest contracting and flexing. His eyes were dark and watchful, as if he was witnessing something he couldn't quite believe.

Such a small touch brought him to this? She increased the pressure, tasting him with her tongue as he'd tasted her. His hips bucked again and she pulled back.

"Is this wicked?" she asked, returning her lips to his skin.

"*Yes.*" He placed his hands in her hair, and she noticed they shook wildly. He'd drawn his leg up beside her on the bed.

"Since I like kissing you here so much, I must be wicked."

He groaned at her words, and then more deeply when she ran her tongue up his length.

"And since you like it . . ."

"*Like* it? Like isn't the word I'd—" He sucked in a breath when she took him fully in her mouth. She glanced up, his flesh still between her lips, to find his head thrown back and his torso rigid all the way down to the base of his manhood.

"Ah, God, Victoria." At once he lifted her and placed her before him. The grip on her arms was hard. "You make me feel like a beast, I want you so much."

The warning in his eyes excited her. "Do as you will."

He made some fierce noise in the back of his throat, then freed her dress and yanked it down. When she stepped out of it, he tugged her pantalets off and tossed them aside.

She'd been eager for him to see her black silk stockings with their provocative openwork stitching, but now embarrassment suffused her. When his fingers traced the lacy patterns on the stockings and then almost playfully tugged on the black satin garters high on her thighs, she reached down to remove them, but he took her hands.

"Leave them." His voice sounded tortured. "*For me.*"

She nodded, eyes wide. He sat then and lifted her into his lap, dragging her shift over her head. He moved her body, her legs over his, laying her back in his arms to stare at her bared breasts. With a growl, he leaned over to put his lips on her nipples, suckling them almost painfully. They soon became numbed until every lash of his tongue on them was felt coursing between her legs. She spread her thighs, and an obliging hand trailed down her belly. His fingers parted her.

"So wet for me," he rumbled against her breast as he fondled her sex. "So perfect."

When he swept a glance down her body, she arched her back, tempting his mouth back to her nipples. She hadn't thought anything could feel better than his stroking her, but then he delved a finger *inside* her. She gave a sharp cry and her hips reared to his hand. He held her sex, stirring his finger in her, making her moan.

"Grant! This feeling . . . Make it . . . *Help me.*"

"How, Victoria?" He placed her on the bed and pressed her back with one huge hand across her breasts. Kneeling between her legs to lift her bottom, he brought her to his mouth as though to drink her.

"Help you"—he kissed her then and groaned against her flesh—"with my lips?"

"Yes!" She raised her hips in offering. *Yes, his lips.*

"Or with my fingers?" He stroked her then, making her moan low. Her head thrashed. When he drew his fingers from deep inside her, she whimpered, opening her legs wider. No relief came.

She glanced up, and saw he'd removed his trousers and returned. He reached up to palm her breasts and massage her nipples, and his manhood rose over her, resting up on her belly. It was thick and visibly throbbing, the head moist. Her mouth fell open in awe. So beautiful, so strange. So *compelling* . . . He looked down to see her staring at him, and she thought his lips nearly curled.

"Please!" she cried.

His whole body was tight, like he was about to explode. "What do you want, Victoria?" Then he leaned down to whisper in her ear, words she knew should be *unspoken.* She couldn't believe the language, yet it wasn't even what he said, but the way he spoke to her, the ferocity, the *want,* that made her moan.

Then he pressed his finger inside her again, making her gasp and shudder. She fell back, arms raised above her as the tension wracked her body. When he withdrew only to push back into her, need spiraled in her, mounting with each push and withdrawal, until it peaked and finally shattered. As her body spasmed and her back arched, he rasped what he was going to do to her after she came from this, places he would lick her, places his fingers would find and rub, how badly he wanted her mouth on him again, sucking him deep. . . .

"*Oh, yes,*" she moaned long and low. She could feel her body squeezing around his clever fingers. He was relentless, continuing to tease her, spreading the moisture in long, luxuriating strokes.

As though another man inhabited his body, Grant teased Victoria inside, testing her, stretching her tightness. After witnessing her abandon, there was no thought of denying himself this. She would be his. At this moment, nothing could please him more. He saw her lick her parted lips, saw her breasts moist from him, and the fair curls covering her sex. . . . *Lost.*

Seizing her thighs, he spread her wider, then gripped himself to run the head of his cock up and down her folds, making sure she was ready to take him. He groaned as she became wetter against the head.

Finally, he allowed himself to push into her, but only just so. She was slick, but still so tight. Every muscle in his body quaked for him to plunge to the hilt, to bury himself in her regardless of how small she was. No, he *wouldn't* hurt her. He *could* control himself.

But she began moving, writhing to make him enter her more fully. He grasped her beneath to hold her still, groaning at the feel of her in his fingers, withdrew, and then entered just the head once more. She was too tight, impossibly so. He feared he would break her. "I don't want to hurt you," he grated in a low, barely recognizable voice.

"Isn't it supposed to hurt?" she said on a breath. "A little?"

A little? Not this time. By the way her body clenched powerfully against his, he could swear she couldn't take more.

"It's going to hurt, sweet."

She sighed. "I worried you'd be too big. And I don't know if I'm quite normal—"

He leaned down to kiss her, his voice rough against her lips as he said, "You are everything a man could want. . . ." He met the barrier and she sucked in a breath. He flexed his hips, surging into her. She cried out—he froze.

"Victoria, are you all right?"

"I-I think so," she whispered.

Grant believed he should be still. Let her body adjust to his size. Wasn't that what you were supposed to do with virgins? He'd never had to worry about this before. "Do you want me to stop?" As if he could. This would be the ultimate test, buried in her tight heat and having to give that up. . . .

"Yes."

No. Damn it, no! his mind screamed. He couldn't give this up. He'd just achieved heaven. But he looked down and saw that her eyes watered. The idea of her hurting tore at him.

His body set with determination, he pulled out, but beast that he was, he withdrew slowly, lingering inch by inch to enjoy what he'd only tasted.

She moaned low in her throat. "Oh, wait. I like that." Stunned, he drove back in. "*Ow*," she bit out.

He pulled out once more, and again she moaned. He was losing his mind. "Love, you can't have one without the other."

"Can you go in slow, like you go out?"

Could he? When every instinct demanded he plunge into her? Shaking, sweating with effort, he slowly, so slowly tortured himself in and out, finding a rhythm that pleased her and made him shudder. Sweat dripped from him onto her trembling breasts where it mingled with her own. He bent down to take a salty nipple into his mouth and drew on it. She moaned again, spreading her legs wider.

"Maybe a bit more quickly," she whispered in his ear. Again, he shuddered.

As she wished, he pushed in faster. When he saw her breasts shaking with each thrust, he knew it was only a matter of time, and when she moaned he took the ground she gave. Over and over, his hips drove into her, his hands trapping her thighs wide or fondling her breasts.

"Ah, Grant, *yes.*" The harder and faster he took her, the more she called his name, until he was pounding against her and she was meeting him.

Then suddenly, just as he'd become so thick in her he could hardly move, she arched her back, breasts pushing against his chest. She cried out and he felt her squeezing around him, all along his cock, her body milking his.

No more. He could take no more. A last pounding shove. Yelling out her name, he exploded into her, his orgasm pumping on and on, relentless.

When he finally was spent, he realized he'd been squeezing her in his arms as he helplessly continued to buck.

Slowly, thoughts emerged from the haze. *I'm holding her so tight, I might hurt her. . . . She's mine. . . . I don't know if I can let go.*

He eased up to rise above her. As though clawing his way from a dream, Grant stared in disbelief at Victoria beneath him, at his body still languorously pushing inside her. He stared down at her delighted face and saw her tears.

What have I done?

• • •

Victoria lay in his bed, curled on her side. She slept lightly, with small twitches and movements of her eyes behind closed lids. Life on the island most likely had awakened that in her—that something deep within, that instinct reacting to sound, filtering the normal from the warning, the slapping of bristly palms in a breeze from the first low hiss of a storm.

He enjoyed watching her sleep, he realized, but she needed to get back. God only knew what he might do to her if she stayed, because he'd realized something about himself tonight. He was becoming more and more comfortable with losing control with her.

He shook his head, still staggered by his behavior. He'd never been free with a woman, never had more than a perfunctory release, certainly had never done what he'd pressed on Victoria—he'd always feared losing control, feared his needs being talked about among the women of his acquaintance. Perhaps that was why he never sought out women, and by no means slept with them more than once. He was far from a rake, but worried that if he ever got comfortable his restraint might slip.

And every time he'd eased the pressure himself, the fantasies and imaginings filling his mind had only reinforced what he already knew about himself and what he desperately wanted to hide. Men of his caliber should be able to control such baseness. But then, the men of his family had never been good at restraint. No one but him.

Until now.

He leaned over and turned up the lantern. When he reached her side, he noticed the four fading half-moon indentions in her palm where her fingernails had dug in during her pleasure. She made fists when she reached her peak.

And when he returned her to the hotel, she squeezed his hand as if in thanks. The memory of the indentions in her palms flashed in his mind. Something so small. It was really such a tiny detail and shouldn't mean so much.

He was lost.

Eighteen

Tori's lips curled up seconds after her eyes slid open to the morning sun. She stretched her body, her soreness making her grin widen. She'd been made love to thoroughly. Oh, the things Grant had done to her. . . . She'd never conceived of actions and words so wicked and stirring.

She shivered in delight. And now they would marry. Her future husband had a vigorous imagination—and a talented, powerfully built body. Reflecting on Grant's perfect pairing made a haze of contentment wash over her. She could now admit to herself that she'd fallen for Grant. Completely.

When she finally dressed and joined Cammy, they enjoyed a luncheon of eggs, rice, apples, and juice, in keeping with Cammy's new special diet. Both were so excited about her health, they giggled over the slightest thing.

But late that afternoon, when Grant still had not shown

up, Tori's contentment and confidence withered. How dare he not come by? After a night like the last, she supposed she should feel used, but that would mean she'd given something up. She felt she'd received something instead. And that was why she was so livid. She wanted to . . . *receive* again!

That night, what was left of her patience was ragged. The second Cammy fell asleep, Tori crept out the door and hurried to the *Keveral.* The guards on deck took one look at her face and backed away, nervously chuckling as she swished her skirts by them. She marched to Grant's cabin and yanked open the door. No sign of him. She made her way toward the salon and heard his voice. Good. She couldn't wait to get this off her chest.

As she neared the door, she heard Ian as well.

"Are you going to tell me again that there's no chance of her having your babe? Because this time, I'm not—"

"No, there's every chance in the world." Grant's words were slurred.

Why were they talking about this?

"Ian, drop it."

"Just because you're foxed? It won't deter me. Listen to me clearly, Cousin. I was going to let you work this out on your own, try to see if you'd put things right, but you haven't. Tori's become like a sister to me and I'm about to act like a brother."

"How's that?"

"I'm going to wipe the floor with your face, if you don't promise to make this right by her. Damn it, man, I keep thinking about how Emma or Sadie would feel in her situation. They're all the same age, Grant. I would hope that someone would help my sisters like this if they needed it."

"You have nothing to fear. Though this lecture is absurd

coming from you, it appears that I am going to do the honorable thing and marry the chit." She heard him clacking a bottle against a glass. "So, wish me well."

Chit? Well, he did say he'd marry her. A grin spread across her face.

She could swear she heard Ian exhale. "Good, you've finally come to your senses."

"No, I've just finally done something that I can't undo, and I'm going to pay the price. I'll own up to my mistakes."

Mistakes?

Ian echoed her thought. "Mistakes? How could this possibly be a mistake?"

"She's not what I want in a wife. She has no respect for rules. I wanted an asset by my side—her wildness will always be a liability. I shudder to think how she'll behave in London."

Tori pulled her head back as though slapped. Hot shame flowed through her, seeping into every inch of her body. Her breaths shallowed. Now everything became clear. She *embarrassed* him. He was *ashamed* of her. Making love to her was a mistake?

Everything she'd shared with him now seemed cheap and sordid. Her wildness? Had she behaved inappropriately with him? Done something unacceptable in his bed? *Oh, God.* The humiliation was so thick she tasted it rising in her throat. She rushed to the gangway and retched.

Wiping her face, she leaned on the rail, her face in her hands. An uncouth girl. A sorry, pitiful woman, following him like a puppy nipping at its master's heels. She was the one who couldn't see what was so plain before her. She remembered Cammy's advice: *Don't confuse love and lust.*

Turning back to town, she ran the back of her hand over her tears until their sheer number defeated the gesture. It wasn't ever about winning him over, just trying a little harder to get his attention. She'd never had a chance.

That's why he didn't *want* to make love to her. That's why he felt so guilty afterward—*because he'd reduced himself by it.*

Oh, God.

She could barely make out her way through tear-clouded eyes, stumbling back to the hotel. Captain Sutherland would never have to worry about her bothering him again.

"Grant, you're an idiot. Mistakes, liability? Do you hear what you're—"

"What if she comes to want another?" His voice was low, hurting.

"So this is what it's really all about?"

"No, the other things are"—he waved his hand as he searched for words—"well, there are other concerns." He slurred the last. "Bloody hell, I'm about to make her mine, give her everything I have, and I'm probably doing *her* a disservice. I can't help but think that perhaps she should have had a chance to find a husband naturally, with more prospects. I think she settled on me because I'm the first man she saw as a woman."

"You're not exactly a bad catch."

"Not financially, but I'm not really what she needs. She needs someone closer to her own age. Someone as fun-loving and carefree as she is, not the killjoy she thinks I am. What if I can't make her happy?" Grant stared down at his drink. "Christ, what if she comes to want another?"

Ian shook his head forcefully. "You run that risk with any woman—"

"No, it's worse than that," he said, raising his face,

uncaring that Ian saw his pain. "You know how women are always accused of trapping a man in marriage? I think . . . I think part of me finally gave in because I wanted her bound to me. I didn't want her to have a choice when we return home." Grant's chest twisted when he voiced what he'd done. "I trapped Victoria."

"I didn't think you'd be awake," Tori intoned to Cammy as she entered their hotel room.

"Oh, I just got a drink of wat—Tori, what happened? Where have you been?"

Tori fought the urge to tell her what she had just learned. The news was just too raw, and if she spoke the words "He is ashamed of me," she thought she'd break down again. She'd never felt shame like this before, and now that man had made her feel it so deeply, she thought she would choke on it.

"It's nothing. I'm just being sentimental about the island."

Cammy looked relieved. "I do that too."

They spent the next hour reminiscing about their times there, calling up good memories, but in the back of her mind, Tori realized one thing she'd overlooked. He *was* going to ask her to marry him. His sense of duty demanded it. She didn't think he'd be easily deterred once he'd made up his mind and his honor was on the line. What to say to him to turn him down? How to approach this to salvage her pride? An idea was forming.

Nineteen

Grant's head was splitting from what he decided was his last hangover. Reality rushed over him in waves. The headache was palpable; his feelings for Victoria were palpable. Both were just facts of life. If Grant drank too much, his head would ache. If Grant made love to Victoria and saw her smile, he'd never settle for another woman. There was nothing to be done for it.

If Victoria came to love another man, it would not be for lack of trying on his part to make her happy. And, of course, it would be over his dead body. He was going to be her husband and, by God, he was going to be good at it.

With his decision made, he felt lighter, more content than he could remember. He couldn't deny that marriage to Victoria was very tempting in certain aspects. Wedding her would give him the right to her body, to do everything he'd been imagining—every touch, every kiss, every way he could join them together—whenever he pleased. He could take what she freely gave him. Only him.

And when the idea arose that she might now be with child, with *his* child, he became curiously pleased.

During the day, he scoured the city for the perfect ring. Grant had to pay an exorbitant amount, but as soon as he saw the emerald, he knew she had to have it. The color was the same as the water around her island, but this stone shone like fire was inside it. He'd never seen anything like it.

He went to her that night, his spirits high. He would get the issue of marriage settled and then take her to bed somewhere. The anticipation of touching her again was maddening. Thinking about what they'd done together . . . His lips turned up in what he knew was a wicked grin. He'd teach her something new tonight. . . .

She sent down a message that she was ill.

Panic flew through him. Had he been too rough with her? Was she embarrassed? Victoria had been grinning ear to ear when he left her the night before, and she wasn't easily embarrassed. She must really be sick. Guilt overrode panic. He'd taken her away from Eden to a dirty, congested city.

He couldn't think like that. After they were married, Grant would make sure she always had room to breathe. He'd make her happy in her new life. He sent up a note asking if they would be able to sail on the morning tide. Her response: *I am more than ready to leave.*

When they sailed the next day, Victoria did look ill. Her eyes were flat. Her face lacked its usual animation. When Camellia kicked her out of her cabin again, Victoria excused herself to his room. He put his hand on her upper arm and pulled her aside. "Are you unwell?"

"Not at all."

Then why do you look as though you hate me? he wanted to rail. He had a fear; he hoped he was wrong. She glared at his hand on her arm, and, baffled, he released her.

Midmorning passed, and Victoria still hadn't made her way to the bridge. She usually brought Grant coffee by this time. Then he saw her. Her long hair was pulled back with a ribbon, and she appeared fresh and young. No sign of sickness.

Anticipation thrummed, but she walked past the ladder and sat on the deck with Ian. She never looked up at him.

Later that day it began to drizzle. Now Victoria would bring him his oilskin jacket as she did whenever it started to rain. He waited for several moments, getting steadily more soaked. Finally, he turned the bridge over to Dooley and made his way to his cabin. She answered his knock in a low, emotionless voice.

Grant felt as though he'd walked into a battlefield when he hadn't known there was a war. He took a chair, though he was unasked.

"It's raining," he said stupidly.

She lay on the bed, curled on her side as she read a book. She gave an uninterested glance toward the porthole and said, "So it is." She licked her finger, then turned a page.

"It's good you weren't on deck. It's going to come down harder." What the devil was he babbling about? She didn't answer, only turned another page.

"Are you feeling well?"

"Splendid." Without looking up, she waved an airy hand at him and said, "Oh, when you close the door, will you lift up on it? It leaks if it isn't in the track. Thanks."

He'd just been dismissed. From his own cabin. But wasn't this what he'd wanted? He'd wanted her to stop looking at him with those adoring green eyes. To stop smiling at him over her cup when she brought coffee.

But that had been before. Before he'd made her his.

What had brought this sudden change between the door of her hotel and the next night? She simply didn't want to have anything to do with him. Maybe it was because she'd expected a proposal, but that didn't explain the *bitterness*.

What if she knew about him now? Perhaps she'd told Camellia what had happened and Camellia had told her how . . . wrong Grant was, how a lady shouldn't have been treated as he'd treated her. He couldn't take it if Tori looked at him with disgust. His mind seized on the idea that she had wished for a proposal—that it wasn't his behavior—and he held on to it desperately.

"I'll leave, but first we need to talk about some things."

Tori immediately put the book down and rose. "Yes, we do."

"We need to marry."

There, he'd asked her. Well, *told* her, concluding the proposal she'd known was imminent. Again, she wondered if she'd misunderstood him when he spoke with Ian. What if he was posturing for Ian? The idea gave her hope, but she wouldn't just blindly grasp at it. . . . "Why should we marry? Do you love me?" she asked bluntly.

He appeared astonished at the idea. Had he never even considered that he might love her? "I am . . . fond of you."

"Fond?" Her heart broke a little. "What kind of marriage would it be, based on fondness?"

"Strong marriages have been built on less."

"Would you be proud to have me as your wife? Would you show me off to everyone?"

The skin around his eyes grew tight. "You would go everywhere I went."

She paced the room. "That doesn't answer the question. Would you want me to change?"

"I'd hope you'd want to acclimate to society again."

In other words, *change.* As in, *you are not what you need to be.* "I wonder if you care for me at all."

"I respect you. I admire your resiliency. I like that you're intelligent and resourceful."

She stood before him, her body tense with anger. "You *admire* my resiliency? You don't love me, you wouldn't be proud to call me your wife—well, at least not in front of others. Though you certainly liked bedding me."

He stood, his eyes seeming to burn through her. *"More than you can know."*

She almost lost her will to him then. Almost. Unfortunately, he was confirming everything she'd overheard.

The answer she most needed to know . . . "Do you feel obligated to marry me?"

He hesitated. "I know the rules, Victoria. I uphold the rules. We must marry."

She wouldn't cry. She couldn't. *Be strong.* "That's the thing about obligations. People come to resent them. I won't marry you."

"Pardon?"

She moved to sit on the edge of the bed, then gave him her rehearsed speech. "Grant, I've thought about our situation a lot. And I believe that you were right about us— that my feelings for you were mere infatuation. It occurred to me that I couldn't possibly suspect myself of having more substantial feelings when I hardly know you and don't know other men at all."

"What?" His whole body grew rigid.

She made her tone businesslike. "You were kind enough to point that out, even when I was so obstinate about it. I've come to my senses, so you have nothing to fear."

"It's a little late for this. I've bedded you," he pointed out needlessly.

She stretched her fingers to study her nails. "And I trust that won't get out to any of my possible marriage prospects when we get back to England."

His eyes widened, then blazed with anger. "You won't have prospects. You have no dowry. Your grandfather is impoverished. What will you do then?"

His words left her shaken, but she masked it. "Cammy and I will live with Grandfather at the Court."

"You won't be doing that either." His tone was ruthless.

"Why not?"

"The Court is mine. It's my payment for finding and returning you."

Her head slanted forward. Could she have misheard him? "You neglected to tell me that I would return to England prospectless, penniless, and *homeless?*"

"You didn't need to know at the time."

Her shock gave way to anger. "You lied to me."

"I never lied."

"You're claiming my family's ancestral home?" she asked in disgust. Her tone was scathing when she added, "Then you were wrong on the island. You *are* some hack delivering me."

"So would you like to tell me about your recent change of heart?" Cammy said over dinner in her cabin the next evening.

When Tori didn't answer, Cammy coaxed, "Please, tell me what you're thinking."

Tori set down the bread she'd just buttered. "I don't want to bother you with petty things—"

Cammy gave a short, humorless laugh. "I'm cabin-ridden for an interminable amount of time. I *need* you to bother me."

Tori took a deep breath. "I made love to Grant."

Cammy sat silently.

"Aren't you going to say something? Show any surprise?"

"I may be sick, but I can still see which way the wind blows," Cammy said, pushing her plate away.

"Aren't you upset with me?"

Cammy shook her head. "No, because Grant is a good man. I know he wouldn't have done that if he didn't intend to marry you. I suspect he's planning a wedding right now."

"He already told me we would marry."

Cammy leaned back and blew out a relieved breath.

"But I won't do it."

"What do you mean?" she asked slowly.

"I think I could hate him."

Cammy got a strangled look on her face "Do explain!"

"I overheard Grant tell Ian that he was . . . that he was embarrassed by me. That he was ashamed of me."

"Did he say those exact words?"

"No, but the meaning was clear. He said he would shudder to see me loose in England. That I was a mistake."

Cammy sucked in a breath. "He wasn't saying this for Ian's benefit? Men sometimes . . ." She trailed off when Tori shook her head.

"When he told me we would marry, I asked him if he cared for me. If he would be proud of me. If he was marrying me for more than his sense of obligation. He answered poorly on all counts." Tori dashed away a tear with the heel of her palm. "Besides, it makes perfect sense. I thought he found me attractive, and I absolutely let him know I was attracted to him, but he usually shied away. And the times he didn't—he obviously felt a deep measure of guilt."

"The *times* he didn't shy away?" Cammy asked in a choked voice. "Just how many times did he not shy away?"

Tori waved her hand as if the information was trifling. "We've kissed and such a few times."

Cammy looked heavenward. "And this before we even get to England."

Tori checked another irritating tear. "Yes, well, our arrival's going to be a bit different than it was presented. He lied about the Court." At Cammy's blank look, she explained, "He gets it—when Grandfather dies, Grant will own it. He'll own my family's land."

Cammy scratched her temple. "Why would Belmont make such a deal?"

"He has no money," she said sadly. "It was the last thing he had to offer."

"Let's think about this," Cammy began in a sensible tone. "Grant did spend more than a year on this mission. He deserves to be compensated for it."

Tori shook her head. "I think it's wrong, and he must too. Why else wouldn't he have told me about it?" She rose to stare out of the small cabin window. "Cammy, for the first time since I could remember, I felt secure. But it was false. We don't know what kind of life we're sailing into. To believe I thought so highly of him. He was only pretending to be this gentleman surfeit with honor." She placed her hand on the cool glass. "I fell for it, but I'll never let down my guard again."

"Tori, what if you're with child?" Cammy asked gently.

She was silent for a long time because she didn't know how to feel about that. She didn't have words to express the turmoil the idea brought her, the joy, sadness, worry, and regret. She faced her friend. "I'll know soon, in the next week, I believe."

Cammy nodded, and they agreed to put off any further discussions until then.

So Cammy spent the week resting and eating her new foods, and Tori and Ian strategized on the best way to make his lady forgive him for disappearing for so long. Their conversations helped break up her misery. He loved to talk about Erica's big, gray eyes, her sharp intellect, her shyness. At least one man on this ship was in love.

Ian couldn't wait for Tori and his sisters and mother to meet Erica. He predicted that all would adore her as much as he did. When Tori remarked that she would have loved to have so many siblings, Ian promised her she was about to have three new sisters, four with Erica, and a quirky yet lovable Aunt Serena. It was the first time Tori had smiled in days.

She sometimes caught Grant observing her and felt him even more, yet he never said a word to her, until on the very day she was sure she would not be having his child, he approached her.

"Victoria, I'd like to speak with you."

She exhaled as though very put out and walked to the cabin, sitting on the edge of the bed. He shut the door behind him, then moved to sit across from her. His blue eyes were somber yet watchful, searching her face—he *seemed* very concerned about her. That thought made it difficult to remain indifferent to him. *But look how wrong I've been about him before.* Obviously, she was woefully ignorant of what people were thinking and how they really felt. Her mind flashed to her bumbling attempts at seduction, and her face flushed.

"I'd like to ask you if you . . . has there been? . . ."

She gathered what he was trying to say. Part of her wanted to make him uncomfortable and force him to say the question. Finally, she said, "Am I with child?"

"Yes."

She fingered the coverlet in snappish movements. "Why do you care?"

"Why do I—? How can you ask that?"

"What would you do if I was?"

"I'd marry you." There was steel in his tone. "At the first opportunity."

She boldly met his gaze. "I wouldn't marry you under any circumstances."

His lips thinned as though he just held his fury in check. "This has gone on long enough. I don't know what I did to cause you to cool toward me, but you shouldn't take that out on an innocent child. You'd make a bastard out of my child to spite me?"

"You, you, you!" She leapt up. "Why does everything have to be about you? Do you think I go about my days thinking of ways I can spite you? You flatter yourself if you believe I think of you at all."

"Then why?"

"Because I wouldn't chain myself to you for the rest of my life. I think you've been absolutely right about me all along. *You* aren't right for *me*. I hadn't had enough experience with men to know what I wanted before. And now, now that I will have that chance, I'm certain I will find someone who'd be better for me. No, we won't marry."

His hands knotted into fists. "You wouldn't have a choice. Do you think you're my ideal bride? I assure you

you're not, but I'd marry you to spare our child any unnecessary hurt."

Oh, she knew very well that she wasn't his ideal bride. She was a *mistake*. Before she began crying, she said, "No."

"No, what?"

"I'm not with child."

He sat staring at her, his eyes dark and . . . hurting? "Very well, Victoria." He exhaled a long breath. "I wanted to make sure."

"There's no child. When we get to England, we can go our separate ways."

Grant turned back to her one last time before he left, confusion plain on his face. She ignored the pain in her heart and told herself for the hundredth time that it was for the best.

Twenty

Tori stood on the bow of the *Keveral,* her excitement at seeing London dimming as the city's mist settled into droplets on her coat. She sighed at her dismal surroundings, breathing in dank air that tasted like soot, surely from the tall chimneys on the horizon choking up black smoke.

"So this is what all the fuss was about," she said loud enough for Grant to hear. He stood close by on the bow, and she told herself it was to pine near her. Not to oversee the steam tug towing them up the Thames.

She thought she saw him flush. The port was not showing well. With a pointed look at the thick, cloying refuse in the Thames audibly knocking about the sides of the ship, she said, "And to think I might have missed this, if not for you."

Grant scowled at her and stalked off to give instructions for docking. As soon as he left, she felt empty. What did that say about her? That she would rather be with him in anger than without him in peace? That was sorry of her, and she didn't want to be like that. No, she didn't, but another part of her mind whispered, *Peace is a relative term, anyway,* and urged her to torment him.

For the last month, she'd been cutting, mumbling insults at him, glaring at him. If she had one wish, it was that he'd stay and *take* her anger, absorb so much that it faded from her. And then he would, of course, apologize abjectly and say that he loved her.

She sighed. It wasn't in her nature to be this churlish. Squaring her shoulders, she resolved that she would endeavor to be civil to him.

This day would mark a new beginning. She frowned up at the sky. This gray, faded day. Regardless, it was a new beginning in a new land and a new life—a life far from the one she'd envisioned for herself, but spiting Grant helped nothing.

She would try to change and make the best of things. Keep what was past in the past. She gave herself a sharp nod. A new start—

Something thumped against the bow. Dooley exclaimed, "That one must've been a body." The crew howled with laughter.

Tori drummed her nails and rolled her eyes. New beginning . . .

How utterly auspicious.

Hours later, as they traveled deeper into what Tori learned was called the "pool of London," she took in one bewildering sight after another. It was like a forest upon the water, there were so many masts from the ships clotting the harbor. Low, nebulous clouds slid along with the gusting wind. The sounds of chains grating, construction, and a multitude of vendors hawking wares assaulted her ears.

The steam tug chugged onward, towing them to a system of wharves and a monstrous warehouse bordering the river. The ship was docked at one of the largest piers as gently as a baby laid to cradle. Sodden flags matching the pennants of the *Keveral* snapped from masts at the shore.

After the crew secured the ship, Tori and Cammy said farewell to them. Tori hugged Dooley with watering eyes, wishing him luck on his next voyage. When Dooley teared up too, Ian quickly conducted Tori and Cammy to the warehouse. They were to wait there while Grant oversaw the details of arrival.

The goods inside were piled so high it was as if they walked a maze. They inspected the spectacular lots of marble, teas, carpets, and spices. In a separate room, the blue room, they saw stacks of compacted bales of indigo powder. Tori knew all these materials were expensive, even without noticing the guards walking the perimeter. "So Grant does well as a captain?"

Ian looked at her quizzically. "He owns half of this."

Her eyes widened. "But I thought he was only a captain, or just owned a share."

"The brothers own it jointly," Ian said. "Rich as Croesus, both of them."

Tori looked at Cammy in shock, then back at Ian. "Then why didn't Grant just buy an estate, instead of make this deal with my grandfather?"

Ian sank onto a roll of carpet. "There simply aren't unentailed estates that large left. Not for sale and not near Grant's family's home."

"Just how big is the Court?" Cammy asked.

"Vast, because the family stipulated it never could be

divided, almost as though it were entailed. So in a time of dwindling estates, the Court still has its parklands, woodlands, downlands, and a village of tenants."

"Why does he want such a large property?" Tori asked as she and Cammy sat in a pair of wrapped antique chairs across from Ian.

He shrugged as if he didn't know very much about the subject, but Tori knew Ian observed and recorded more information than anyone suspected. He finally explained, "Grant's clever and ambitious. He knows that in England, land means power. As a younger son, Grant never hoped to acquire an estate like your family's, but if he did, he'd have a seat of power."

When Tori gave a cynical smirk, Ian said, "I want to be clear about this. Land means power but it also means responsibility, and I swear Grant's the only man in the kingdom who wants the latter more than the former. I don't want you ever to doubt his motives in this."

She would always doubt his motives. She feigned a smile and Ian relaxed, apparently convinced that she did in fact understand him.

While she pondered this new information, Ian waved his now calloused hand around the warehouse and said, "The family didn't see fit to cut ol' Ian a piece of the pie when my mother, Serena, inquired years ago. Told her some nonsense about 'unfortunate predilections' and an 'absurd disregard for fiscal responsibility.'" He shook his head. "Picky, picky."

Cammy remarked, "Your mother was good to ask for you."

"She didn't give a whit about the money." He chuckled. "She just wanted the brothers stuck watching out for me as they always had, keeping me straight . . ." He was about to say more, when they heard Grant's voice carrying from somewhere in the warehouse. Ian rose and stretched his long arms above his head. "I'll just go check with Grant and see if he's ready to escort you from here."

"Are you certain you can't accompany us to the Court?" Cammy asked. "We will miss you, Ian."

Ian leaned forward to kiss her hand. "I have to go find Erica. Still, I wouldn't leave you if I didn't know Grant would care for you both."

When he took Tori's hand, she said, "You must write and tell us how you're doing."

"Write?" Ian scoffed. "As soon as I find Erica, I'm introducing her to Serena and my sisters, then dragging my gaggle of females west to see all of you." He looked very young, but so sure when he said, "You won't get rid of me that easily, I'm afraid."

Grant was as ready to be on his way as any of them. He figured his best chance at sanity was leaving Victoria at the Court. Apart from her, his feelings would fade. They had to. He worried that they hadn't already. He had, after all, dodged a bullet. He'd bedded her and didn't have to pay the ultimate price. So why did he feel like he wanted to be shot at again?

"What are you so nervous about?" Grant asked Ian when he joined him outside Peregrine's office. For the past two weeks, Ian had seemed more anxious about landing than any of them.

Ian shrugged. "Nothing that concerns you."

"If this is about those creditors, I can lend you some money. Again."

"It's not about them," Ian said coldly.

Grant raised his eyebrows, but changed the subject.

"I'm still surprised you don't want to accompany the ladies, although I'm not complaining."

Ian glared, then said, "I want to, yes. I feel like I'm abandoning them. Especially since Tori appears to despise you." He cast Grant a confounded look, as though he'd never figure that one out. "But I've got other things I need to see to."

"Like what?"

Ian scrutinized Grant, as though determining if he could trust him. He apparently decided he couldn't, because he ignored the question, and asked, "Are you going to send word to Derek and the family?"

"No, just to Belmont. The papers would have a field day with this story, so I'm trying to keep it under wraps. I'll visit Whitestone afterward."

Ian nodded, then said, "We're returning Cammy home, but for Tori this will be as new and you'll have to be patient. We can't even begin to understand how she feels about all this."

"I can't believe *you* are lecturing me on the care of a woman."

"Since I can't go, I'm going to have to trust you to care for her."

Grant made a disbelieving sound, then grated, "*I already care for her.*" His eyes narrowed. "That didn't come out as it should."

"Didn't it?"

Grant turned to the object of their conversation as though searching for some idea how to respond. Victoria and Camellia waited across the busy street by Grant's carriage, taking in the confusion and riot of the London docks with eyes wide.

A group of towering, foreign sailors with blond cropped hair stopped in their tracks when they spotted

Victoria. In their strange northern language, they chattered to her, surrounding her. She half-smiled, unsure what to make of the men, some holding their hands over their hearts, others bowing with great solemnity.

Ian chuckled. "Looks like they've found their Scandinavian princess."

"The hell they have. . . ." Grant started for them, intending to crack skulls. Before he could get near, Camellia raised her umbrella warningly, and the group dispersed, throwing kisses back in their wake, while Victoria smiled and waved. Grant didn't slow, but made his way in front of Victoria to glower at the men until they disappeared from sight.

After Ian joined them and gave his farewells, Grant helped Camellia up into the carriage, then turned for Victoria. She ignored him and offered her hand to Ian.

"I wish it were you taking us to Belmont," she said in a not-low-enough voice.

Here, Grant wanted to rail. *I'm directly here and can hear everything you say.*

"I wouldn't leave you with him unless I trusted him to care for you."

"I know," she said, but a tear fell anyway.

"Ah, come here, Tori."

He hugged her; Grant was certain he'd kill his cousin in the street.

"It's going to be fine. You'll do fine."

They finally parted, and Ian helped her in, closing the door behind her. He stood back, looking more determined than Grant had ever seen him, as if anticipating a fight he *had* to win. He saluted Grant, then gave a last wave to the ladies before charging into the swirl of people.

When they pulled out into the traffic, Victoria was still

twining around to see Ian. Grant knew they were just friends, that Ian had "adopted her" as a sister and planned to have her meet Emma, Sadie, and Charlotte as soon as she settled in at the Court. Still, had he not known better, they would've looked like parting lovers. Grant wished he could comfort her, say the right things, but that chance was gone.

He sensed Victoria's unease, but she hid it well. Compared to Cape Town, London was a hundred times louder and more congested. Aproned fishmongers, boot-black peddlers, and a boy screaming, " 'ot eels!" all descended on the carriage, startling her. She looked at Grant in bewilderment before turning away.

When they finally made the covered drive of the Sutherland town house, Victoria exhaled a breath and rushed inside, pulling Camellia with her. Grant followed and had the housekeeper show them to their rooms. After arranging for food to be brought up to them, he adjourned to his study intending to take care of his most pressing business. Yet after two wasted hours he realized he couldn't focus with Victoria just upstairs, not with thoughts about her plaguing him.

Grab her. Pull her into my room and take her in my own bed. Until neither of us can walk.

As though chased, he left his home and made for his club to catch up on months of news. He did not expect to see Ian—much less a miserably drunk Ian.

"Good God." Grant couldn't hide his surprise at his cousin's condition. Ian was a drinker, and often a drunk, but never had Grant seen him this bad.

"Gran'!" Ian's face brightened. "How's m' girls?"

"Fine. Camellia's sleeping and Victoria's managing."

"Good girls." Ian's face fell.

"What's the matter with you?" Grant asked.

"Can't find somethin' I want," Ian slurred.

"I see." Grant looked around for somewhere else to be.

"Hope I haven't lost it."

Grant was hardly paying attention to his cousin's drunken ramblings. "I daresay if you can't find it, then it's lost." Grant heard a sharp breath. "Ian?" Grant was unsettled by the utterly lost look in his cousin's eyes. Ian appeared devastated, which couldn't be right since he rarely cared about anything enough to be even mildly distressed. "What is it, Ian? What's wrong with you?"

"It's *her*."

"Ahhh," Grant said as if he knew what the hell Ian was talking about. "Time to go home, Cousin."

Twenty-one

Camellia and Victoria had already breakfasted and had their belongings loaded into the traveling coach when Grant came down the next morning. Victoria's face didn't light up as it used to. Instead, she gave him a businesslike nod, the same nod Grant might give someone at a party whom he didn't particularly like. Camellia immediately quit the room to wait in the coach. Grant's mood—already at an abysmal level—sank.

"You don't have to accompany us to Belmont Court," Victoria assured him over her shoulder as she strode to join Camellia. "We have detailed directions."

That would be the end then. Part of him was tempted to test his theory about being away from Victoria, but there was no way he could surrender them to the dangers of coach travel. "I didn't sail thousands of miles to lose you somewhere in England. I'll go on to the Court."

He heard her mumble, "The estate. Always the estate."

He scowled. "I don't want you hurt."

She twisted around and smiled meanly. "And I think I know exactly why." With that, she climbed up the steps to slide onto the coach's squab seats. Grant shook his head and followed her in.

Three hours into the journey out of London, Victoria had become much more animated. The more rural or wild the countryside, the more excitement she showed. She obviously didn't like crowded cities, and Grant was glad the Court was far from any. But the excitement he sensed in both women wore off as the snowy roads continued to worsen. "We need to stop," he said, and was about to call new directions to the driver.

"Nonsense. Not on my account," Camellia said in what might have been an attempt at crispness.

"You need rest," Victoria said.

"We can stop in the next town," Grant suggested. "I don't think they have an inn, but we can try—"

"No," Camellia protested. "The only thing that is getting me through this journey is thinking about warm food and a warmer bath."

"Cammy, are you certain?"

"I am asking both of you to continue on."

Victoria looked at Grant. "Very well."

So they did, but with the next lurch of the coach, Camellia's lips thinned.

With the nearest inn still some distance away, Grant thought to detour to Whitestone. Nothing could compete with the comfort they'd find at his brother's estate. He hadn't wanted to go there and entangle his family in his affairs. All would ask him questions that he wasn't prepared or inclined to answer.

He looked over his exhausted charges, at Victoria petting Camellia's hair while the woman slept, her face drawn with worry, and realized that avoiding his family wasn't important. Certainly not more important than watching out for Victoria and Camellia. Decided, he gave the new directions to the driver.

"Is that your brother's estate?" Although Victoria finally spoke to him, she still looked out the window.

"Yes. It's closer for Camellia."

She nodded her assent, then put the back of her hand against the glass. "Will your family be there?"

"This close after Christmas, I imagine they will."

"Aren't you worried I might embarrass you? My ways are beyond backwater, aren't they?" she asked.

He frowned at her, puzzled that she would ask. To be honest, he was worried. His voice low, he said, "I won't be embarrassed if, for instance, you could refrain from skipping up to my brother to ask if your breasts have grown."

Camellia stirred. Victoria put her finger over her lips, then faced the window again. Grant stared at her long after she'd turned from him, knowing he would never understand her.

A few hours after dusk, after they'd traveled far into the Surrey hills, their coach rolled into Whitestone's lamplit gravel drive. Grant felt a welling of relief, and when his family rushed out to meet them, he knew he'd made the right choice.

"Grant! You're home," his mother cried, hugging him the second he stepped out.

"Looking as fetching as ever, Mother."

Derek stood next to her and extended his hand. Grant took the hearty handshake, nearly wincing as his large brother slapped him on the back. "I'm glad you're back,"

Derek said simply, but Grant knew what wealth of sentiment his words held.

"Grant!" Nicole rushed up and hugged him as well. When she stepped back, her attention was drawn behind him and her eyes widened. She plowed past him. "Oh, my Lord. Is that? . . . Is she? . . ."

"This is new. My wife is speechless," Derek joked, but he turned serious when he saw what had caught her attention. "Why didn't you send a message? My God, you found her."

Victoria was just emerging, and Grant rushed to help her down. When he set her away, he reached in to help Camellia out. "I was worried the message wouldn't be safe. I imagine the papers would like to stumble onto a story about castaways."

Everything went quiet. His family stared at his charges as though they were ghosts. Just as the situation grew uncomfortable—

"Castaways!" Nicole squealed. "Things just got interesting!"

"Don't you want to introduce us?" Derek said under his breath.

Grant felt himself flush as he made introductions.

Nicole immediately asked, "You really were stranded on an island?"

Victoria nodded, though she looked overwhelmed. Camellia clasped her arm for support. Grant saw his mother focus on that, then look questioningly at Camellia. For the most part, his mother acted as if she had a head full of fluff, but she actually missed nothing.

"Dear, are you feeling all right?"

"The traveling must have caught up with me—"

"Grant, get her inside!" Her tone was strident, her movements brisk. "I know just the thing for Miss Scott. Marta's chicken soup."

Grant heard Camellia mumble, "Anything but fish."

Grant's mother, the dowager Lady Stanhope, went straightaway to have food sent up for Cammy and Tori, while Nicole showed them to their rooms. Tori had been successful in hiding her awe at the Sutherland town home, at the rugs, paintings, and gold, but now she couldn't stop gawking at the magnificence of this residence. Even Cammy appeared distracted from her fatigue by the wonders around her. Tori couldn't remember ever seeing such high ceilings or such intricate detail in a home's design. She wanted to stop at each set of moldings and trace the minute impressions carved in the soft wood, or run her fingers over the textured silk wall coverings.

Nicole showed them up a carpeted stair to their rooms, set in one apartment. "I thought you two might want to be situated close to each other, but if you'd like separate apartments, please let me know."

Apartments, as in a suite of rooms to oneself. Tori felt like a royal. "No, this will be fine. Besides, I'm already lost."

Nicole chuckled. Tori could tell she wanted to stay and ask questions, but she said, "You two probably want to eat and tidy up in private. I know I would. The food will be up shortly, and please don't hesitate to ring if you need anything." At the door she added, "And do join us downstairs if you feel up to it."

Short minutes later a smiling servant brought up a tray and laid out an informal repast of soup, cheeses, breads, and fruits served on china as delicate as eggshell.

Cammy ate a surprising amount, exclaiming over the soup and the pleasing flakiness of the bread. "Are you going to eat that roll?"

Tori knew she looked startled as she surrendered the roll. "Would you like the rest of the soup too?"

"Oh, I didn't want to ask, but yes, very much."

Later, just as Cammy was eyeing the plush coverlets on the antique-looking four-poster bed, a servant knocked to warm the sheets while another unpacked Tori's trunks and hung up her clothes in the next room.

She and Cammy stared at each other. "This just gets better and better," Tori whispered.

Minutes later, Cammy drew the toasty covers up to her chin. "Oh, my word, I missed this. Tori, you have to sit here. Even better than the town home."

She sat. Her eyes went wide when she sank down in what felt like a cloud.

"I could get used to this," Cammy continued. "My belly's full. I'm warm and sleepy and in a bed that I should like to keep when we leave." Her eyes were starting to close. "Sometimes, I remember things so clearly. Anne and your father would be so happy to know you are about to be with your grandfather." Her eyes closed, she sighed, "Have you ever felt anything so . . . soft?" and fell asleep.

Tori pulled the cover up more snugly, then went to her own room next door. But after examining the elegant lace of the counterpane and the curtain fringe, then sweeping her hand over the upholstered chintz headboard and investigating under the furniture and searching the closet—which took some time to walk through—she grew bored.

She washed, repinned her hair, and changed into an emerald green silk dress, then made her way downstairs, patting the spiky ropes of garland artfully twined around the railing. She heard conversation and walked in that direction.

When she entered the great room, she drew in a quick breath at the beauty of the scene. Redolent with evergreen, the area shone bright from Christmas candles and from a roaring fire in what had to be the largest fireplace she'd ever seen. But the focus of the room was a spiring fir tree. Throughout its boughs were lighted candles, candies hanging from strings, and ribbons tied in graceful bows. She could hardly take her eyes off it.

Nicole saw her first and stood with a wide smile, the men following. "Please, won't you join us? I'll pour you warm cider with raisins."

Tori noticed how striking Nicole's cobalt velvet gown was, how it emphasized her dark blue eyes and highlighted her red hair, already tempered with gold, and was suddenly very thankful that Grant had bought her new clothes. She might be uncouth, but she'd be damned if she'd look it. "That would be lovely."

Nicole handed her a silver cup, aromatic steam rising from the liquid, and when she motioned for everyone to sit, Tori perched on a plush settee.

"Oh my, you are so beautiful. And so tall." Nicole sighed wistfully. "But then, everyone is taller than I am."

"Not everyone, sweet," her husband said from his seat by the fire. "You tower among young children, for instance," he supplied helpfully with a glint in his eyes.

While Nicole bantered playfully with him, Tori took a sip of her cider, scrutinizing Grant and Derek over the rim.

Grant looked a lot like his brother, both so powerfully built and tall. They both had thick, black hair, but Grant's eyes were blue to Derek's gray, and Tori knew those blue eyes could be cold. Grant was perhaps a bit leaner and more classically handsome than Derek, but it was hard to justify that distinction as he had not smiled once since Tori came down.

"You know, I've sailed near your island," Nicole said to Tori. "That part of the world is breathtaking. It must have been hard to leave it."

She had no idea. Tori could adjust to traveling halfway around the world and to all the jarring sights and confusion, but she couldn't help but reel when she let herself think life for her was going to remain just as uncertain. Tori felt tears pricking her eyes.

"Oh, Tori." Nicole grabbed her hand. "I didn't mean to upset you."

Nicole had called her by her nickname without permission or hesitation, as if they were the oldest of friends. Tori felt strangely comfortable with the thought.

"Amanda—Lady Stanhope, that is—wanted to come down this evening but she's tired out from"—she turned to smile at Derek—"from the day. She hopes you're settling in?"

"It's been perfect. I've never heard Cammy so content."

"Good. Now that you're both here," Nicole said, looking from her to Grant, "I want to introduce you to someone." Nicole grabbed Tori's hand, pulling her up. Tori gave Grant a questioning look, but they both followed her up the stairs. She placed her finger over her lips and gently pushed open a door to reveal a nursery, decorated with light blue draperies and pillows, and clouds painted across the accent wall.

"Well, so much for being quiet. He's up!" Nicole lifted a baby from the crib. "Tori, Grant, meet Geoffrey Andrew Sutherland."

Grant's eyes went wide. "You mean I've got a nephew?"

She grinned proudly. "We've been busy while you were away."

"He's precious," Tori said on a breath, noting the already expressive blue eyes of the boy.

"He's a handful. Amanda, who proclaimed herself expert at baby boys, begged for her bed tonight. So, who wants to hold him?"

Grant put up his hands. "I think Victoria should. I'll just watch and learn, if you don't mind."

"Oh, no, I couldn't. I—"

"Haven't you ever held a baby?"

"Well, yes, some time ago—"

"So you know to cradle his head"—Nicole handed him over—"and hold him close. Perfect. See, you never forget how to hold a baby."

He gurgled in her arms and Tori smiled. She hadn't forgotten how to hold one, but she had forgotten how much she loved them.

She caught Grant looking at her with the baby, his eyes soft. She knew he didn't even realize it. Nicole must have seen it as well, because she said, "Is that Derek calling for me? That man can't do for himself for three minutes. Just put Geoff back down when you're through visiting." With that, she breezed from the room.

Tori's eyes grew wide. She was leaving them here with the baby?

She and Grant stared at the door. "I think you're doing fine," Grant said, facing her. "I think."

"It's just that . . ." She faltered. "It's been so long."

Geoffrey grasped a curl and tugged.

"He likes you."

She lifted her chin. "There's a lot about me *to* like."

His voice low, he said, "Yes, there is," and completely deflated her challenge.

She recalled that she was being civil to him now. "You should touch his cheek. There's nothing like a baby's cheek."

He did, and Geoff grasped his finger. Grant looked down at him in a way Tori could never have imagined, and her heart twisted. When the baby's hand drooped and he fell back to sleep, they laid him in his crib and silently returned to the great room.

For the next hour, Tori studied Grant and his family. Derek was obviously smitten with his wife. Looking at Nicole, Tori wondered how he couldn't be. Besides having a unique beauty, she was clever with a cutting wit that she used to tease and cajole laughs. She made what was an uncomfortable situation enjoyable. Except with Grant. He didn't join in the conversation, but stared down at his drink.

To Tori's amazement—and approval—Nicole beaned him with a chestnut. He jerked his head up, glowering, but before he could say anything, she related, "You just missed Lassiter and Maria. They came over before Christmas but left right after for their honeymoon."

"Your father married his business partner?" Grant asked in a surprised tone.

Nicole nodded happily.

"Yes, Grant," Derek began with a feigned look of disappointment, "as you can imagine, I was crushed that Nicole's father couldn't stay longer."

Grant reluctantly explained to Tori, "Derek and Lassiter didn't get on well—"

"They despised each other," Nicole interrupted, "but now they only *act* as though they don't like one another."

Derek coughed suspiciously.

Nicole eyed him in mock stern fashion, then turned her attention back to Tori. "So, how long can you stay? Tell me you'll stay for New Year's?"

Tori looked to Grant. He answered, "We need to get her to Belmont. The earl's waited long enough."

"The roads to the Court are tricky," Derek said.

Grant frowned. "They were passable here."

"There's not much traffic up there." Derek cast a look at Tori as if deciding how to word his concern. "There's simply no maintenance on those roads."

"How long?"

"If more snow doesn't fall, I think a week or so."

"A week." His tone was aghast.

Tori stood in disgust. "Your estate will still be there." Spine straight, she strode from the room.

She could still hear Nicole say, "Grant! She's going to think you're anxious because you don't want to be around her."

"She'd be right."

Tori ran to her room, covering her face as tears streamed down.

Twenty-two

Just what do you find so distressing about her presence, Grant? Her courage and strength? Her beauty?" Palms up, Nicole demanded, "What?" When he said nothing, she looked at Derek and then Grant, glaring at both before following Victoria.

Derek raised his eyebrows. "I'll bite. Why wouldn't you want to be around her?"

"I'm hoping my life will return to normal when she's gone. I'm hoping I'll sleep through the night and that I'll be able to—" He stopped himself. Be able to not have his thoughts on her each hour of every day. "Victoria's too tempting to have around."

Derek scoffed, "*You?* Fighting temptation?"

He rubbed his palm across the back of his neck. "Fighting it like a doomed man."

"I thought you weren't bothered by what plagues us mere mortals. Well, why fight it?"

"Myriad reasons," Grant said, trying to end the path of the conversation.

"Such as . . ."

"I think we're mismatched. I worry this would end up like you and Lydia."

"Not unless she's *evil*." At Grant's scowl, he continued, "Nicole had a point. The girl seems sweet, and you can't keep your eyes off her."

Grant exhaled. "Yes, that's true. But she's not the type of woman I'd marry. I need a proper English bride, someone less"—he paused as he cast about for a word—"less . . ."

Less what? Extroverted? Grant rather liked that about her. Outspoken? He'd grown used to that and wouldn't change it. Less self-confident to the point of arrogance? No, he loved that. "I just need someone who's *less*. Someone who is constant and pleasant. Someone who is, above all else, *predictable*." So he wouldn't have this turmoil.

"Where have you gotten this distorted view of women?"

Grant shot to his feet. "The example of my brothers! Your life was devastated because of a woman. William's was *ended*."

"William's was ended because he drank too much and fought a duel when he was sauced."

"He was fighting over a woman."

Derek shook his head. "He was fighting because he was proud and reckless. He could have backed out of it. And I should have handled things differently."

"Both those paths would have been dishonorable." He pressed his fingers against his forehead. "And what about Victoria? I worry that she only thinks she wants me because I was the first man she saw as a woman. What if she later finds another? Someone she wants more than me?"

"That could happen in any marriage," Derek insisted.

"But I've seen her looking at you as well, and I see more than simple infatuation. Besides, didn't she spend several months with Ian? For some reason, women can't resist him. Since Victoria did, well, your theory's flawed."

"She and Ian acted like mischievous siblings the entire voyage. There's a bond there, but it's not romantic."

"So? . . ."

"So, that still doesn't change the fact that Victoria didn't have a real childhood, she was cheated out of parents, and now I'm to cheat her out of courtship as well? And she's clearly told me she wants to experience that with other men. If I married, I would never divorce. I don't want to wake up every morning knowing I have an awful marriage, but am still trapped in it." He stared at the fire. "Just a simple English bride for me."

"There's something that might get in the way of your marriage to the imaginary paragon."

Grant raised his eyebrows at him.

"You're in love with Victoria."

As Tori sat yanking her brush through her hair, giving the mirror black looks, she heard a light knock on her door.

"Are you awake?" Nicole asked.

Embarrassed by her behavior, Tori debated not answering, but in the end she welcomed the new company.

"I'm awake. Come in."

Nicole strolled in—again as if they were old friends. Or even sisters, when she asked to finish Tori's hair. She picked up strands and brushed them to the ends, humming, lulling Tori, and then . . . "So, how long have you been in love with Grant?"

Tori's gaze leapt to the glass to meet Nicole's. But could she really be surprised? She loved him so much, she wondered why others couldn't feel it bursting out of her. She shrugged as though it were unimportant. "He doesn't return the sentiment."

"I think he does," Nicole said with a quick stroke of the brush.

"It matters little anyway. I've moved past him."

The brush slowed. "Uh-huh."

"Perhaps not completely, as in the utterly sense. But he doesn't like me." Tori felt questions bubbling up inside her. Nicole was a woman her age. One who understood love and marriage. "I don't understand it. He thinks I'm physically attractive, but then he doesn't like how I behave."

"Why would you think that?"

"Because I overheard him say it."

Nicole grimaced and muttered, "Grant, you dolt." Moving to Tori's side, she grabbed her hand. "I've never seen him look at anything like he looks at you. He's in love with you," she said in a satisfied tone.

Tori shook her head. "If only that were true."

"You'll see that it is. Now get some sleep." Nicole patted her hand, then rose. At the doorway, she turned back and said, "Just give Grant time."

After Nicole left, Tori dropped into her new bed and gazed up at the patterned ceiling, but against her predictions, she didn't sleep. It was as though her body protested the softness. Or that she was restless when she thought about how much her life had changed in the last few months. She eventually dozed off in the strange room, wondering where Grant was and if he was sleeping better than she.

Their first full day at Whitestone was spent at leisure. Tori joined Derek and Nicole for breakfast, and made her excuses for Cammy, who hadn't yet risen.

Between bites, Tori observed the married couple. Derek whistled at the sideboard and gave his wife long looks, at which she would flush and bite her lip. Tori gathered they were a passionate couple. She'd always wondered if others were like her own parents—holding hands, laughing, sharing smiles they thought were secret. She'd shared passion with Grant but never the smiles and teasing. Never the ease.

When Grant came down, he eschewed food and took only coffee. Tori wondered how he could pass up the sideboard laden with sausages, breads and jams, eggs, and creams, then realized he was anxious to get away from her. Their silence became strained. Derek and Nicole had shown her every kindness, and she didn't want them made uncomfortable because of Grant's and her discord. Tori determined to be polite. "Did you sleep well?"

So much for politeness. His eyes narrowed, and he looked at her as though she should have known he hadn't. "Not particularly. And you?"

Not wanting to insult her hosts, she stretched her arms in front of her, and lied, "I slept very well." She didn't know if it was the words or the contented sigh that accompanied them that irritated him so much, but he pushed out of the chair so fast it grated, resounding across the tiled floor, then stalked from the room. Nicole gave her a sympathetic smile, while Derek stared at the door as though he didn't recognize the man who'd exited it.

Later, when Derek and Grant rode out to inspect the property, Nicole led Tori on a tour through the home, culminating in a spacious library. Tori spun around in wonder. *Books. Beautiful books. So many.* She ran her fingers down the spines, marveling at the impressions and intricate designs.

Tori eyed the floor-to-ceiling shelves. "There are more than you could possibly read in a lifetime."

"That's true. So I'll point out my favorites that you might enjoy, especially the lurid, titillating ones," Nicole added with a chuckle.

When they'd collected a stack of books for Tori, they drank tea, looked at fashion plates, and ate succulent oranges from Whitestone's orangery. They played with Geoff, who was the winningest baby Tori had ever known. She felt disappointed when his nanny, a cherubic older Scotswoman, took him for his nap. The woman, whom everyone called Nanny because she'd cared for so many babies over the years, clearly adored the boy. In fact, when Lady Stanhope wanted to take him, Nanny cheekily said, " 'Tis no' your turn, milady."

And when Cammy woke for each of her *three* luncheons, Tori and Nicole joined her. That night, Cammy made it to dinner, and the mood became celebratory. Though her hair was as fiery as ever, her skin seemed translucent against the gray of her silk brocade dress. But she didn't look like she'd have to bolt from the table at any moment. In fact, she ate more than Nicole and Lady Stanhope combined.

Tori found herself looking for Grant a few times early in the evening, but he never appeared. She hated that she'd been looking. Worse, she'd been caught looking by his eagle-eyed mother.

The next morning, Tori went straight to Cammy's room and found her just finishing breakfast. Dishes of food, empty dishes, cluttered a tray.

"Good morning, Tori."

"To you as well." She couldn't say if Cammy looked any better, though she certainly didn't look worse.

Cammy saw her eyeing the tray, and blushed. "It's just all so good. I don't think I've ever *tasted* like I do now. The food textures are so vivid."

"I'm proud of you! Let's set a goal to clean Whitestone out of food," she said with a laugh. "Do you feel up for a walk?"

"Yes, I believe I do."

"Good. We can walk the halls. The house is as large as"—her brows drew together—"well, it's big."

"I was thinking outside," Cammy said.

Tori had been getting increasingly restless and felt a jolt of excitement at the idea. She walked to the window and opened the heavy damask curtains. "There's snow."

"I used to love the snow," Cammy admitted. "I miss the odd, hollow quiet of it."

"I don't know if this is a good idea."

Cammy's tone became brisk. "Tori, it'll either cure me or kill me, and frankly, I'm ready for a decision to be rendered!"

Half an hour later, Nicole was making sure they were bundled in cloaks, scarves, and gloves, entreating them to take a nice *long* walk. They wanted Nicole to join them, would've insisted on it, but she seemed very excited about staying. Little wonder. Lady Stanhope was with Geoffrey in her apartments. Grant had disappeared and Nicole's two guests were setting off for the morning. Tori would have laid odds that Nicole found her husband directly after their departure.

So Cammy and Tori strolled the grounds, Cammy pointing out a few trees or birds unfamiliar to Tori, but she confessed she'd forgotten most of them herself. They came to a small hill, small to Tori, but Cammy was sizing it up as if they'd met a mountain.

"I think I can do it."

"But you might—"

"Then it's settled," Cammy interjected as she started forward.

I know the ending to this story. Tori rolled her eyes and had no choice but to follow. She could hear Cammy's labored breathing, but Tori knew she had a determination unparalleled. When Cammy took the last slow step to the top, her color was high, but she didn't look the worse for it. She appeared . . . triumphant.

"Oh, look, there's Grant," Cammy said between breaths.

Tori's head whipped around. She spotted him on a huge horse, just emerging from a snow-covered orchard in the distance. He directed his horse to the riverbank and then appeared to give it free rein.

"And look at that orchard. Would've been nice to have on the island, wouldn't it?"

Tori dimly heard her. She was rapt, watching him.

"Tori, it's clear your feelings haven't faded."

"Hmmm?" She dragged her gaze from Grant. "What was that?"

"Your feelings for Grant. Still as powerful as before?"

"More's the pity." Tori sighed. "Unrequited hurts."

Cammy shook her head. "No, he's in love with you. Anyone with eyes can see that."

Tori gave her a cheerless smile. "He made his feelings toward me more than clear."

"When Ian comes to visit, you should ask him about it," Cammy suggested.

"I will, but I think in this case, the reality is as simple as it appears," she said sadly, then turned to descend.

On the return to the manor, they came upon the head gardener's children playing fetch with a bounding, white dog. Their laughter and play trickled over Tori, easily altering her mood, and soon she was rolling in the snow with them, learning to make snow angels. Cammy clapped when the dog rolled with them, making his own rendition.

When Cammy grew chilled, Tori escorted her back. The cold hadn't bothered Tori as she'd expected. She found it bracing and loved that her breath came out as smoke. She could happily go run about some more.

They met Grant at the front entrance to the house, and his brows shot up at her appearance. It was only then that she noticed her hat was askew and her hair had fallen from what had once been a bun. The back of her coat was wet and white fur layered the front of her dark skirt. Something suspiciously like dog drool coated her sleeves. But he didn't remark on it. Instead, he asked politely, "Did you enjoy your walk?"

Cammy looked to Tori to answer.

"Very much," she said, making her tone civil. What was she saying? Civil was getting easier, while wistful was proving a problem. "How was your ride?"

"I missed the land," he said simply.

Tori thought back to what Ian had said. Did Grant miss the responsibility, the protection of so many people? Looking at him now, his eyes so clear and direct, she felt that Ian was right—that was why Grant wanted the Court. Not to have a place to own, but to find a place to belong. . . .

Her thoughts were interrupted by the clomping of hooves on the gravel drive as a stately carriage pulled in. Nicole and Amanda walked out shortly after to greet their unexpected visitors. Of course, Tori thought, the Sutherlands *would* receive guests just when she appeared to have been mauled by a mad dog who slavered instead of bit.

"Oh, it's Lavinia," Lady Stanhope muttered. "And Lady

Bainbridge. I've spent the last eleven months around those tabbies, and then when I visit my family for just a few weeks, they track me here."

As the carriage halted, Grant helped two extravagantly dressed women down and made introductions. Tori and Cammy were styled "distant cousins."

The new pair gaped at Tori. Even after they'd recovered from their surprise, they stared, and Tori nearly flushed with embarrassment. Then her eyes narrowed. As Tori studied them studying her, she recognized something she could hardly believe.

They were jealous.

The two looked at her like women in England used to look at Tori's mother. Well, not exactly. Most women fawned over Mother—she was a future countess—but underlying it was always a jealousy that Anne would soon leave on yet another journey to roam, explore, and live utterly free.

To break the silence, Tori said, "We just had the most delightful time! I learned to make snow angels, and Cammy and I practiced the intricacies of the perfect snowball. Just delightful, wasn't it?"

Cammy's forced, tight smile for the ladies softened, and she answered with obvious honesty, "I can't remember the last time I had so much fun."

Nicole beamed at them, and Lady Stanhope grinned. Not surprisingly, Grant's brows slanted in a deep frown.

"Well, if you'll excuse us," Tori said. "We're about to have a feast. Laughing like that builds such an appetite." She looped her arm through Cammy's. "It was a pleasure to meet you!"

Inside, she and Cammy divested layers of clothing and their overboots, chuckling the entire time at the women's pinched expressions. They agreed to wash up and change, then meet in Cammy's room for a late luncheon.

When they sat down to their meal of steaming game stew and hot buttered bread, Cammy remarked, "You reminded me of your mother down there."

The compliment made Tori pause. "I was thinking of her," she admitted with a smile, then motioned for Cammy to begin their meal.

"The walk made me famished," Cammy said between bites. "I think I can fit three more bowls in. Isn't that awful?"

"It's fantastic!" Tori said, and raised her glass to Cammy. "I don't think I've ever seen you eat like this."

"I just feel like my body's growing and screaming for nourishment. My mind, too. It's like my clarity is directly proportional to how hungry I'll be later."

How could Tori express the relief she felt without letting Cammy know how afraid she'd been? "Then we shall make you plump by Easter."

After they finished, Cammy patted her belly, yawned, and lay down, planning to sleep for hours. Clean, crisp clothing didn't prevent Tori from going right back outside, but she failed to find any of her new friends. She settled on a bench under a sprawling oak near the manor, and some time later, Nicole found her still there, studying the birds that had gathered near her feet hoping for food.

"Oh, dear, it looks like you've given in to contemplation," Nicole quipped with a grin.

Tori smiled, happy for the company.

"I've come to announce the tabbies' departure," Nicole said with flourish before sitting beside her. "And look what I've brought." She lifted a bag of bird feed in one hand and a bag of sweets in the other. "Bird feed and lady feed."

"I'll just pass on the sweets," Tori said in a pained tone.

"I bought a bag of them in Cape Town, ate them in one day, and nearly made myself sick."

Nicole chuckled and handed her the bag of seed. "You handled them perfectly today, by the way."

"I'm glad you approve," she answered honestly.

"So, aside from snobby women, how do you like being back in England?"

Tori scratched her ear. "It's not what I remembered."

"A very diplomatic answer. But you can tell me the truth. I'm not a native."

Tori frowned. "It's rather bewildering. The city was frightful in places, especially since I'm so unused to noise and people." Tori dug in and spread food for the suddenly animated group of birds. "But Whitestone is like a fairy-land you read about. I'm happy to have seen it. Do you like it here?"

"I love this place," Nicole answered. "When Derek first brought me here, I felt I was coming home."

"Do you miss the sea?"

"I miss the tides."

Tori turned to Nicole, surprise plain on her face. "I do too! I didn't think anyone would understand it. I miss their pull and their steadfastness. I lived my life by the tides, and now they're gone."

Nicole patted her arm. "I feel the same way. But you know what helps? I look over the fields and see the hills and valleys like waves. In the spring when the grass and leaves grow green, you'll want to weep from how dazzling it is. It'll be as green as the waters around your island."

"Really?"

She nodded. "Plus, we'll take you to the coast in the summer. I get just what I need from the sea and then I return here feeling full." She smiled at some memory.

"I would love to go. It sounds wonderful."

"Amanda used to take the boys to the seaside when they were little." Nicole dug into her own bag and popped some candy into her mouth, but it stuck to her woolen mitten and she had to nibble it off.

A thought occurred to Tori. "Grant·must get his gravity from his father. Lady Stanhope's so easygoing."

Nicole laughed and said, "In the past, she wasn't that way. . . ."

Tori almost heard the *at all* omitted from the end of that sentence. If Lady Stanhope could change, perhaps Grant could?

Nicole's expression turned serious. "So have you talked, really talked, to Grant?"

Tori shook her head. "He's never around."

"He's got to work through this one on his own, I'm afraid. With a man who takes his commitments as seriously as Grant does, he'll take his time jumping in. But then it's forever."

"What if it shouldn't be forever?" Tori wondered.

Nicole's brows shot up.

"I mean, what if we shouldn't even be together? We're so different, and he wanted me to change. I determined today that not only *couldn't* I change, I didn't *want* to," she said fiercely. "Shoes will always be an optional accessory. Whenever I play with children, which I hope will be often, I will return as dirty as they are. I will never be able to partake in a ladylike stroll—I'll more likely need to range over miles." When a bird pecked close to her boot, Tori showered him with food for his bravery. "And Grant. Do you know I've never heard him laugh? Ever. I thought I could fix that, because I would never dream of marrying someone so grim."

She wanted Nicole to say that Grant would ease up and be less dismal, but she didn't. Was Tori growing wiser? Realizing her love wasn't strong enough for two and shouldn't have to be? "I can't imagine life without laughter." Tori sighed. "And today. I thought his face would freeze into that scowl. Still, I miss him. Isn't that odd?"

"It's not odd since you love him," Nicole insisted. "And you'd be surprised how love can smooth out the rough spots in a relationship."

"Doesn't it have to come from both sides?"

"It already does, even if he doesn't realize it yet. Take my father, for instance. After my mother's death, it took him years to figure out he might love again. He finally saw he was in love with Maria. She waited for him, and now they're married."

"How long did she wait?"

The birds captured Nicole's rapt attention.

"Nicole . . ."

"About sixteen years," she muttered.

Tori's face tightened. "I won't wait the week out. If he doesn't come around, I'll put him in my past, and once I do that, he'll be gone from my mind forever."

Twenty-three

"Grant, do you think I'm doing a good job as the new countess?" Nicole asked sweetly before he could flee the breakfast parlor with his coffee.

"Excellent. You're doing a fine job." He pulled at his collar, wishing someone else were in the room. He suspected this conversation was going somewhere he mightn't want it to go. It was alarming, like being in a runaway coach and having no idea of the destination.

"Do you think I'm a gracious hostess?"

"Most gracious."

"You wouldn't expect a gracious hostess to allow one of her guests to be rude to the others?"

Aha. I can see it—the edge of the cliff draws near for the doomed coach.

"So this hostess will tell you to stop being an ass and behave like the gentleman you profess to be. It's insufferably rude of you, the way you're treating Victoria. For someone who's always displayed such *faultless* manners, this lapse is puzzling. *Very* puzzling."

"I've been busy." He sounded like a scolded schoolboy. He had an impulse to tell her to mind her own business, but knew that if he did, Derek would be cleaning his clock within the hour.

"The family will expect your presence. Especially today."

"What's so God all important about today?"

"It's New Year's!" When she stomped off, he heard her mumble that he was a clod.

He'd been so close to escape. Tomorrow they planned to leave for Belmont. Being near Victoria was hell for Grant, knowing she didn't want him, had bedded him and chosen the *possibility* of another over marriage to him. He'd avoided her, but thoughts of her still plagued his mind. Now he would be forced to interact with her.

Yet when he joined everyone that evening, his gaze immediately lit on Victoria, and he grew mystified by why he'd sought to avoid her in the first place. She wore a satin gown the color of claret, which he hadn't remarked much when he bought it because it didn't shine as it did when she wore it. It made her lips look red, sensually red. He noticed she was in stocking feet, her shoes discarded somewhere. With a glance around the room, Grant spied them tucked behind a curtain fold.

He regarded the unconscious skimming of her fingers over the facets of crystal on her glass as she laughed at Nicole's stories. Captivated, he thought he'd never seen anyone so desirable or so alive. No wonder the biddies envied Victoria. Yesterday, he'd been surprised to discover that their censorious looks barely masked their jealousy. The encounter had brought a hard question to mind. Did he criticize Ian's easy ways because he envied them?

The dinner bell interrupted his thoughts. For New Year's, the family dined on a traditional feast. They began with asparagus soup and dressed salad, omitted the fish course, then enjoyed creams, sauces, duckling with gooseberry, braised venison, and roast goose—all of which Grant thought should have been placed directly in front of Camellia for her lone consumption.

She devoured every entrée, then made short work of the hothouse grapes, pineapple, and puddings. He knew she probably subscribed to the belief that ladies shouldn't have such large appetites, so for her to put away the food she did . . . He couldn't imagine the hunger driving her. But something here was working for her health. Apparently, her walks in the snow and piled plates of food were pushing her to turn the corner.

Victoria nearly preened, she was so happy about Camellia, and he liked to see that. He *did not* like to see everyone catching him looking at Victoria.

When they'd finished dinner, they all returned to the sitting room and visited with Geoffrey until Nanny insisted it was his bedtime, "holiday or no." Afterward, Nicole, Amanda, and Camellia played cards, laughing at Geoffrey's earlier antics. Already, the boy was a favorite with the ladies.

Victoria excused herself to go to sleep shortly after, so Grant deemed his presence no longer mandatory and made his way to the nursery to look in on Geoffrey. He hadn't thought he particularly liked children, but after he'd held the boy and seen him look up as though in recognition, something inside him shifted.

He found Victoria in the rocking chair singing softly to the baby.

"Grant!" she whispered, startled.

"I didn't mean to disturb you."

"You weren't. I just wanted to say good-bye. I don't know when I'll see him again." She pointed to a nearby chair. "Why don't you sit?"

"I, well, I don't—"

"This is silly, Grant. We're both adults. After all we've been through, I would hope that we could be friends."

His voice low, he said, "I can't be friends with you."

"What?" Geoff curled sleepily in her arms, so she walked to the crib and tenderly placed him back in.

"Forget I said anything."

"You can't make a statement like that and not explain."

"I refuse to argue with you in my nephew's nursery," he said over his shoulder as he strode out.

She followed, closed the door, and was right behind him, nearly running into him when he stopped abruptly and turned to her. "You are not going to do this to me." She poked his chest. "Tell me we can't be friends and not explain why."

Grant's temper was boiling. How to explain that he couldn't be friends with her because he simply couldn't be near her? Not when all he wanted to do was kiss her and stroke her luscious little body, and not when he was so bloody tired of denying himself. When she went to poke him again, he snatched her hand and laid it on his chest, trapping it there. *Don't explain. Show her.*

He grasped the back of her head, hands tangling in her hair, bringing her roughly to him.

His lips on hers. His memories of touching her were vivid, but had her lips always been so lush? *How* had he possibly kept himself from doing this earlier?

She moaned—from the mere contact of their lips—

and hunger shot through him, too burning to deny. Without thought, he pinned her arms over her head against the hallway wall, and lowered his mouth to the swells above her bodice. The feel of her breasts beneath his lips, so plump, shaking with her trembling and panting breaths . . . He rasped against her flesh, *"You make me crazed."*

His mouth grew wet as he set to them, nipping the tips through the cloth of her dress, reveling in her response as her gasp turned into a low cry. She rolled her hips to him, pushing against his rigid shaft, and with each sweep of his tongue or nip of his teeth, she writhed against him more wildly. He had to have her, here against the wall, or surely he'd die from this. "You introduced me to something, Victoria, and I want more." He claimed her mouth again to stifle her cries, and his erection pulsed harder with each lap of her tongue against his. Freeing her hands, he seized a fistful of silk, hiking it up.

She grasped at him, urgently petting and clutching his chest and hips.

All at once, she froze. "Wait," she mumbled, breaking away from his lips. "I hear something."

"No, love, there's nothing." He kissed her again, bunching up her skirts.

But out of the corner of his eye and only dimly comprehended over the pleasure of Victoria's body molding to his, Grant saw his brother enter the hallway. Derek shielded his eyes as though struck by a bright light. "Hell, I'm sorry. Grant, I'm going! Sorry."

Grant could *hear* Derek smiling.

Tori's head fell back against the wall. "Is there a cliff nearby I can hurl myself from?"

"I'm just pleased he didn't see us two minutes later." His voice was low and rumbling.

"Oh, and you're just sure I would've continued with this?"

"Wouldn't you have?"

She pursed her lips. "That's not what's at issue. Just because I feel a certain way doesn't mean I have to *like* feeling that way. And why do you even desire to kiss me? You made your feelings about me clear."

"And you made yours equally clear." He frowned. "Wait a moment, when did I make my feelings clear?"

"Let's see. . . . You said making love to me was a mistake"—she began ticking off points on her fingers—"that I would always be a liability. And that you shuddered to think how I would behave in England."

His face tightened. "Ian told you that? I'm going to smash—"

"I overheard the conversation."

"All of it?" He flushed, suddenly looking very uncomfortable.

What else was said? She searched his face, but his eyes were shuttered. "I heard enough to know that you were going to ask me to marry you because you would own up to your mistakes."

He flinched.

"And then when you informed me we had to be married, you confirmed *everything* that had been said." She shook her head. "How could something I saw as so wonderful be a mistake to you?"

"Because it *was*. By doing that, I abused your grandfather's trust. And that's something I swore I wouldn't do. I wanted you so badly that I turned my back on my promise, my honor."

"You wanted me ... badly?"

"You couldn't tell when I completely lost control?" His voice grew low. "Or when I grew hard in you immediately after?"

Her face heated, remembering. "I didn't know if I was just another woman for you," she whispered. "How could I have known it was different for you when I'd never experienced it before?" But she had thought it was special, exquisitely so.

"Victoria, no woman could have tempted me, has ever tempted me, like you."

A rush of pleasure sped through her at his words. Then her face fell. "That doesn't change the other things you said."

"Since I've seen you with my family, I've realized you did a lot of brazen things on the ship just to irritate me. Even if I was still hung up on your behavior, which I'm not, I know now why you acted as you did."

"Oh." There was that. She *had* done much to needle him then. "And those women this morning? You saw the way they looked at me."

"They looked at you like that because you look tumbled and breathless and alive. More than they've ever dreamed of being." His brows knitted as a thought occurred. "Wait, you knew I was going to ask you to marry me?"

She examined the hem of her skirt.

"Is that why you said those things to me? About finding someone else?"

"Yes." She looked directly into his eyes. "You hurt my pride. You hurt me so much. There was no way I was going to marry you."

She thought he would be furious, but he just seemed lost in thought. "You couldn't have said anything that would have unsettled me more. You played on a fear of mine."

"You'd brought it up in the past and seemed bothered by it."

"You didn't feel that way? You would have been content with me?"

She thumped his chest with the back of her hand. "Just how many more ways could I have shown you that?"

He caught her hand and kissed her fingertips. "We have to marry. I can't be lifting up your skirts and taking you in the hall."

"We have to marry? Because then you can?"

"Then I wouldn't need to." His lips curled into a lazy, seductive smile that made her chest feel too small for her heart. "We'd be sated by morning if we shared a bed." As soon as he said it, he frowned and muttered to himself, "I don't think I'll ever be sated of you."

Words bubbled up in response, words she was helpless to contain. "I love you."

He made a low sound, then kissed her deeply, lovingly, but he hadn't said the words back. She pushed him away.

"I told you I loved you. Those words deserve some answer just as if they were a question."

He ran a hand through his hair.

Like a slap, she recognized he did not feel the same way. Well, she'd thought that. But she'd also expected he might say that the feelings would grow. That he *could* love her. *Just give me something more to hold on to,* her mind cried. The absence of those words was like a blow so sharp, she wondered if she could remain standing. "It's obvious you don't feel the same way."

"I admire you. I respect you."

Just give me something more than that! She envisioned

a lifetime of being compelled by feeling to say "I love you" and his reply of "Uh-huh." She shuddered. "Both those declarations sound wide of the mark in response to mine."

"Why are you seizing on this?"

"Because we are mismatched. Oil and water." Just as Nicole had said—nothing smoothed out the differences like love. Without it, their relationship wouldn't survive the clash between their disparate personalities.

He waited for her to explain.

"I'm fun-loving—you're not. I'm optimistic—you're pessimistic. I'm impulsive—you're . . . *predictable.*" She caught his gaze. "I welcomed and accepted that I want you so badly, and you've fought it with everything you are."

He shook his head, but he didn't deny it.

"There's no ease between us, no affection."

Realization showed on his face. "You've been studying Derek and Nicole."

She put her chin up.

"They're an anomaly. They had to go through hell to get what they have."

"Well, I would as well. All we've got between us is lust. You can't build a marriage with just that."

"It's a bloody good start."

She shook her head. "There has to be love between a pair like us."

"*Love?*" He skewered the word.

"Yes. I won't compromise on that."

"Goddamn it, Victoria, you can't have everything."

"Why not?" she asked, sounding baffled even to herself. "Besides, I've missed out on a lot of things in life, and I won't forfeit that."

"You can't have everything *your way*. I asked you after

Cape Town, and I'm asking you now. But if you say no, I'm not asking you again."

"So, it's to be marriage your way or nothing?"

"Yes," he answered without hesitation.

"I say it's to be marriage my way or nothing," she retorted.

His eyes narrowed and his lips thinned. "We've blundered and scraped our way through this, and now you choose to raise the stakes." She'd never seen him so enraged. "Never again, Victoria."

As he strode away from her, he hit the wall with his fist, crushing the plaster.

We finally get on the same page and she throws the bloody book out.

Grant had never felt such frustration. He was embarrassed for her. For saying those things that he couldn't answer. What compelled people to profess love?

She was going to deny them over a petty word, a driveling sentiment. Damn it, love was an untidy emotion.

Furious with her, Grant had stormed away, but as the hours dragged by, he had nowhere to go in the quiet house. With everyone asleep, it sounded hollow, like he felt. He nursed the anger. Anger was better than emptiness.

Since the day he'd met her, Grant had not had one single restful night's sleep. Tonight was the worst. He didn't even go through the motions, but sat in a chair, drinking brandy, remembering times on the island and analyzing. Always analyzing. When dawn rose, he did nothing but wash, then change his clothes.

Bleary-eyed and still fuming, he made his way downstairs, planning to guzzle coffee. Surprisingly, Derek was already up reading the paper. The paper drooped to reveal

Nicole in his lap, her hand ensconced in Derek's shirt by way of a loosened button, drawing lazy circles on his chest as they read together. Fresh irritation simmered. "*Must you two?*"

Nicole and Derek looked up. Nicole tilted her head at him; Derek glowered. "As a matter of fact. Good morning to you as well."

"The two of you aren't bloody typical," Grant said as he absently poured coffee. "Odd, that's what you are. Peculiar even . . ."

"Should I even ask?" Derek inquired of Nicole.

Nicole popped to her feet. "I'll just let you two talk." She kissed Derek atop his head. "I'm about to relieve Nanny of a fussy morning baby, and I think I'll have more fun than you're about to."

When Nicole left, Derek folded the paper. "You look like hell."

"No better than I feel."

"I take it you and Victoria haven't gotten anything resolved." He poured himself more coffee, clearly anticipating a long conversation. "Though you certainly seemed to have last night."

Grant glowered. "What's resolved is that I'm going to drop her at the Court, and for the first time in months I'm going to sleep well."

"If you say so."

"What's that supposed to mean?"

"Why wouldn't you just ask her to marry you?"

"*I did.*"

Derek opened his mouth and said nothing. Then he chuckled. "And she said no?"

Grant rose in disgust, but Derek grabbed his arm. "Sorry. Did she give a reason?"

"Yes, she won't marry without *love*." He spat the word. "She wants what you and Nicole have."

"I don't see what the issue is. Everyone knows you're in love with Victoria but you."

"I am *not* in love with her."

"Keep telling yourself that."

"Love's turned you into an imbecile."

With a smug smile, Derek raised his cup and remarked at the rim, "Then there's much to be said for imbecility."

"She drives me mad. I can think of nothing else! I never sleep; I hardly eat." Grant's fingers were white on his cup. "I can't live like this. If this is love, then I can certainly do without this misery."

Derek reached for Grant's cup and pried it from him before it cracked. "That's because you're crossing swords with something you shouldn't fight. Just go tell her you love her."

"*No.* Love is pleasant. Not this fever-pitch feeling twisting my gut whenever I'm near her."

"Pleasant?" Derek laughed without humor. "Nicole and I had something, or rather someone, between us. Loving each other was out of the question. But you have it so damn easy. A lovely, intelligent woman loves you, and all you have to do is accept it."

"I did. I asked her to marry me. Now she's made new demands." He ran a hand through his hair. "I should've just told her I loved her. I could certainly act like it." His voice grew excited, as though he'd hit on the perfect solution. "She'd never know."

"Listen to yourself. If you can act like it . . ."

Grant pounded his fist on the table. "You're right. She couldn't have conceived of a better way to drive me mad. She knows I'm an unemotional man. Detached, even. And she's asking for the one thing I can't give her."

Derek eyed Grant's still clenched fist. "You might want to reevaluate your, uh, dispassionate nature. Yes, in the past, talking to you was sometimes like talking to a wall. I remember how enraged you were when I told you I wasn't sailing the Great Circle Race. I wanted you to swing at me. I was praying you'd finally lose your temper."

"Why?"

"To confirm that you were still alive. Not a machine and not dead inside. And now I know you're miserable, but I can't help but be glad that she's awakened *something* in you. What you feel for her has taken over your life, and I can't be unhappy about that."

That made Grant even angrier. Nothing interrupted his ordered life unless he desired it to.

And this love that she wanted . . .

He was no coward, but this, this *giving* of your heart to someone else's care, where they could tread upon it or let it atrophy . . . The prospect was fearsome because he knew instinctively that should Victoria abuse his trust with it, he would never know happiness again. Any sane man should be afraid to give up control of his own happiness. To become dependent on someone else for the first time since he'd become a man. He felt as if he were strangling. . . .

"What will you do?"

"What I've always planned. I will deliver her to Belmont, and then in the future when he passes, I'll return to claim my payment. For now, I'll endure one night there, then I'm going to get my bloody life back."

Within the hour, Amanda, Derek, and Nicole with the baby all gathered at the carriage to see them off. "You're only half a day away when the weather's good. We'll visit soon," Nicole promised as she handed little Geoffrey to

Victoria. Victoria cradled him close, spilling a tear on his blue cap. When she kissed him and returned him to Nicole, Derek caught Grant's eye, giving him an expression that said, "Well?"

Grant returned a quick, restrained shake of the head.

Twenty-four

As Grant's coach rolled onto the drive of Belmont Court, sheepdogs bounded through the snow beside it, delighting Victoria and Camellia along with all the new sights.

White covered the manor house and the downs surrounding it, painting an idyllic picture—and masking the decline of the earl's home. Grant had been here just before the voyage and had been struck by the work the battered graystone needed, by the gardens blighted by neglect.

Yet, on this day, it looked like any other grand property. Stately trees lined the winding drive. Farther out, hills and vales, softened by snow, all rambled down to the riverbank.

The splintered front door brought him back to the reality of the situation. The Court was dying and needed an infusion of capital to survive. He reached for the knocker, and as it had before, it shone, freshly polished. What was left was tended as best as the earl's people could.

The door opened to show an older man. He had a tuft of red hair—red bordering on orange—that was graying at the sides and down his muttonchop whiskers.

"Dear me, dear me. It's really you. We scarcely believed the messenger. Come in, come in. I'm Huckabee, the manor steward," the man said with a little bow. "And this is Mrs. Huckabee, head housekeeper." He wrapped an arm around a round, matronly woman who'd waddled up beside him. Her hair was wholly gray though her face was unlined. "Don't suppose you remember us?"

Victoria thought for a moment, then said, "Don't you have a lot of children?"

"She does remember us," Mrs. Huckabee said, clapping her hands in excitement.

Victoria introduced Camellia—Grant, they already knew. Before Huckabee shut the door behind them, he pointed out a redheaded boy tearing off across the yard. "That'd be the youngest of nine Huckabees—he's the stable lad, and a late one at that."

"The villagers call him Huck," Mrs. Huckabee added. Then, casting a worried glance at Camellia, who'd paled on the jostling trip over, she said, "You all must be sorely put about with so much traveling and the roads so wretched poor. I'll put on dinner and Mr. Huckabee will show you straightaway to your rooms."

As they followed Huckabee up the bare steps, Victoria asked, "How old is this place? I don't remember it looking so . . . old."

"The Court as it stands now was built in the early seventeen hundreds, but a residence has been at this site since the late fourteen hundreds," Huckabee replied.

The Court's design had always impressed Grant. Since it was hollow, built around two central courtyards, most of the rooms on each of the three stories had views of either the upper or lower courts, as they were called, or of the surrounding countryside. But now the manor was just a shell, even emptier than Grant remembered. As Huckabee directed them along, Grant again noticed the blank walls and lack of carpets. After they'd accompanied the ladies to their rooms and reached Grant's spacious but nearly empty quarters, he raised his eyebrows at Huckabee. The man proudly lifted his chin and acted as if nothing was amiss.

Grant washed up and met the other four downstairs in a room just off the kitchen, arguably the warmest room in the house.

Victoria had changed dresses and combed her hair into an elaborate knot at her nape. She looked beautiful—a given for him to think so—but she also appeared anxious. Grant hoped she and her grandfather, whom she was to meet momentarily, would get on well.

With the Huckabees busy in the kitchen, Victoria looked out at the vacant front hall. "This place is so different from Whitestone," she whispered to Camellia. "I remember the Court being warm and full of fine things."

Grant explained, "It hasn't been maintained. The earl spent his fortune searching for his family."

Victoria squared her shoulders. "Then I will have to help him make it nice again."

Grant had to look away. She had no idea.

At just over eighty-five, Edward Dearbourne was a frail man, his body insubstantial in his huge bed. Tori knew he was bedridden, knew he'd never recovered since his family had disappeared, so she was startled when she looked at his eyes. Though faded from age, they blazed with will and intelligence.

"Tori! Is it you? It's you!" He could scarcely rise up from his pillows.

"I'm here." She felt nervous with him, her last immediate relative.

"Sit. Sit, please."

Tori dragged a chair to his bedside, settled in, and wondered what to say.

Her grandfather wasted no time. "Do you remember me? You were so young the last time you visited. How old were you? Eleven or twelve?"

"Eleven, but I remember you. You built a tree house for me. We stole food from Cook."

His hearty laugh stuttered and pitched into a deep cough. Tori could tell he fought to suppress it. "You do remember," he finally managed. "What happened out there, dear? I've lain awake so many nights wondering."

Tori took a breath and swiftly described the wreck. She highlighted her father's bravery and quick thinking and her mother's courage, and, of course, downplayed the horrors of herself and Cammy struggling to find water and food. But she didn't think she fooled the man before her, with his clear, lucid gaze.

"My boy. My poor Anne . . ." His voice trailed off, his eyes watering. Though she thought she'd be well past it by now, Tori's eyes did as well. "And what you must have gone through."

"In the beginning it was hard. But after a while it was very comfortable living there."

He studied her as if to determine how truthful she was being. Satisfied, he sank deeper into his pillows.

"They loved you very much," Tori said. "Before she died, Mother told me that you would come after us and wouldn't stop until you found us."

That seemed to please him very much. "She told you that?"

"Told me to count on it."

She could swear his chest puffed with pride. But then a cloud passed over his face. "I'm afraid I used up any legacy for you and your children." He looked away. "It's almost a blessing that Edward didn't come back. Letting go of this place would have broken him. He loved it so." He fell silent, alone in his thoughts until he turned to study Tori. "You know I promised Sutherland this estate?"

"I know," Tori said with a harsh laugh. "Believe me, I know that."

He frowned at her, then said, "When I die, he's going to take it. I've got to see you married and secure before then. I didn't bring you all this way to leave you in a vulnerable position."

Tori felt her heart drop. She didn't want to marry some stranger. Her emotions were raw, and she couldn't even contemplate a husband. She forced a smile and said, "We've got plenty of time to worry about that. Right now I'm wondering if the tree house still stands. . . ."

And so for another two hours, Tori and her grandfather asked and answered questions, until she watched him resist sleep and lose. She surveyed her aged grandfather as he slept. Here was the man who'd set Grant into unwavering action.

He'd altered the course of her life, giving up everything for them, and she was, for the first time, truly humbled by his gift. She smiled, recalling a time when they had been friends planting thorny bushes to protect their fort, or coconspirators stealing whatever was warm and sweet cooling on the kitchen window ledge.

She leaned down and kissed his cheek, then left him to his dreams.

When she walked out into the hall, she realized the rest of the house was abed. She was too conflicted to sleep, so she checked on Cammy, found her softly snoring, then set off to explore the main wing of the house in the dim light. She came upon a battered vase prominently displayed on the center table in an empty salon.

Seeing it brought on a flood of memories. She remembered her mother had told her not to play in the house. Tori had disobeyed and broken what must have been a very old vase. Grandfather arrived at the scene first—Mother and Father a few moments later. Mother had looked aghast at the ruined pile of fragments. "Victoria Dearbourne! I told you not to play inside."

Grandfather had interrupted, "Anne, it was I. Getting so old I'm running into things." Mother had eyed him doubtfully, but before she could say anything, the earl grabbed Tori's hand and took her off to search for help to clean up. Tori had nearly forgotten that the next night when they'd all retired to the salon, he'd winked at her and then pushed another vase off a table to solidify his tale. "*There I go again. . . .*"

But she had felt awful for breaking something of her grandfather's. To dry her tears, the earl had collected all the pieces of the original vase, and for the rest of the summer they'd spent evenings patching it back together, in a rough facsimile of the original, but whole again.

When Grant woke, he lay for some time under the frayed coverlet, staring at the peeling ceiling above him. Staying in this manor, so full of potential, and essentially his, was awkward. He should be glad that his mission was finally complete, but as was usually the case since he'd met Victoria, he felt unsettled, conflicted.

That was how it was with her in his life.

This was not how he wanted to spend his life.

After wearily rising and dressing, he made his way to the earl's apartment and found Victoria and Belmont playing chess, with Camellia reading before the fire. Grant would've been content to watch the game, perhaps spend the morning with them. He had to admit he liked the old earl. Still, some instinct of self-preservation screamed for him to leave Victoria.

"Lord Belmont, I'm going to show myself out."

"No breakfast, Sutherland?"

"I've been gone for more than a year. I need to get back and get my affairs in order. Good-bye, my lord." He bowed. "Camellia, Victoria."

"Actually," Belmont began, "I think I'd like to ask Camellia about her hometown in Kent. My best friend hailed from those parts. Tori, why don't you show our guest out?"

"Certainly. I'll just see him on his way." She smiled at Grant, too sweetly.

At the front door, Grant hesitated. "Are you going to be all right here?"

"Yes, I believe so." He knew her well enough to know she wasn't saying what was on her mind. What was she thinking? Did she regret pushing him the day before? Against his vow, he decided to broach the subject once more. "Can I convince you to marry me?"

"Can I convince you to love me?" she countered.

He leaned his forearm against the doorway. How had he ever dreamed that he could wrap this up with a speedy conclusion? "We've been through this."

"Well, I'm not satisfied with what *we* decided."

"So this is it. It ends here. You made your decision."

"And I stand by it."

He straightened. "When I leave now, there will be no second chances. This, whatever is between us, is over."

Her eyes slit. "Good. Because I don't suffer fools gladly. And I don't want a husband who's so stubborn he can't see what's just before him. As for second chances, there is no need. We've said all that needs to be said, I think, except good-bye."

"Fine, Victoria. You're making your bed," he grated, but he didn't turn to leave.

"Are you leaving now?"

"I'm going."

"Why won't you leave?" Before he could, he saw her expression change to one of realization. "The estate," she muttered. "For pity's sake, you'll just have to wait until he dies. Perhaps you can go count the sheep to make you feel better."

Grant was taken aback by her words. Though it had taken months for him to decide to make the voyage, in a heartbeat he knew he couldn't take the Court from her. "I don't," he bit out, "want it."

She was obviously shocked, but retorted, "Well, I assure you I don't either."

"I won't come claim it."

"I won't stay."

They stared at each other, neither prepared to back down. Why did everything have to be so bloody complicated with her? It was a constant test he was ill prepared for. "Just end this idiocy and marry me."

She recoiled from him, then leaned in aggressively. Her eyes glittered with fury. "Idiocy?" she hissed. She drew herself up to her full height and glared at him with will firing in her eyes, resolve powerfully thrumming through her. She'd made a final determination about him, here on this doorstep, and she would be unbending about it. He half-feared what she would say.

"I waste my time with you. I never want to see you again."

The door was towering and heavy, but it rocked on its hinges when she slammed it in his face.

Grant stared at the battered door for many moments. Damn it, had she wanted him to promise something he didn't feel? To lie to her and say he loved her?

How the bloody hell should I know if I'm in love when I've never felt it before?

He'd chosen the only path open to him, so why did the finality of their parting make him ache?

He was lost in thought as he drove away, leaving this place for good. He'd been surprised to hear himself relinquish the Court after dreaming of it for so long, but as he'd said the words, he'd known them to be true. He would never drive her out of her ancestral home, and he sure as hell couldn't live there with her.

Why did she have to be so stubborn? Wasn't it enough that he respected and cared for her? He was continually amazed at her intelligence and charmed by her humor. He could make love to her every night for the rest of his life and die a happy man. He wanted a passel of children with her—sons with courage and daughters with inquisitive green eyes. Wasn't that enough? Thinking of a future without her made his mood blacker than before.

Think of something else. Like what to do with his life now that he'd given up the object of his longstanding quest. He supposed he'd start at Peregrine again. His brother and Nicole had kept it running smoothly, even gaining accounts since her father's shipping company had bowed out of their market.

If he worked hard over the next several years, he could build a place like Belmont Court. A place of his own. And fill it with a wife and children. Damn it, Victoria was the most unreasonable woman he'd ever met.

When he returned to Whitestone, he avoided his family and the questions he knew they'd ask, but Amanda was not deterred.

"How did they settle in?"

"She and Camellia hit it off with the old earl."

"I'm glad they're comfortable there. Nicole and I are going to go make sure they are all right, but I suppose we should give Tori time to bond with her grandfather."

"Probably."

"Tori certainly is a charming young woman," she said, openly gauging his reaction.

Grant shrugged. *Here it comes.*

"I know you agree. So why don't you like her more?"

What to say to that? That he *liked* her to the point of madness? That he was so furious with her right now he could hardly speak? "I want a more conventional bride."

"Conventional?" She nearly spat the word, all her politeness gone. "I really had better hopes for you, but apparently you're going to do this the hard way. Like your brother," she added. "He didn't know how to go about getting what he wanted, but at least he could *see* what was just before him."

Goddamn it. He was doing the best he could with the tools he had.

Something in his look made her suck in a breath and catch his arm just as he was turning from her. "Oh, Grant, you really don't know what to do with this. You've never been in love, have you?"

Never.

He wiped any expression from his face. "Love? Not in the least."

"I'm not blind. I can see what you feel for her. I hope you won't let this lie for too long."

He gave her a stiff bow and strode away. But over a late lunch, Nicole made sure that all talk was centered on Victoria. Grant was uncomfortable at first, but then his anger receded and talking about her ceased to grate on him. He found that telling them about her beat brooding over her alone. He described her clever contraptions on the island and related how brave she'd been on the ship.

After the meal, the family settled in the great room in front of the fireplace. His mother and Derek read, while Nicole sat on a blanket playing with Geoffrey. She clapped his hands and feet, and he flashed his toothless smile. Finally Derek, who'd probably been trying to act as though he weren't a fool for that boy, couldn't take it any longer and went down to play with them as well.

Grant had never seen two parents so fascinated with their child, as if they couldn't quite believe they'd created him. And they should be delighted with him. Grant didn't believe he was biased, but Geoff was just about the best baby he'd ever seen. He was inordinately proud to be his uncle. A sudden thought made him scowl. He wondered if Geoff would grow up thinking of Grant as his somber, staid uncle.

How utterly depressing.

Victoria had said he was predictable, but he couldn't help but think she'd passed over the words *plodding* and *boring* before settling on the less hurtful *predictable*. They all sounded bad to him.

He cast about for something else to think of. Before long, the fire drew him, the flames reminding him of the island. Of what he felt for Victoria. Was it love? He'd never anticipated that for himself, never thought to enjoy something like what his brother had.

He shook his head. Victoria had another guardian now and was no longer his responsibility. He wanted to visit with his family, play with his new nephew, but he was distracted, only half there. And everyone seemed too understanding. . . .

His eyes were drawn to the mantel to the intricate, spiraled shell Victoria had given his mother. Victoria had labored to keep it unbroken the entire voyage. She'd told him it was exceptional among all that she and Camellia had ever found.

Victoria had little to remind her of the island, and yet she'd given a piece of it, of herself, away. She was generous. And kind. Lovely beyond his most fevered imaginings.

A log crashed in the fireplace, snapping him out of his reverie. His breaths were shallow. *I can't be in here any longer.* "Going out," he mumbled to no one in particular, then strode to the front hall.

He stabbed his arms into a coat and rushed out the front door—immediately colliding with his aunt Serena. She grabbed his collar, eyes wide and swollen from tears. "You've got to help me," she cried. "I need a ship!"

Twenty-five

$\mathcal{T}$hat Sutherland boy is a fine young man," Belmont remarked to Tori and Cammy over a game of cards that afternoon. "A fine young man."

Tori's fingers clenched, nearly wadding her cards like paper. All morning, she'd tried to conceal her anger over her and Grant's argument and had been having a hard time even when Grant wasn't the subject of the conversation. She didn't glance up, but knew her grandfather and Cammy were studying her quizzically. She forced herself to say, "I understand that many people have that opinion." *That mistaken opinion.*

Though Grant was *the* finest when it came to making her miserably angry and hurt. Luckily, no one could infuriate her as he did, and now that he was out of her life . . . Tori frowned when her bent cards refused to be smoothed.

"Yes, yes, he has a sterling reputation," Grandfather added, ending his statement in such a way that it sounded like a question.

Tori was saved from answering when he suddenly realized he'd won. "Observe a master at work," he said when he laid out his winning hand. Tori couldn't help but smile.

Cammy chuckled, but stood when Tori proposed a new game. "You'll have to play without me. I think I'll just go for a walk, stretch my legs a bit," she said. "Besides, I can't take another terrible trouncing from him." She pointed to the earl, who responded with a wily grin. Leaning down, she pecked a kiss on his forehead. "Have mercy on her," Cammy called over her shoulder as she left.

Once they'd dealt fresh hands, her grandfather continued in a casual tone, "I had hoped that you two would hit it off a bit more." His bushy brows drew together, indicating his weak hand.

She sighed. "Oil and water—that's what we're like. Two people couldn't be more mismatched."

"That's a shame." He forced a short laugh. "I'd, well, I'd thought you two might marry. And live here at the Court."

"If he wasn't obstinate and thick-skulled and incapable of laughter or feeling, that might have been a possibility."

He scrutinized her reaction, but she wouldn't volunteer more. What to say? That she loved him beyond measure, but he didn't return the sentiment? That he wanted a marriage without love? That she'd missed out on so much that she refused to abandon the possibility of love as well?

"Then we must start thinking of someone for you to marry. I can't stand the thought of you and Camellia not being secure."

"He told me he didn't want the Court any longer."

"What?" In his surprise, he lowered his hand until she could make out every card.

"That's what he said."

"Tori, I signed an agreement with him. It's binding." He hiked up his cards and bunched his lips at her. "Let's just hope that what he says and what he does are the same."

She didn't want to think about that now. She wanted to think about how to let Grandfather win without him knowing she'd thrown the game. She wanted to think about Cammy's growing restlessness and what to do about it.

Besides, she was *done* with Grant. His rejection had stung. She'd fought tears this morning after she'd slammed the door in his face because she now knew it was over forever. Even if he came around and begged forgiveness, declaring his love, she wouldn't take him. They'd had something special together—she knew it down to her toes—and for him to walk away? . . . He no longer deserved it.

After tea, Tori left her grandfather sleeping peacefully, and walked about the manor, surveying the vacant halls and rooms. She called out, "Echo!" in the ballroom, and her voice answered. She imagined what this place had been like when her father grew up here or when her parents had stayed here for the visits her mother remembered so fondly.

She returned to the nursery Mrs. Huckabee had shown her and again marveled at the expanse of mullioned windows overlooking the upper court, letting in prism-cut sunlight, but even with the warm sun shining in, she shivered. The room seemed to ache for the sound of children's laughter.

During her exploring, she found Cammy standing by a window and again was struck by how vibrant she looked. Her hair was thick and shiny, and her skin had a creamy tone to it. "Cammy, you look lovely."

She whirled around. "Oh! You startled me."

"I suppose it's been happening for a while, but I didn't notice until just now."

Cammy blushed, increasing the rosy hue of her skin. "Tori, don't be ridiculous," she said, but patted her hair as if wanting to believe it was even partially true.

Tori frowned. Her friend had been staring out the

window. Tori found herself doing that on most days. Did Cammy do it for the same reason, because she longed?

"Cammy, why do you stare out the window?"

She answered in a light voice, "I've missed the English countryside. Why do you ask?"

Tori didn't answer. Just searched Cammy's face.

Her smile turned sad. "Even an old maid like me can get lonely."

"Old maid?" Tori sputtered in disbelief. "You look all of twenty! We look like the sisters we've become."

Cammy grinned at Tori's expression, then hugged her. "There. I feel better already. You are a good friend and sister, Tori."

"You make it easy to be," she replied, still concerned.

Before she could say more, Cammy changed the subject. "We should check to see if your grandfather's awake," she advised, knowing Tori had determined to spend every hour with him that she could.

Tori reluctantly dropped the subject and nodded. They both feared he couldn't last much longer.

"It's been days," Serena sobbed, her sausage curls bouncing with emotion. "Ian told me he had someone for me to meet on the morrow, but he never arrived. I sent a footman around to his bachelor apartments, but he couldn't find Ian. A neighbor told him they saw my boy getting knocked about." She made a wailing sound behind her lace handkerchief. "By a crimp gang!"

Grant saw Derek trying not to laugh. And it *was* almost funny. For Traywick to be crimped—his spendthrift, indulged cousin to live as a common sailor. It could be argued that this was the ideal punishment for his wild ways.

Amanda sat beside her sister, as close as possible considering Serena's jutting hoops under bright satin skirts, and patted her hand. "Serena, you must be calm."

Grant felt like snorting. As if his high-strung, hypochondriac aunt had ever lived up to her name.

"We'll devise a way to find him."

"Someone's got to, and quickly! I'll have a brain spasm before this is all through."

Grant mouthed *brain spasm* to Derek, and his brother coughed into a fist.

"You know Ian! He won't last a week taking orders from someone else." Serena punctuated this with another wail.

When all eyes turned to Grant, he exhaled slowly. He was the most logical choice to retrieve his cousin, having just spent more than a year in his close company. And he'd ignored Ian's repeated attempts to confide in him. Something had been developing, and Grant hadn't been there for him. Guilt seared his chest.

He let out a long breath. "I actually saw him home that night because he'd, well, overimbibed. I don't know what could make him go back out in his condition. Aunt Serena, I'll go after him. They can't have gotten far in a fully cargoed ship."

"That's true," Nicole said. Turning to Derek, she asked, "When will you two leave?"

"I can handle this alone," Grant told her. "I'm sure Derek doesn't want to be separated from you and the baby."

Derek looked to relax again, apparently thinking the debate was finished.

"Ian's your cousin too, Derek. And it'll be good for you to visit with Grant after so long. Besides, it should only take you a few days to track him down."

Derek exhaled loudly. "Aunt Serena, you have nothing to fear."

Twenty-six

"Tori, do you regret it?"

"Hmmm?" she murmured from her grandfather's window. Forehead against the cool glass, she looked out over the land through the misting rains that had persisted for weeks. She tried to picture it as Nicole had suggested—with flats and swells rolling to the horizon like waves on the sea. It did look like a body of water, at least. A river of flowing mud. She turned to her grandfather, who had just awakened, and smiled. "Do I regret what?"

"Being brought back here?"

"Of course not." She sat next to him and took his hand. His skin was cool and papery. "I am so grateful you did what you did. You never gave up on us. We'll always love you for that."

"But there's a sadness about you, Tori, that wasn't there when you were younger," he said. "I understand about the wreck, of course. You don't know how much I hate that I wasn't able to protect you from that—"

"That's not why I'm sad now," she interrupted, never, never wanting him to feel guilt for that. She softly admitted, "I fell in love with Grant."

He gasped and squeezed her hand. "You love him? I was worried you were so angry with him that you wouldn't see that. Oh, this is good news, indeed."

Surprised by his eager tone, she informed him, "He doesn't feel the same."

He gave her an incredulous look. "Boy's mad for you," he said, then snuggled back into his pillows. Seeing him like this, she realized he'd never truly relaxed before now. "Just as I've hoped—you'll be married to Sutherland by May," he rasped happily.

Though Tori knew it was untrue, she couldn't help giving him an affectionate smile and putting his hand to her cheek. He sighed in contentment and drifted to sleep again.

Her grandfather's funeral was to her mother's funeral like day to night.

She had only the two to compare. Tori remembered when they'd buried Mother, when she and Cammy could only recite simple prayers. How she wished she'd known the pastor's comforting words then. She wished she'd done better by her mother. She wondered if she'd done everything possible for her grandfather.

He'd been so loved. Even with the continued rains, scores came to wish him farewell. And of the many villagers who had showed up in their best, only one or two managed dry eyes.

Tori was thankful he didn't suffer in the end. When she'd realized he was fading, she'd stayed by his bed, holding his hand, hoping for some last words. But he passed from sleep into death without a whisper. As though he could finally rest.

After the funeral, Tori returned to her room, planning to stay there for several days and cry until she didn't feel this cloying emptiness. In the short time she'd been here, she'd remembered her grandfather from her early childhood more clearly and remembered how much her father and mother had looked up to him, how both had loved him. Tori had loved him too. And now he was gone.

She'd wager Grant would be taking control of the estate soon. There was nothing left for her here.

The rain continued to fall, coming down in torrents, seeming to give Tori permission to lie curled up in bed, crying, feeling sorry for herself. Cammy had been so helpful, a bedrock of strength for her, but Tori didn't want to burden her further. Alone would be best.

But after she'd spent three days taking her meals in her room and avoiding everyone, the Huckabees begged a word with her and would not be dissuaded. When Cammy told her she wanted to have a serious talk as well, Tori agreed to meet the three of them at breakfast the next day.

"Mrs. Huckabee and myself," the steward began uncomfortably when they'd all convened around the breakfast table, "we was wondering what you ladies planned to do now."

Before her grandfather had determined that Tori would indeed marry Sutherland, he'd become increasingly concerned about her future. She'd brushed it off, wanting only to enjoy her remaining time with him. Now Tori struggled with the idea of what she should do with her life. "I don't know. I know there isn't much money." She plucked a hot pastry from a basket Mrs. Huckabee handed to her. Cammy blushed when she took two for herself.

"Actually, there's no money. At the last, even the earl didn't know how bad we were, 'cause everyone agreed to shelter him. But we can help you sell the remaining furnishings and set up a nice little house in town."

Tori dropped the bun. "Town?" She hated towns. They were so loud and cramped. "What will you do?"

"We've got positions at an estate near Bath."

"You won't stay on?" Cammy asked.

Mrs. Huckabee answered, "No, our families have worked for the Dearbournes at Belmont for over a century. Without Lady Victoria or her young ones here, there won't be any Huckabees about."

"But we won't leave till we find a place for both of you." Huckabee scratched his head. "Though we might need to be quick about it, because that creditor gets the Court in forty-five days if Sutherland doesn't claim it."

Tori asked slowly, "You mean it's not just automatically his?"

"No, no. Their agreement was an amendment to the earl's will. Unless Sutherland exercises the codicil within forty-five days, the will settles as it normally would, with you inheriting the estate."

Grant often accused Tori of ignoring him. But she'd been attending every word he'd said that last afternoon. *I won't come claim it.* "What if he doesn't?"

"Then you'd have one day after that to pay the creditor's notes or he'd claim it from you."

Her brows drew together. What if Grant really did give it up? Her grandfather had loved this place. He'd told her he *loved it with his soul.* At the time she'd listened to his words, she'd been struck only by the remarkable sacrifice he'd made for his family. Now she wanted to know *why* he loved it. Why it would've broken her father to lose it. And why her mother talked about the peace she found here. Could this run-down estate be her destiny? Was that why she had been brought this far?

There was one way to find out. She shot up from the table, then marched toward the doorway, calling over her shoulder, *"Be back soon."* Hastily, she donned her cloak. When she opened the door to head for the stables, her eyes hurt from the shock of sunlight after so many days inside. Blinking, adjusting, she finally opened them; they widened at the change in the landscape. Her breath shuddered out.

Green. Everything is a startling green. "Oh," she breathed as she twirled around to take in the hills carpeted in new grass, at the flowers bravely sprouting between rocks. So this was what Nicole meant. She'd wondered. When the snow melted, they'd been left with rain and runnels of mud, and Tori had been consistently unimpressed. Now ... *Breathtaking.*

Even a timid rider like her couldn't wait to get on a horse and *go.* To explore this place that was like new. Determined, she swallowed and marched into the stables to find young Huck. "I need something that won't run," she explained. "Something short. With tiny little legs."

Huck assured her, "The way things've been around here, that's about all what's left of the Court's horses. Used to have a foin stable, we did. Here's Princess." And he led out a squat mare. Princess looked as if she had ingested some soporific. *Perfect.*

Once Tori got accustomed to the horse and they ambled out into the pastures, she came to see what Nicole had found so special. And she did get the sense of freedom she'd enjoyed on the island. The wide expanses of land *were* as splendid as the greenest seas she'd ever swum.

Yes, it was a world away from what she was used to, but it appealed to her in an unexplainable sense. Were her roots drawing her to this place? Some unknown force pulling her to love it, though her every sense told her it was unfamiliar, foreign?

Could she at least try?

Lost in thought, she gave the horse free rein, and they descended the downlands into the village. A picturesque little hamlet in the valley, it consisted of four or five rows of timber-framed cottages amid their own penned-in gardens. Sheep roamed with impunity and trotted after children as they played.

Tori passed the common area, where most of the villagers took their noontime break. As soon as she was spotted, a group of tenants begged her for her time.

After polite small talk, they descended on her. "If'n we don't get some seeds this season, ye can expect nothing from our fields."

"Ol' Mr. Hill broke his arm—he'll not be shearing this year. Who's to replace him?"

"Me boy's stout enough," one woman volunteered.

"Hush up! He's a wee twig still—"

"He's the best we got since all the young bucks went to greener pastures to find work."

Tori had noticed that only women, children, and much older men inhabited the village. So the young men had been forced to leave their families when the work withered away? She sighed, remembering that Huckabee had told her eight of his nine children had gone to work in the cities. She hadn't realized until now that they hadn't had a choice.

While they quibbled, the youngest of the old men introduced himself as Gerald Shepherd and said, "We bred the ewes last fall just as we always done. But who's to be here to help during lambing? And the roof's got to be fixed on the sheep barn. Wool's perishable and can't get damp. Warm and dry it's got to be, for shearing and lambing."

Shepherd grew quiet—she thought because he'd said all on his mind—but he'd only been catching his breath. "And the acres by the creek flooded this fall. What ye got is a marsh out there. That land was where most of our food was grown, since the other fields were taken with sheep."

This alarmed her more than anything. Food was the first priority—anywhere you were. "So if I don't get those acres drained, we'll have no food?"

"That'd be the right of it."

"There's no other land free?"

"Not unless you count the rose gardens," he quipped, and everyone chuckled.

Trying not to look as panicked as she truly was, Tori said, "I will have it figured out tomorrow."

"Time's a-wasting," one of the older men grumbled.

"*Time's a-wasting,*" Tori mimicked when she got back to the house. She tracked down the Huckabees.

"I've decided I want to stay here and try to make the finance payments. So, we've got a lot of work to do," she began, then launched into a litany of the villagers' complaints.

The couple eyed each other uncomfortably, then Huckabee coughed. "To be blunt, there's nothing here to work with. Not unless you can get a loan. And there's simply no collateral left. The creditor was lending the earl money, but now that he's passed away, there'll be no more credit."

"What if I appealed to them?"

"West London Financiers, that's the name of 'em.

They're as hard as they come. About a year ago, we wrote, begging for an extension, and the same day they sent a payment due notice upon threat of foreclosure."

Her heart sank.

"Mrs. Huckabee and me, well, we like to work and need to follow it. But like I said, we'll set you up in a nice place in the city somewhere. You could live well, if you were frugal."

Without the land . . . A bitter taste rose in her mouth. Why was it that when she was just starting to see the possibilities of the place, she saw how impossible it was to hold on to it?

She cleared her throat to ask him when she should expect their departure, but an insistent thought arose. When Tori had first arrived, Mrs. Huckabee had shown her the room upstairs where Tori's father was born. And his father, and his father. And while Tori stood there, she'd had the oddest thought that came from nowhere. *My children will be born here.*

Brows drawn together, she abruptly asked, "Mr. Huckabee, what if I could get some money to pay the first finance payment?"

He shook his head sadly. "I think it would buy just a little time. Even some of the villagers are already asking me when Sutherland is to take up the place."

"What did you tell them?" Tori demanded.

"The truth. That I didn't know what was happening. But maybe it's for the best. Those Sutherlands got a heap of money."

He began to say more, but Tori cut him off. "Listen to me. He's not taking this place. No one's taking this place!" As soon as she said it, she knew it was true. She would fight.

This was *her* birthright—her family's memories were

woven throughout. She liked the people here. Her best friend was blossoming in this cold land. . . .

"What if I could come up with a larger sum of money? How much would you need to get us over the hump?"

He hesitated, then seemed to be doing calculations in his head. "We'd have to get the wool shipment off to McClure, the wool broker. We'd need a load of cash just to harvest and move it."

Cash. She took a deep breath. "Say I can get some?"

"We'd have to contract a shearing crew." Mr. Huckabee raised his eyebrows. "It might—it might just work. If we come up with some ready money *and* can get this year's wool shipment off, then we can meet our more pressing loans with West London. We'd be safe for a couple of months, maybe three."

"Can you tally up how much I'd need?"

"Yes, but it's going to be dogged hard to make it all work. Even if you could get the money."

"Huckabee, I'll take care of the money. You just find out how much I need to get."

"Yes, milady!" he vowed before he rushed off to the office, obviously very pleased to have something meaningful to do.

Later, when Tori met Cammy in the study to explain her plan, Cammy said, "Count me in. I can work. But where would you get money from?"

"There's actually some more furnishings left inside—the Huckabees wanted to spare Grandfather the reality of his situation, so his room is virtually unchanged. There are some paintings left." She rose from her grandfather's worn leather chair and walked to a safe, pulling out a box filled with various cases and rolls. "And some of Grandmother's jewels that he couldn't bear to sell." When Cammy joined her, she unrolled the velvet jewelry pouch, displaying glittering stones set amid rare antique settings. "And I have one other possession."

She thought of the ring stowed in a drawer in her room.

Cammy gasped. "You can't," she sputtered. "Surely you wouldn't."

"I wouldn't what? Do what absolutely has to be done? If that ring had meant food for us in one of the first days, would you have sacrificed it?"

After several seconds, Cammy nodded. "But this isn't the same."

"It is!" Tori insisted.

"You could write Sutherland. He wouldn't want this to happen to you."

"Then why isn't he here, making sure we are well? Because he doesn't care. The only way he'll come back here is to claim the Court. You know how much he wanted it. Why would he give it away just when it was in his grasp?"

"Maybe he did it because he loves you."

She folded the jewelry in its pouch. "He very succinctly told me he didn't the last time I saw him, but he did tell me it was over and that there would be no second chances."

"His family?"

"Would help us, I've no doubt. But they'd inform Grant. I don't want him back here until I can get my resources together to put up a good fight. There was a signed contract, Cammy."

"Well, we just haven't thought hard enough about it then. There's got to be a way for you to live without this place—"

"London frightened me, but I was able to tolerate it because I knew I would be leaving soon. The idea of being stuck in a city, even one a third of the size of London . . ." Tori shuddered. "I have to make this work. My back's against the wall just like on the island. If you look at it that way, things become so clear. I see potential in everything. I have to." She touched the heavy pieces in the roll. "I'll send Huckabee to London tomorrow with everything I have."

Cammy's eyes were wet. "Oh, Tori, can you do it?"

"Yes. This is my lot." She took it with a heavy heart, but she would accept it with resolve. "I must make it work."

When their first visitor knocked on the front door, Cammy rushed to answer, but Tori beat her to it. "Let me guess," she called in the foyer, "some news of a broken pump, or some seeds gone bad, or the eighty-year-old natives are restless—" She opened the door to a man they didn't know. "Yes?"

Cammy stared at the stranger, at the six feet of powerful man standing just there, seeming to fill the doorway. Salt-and-pepper hair, sensual gray eyes. He could rival even Ian's good looks.

He explained that he was Stephen Winfield, their neighbor to the north. "I'm terribly sorry that I missed your grandfather's funeral. I was away."

Winfield? He must be the baron the Huckabees had spoken so fondly of. Cammy leaned in closer to hear his voice, deep and resonating. . . .

"I've brought some stores from my estate."

The conversation was the oddest Cammy could remember. Incredibly, Tori behaved as if this was just an ordinary man, using the same tone and words she might use with Huckabee. Cammy marveled, knowing she herself would babble incoherently if he looked down at her. No, actual words left Tori's lips: "We don't need your charity. We're fine."

His brow creased. "I would hope your estate would help mine if I needed it."

I'd help, Cammy's mind cried.

As if he heard her, he turned in her direction. His eyes widened, then focused on hers.

"It's incidental whether I would help or not," Tori rejoined. "We don't need your assistance now."

He opened his mouth to speak, then closed it, seeming at a loss for words. Finally, in a low voice, he said, "Regardless, I will return." He wasn't looking at Tori when he said the last, having never taken his eyes from Cammy.

Twenty-seven

"Sell the books, milady?" Mrs. Huckabee asked in a choked voice. "Many are antique first editions."

Tori sighed. "Then sell them, but *charge extra*. Every one that doesn't have to do with business or commerce. I suppose I'm going to need those directly."

In fact, once Huckabee returned from selling the jewels, Tori began wading through those tomes, studying business and negotiating as diligently as a young lady preparing for her first season. The Huckabees also advised that she study sheep farming because, as they related to her horror, they didn't have anyone in charge of the wool operations.

"When the man quit, we couldn't find another to hire on," Huckabee explained. "I took up the books, but the truth is—I just don't know sheep. Crops, yes. Sheep, no."

"So no one here knows about sheep farming?"

"The villagers do, but they don't know the business end."

"We've got to find someone. Place an advertisement or something. Find me a sheep man!"

And during this time, when she wasn't having Huckabee point out everything—anything—that could be converted into money without affecting future production, she was following Gerald Shepherd around. As he fed and examined the ewes, she clomped about in her borrowed heavy boots and peppered him with questions. One thing that struck her in particular was that the sheep didn't act very . . . *sheepish*.

In fact, she would swear she'd heard one *growl*.

When asked about them, Gerald answered, " 'Pon my word, we dunno how that came about. Even the lambs can make some of the smaller dogs skittish. Confounds the poor pups."

Gerald scratched his shaggy beard and Tori gawked as they stared out over the nearest field—a dozen sheep were climbing atop the stone walls that were supposed to fence them in, using them as walkways.

"Nicole!" Amanda called, shaking a letter in the air. "The earl of Belmont passed away a week ago." She ran down the lawn to where Nicole and Nanny had spread a blanket to play with Geoff after breakfast.

"*What?*" Nicole jumped up. "Why didn't they say anything?" Last week, they'd received a missive saying that Tori and Cammy were settling in just fine.

"I don't know, but I'm going to find out."

Nicole turned to Nanny. "Will you be all right?" Amanda heard the Scot burring in an amused tone about *the wee bairn being such a doddle* so not to *fash yerself*.

Amanda was mystified when Nicole nodded in understanding. She gave Geoff a quick kiss before she and

Amanda stormed to the carriageway. Amanda asked, "You or I?"

"Me. *Carriage!*"

When the two rolled into the overgrown gravel drive of the Court, they saw the oddest thing. Tori dug in the dirt, then ran around the corner of the home, then back to her excavation site. With a swift glance at each other, Amanda and Nicole descended from the just halted carriage and followed.

"I don't care what you have to do, do it!" Tori shouted. "The stone's not important. Just get that iron out. Does it look like I care about how this place looks?" she asked with a wave of her hand, indicating the walled rose gardens of the estate that were now tilled, hoed, and in the process of being planted. With crops.

The girl, who before had only had eyes for Grant, was now a self-sure woman.

And a tyrant.

"Ahem."

Tori whirled around. "Nicole! Lady Stanhope!" She greeted her friends, then sighed. "I suppose you heard?" When they nodded, she said only, "It's a long story." She was saved from further explanation when Cammy arrived to welcome them.

"Cammy, will you take them up to tea?" Tori asked in a distracted voice. "I've got to get this iron out today or we won't get paid."

"Certainly," she said with a light smile, but it was clear Cammy was worried.

Amanda and Nicole made small talk as Cammy showed them inside to a sitting room. Only four chairs, a tea caddy, and a small table occupied the vacant, echoing room, and large squares of unfaded wallpaper stood out on the walls indicating sacrificed paintings.

The three settled the chairs so they could watch Tori lead the horse pulling at the wrought iron gate.

"Please tell us what is happening here," Amanda said.

Cammy started the tea in a chipped service. "It's not as bad—"

"Don't sugarcoat it, Cammy," Nicole interrupted in a no-nonsense voice.

"Very well. It's been awful." The cup and saucer she held out to Amanda shook in her hand. "For days after the funeral, Tori cried, cried enough to break your heart. She lost her grandfather and then was going to lose her new home to this awful mortgagor even if Grant never got around to claiming it. She felt so betrayed because Gr—" She broke off. "Because she was taken back here and then, in her mind, abandoned."

Amanda shot Nicole a look.

Then all three peered out to see Tori shouting something, brow drawn in concentration. Like a shot, the iron gave, launching her backward in a heap of skirts. The women tensed to run to her, but Tori sprang up with a laughing squeal, grass radiating out from her hair and the back of her dress. She skipped to Huckabee and slapped the man on the back.

"Anyway." Cammy faced them again. "That night, she just snapped out of it. She was no longer sad. Just very, very angry. She sent Huckabee to sell her grandmother's jewels that her grandfather hadn't been able to part with. She sold saddles. She's been selling everything that isn't nailed down."

When Cammy paused, they all peeked out to see Tori directing workers with strong arm movements.

"It still wasn't enough. So she . . ." Cammy bit her lip.

"Go on," Nicole prompted.

"She sold her mother's wedding ring."

"Oh, God," Nicole whispered over Amanda's gasp.

"Why didn't she contact us?" Amanda demanded. "Why didn't you?"

"Because she knew you'd give her money," Cammy said simply. "Tori's very proud. Plus, she didn't want Grant to know the earl had died. She wanted to prepare herself so she could fight his claim—"

"But Grant told us he gave it up," Amanda said.

"He told Tori that, but there was a contract," Cammy pointed out. "Tori can't see how he would just dismiss something he'd worked toward for so long. I believe Grant, but his behavior is rather puzzling."

"Unless he was in love," Nicole pointed out. "He might not even have known it."

At luncheon, Nicole explained Grant's absence to Tori and Cammy. "Grant set off to find Ian. Apparently, he was taken by a crimp gang."

Tori's eyes went wide. "Poor Ian! I can't believe he's going right back out to sea. What can I do?"

"With any luck, Grant will find him and bring him back," Nicole assured her. "And you know how meticulous Grant is."

"So he had a reason for not coming by?" Tori asked.

Nicole nodded happily.

"Then why didn't he send word? Why didn't he tell me about Ian?"

Nicole's nod stilled. "He probably didn't want to worry you. From what I understand, you and Ian became friends?"

"Yes, we did."

"And apparently Ian gets into scrapes. Sometimes there

are embarrassing situations that Grant's always managed to keep under wraps."

Tori tried not to sound too hopeful when she asked, "Did Grant tell you to tell me anything before he left?"

Nicole scratched her inner elbow. "Not specifically. But it was damn well implied."

Tori frowned at her.

"Very well. He left hastily and everything was so rushed. He could have said something. I was just so busy wishing Derek good-bye."

He might have said something or he might not have thought of her at all. She'd put good money on the latter, money she had very little of—though not if the Sutherland women had any say.

Throughout the meal, Tori had to turn away offers of money—some veiled, some clever, some imperative—a total of fifteen times.

And when Tori and Cammy were seeing them out, Nicole put her hands on her hips to announce, "We're not leaving until you agree to let us help."

"I'm so close," Tori said. "We're right at the breaking point. If everything falls into place, then we can hold them off." She looked from Nicole to Lady Stanhope. "I want to do this."

Lady Stanhope cleared her throat. "You've turned into a damn fine . . . capitalist, Tori. But we can't sit back and watch you lose your home."

"Please, listen. I've read a few stories that had a hero who couldn't take money from friends, even if it was his downfall, because his pride simply wouldn't allow it. When I read them I didn't understand the importance. I thought, 'Well, if you say so—I'll go along with it,' and I turned the page. Now it's clear to me. I know I'm not a hero, but I think I have pride like one."

"Oh, Tori, there's no shame in taking a loan," Nicole pointed out.

She sighed. "There is if I can't pay it back."

Twenty-eight

The trail went cold in France.

The two brothers pulled their collars up against a wild wind off the Atlantic, shuttering their eyes to the dead leaves darting in the air. They trudged into a narrow alley, then escaped into an inn.

Day and night, Derek and Grant had chased down every lead, doggedly following their cousin's trail. And now on this blustery eve, they'd bitterly concluded that there was no new direction to follow.

After they sank down and muttered an order for food, Derek said, "We need to look on the bright side. Hell, this might be good for Ian."

"Might be," Grant echoed, without thought. On a night like tonight, he should be curled up in bed with Victoria.

Derek snapped his fingers in front of Grant's face. "Damn it, Grant, you've been like this since we left

Whitestone. I know what you're brooding over, so why not just speak about it."

Grant pinched the bridge of his nose. "I left things . . . bad with Victoria."

"Why should that bother you?" Derek asked in a reasonable tone. "You're unemotional, incapable of love, et cetera."

"That doesn't mean I didn't want to marry her," Grant answered. "But she issued that damned 'love' ultimatum." His brow furrowed. "How did you know you were in love with Nicole?"

Derek didn't have to think. "I knew it when I realized I'd lay down my life for hers."

"But a gentleman would lay down his life for a lady—"

"*Gladly*. I'd do it gladly. Plus, when I knew I'd lost her, I couldn't plan for the future, and didn't want to. 'She's not to be yours, get on with your life,' I told myself a hundred times. And right when I decided that I needed to return to Whitestone, the first thing I thought was *Nicole will like it there*."

Grant was certainly incapable of planning a future without Victoria. It was as if his mind rebelled against the thought. He mulled this over until their meal was served. As they'd experienced from most of the roadside pubs, the food was ridiculously bad. What should have been hot was cold. Soft staples were hard.

Derek picked up some indeterminate foodstuff, frowned at it, and said, "I still say we should have hired investigators."

"I didn't think he'd really disappeared," Grant said. "I thought I could return him home as I have several times before."

"As of today, we can be certain he's gone. We're going to have to set the runners loose on this."

Grant exhaled in resignation and nodded. "Ian's like a bad penny—he should have turned up by now. He'd been acting strange the whole voyage."

A buxom maid sashayed to their table and leaned down. "Is there anything else you fine gentlemen might want?" she purred.

Neither looked up. Both said in unison, "*No.*"

When she stomped away, Derek said, "I'm going back, tomorrow."

"I understand," Grant said honestly. "I need to tie up some loose ends, try to squeeze something out."

"Then I'll return and handle Aunt Serena." Derek grimaced. "Alone."

Grant was aghast. "You'd do that?"

Derek nodded. "I need to see my wife. I miss Nicole and the baby. I miss her as I would air," he admitted quietly.

Grant wondered if Victoria missed him at all. He was sure her days would be busy playing chess, exploring the estate, perhaps relearning to ride now that spring was here. When he left, she'd looked comfortable and secure with Camellia and the earl playing games by the fireside. Yet Grant knew the old earl wouldn't last much longer. When he died, Grant would make sure Victoria had everything she needed.

Grant hit on an idea. "Could you send Victoria a horse when you get back? And tackle. Spare no expense."

"I'll do it, but I think she'd prefer you over the gifts."

His brows drew together. "I feel responsible for Ian. He tried to talk to me several times on the voyage and I rebuffed him at every turn. I'll return as soon as I can, but it can't hurt to keep myself on her mind." He folded his arms over his chest. "And I think being away might work to my advantage. She'll have weeks to get over her pique. She'll have time to get to know her grandfather. Most important"—Grant smiled, a confident curving of his lips—"she'll realize how much she misses me."

"I hate him!" Tori muttered, when Huckabee delivered a gift from Grant.

Cammy tsked. "You don't mean it."

"Oh, but I do." *A sleek mare.* What was he thinking, sending her something so expensive? Had he sent the gift out of guilt? Her brows drew together and she shook her head. She couldn't understand the purpose and that irritated her. It was a communication that she'd be damned if she could decipher.

He'd sent no word, no letters, no inquiries—just a *horse.*

Cammy was already running her fingers down the animal's tawny neck. But she *was* a splendid horse, Tori thought, when she looked into her intelligent eyes. The mare whinnied softly and brushed her head against Tori, and she couldn't help but smile. "I think you like us," she cooed. "I know we like you." But she needed a workhorse, not a graceful runner. She stiffened and forced herself to look away.

"Huckabee, get what you can for her. And the tackle as well."

Cammy looked longingly after the mare as he led her away. "Do you still think we can pull this off?"

"Now more than ever, Cammy."

She sounded so confident to her friend, but that night when she lay awake in the dark, doubt resurfaced. She didn't know how much more she could push herself.

At the end of each day, when she eased herself into bed, there were a few moments when her body ached worse at rest. She was too weary to stand again, or even to cry. At least her exhaustion helped deaden her desire for Grant. Though it couldn't extinguish it entirely. She still dreamed of him each night, erotic scenes piercing her murky thoughts.

She was beginning to wonder if she could ever put him in the past. Where he belonged.

Camellia Ellen Scott was *the* finest horsewoman in the world.

Cammy was sure of it as she and the new mare flew over fields and fences, hedges and streams. She could feel her blood pumping, making her mind sharp.

The horse's hooves pounded into the earth, the sound reminding her of her childhood spent riding every moment she could. She was glad they had the horse for two more days before the new owner picked her up. Cammy planned to be on the back of that horse for every hour of those days.

She'd long thought she was dying, but today, now, she knew that she was alive and staying that way for quite some time. Cammy felt . . . strong and *revived*. Laughter burst from her as they took a higher hedge and approached another.

She was flying. *Really* flying. Backward.

The horse had slowed, balked, and reared, sending her tumbling, one leg catching over the pommel of her side-saddle. When it dislodged, she crashed down. After a stunned second, she gingerly rolled to her knees, then stood. Pain flared high on her inner thigh and her palm darted to rub her aching backside.

"May I help you with that?" a deep voice inquired.

Cammy yanked her hand away and whirled around,

lips pursed in irritation. Her breath left her in a whoosh.

It was the baron.

"I meant the horse." His gray eyes were bright with laughter. At her. "Shall I help you with her?" He'd dismounted and was leading his own, but hers was nowhere in sight.

Speak, Cammy. This is where you return talk. "I, oh, yes. She spooked."

"We can walk a ways and see if we spot her."

When she took a step and winced, his eyes widened. "What's injured?" the man barked.

What's injured, indeed. A spot on her body she'd be loath to tell a physician about, much less the charismatic baron.

She'd just have to lie. "My ankle." Weren't ladies always turning their ankles? Before she could finish the thought, he was kneeling before her, pushing up her skirt! "I—what? Stop that!"

"Well, you're obviously not that hurt, but I need to see if you've a break or a sprain."

"You drop my skirts, sir!"

He glanced up, looking as if he was just holding in his laughter.

Her face flamed. He might be wonderful to look at, but she didn't like that he found her amusing. Chin in the air, she said, "I will examine it." To prove her point, she limped over to a stump and sat with her back to him. She thought she heard him chuckling.

As she pretended to probe her ankle, he said, "I was up on the ridge and saw you tearing across the county. Very talented riding."

She looked over her shoulder. "Very talented riding doesn't leave you horseless and hobbling."

Now he did chuckle. He walked around and bent down to catch her gaze. "Well, what's the verdict?"

She stared at him blankly. *Verdict? Infatuation.*

"Your ankle? Sprained?"

"Oh! Yes, just a sprain."

"I'm Stephen Winfield. May I have the name of my distressed damsel?"

She did laugh then. He had no idea. "Sir, you can't *imagine* distressed when it applies to me. This, I assure you, is but a hiccup."

"Ah, so the name of my damsel? . . ."

Oh, he is too charming. She felt fluttery, as if her body were melting inside, which wasn't helping her remember how small talk was done, especially small talk with a man one found remarkably attractive. "I'm Camellia Scott."

He took her grubby hands, brushed them off against his coat, and kissed one. "My pleasure."

They stared at each other for what seemed a very long moment until she heard a high-pitched nicker. "M-My horse! Thank goodness."

Cammy rose, intending to hobble over and mount. She could do it, despite her pulled muscle and hurting backside, but she'd look like a buffoon in the process. She turned to Winfield. "Thank you for your help, but you can see I have everything I need."

He gave her an amused look. "I *will* be seeing you home."

"I *won't* be needing an escort." He raised his eyebrows at her. Cammy, as a stubborn person, recognized his stubbornness immediately. She wasn't going to win this one. "Fine!"

He mounted, reining his horse around to her. Before she could even form a protest, he'd lifted her and placed her gently in his lap.

"Th-This isn't proper. I thought you were escorting me, not carrying me."

"This seemed appropriate, considering the circumstances."

She blew out a frustrated breath and turned her head. "Then to Belmont Court!"

"I know where you live. I saw you the other day, remember?"

Of course she did! But how had he remembered *her*?

"Are you a relative of Belmont's granddaughter?" he asked.

"No, I was her governess when she was young."

He inhaled sharply. "You're one of the castaways?"

She stiffened and up went her chin.

"You are. It's an honor to meet you, Miss Scott."

She turned in his lap to face him better. "You don't think I'm odd?"

He shook his head. "I think you were right. A spill from a horse must be a day's play for you. I also think you must be one hell of a woman."

She was flustered. The way he said those last words, so low and intense, nearly made her shiver. How could she respond to him? What to say?

She inwardly shook herself. He made her want to say even more silly things, so she pressed her lips together, determined to be silent the entire way home. When they were just beside the entrance, he helped her down, but not to the ground. He scooped her into his arms, leaving her no choice but to hold him around the neck.

"You can't carry me in!" Oh, he was so strong. She could feel his muscles working. "You can't come in the house!" My God, he smelled *incredible*. "Please, put me down!"

He kicked at the door with his boot. She groaned. She'd

just wanted to go for a simple ride. Huckabee opened the door, and his dropped jaw made her face flame again.

"If you'll direct me to a settee?"

"Of course, my lord."

Winfield shifted her in his arms. She thought he was just finding a more comfortable position, but he'd actually pulled her closer. Could this situation become more unbearable?

Apparently. Tori strolled in, saw she was injured, and ran for them, looking like she'd do Winfield harm. "Are you hurt? What happened? Why is he holding you?"

He answered in a patient voice, "Miss Scott's a little banged up. She fell from her horse. I'm holding her because I don't want her to walk."

He placed her lightly on the settee in the parlor and called for ice, pillows, and tea. Tori hesitated, eyeing the baron, but when she saw Huckabee starting in the direction of the icehouse, she glowered at Winfield in warning and went for pillows.

He propped up Cammy's pitifully unswollen ankle with the small cushions available. She swished her skirts over it as though modest.

"May I call on you and check on your recovery?"

He'd already helped her so much. "That really won't be necessary."

"I insist."

She shook her head. She didn't want him *obligated* to come see her and certainly didn't want him to know she'd lied about her ankle. "I don't think that would be a good idea."

For the first time, his face fell. "Of course." Almost to himself he said, "I tend to forget how old I am."

"Old," she scoffed, rubbing a smudge from her hand.

"You're in your late thirties, if that, and most virile." She glanced up just as she gasped at herself. The earth would swallow her now, if it did as bidden.

His eyes were merry, his expression pleased. "Early *forties*. But I fear you're too young for me."

"I am not too young for you."

His smile widened.

"I meant, should two people of our ages . . ." She trailed off with a frown. "I'm simply saying that should circumstances . . ." Her face was on fire. "I'm quite near thirty!" Maybe he wasn't just amused *at* her. It could be argued that he was delighted *with* her. Or both. She just didn't know.

"I don't see how that could be possible, but as it works to my favor—"

Tori returned then with blankets, pillows, and Mrs. Huckabee bearing Cammy's favorite tea. Tori scrutinized Winfield looking at Cammy and didn't seem too pleased with the situation. He must have sensed Tori's animosity because, with a last lingering kiss on Cammy's hand, he turned to show himself out. But not before he said over his shoulder, "Friday, Miss Scott."

Both she and Tori stared at the doorway for some time after he left.

"Tell me everything," Tori finally said.

Cammy explained her fall and detailed his kindness. And she didn't omit the inane things she'd said. By the end, she and Tori were laughing.

"Oh, Cammy, I was so rude to him. Again. I was just worried about you. And the way he was holding you. *Possessive.*"

"Really?"

Tori nodded. "Absolutely."

"I can't believe I called him virile. And that's only one of the dim-witted things I said to him. I was rattled to find that I can't converse."

"I think you're brilliant at conversing if the way he was looking at you is any indication. So what shall you wear Friday?"

"Don't be ridiculous," Cammy scoffed. "You make it sound like he's coming to court me."

"That's exactly what he's doing. Mrs. Huckabee said he's been a widower for over ten years."

Cammy hardly knew him and yet she felt so sad for his loss. "He's just being polite. Handsome, powerful men like that don't court emaciated, pale, formerly out-of-their-mind redheads."

"None of that is true but for the red hair," Tori insisted. "But I have a feeling that even if all of it were, this man would."

Winfield returned on Wednesday.

After rushing up to her room and trying on as many different dresses as she owned, Cammy chose a royal-blue walking dress, smoothed her hair, and then calmly descended the stairs. The pain in her legs and backside that she'd complained of only that morning had vanished.

He sucked in a breath when he saw her and seemed so admiring that she concluded the poor boy was losing his eyesight.

"I had an excuse ready about how I didn't think you could get around easily and it was such a fine day I'd hate for you to be inside. But the truth is, I didn't want to wait till Friday. And I liked the idea of carrying you again."

"Oh," was her rejoinder. She barely left off the breathy *my*.

"So, I've a blanket, some wine, a bit of food, and an early-blooming cherry tree to enjoy them under."

She nearly sighed, it sounded so wonderful. "I'll go with you, but I must insist I walk. My injuries feel better after moving around."

"But your ankle . . ."

"Hardly a twinge. Like I said, just a hiccup."

She saw him hesitate and knew he was suspicious, but she poked out her chin and defied him to say something. Surely, as a stubborn person, he recognized her stubbornness.

"As you wish."

They strolled, slower than she would have liked, up in the hills to a spot overlooking the valley and set out their luncheon. Though she struggled to limit herself to only a few grapes, he plied her with wine and delicacies, candied apricots and roasted apples, cheeses so good she wanted to roll her eyes in delight, and brown and white breads wrapped in cloth and still warm.

The more wine she drank, the more loquacious she became. The wretch took advantage of her state to ask her questions about the island. How to tell him she was previously addled in the head, could never eat fish—a main staple of the English diet—and didn't remember a great deal of the last several years? How could she confide that there were things she wished she couldn't recall? She put him off by describing the flora and fauna.

At the end of the day, a singularly lovely day, he said to her, "The time passes too quickly when I'm with you." He reached for her hand. "I want to see you tomorrow."

Cammy stared at him, perplexed because he really did seem to like her. One could get used to having a magnificent man smiling at her as if she hung the moon.

Yet, she worried. How could she find someone, be *courted*, when Tori was mourning her grandfather? And the love of her life?

As promised, Winfield came around again on Thursday. But when he talked about what they would do the next day as though it was inconceivable that they wouldn't be spending it together, she said, "I would like to see you tomorrow, but circumstances at the Court are very delicate just now."

"How so?"

"Lady Victoria has been under a tremendous amount of strain. I don't know that this won't add to her worries."

"Wouldn't she be happy that a man, a good and decent man, I might add, is besotted with you?"

She thought he teased her. "Are you besotted?" she asked lightly.

His expression grew serious. "Since the moment I first saw you."

Her mouth parted in disbelief. She wanted to cover up her amazement, to say something witty. But his lips covered hers and saved her the trouble. Slow, tender, yet urgent. He communicated more to her in those brief moments than she'd ever dreamed. He pulled away, his gaze catching hers. "Tell me you feel the same way."

"I do," she whispered, then brought her lips back to his, gently clasping his face to answer him in kind.

Twenty-nine

*T*hough the scenery on the Atlantic coast had been striking for the last few days, Grant hadn't enjoyed it. Tonight he was treated to the sun sinking into the azure sea, the clouds strewn around painted scarlet. Grant slowed his horse, and felt the familiar pang he suffered whenever he saw something so appealing. His first thought was that Victoria should see it as well.

The night before Derek had left for home, he'd said he missed Nicole as he would air. Grant now understood that feeling completely. Victoria should be where he was. Period.

How could I know I was in love when I'd never felt it?

The sun hissed when it met the sea. The sky burned with afterglow.

"Ah, bloody hell." He winced, then dropped his forehead into his hand.

It was *because* he'd never felt this way before that he

knew. He shook his lowered head. "I'm in love with her," he mumbled to himself, noting that his voice sounded bewildered. Looking back at the sky, he said more clearly, "I love Victoria."

His discovery made him near frenzied to get home to tell her, but he forced himself to painstakingly follow any semblance of a lead to the end. When he concluded that he'd missed nothing that could help them with Ian's disappearance, he allowed himself to turn back to England, riding day and night to the channel, then pacing on the short voyage across. Every mile closer to home, the guilt he felt for not finding his young cousin grew heavier to bear, but he simply couldn't find another direction to investigate.

Once he'd made it to Whitestone, he took his lathered horse to the stable and ordered his mount rewarded and another saddled. He hurried past Amanda in the garden and tossed a greeting to her.

"Grant," she replied curtly.

Puzzled by her cool behavior, he strode into the house, starving, coated with road dust, and impatient as ever. He grabbed two apples for his dinner, then nearly walked straight into Derek. Grant noticed the tight look on his brother's face and narrowed his eyes. "Did you break the news to Serena?"

Derek gave a distracted nod. "She's sure she's dying of an equatorial disease she read about in the *Times* and rounded up the daughters to accompany her to Bath."

"Poor chits."

"But I've unleashed the runners," Derek added. "They said they should have news soon."

"That's good, because I found nothing new." Grant jerked an apple in Amanda's direction. "Why isn't she talking to me?"

"I'm afraid it isn't just her," Derek admitted. As if to illustrate his point, Nicole walked in, spotted Grant, and immediately quit the room.

"What's this about?" Grant demanded.

"I . . . it's about Victoria—"

Grant dropped the apples to fist his hands on Derek's shirt. "Is she hurt? Is she in trouble?"

"She's not hurt," he rushed to assure Grant. "But the old earl passed away while we were gone."

"He died?"

"Yes, he died." This from his mother, who'd just entered the room. "Leaving her with nothing. Less than nothing. She's been working like a field hand and selling everything that isn't nailed down just to keep the creditors from taking the Court. And actually, *not nailed down* is no longer applicable."

Grant sank down in a parlor chair and exhaled a breath.

"She had to sell her mother's wedding ring that Camellia took from Lady Anne before they buried her." She glared at Grant. "You brought Victoria here. Then you abandoned her."

Instantly, he was on his feet. "You know why I had to leave—"

"Then why didn't you make sure she had enough money before you left? Get someone to watch over her? You alone knew how destitute Belmont really was. None of us had any idea. You'd seen that the place was falling down around their ears."

"In case all of you hadn't already noticed, I don't do my best thinking where she's concerned. I just never conceived he'd die so soon."

"He did, and you stranded her—that's how she looks at it, as another stranding. And just like before, she's doing whatever it takes to survive. Believe it or not, she's making a go of it. But then she had to—"

Grant was out the door before she could say another word.

He made the Court in well under half a day. Energy surrounded the place and changes had been made, but he didn't hesitate to study anything in particular, only rushed to the entrance. The knocker was missing. Grant's brows drew together. Surely Victoria wouldn't have sold that too.

Strangely nervous, he banged on the door, but no one answered. Finding it unlocked, he let himself in and searched the manor until he came upon her in the study. Grant had thought he was prepared to see Victoria, but his chest tightened when he caught her rubbing her forehead, her face pensive as she inspected the account books before her.

He didn't want her pensive. Especially not because of account books. If there was one thing Grant could help her with, it was finance. He reminded himself that she didn't need him to take care of her.

Damn it, *he* needed him to take care of her.

A thought arose that made his nervousness return tenfold. There was a possibility—albeit slim—that he could mend the rift between them and have her in his arms within the hour.

So much work to be done, and already Tori's head was aching as if her temples were in a vise. Even the birdsong outside—which she had set up a feeder at the window to attract—grated on her nerves.

She put her arms up to stretch, to try to work out the tension creeping up her back into her neck. Her breath left her and her arms fell limply. *Grant?* He was leaning in the doorway staring at her. How long had he been there? She frowned. That man could not have chosen a worse day.

Without invitation, he entered her study.

Who did he think he was, walking into her home like this?

Like he owned it.

He stood for a moment at the desk, no doubt shocked at how tired she looked or how fierce her expression was when she faced him. If she looked tired, he appeared exhausted, his face drawn with some emotion. His clothes were covered in dust, his boots scuffed. He'd ridden here without even taking the time to shave. Her brows drew together in interest, until he casually laid his hat on her desk and took a seat. The gesture infuriated her and brought out a violently strong possessiveness of the Court.

"We need to talk."

Please, don't be here about the Court. Don't want it like I do. . . .

"I need to explain what's happened in the last few weeks—"

"Did you find Ian?" she interrupted.

His face tightened. "No, I didn't."

She glanced down, not wanting to share her sadness with him. She'd assumed Grant would find Ian just as Grant had found her, and was crushed to hear otherwise. "Is that why you came here?" She faced him again. "To tell me you hadn't found him?"

"No. Not completely."

"What else did you want to discuss? I'm afraid I don't have the time or the inclination for social calls just now," she said, her voice cold and pleasingly steady.

His eyes widened a touch. "We haven't seen each other in weeks. You can't spare time for me?"

"Is that why you're here? To visit? You should have left your card."

"You know that's not why I'm here—for a simple visit."

"How can I possibly know what you could want here?" She put her palms up in true frustration. "The last time you left here, you swore you wouldn't come back—"

"I behaved like an ass, and I regret that."

He regretted that? *I'm sorry,* her mind cried. *Say you're sorry.* Her headache had spread to a band around her entire head. She remembered vowing that she wouldn't take him back even if he swore eternal love and begged forgiveness. He wasn't even close to that with this stilted, pulling-teeth conversation.

"I just don't have time for this," she said, stacking papers in snappish movements. "You need to leave."

"I don't want to leave yet." He irritably raked his fingers through his hair. "I have to speak with you."

She stood. "*I* don't *have* to speak with you. And by my calculations, you've had your way every single time we've been at cross-purposes, so I believe I'm due. Good-bye, Grant."

He gave her a disbelieving look.

"It's over. I said good-bye." She walked to the front entrance to show him out, and heard him follow. When she opened the door, he exited, secretly disappointing her. She'd hoped for a groveling apology. Without warning, his hand shot out to drag her to him. Then his lips were on hers, the mere contact as explosive as ever. She didn't slap him or struggle, but was motionless. After moments passed, she couldn't resist moving her lips under his just slightly. He groaned, she gasped. Their hands collided as they reached out to grab each other.

But he was breaking the kiss, seeming to drag himself

away. She heard herself give a little whimper of protest. When she opened her eyes and they cleared, she stiffened.

He scrubbed a hand over his face. "It damn well isn't over."

"That means nothing," she blustered. "We've always been good like that. If you were listening to anything I said before, you'd know I wanted more."

"I'm ready to give you more," he said, the words like a promise.

She shook her head, furious. "Don't you dare toy with me. I would hope you knew your own mind enough that you wouldn't go from 'a lusty marriage only' to 'anything you want' in the space of a few weeks. A few weeks that we were apart and not working through this together, I might add." She pressed her fingers to her temple. "You made everything clear to me the last time we saw each other, and although I disagreed at the time, I've come to see that you were right about everything."

"No. No, I wasn't. I was a bloody—"

"I want you to know that I wish you every happiness," she interrupted coolly, and closed the door on his achingly handsome face.

But it only bought her a day. The next, he was back like a dog at a bone, continuing his pursuit. As there were only weeks left until the Court was hers, she resolved to avoid him at all costs.

Eluding him was as easy as it had been on the island. Anytime the dogs barked, she left the house or read in her closet by candlelight. Once, she and Mrs. Huckabee were in the kitchen when they heard him striding through the house. The woman had cocked a meaty hip into Tori, sending her flying into the larder just before Grant walked in. Another time, Huck had hidden her in the hayloft where she was silently trampled by a litter of adoring barn kittens.

The growing number of days she evaded him was satisfying.

Curse it, it *was*.

Victoria had accepted life without him, which was unacceptable.

As Grant drummed the door at the Court, he replayed for the hundredth time the unflinching look Victoria had given him the first day he'd returned. Grant had prepared for her anger. Her resignation was far worse. But she'd fought for him; he would do no less by her.

Plot, organize, fight, conquer. It worked in business. After much coaxing, he'd garnered support from his mother and Nicole, and if he couldn't find Victoria, he'd run Camellia to ground and recruit her as well.

But Camellia did not seem pleased to see him. Actually, at the front door she said, "I can't say I'm pleased to see you." She let him into the house, at least.

The difference in her appearance floored Grant. Gone was the thin, ailing woman, replaced by a comely, vibrant one. "Miss Scott, you're looking well."

He thought she would smile or thank him. Instead, she glared. "Why should I even speak to you? You've hurt Tori terribly."

"I know—I can explain that. I had to go after Ian—"

"She knows *why* you ran off. But not to even send word? To check on her?"

"I thought she felt well rid of me. Especially when I left here that last morning."

In a saucy tone, Camellia mumbled to herself, "She feels that way now."

"Damn it, Camellia. I thought the time apart would

dim her anger toward me. And it would have if the earl hadn't died before I returned."

"The only reason I'm speaking to you is because your mother and sister-in-law wrote and asked me to," Camellia said as she led him into the parlor. "You're lucky Tori's out for the entire day."

When she took her seat in one of the few chairs, Grant sat as well. "This isn't easy for me to ask for your help."

"Why on earth should I help you? You broke her heart."

He frowned, thinking of Victoria's cool words to him. "She's not behaving like her heart's broken."

"No, but you're looking it."

He nodded, knowing she was right.

"No more than you deserve." Her tone was cutting, shockingly so.

"My God, I liked you better addled."

She narrowed her eyes.

He pinched the bridge of his nose. "I'm sorry. I just want to marry her, spoil her—"

"Love her?"

He looked her in the eye. "More than anything."

"So that's why Amanda and Nicole were so adamant. I'm surprised you told them."

He threw up his hands. "I talk about this to anyone who'll listen. The bloody stable boy knows I'm devoted."

"Well, what do you propose?"

"She said before that there was no affection, no ease between us. I know no one will trick her into meeting me. So what can I do? I want to show her there can be affection between us, but it's impossible when I have to hunt her down. And the one meeting we had since I returned was rushed."

"And, of course, you were nervous."

"I was not nervous." At her disbelieving expression, he grumbled, "There's a lot riding on this." Moving them back to the subject, he said, "I want to be with her alone and uninterrupted for the remainder of the month at least."

She shook her head. "Tori won't leave, and if she did, she'd be so distracted thinking about all the work she needed to be doing that it'd be like she was still at the Court anyway."

"Then I have to be here. With her alone."

"You'll ruin her reputation," Camellia pointed out. "You can't just *live* with her."

Grant had already planned for this argument. "The Court is isolated. I know you don't get visitors. The villagers and the Huckabees are loyal to their bones. Think about it—if they weren't, the papers would have been here to follow the story of the castaways. And I know your nearest neighbor, the baron. He's a good man who would never gossip."

Camellia was silent for some time, clearly torn.

Grant saw her waver, and pressed. "If worse comes to worst, my mother has agreed to say she was chaperoning here the entire time."

Finally, Camellia said, "Tori's had some papers drawn up. She wants you to sign them and swear off your claim." She studied him. "I might help if you signed them—"

"Done."

"—and left them with me." Camellia raised her eyebrows. "If you don't make her fall for you in two weeks, you lose her *and* the Court. Are you willing to do that?"

"I want *her*." His hands clenched. "*Bugger the rest.*"

Camellia coughed delicately at his language, then said, "I'll trust you on this, but only because I *know* she loves you. But if you hurt her . . ."

"I won't."

She pointed her finger at him. "And don't you dare offer her money or try to fix this. She wants—she needs—this for herself."

A quick nod. "Agreed."

"So, alone, you said?"

"If possible."

Her brows knitted in thought. "The Huckabees moved back into their cottage recently. They'd only been in the manor house to care for the earl. And as for me . . ."

"Perhaps you could visit Whitestone?"

"Oh, I'll just tell her I'm having a torrid affair with that baron and am going to his hunting lodge for a couple of weeks."

Grant straightened. "I wouldn't ask you to lie."

She blinked up at him. "It's not a lie."

Thirty

*T*he roof on the sheep barn?" Tori asked Huckabee in one of their thrice-weekly office meetings.

"We're still getting estimates for materials."

"The shearing?"

"We've got a crew coming in later this spring. But they're going to want half their fee up front."

She sighed loudly. "I'll find it somewhere. The low acres?"

"We've contracted to have them drained by the end of the month."

Her eyes narrowed. "In time for planting?"

He checked a smile. "Aye, miss."

"Let's meet at the barn tomorrow and go over the repairs."

"Right after breakfast, then?"

She nodded, amazed at his unwavering enthusiasm. For some reason, Huckabee was delighted with how she was doing. Mrs. Huckabee related that he'd said he'd never worked for anyone as involved and knowledgeable as she was coming to be. He charged out with a spring in his step and his shoulders back.

She was already lost in thought on what else she had to get done that day when Cammy passed through the doorway a moment later. "So how has your day been?" she asked, taking the seat across from the desk.

"Well enough, I suppose."

"Huckabee certainly looks pleased with the progress."

Tori nodded absently. *That barn is going to be the death of us and timber is so expensive right now. . . .*

"I wanted to let you know that I'm going on a trip for a while."

That snapped Tori's attention back. "What? Where?"

"I was going to tell you this sooner, but Winfield and I have been seeing each other. A lot."

"I gathered that. And if your humming and rosy cheeks are any indication, this is more than an infatuation?"

Cammy nodded. "He wants me to go with him to his hunting seat in Devonshire for the last half of the month. It's supposed to be beautiful there."

Tori was too jarred to say anything, though she wanted to appear happy. Two weeks in a lovely part of England, doing nothing but relaxing with the man you love . . . Part of her was jealous. But Cammy deserved this more than anyone. "You're going to have a wonderful time."

Cammy leaned in to whisper, "I told him everything, Tori. Everything that happened on the island. And he said he was proud of me for what I did."

"He should be," Tori said fiercely. "You saved my life."

"Well, you started it by saving mine." When Tori gave her a watery smile, Cammy asked, "Will you be all right for two weeks?"

She hadn't thought about that. Two weeks alone. "I'll be fine."

"Then it's settled. He's to pick me up tomorrow afternoon."

"Tomorrow?" Tori swallowed.

"Is that all right?"

"Of course," she said casually. Yet when she saw Cammy off the next day, she thought about asking the Huckabees to move back in. That would be silly. She was the mistress of her home, a woman grown who'd conquered a damn jungle, and could be here unattended. Still, as noon approached, she dreaded the night alone in the big desolate house.

"Where the devil have you been, Grant?" Amanda cried when Grant ran in the front door after a three-day absence. "You're supposed to be at the Court this afternoon."

"I know that," Grant said, then nearly groaned when Nicole entered the room as well. He didn't need this. He was already unsettled by his travels and running late. "I don't have time just now—"

He tried to pass Nicole in the doorway; she crossed her arms over her chest and blocked him. "Yes, why don't you tell us where you've been? We have an interest here."

He feinted left; she blocked him. He ran a hand through his disheveled hair. "Damn if I didn't like my life better without a sister."

That seemed to please her, but she still wouldn't move.

"If you must know, I've been riding around the country"—he paused and his voice became embarrassed—"trying to buy back everything Victoria sold."

They smiled at him like at a dog who'd done a good trick. He leveled a scowl at both of them, then tore off to change shirts and get a fresh horse for his trip to the Court.

• • •

Deep in thought, her mind clouded with myriad concerns, Tori nearly ran into the strange man carrying bed slats into her home.

"What is this?" She didn't like surprises. Too many new ones greeted her each day at the Court.

"Furniture we're moving in."

She noticed another man walking past them with the headboard. "Where did it come from?"

He pointed an elbow at a moving wagon in the drive. "Sutherland."

So now he was buying her furniture? How embarrassing that he'd noted their lack and sought to fix it.

"Please remove this at once and tell him that we won't accept these gifts." Although that dresser she spotted near the back would look perfect . . .

"They're not gifts. He's moving in."

A slap couldn't have rocked her more. "Stop. Just stop what you're doing! Move your little ant line in the opposite direction." She stiffened when she heard chuckling from behind her.

"Ant line?" She didn't have to turn to know it was Grant.

Victoria whirled on him with a withering look. "What do you think you're doing?"

"Moving in."

"This place is mine." She hiked a thumb at her chest. "*Mine.* You can't just come in here like this."

"The deed says it's mine," Grant said in an even tone.

"B-But you said you didn't want it. That you wouldn't claim it."

He raised his eyebrows. "You said you didn't want it either."

Biting out each word, she said, "I changed my mind."

"As did I."

He walked in the direction of his new room. She was right beside him. "No! You can't do this. Do you know how hard I've worked? I worked myself to the bone. I earned this place."

He slowed. He couldn't do this. He couldn't hurt her. And still part of him was so eager to be near her. "I earned it too. I gave up more than a year of my life for it. I'm staying."

"You're kicking us out?" Her voice was broken.

He stopped then, rushing to assure her, "Who said anything about kicking you out? You and Camellia are welcome here for as long as you like."

She looked as though she were strangling on her words. "You expect me to live here with you?"

"From what I understand, the place needs someone to oversee and expand the sheep operation. I'm hiring myself."

She was bristling now. Good. If she had cried, if her bottom lip had trembled whatsoever, he wouldn't have been able to do this.

"I'll make you rue the day you concocted this scheme. I'll have you out of here within the week."

He ignored her and directed a workman, "Take this up to the second story, fifth door on the right."

"That's adjoining my room!"

He gave her a smoldering look. "Is it?"

She'd fought so hard not to cry. But later in her room, while she paced back and forth, the struggle became harder. Cursing him helped. Kicking things helped more. How could he do this to her? Hearing him next door, walking about "his" room, she thought she couldn't feel more fury.

If she'd ever doubted her decision to stay, she was filled with new resolve. Her territorial feelings were staggering. And for him to interfere now, to take his time claiming the place—it was insufferable. And dear Lord, she could hear him washing up. This wouldn't do, this thinking about him shirtless, wet . . .

She shook her head. She would move to another room! But she dismissed the idea. First the room, next the Court itself. She had to take a stand. Besides, nothing would prevent him from moving right beside her again.

A knock sounded on the door. On the adjoining door. The nerve!

She yanked it open, every ounce of will used to prevent herself from kicking him.

His nonchalance didn't help. He leaned his tall body against the door frame, and ran his gaze over her face, then her breasts, sweeping down her body and up again. His eyes darkened as they did when he wanted her.

A look like that could make a woman forget why she was angry. . . .

"What do we do for sustenance around here?"

We? We! "You don't really expect me to help you? Or to even talk to you, for that matter?"

"Would you deny a starving man?"

"With you as the man? Gladly." She moved to slam the door. He placed his boot in the way.

"Listen, Victoria. You believe you're going to find a way to make me leave?"

She lifted her chin. "Depend on it."

"So why not use me while I'm here? I'm strong—I could help you. I can work."

She saw where this was leading. "But if you work here, it would give you even more claim."

"What if I swore I'd never use that against you?"

"You also said you didn't want the place. Strange, but aren't you here because you 'changed your mind'?"

"I'd give you my word."

She frowned at him, confused by the fact that she knew she could trust him on this. She didn't know how, but she knew. And help would be so critical right now.

She exhaled and said, "We retire early at the Court and had dinner some time ago. And you won't find your meals at the end of a bellpull around here."

"I understand." He gave her a quick nod. "Does this mean you'll help me tonight?"

"Unwillingly. But rest assured I'll be paid back."

His smile was heart-stopping. Cocky and sensual and as powerful as a weapon.

She yanked her gaze away and scuffed to the kitchen, helping him to stew and bread, which he obviously found delicious. "What shall we work on tomorrow?" he asked.

She hesitated, feeling she was about to capitulate more than she ought. Her voice pained, she said, "Be at the north fence tomorrow morning."

Though Grant arrived not long after sunup, Victoria, Huckabee, and an elderly villager were already at the downed fence waiting for him. Victoria looked adorable in her work boots and straw hat. The rough gloves she wore swallowed her hands.

He grinned at her; she glowered at him.

Turning to survey the job, his eyes followed the line of damaged fence as it went on. And on. He scanned in all directions looking for more workers. Irritation sniped at him.

No wonder she'd been working like a field hand. She *was* a field hand, and unnecessarily so. Victoria had been through so much in the last few months, and he'd be damned if he'd let her run herself into the ground.

He grabbed her hand and pulled her aside. "This will take days to finish. Why haven't you recruited more men?"

She glared at his hand.

"Why?" he repeated, before reluctantly releasing her.

"Can we not get started?" she said.

"You'll lose sheep. Penny sure and pound foolish."

Her eyes narrowed. "Proverbs? You can't take blood from a stone. And even if we had the money, there isn't anyone to hire. All the young men in the area went off to find work when no money was being put into the estate." Her voice went low. "How dare you question my decisions?"

Great start, Grant. "I'm"—he swallowed—"sorry. It's just that I'm concerned about you working a line like this without help."

Her mouth parted at his apology. She turned away and mumbled something about a long day ahead.

So for the next several hours, Grant worked as though possessed, mainly to keep the others from it. The old man, Gerald Shepherd, looked as if he could keel over at any moment, Victoria swayed on her feet when she rose too swiftly, and Huckabee's face was a constant alarming shade of red.

One other thing helped sustain him: Victoria seemed eager to stay by him and examine him working. Once, when he pulled up his shirt to wipe his brow, he caught her staring at his chest and lower. Before she hurriedly glanced up at him, she'd unconsciously licked her lips, sending him into a working frenzy. And then when she'd realized they were going to complete the repairs that day, she'd looked so proud, her eyes snapping with it, that he would have worked himself to death.

Just after dusk, when he'd planted the last pole, Grant was almost too exhausted to think of bedding her. Almost. As it was, the compulsion to pull her into his arms to sleep was overwhelming. Just to lie with her. Just to stroke her hair until she fell asleep. He wiped his brow and neck and strode over to where she perched on the end of a pony cart. "We work well together."

"You seem fairly pleased with yourself."

"I am."

"From what I understand, shearing will make the fence look like child's play. Of course, you won't be around long enough to know."

"I'm very familiar with sheep," Grant reminded her. "I ran Whitestone for four years."

She shrugged at him, stifling a yawn as exhaustion caught up with her.

"We need to get you back," Grant said, then called good night to the two men. He grinned, knowing Huckabee and Shepherd were going to indulge in the jug of ale Shepherd's wife had brought them at luncheon. The men deserved it.

One thing Grant had noticed was that Victoria wasn't the only one overworked. The Huckabees were playing too many roles on the estate. Huckabee was not only a steward, but a manual laborer and field hand. Mrs. Huckabee was dairy and scullery maid, housekeeper, and laundress.

When Victoria yawned again, he caught her under her knees, and before she could protest, he'd swooped her up on his horse.

Her eyes went wide. "T-Too high," she sputtered. "Too big!"

"I'll lead him. You're too done in to walk all the way back."

She relaxed marginally when she saw he wasn't letting go of the reins, but still had a hank of the horse's mane in her fist. "Why should you care?"

"I care very much."

She frowned at him as though he confused her. He confused himself. Now that he recognized his feelings for her, he was baffled that it had taken him so bloody long. He was silent the rest of the way and made no advance when he lowered her from the horse.

After Victoria retired, Grant wrote to Nicole about sending qualified people from Whitestone to work here. He knew Victoria would be furious when she found out what he'd done, but in the morning, Grant whistled for the stable lad to have it delivered anyway.

In the middle of the next two nights, Tori ensured that some calamitous noise would wake Grant. She shoved her sparse furnishings around her room or worked on fixing her sticking window and squeaking hinges. Then early in the morning, she'd kick at his door to rouse him, but ultimately, her tactics only managed to exhaust her. He never wavered from being good-natured and complimentary as he followed her around each day, learning how she did things, and he never offered advice after the fence incident, though she could see that holding in his words was killing him. Good.

Yet it *was* pleasant having someone there to open things she couldn't budge or retrieve things she couldn't reach. She had only to show her difficulty, and he was there to help.

"I knew you were driven," he said one afternoon as they moved one of the transferable sheep pens piece by piece.

"But I've never seen anyone go after something with such single-minded pursuit."

I went after you like that, she thought. *And look what it got me. Hurt.* "How else would you go after something? And why go after a prize like you don't expect to get it?"

"Why indeed?" He looked as if he derived a different meaning. Had he read her thoughts?

Being around him constantly, viewing that towering, muscular body at work all day was unbearable, but now something much, much worse was occurring.

He'd started to show a sense of humor.

When a ram butted him, she'd howled with laughter, *and he'd joined her.* She'd frozen, stupefied. His laugh was deep and hearty, and his smile—she'd gaped at him, inwardly cursing, knowing there was no defense against something at once sensual and relaxed.

Then when her dress had caught on a nail and she'd nearly stripped herself in the sheep barn, he'd laughed again. To his credit, he'd caught one look at her face and fought to suppress it, wiping his eyes as he disentangled her and handed her back part of her skirt. Later, she noted, curse him, that he'd removed the offending nail.

That evening before it got too dark, she made her way to the stable to deliver scraps for the barn cats and was forced to pass Grant and Huckabee out on the terrace. As they awaited dinnertime, the two smoked cigars and drank ale, talking about grains and crop yields. She didn't even think Grant saw her hurrying past, but as soon as she called the first "Heeere kitty," he was behind her.

Setting down the plate, she turned and smirked at his expression. Grant Sutherland was foxed. She raised her eyebrows. "I take it Gerald shared some homemade ale with you and Huckabee."

"Potent stuff, that." He rubbed his chin, drawing her attention to the stubble he sported.

"I thought you shaved every day."

"I've been far too tired to even contemplate it. For some reason," he said with an engaging grin, "I sleep poorly here."

She gave him a smug one back. "Even an animal knows to leave a place that makes him uncomfortable." He chuckled—*bastard*—looking relaxed and at home and not at all like the grim Grant she'd balked at marrying.

Closing in on her, he murmured in her ear, "The only thing that could make me shave is if I thought I might get to kiss you." He brushed his fingers over her cheek. "I wouldn't want to rasp your soft face. Or thighs."

Her breath left her like a whisper. *I wouldn't mind,* she thought, then inwardly berated herself. She backed away, blathering an excuse about dinner, and fled.

Grant showed up at dinner half an hour later. Cleanshaven.

She knew what he was doing. He couldn't love her, so he was out to seduce her. And Lord help her, each time she glanced at his face, at his strong jaw and chiseled cheekbones cleanly shaven, a flutter erupted in her. Had he made plans that included kissing her this very night? She shook herself. She would not get aroused just looking at his face! Still, dinner was an ordeal, and she excused herself before she was finished, ignoring his obvious disappointment, to retire to her study.

Leaning back in her chair, she analyzed his strategy. She'd already told him she needed more than lust, and he'd told her that he couldn't give more. *Impasse.* And who was about to get his way, just as he had at every other impasse?

He was mixing their lives together, intertwining them

until she didn't know where hers began. And not just in work. He even planned to go to the wedding in the hamlet next Saturday that she'd been looking forward to. She'd never seen people in their eighties marry; now she probably wouldn't attend.

She muttered a curse. The villagers already saw them as co-owners, everyone looking at them as though they were working as one. There was no *one*. She wasn't a *half*. She owned this place. It was hers by right in less than a week. She would get rid of him and not live a loveless life of unanswered compromise after compromise. She wanted him gone before her desire for him made her forget why love was even important.

That wasn't the only reason for her anxiety. She knew it wasn't fair to keep control of the property when a better owner, better by virtue of wealth, was waiting to take over. She needed to squeeze out just a bit more money for that shearing crew. Tori went over the books until her eyes felt like crossing. She reviewed wordy, bloated contracts with McClure, the wool broker, but couldn't make sense of them.

After long hours, she dozed off, her head falling to a desk littered with historical wool prices, contracts, and reports she'd had Huckabee compile, entailing all the assets of the farm—what they produced, when, and how.

Tori dreamed of sheep, though these days she loathed the bleating little beggars. She jerked awake, rubbed her eyes, and rolled her head on her neck. She couldn't think. She wasn't a businessperson and demonstrated that fact daily.

But curse it, I have to be. Her brows drawn, she organized everything to begin again. It was in this midnight hour, when her vision blurred, that she saw it.

The most wonderful mistake.

She riffled through the thick pile of contracts, focusing on that line only. Every one had the same error; how had they missed it? For years, McClure had paid her grandfather's farm for cheviot wool. They did not produce cheviot, but something much, much more expensive.

They produced . . . Anglo-merino.

Thirty-one

*T*ori called a secret meeting with the Huckabees right at daybreak to tell them about her discovery, but she wrestled confusion and even guilt for not including Grant. Why did she want to share the news with him? Because she wanted him to know that she was shrewd, that she'd found something no one else had?

No, that wasn't it. She just wanted to see him smile at the news. And he would. His breathtaking grins came easier these days. He was becoming integral to the Court. And to her. Yet even when he'd been foxed the night before, he hadn't confessed tender feelings, much less the love that she wanted. *Impasse.* This new information was her way toward complete ownership, and she'd keep this card close to her chest.

After she'd explained the details to the couple, she said, "I'm going to write McClure and tell him about the mistake. He owes us thousands of pounds *in arrears*." She gave a sly grin to Mrs. Huckabee. "I learned that term the other day."

They clasped hands, joyous over the discovery. Then Huckabee's expression dimmed. "What if he meant to cheat the earl? Think about it—the farm's wool manager was gone, the earl was sick and didn't handle business anymore, and I was barely holding things together. It seems unlikely to me that this man made an honest mistake over a four-year span, right when the farm was most vulnerable."

Tori sank back in her chair. "You're right. You're absolutely right. So what do we do? Do we go to the authorities?"

"If you go the court route," Mrs. Huckabee began, "you won't see any money for years."

Huckabee slapped his hand on his knee. "I've got it. We could go the 'gentleman's threat' route." When she frowned, he explained, "Make copies of everything and send him the proof, then write 'Govern yourself accordingly.'"

"Gentleman's threat." She tapped her chin. "Let's try it. What do we have to lose?"

So she worked most of the day copying contracts, then sent the package out for delivery. If Huck caught the mail coach, the documents would arrive at McClure's in the morning.

The next day, nervous and tense about the outcome, Tori decided to work herself into oblivion, but a commotion in the drive interrupted her.

She met up with the Huckabees, and the three strode to the entrance. Grant was there, greeting a carriage from Whitestone that brought a laundress, a cook, a maid, as well as a carpenter to work on the roof of the sheep barn. The Huckabees were overjoyed—Mrs. Huckabee nearly swooned with relief—with everyone beaming at Grant.

Tori stomped off, out of sight of the new help and the Huckabees, but Grant followed her to the salon. When she turned around, he was very close, reaching out to gently touch her arm.

"You look done in."

She backed away. "As if I needed you to tell me that."

"You should have a bath drawn for you," he suggested, his voice deep, lulling her. Her mind was so muddled. Heaven forgive her, but a bath in her room's big marble plunge tub did sound divine. Soaking in steaming, scented water up to her chin . . . Her weakness made her even more furious. "I don't want a bath, and I didn't want servants. I don't even know where to put them."

"They can stay on the third floor of the lower Court."

She put her fingers up to her temples. "We can't heat it."

"Summer is coming."

"Still, their wages—"

"I'm paying for any additional cost."

She stiffened. "*I don't want that.*" He looked so reasonable, and the gesture was so logical, yet she wanted to screech her fury at him. Instead, she said, "Clever Grant, finding another way into the Court. Do you think I don't see what you're doing?"

His face registered disbelief. "You would believe that I brought help here to undermine you, before you would believe I brought them to make your life easier." His voice was hard. "Do you know me at all?"

"I've had to learn that you'll do whatever it takes to get what you want. And now, with this move, everyone will look to you for decisions to be made."

"You must really want me gone," he said, then shook his head. "Damn it, Victoria, deny it."

She said nothing.

"I thought you were beginning to see that we worked well together, that we could make a go of this." Disappointment laced his tone. "I was mistaken."

Grant strode out to the stable to ready his horse. He spotted her at the window, biting her lip and nervously fingering the edge of some ancient curtains, and he wondered if she thought he was leaving for good. What he'd said was true—he had thought she was coming around. He'd stormed out, furious and full of regret, but he was more angry with himself. He must have hurt her deeply for her to have this continued animosity. The idea that he'd hurt her made him crazed.

No, he wasn't leaving her. Not today, not ever. He hitched up a cart of supplies and rode to work on another line of fence. This one wasn't downed, but it *could* be soon, and he needed the work.

By the time he got Victoria to marry him, she'd have the best bloody fences in the county.

When he ran out of materials near sundown, he ambled to the stream to wash off. He skipped stones, finding himself staring after them long after they'd sunk to the bottom.

When night fell, he lay on a rock by the bank looking up at the stars. Their placement was what he was accustomed to; he was in England, listening to the countryside prepare for sleep, his body weary from work. His heart should be glad, but he knew as long as he was away from and unmarried to the only woman he'd ever loved, nothing would be right.

Damn it, he missed her.

He stood and stretched his sore back, wondering if she

could possibly miss him too. He wondered if she was so strong and self-assured that she'd cast what was between them into the past, never to be retrieved.

He turned in the direction of the Court, as if to *see* her. What he saw out of the corner of his eye made him suck in a breath. He turned to the eerie light, scrubbing a hand over his face, unbelieving.

Fire lit up the valley.

Thirty-two

*T*ori lay in bed, staring at the peeling wallpaper. She was like this old room, worn and neglected. After Grant had left, she wondered each hour if she could feel emptier, and each hour she did. Her sadness was escalating, and she feared where it would end.

Had he left her? For good? She hadn't given him any reason to stay. Curse it! He couldn't give up—not when he'd shown her what she couldn't live without.

Him.

That utter, utter bastard.

Realizing she'd never get him off her mind, she rose and walked into his room, pilfering his pillow. She lay down again, bringing it up to her chest and hugging it. It wasn't as if his scent would bring more dreams throughout the night. There couldn't be *more* dreams about him.

She heard noises downstairs and jumped out of bed once more, hoping he'd come home. But when she lifted

the window sash and surveyed the drive, a light in the distance caught her eyes.

Panic clogged her throat. The sheep barn was ablaze.

Sprinting down the stairs, screaming for help the whole
way down, Tori ran for the barn. They had sick ewes in
there mending, pregnant ones needing extra food and care.

When she'd charged breathless into the valley, several
villagers were already working a fire line, although everyone had to know the fire was too intense and spreading too
rapidly for anything to be done. Her knees threatened to
buckle. Yet she forced herself closer to the fire to see if she
could help, then blinked her eyes in incomprehension.

Looking past the flames inside, she spied Grant on the
other end of the barn. She cried his name—he couldn't
hear her. She ran for him, but the heat drove her back. He
had his coat off, swatting at the few ewes left, forcing the
confused animals to escape. As if having received a blow,
she watched him drop down and vanish behind a wall of
flame. Then he stood again—only to disappear once more.

Hiking up her gown, she ran around the entire length of
the barn, through high wet grasses, slipping as she went.
When she reached the south opening, she peered in, but
couldn't see him at all. The air left her lungs as though
she'd been hit. She sucked in a smoke-filled gasp and
screamed his name, yet received no answer. No, she
couldn't panic. *Find him and drag him back.*

Determined, she walked into the flaming entrance.

An arm like steel wrapped around her waist and hurled
her outward, her body pushed far from the barn and
shoved to the ground. She landed, wheezing, Grant falling
on top of her just as the roof gave in with a shuddering
boom and a shower of sparks floated up to the sky.

When she reclaimed her wits, she rolled on top of him,

sitting up to straddle him, wondering where to hit him first. How dare he risk himself like that! Didn't he know she couldn't live without him?

"Christ, Victoria," he bit out as his hands flew to her hips. "If I'd known this would be the outcome, then I'd have set the fire myself—"

"You stupid, stupid man," she said with a slap. "Obstinate! That's what you are." Punch. "I ought to kill you myself." She beat at his chest like a drum.

When she pinched him—hard—he rolled her over, pinning her arms above her head.

"No!" She struggled to free her arms. "I'm not through hitting!"

"I'm through being hit."

She bucked her hips beneath him, making him groan. "Love, that doesn't have the effect I think you intended."

Tears flooded her eyes in a rush. "Why did you stay in there? Why didn't you run away the first time you fell?"

He released her hands and leaned down beside her. "I didn't fall."

"I saw you go down twice."

He frowned. "I suppose it'd look like I fell. But I was retrieving some things."

"What things?"

His face tightened. "Just some things."

It was then that she heard mewing sounds. "The kittens!" She twined her head toward the sound and saw several shaky balls of fur crawling out from under his coat to their mother. "I thought for sure they were dead—they were up in the hayloft."

"The cat was moving them one at a time to the ground. But then the fire spread. The grayish one—"

"They're all gray now."

"Then the small one who is *still* hissing . . . he was not cooperative with my rescue."

Tori was grinning now. "That's why you went down a second time? To rescue one last kitten?"

"In for a penny," he muttered.

Tori saw the mother cat blink at them with a kitten in her mouth, already setting to work transporting, "I think you've just become my hero. My rescuer of kittens."

"That's enough," he grumbled.

She kissed his face. "I didn't know how I was going to get to you."

"Damn it, Victoria. You need to promise you'll never do anything dangerous to help me."

"Can't," she mumbled.

He put his hand on her face, and brushed at the tears on her cheeks. "Why?"

She caught his gaze. *Because I'm in love with you. More than ever before.* . . . She knew she couldn't bear to live without him—no matter what the circumstances—and drew a breath to tell him—

"Miss!" Huckabee called as he trotted over. "Are you all right?"

Grant groaned and rolled on his back as though stunned from the intimate contact with her.

"We're fine," she said, but now that she and Grant had separated, she began shaking in the cold grass.

Grant shot to his feet. "Huckabee, get a bath heating," he barked.

"The new girl has a heap of water on."

"Good." Grant pulled her up and grabbed his coat from the ground, then wrapped it around her shoulders, bringing her close to his side. Even through the smoke and soot, she imagined she could smell his skin.

Halfway up the valley, she stumbled, and he swooped her into his arms. When she moved an inch to be more comfortable, he mistook the motion as a protest.

"Just let me have this," he rasped.

She relaxed in his arms. Did he think that would be all she'd give him tonight?

He carried her into her room, booted open the door to the bathing closet, then raised his eyebrows when he saw the massive marble bath situated before a stoked grate. Steam rose from the water.

He deposited her at the side of the basin. "Will you manage?" His voice was low and rough.

No, she wouldn't. She didn't want to let him out of her sight and knew a grand way to keep him here. She looked down shyly, gliding her finger back and forth across the water. "We both smell like smoke, and there's a bath big enough for two. All this inviting water . . ."

She bit her lip nervously, wondering what he would do, but before she glanced up at him he was already kicking off his boots. She jumped up to help him with his shirt, then lifted her arms for him to draw her ruined nightdress from her.

Her fingers sought his trousers and grazed his skin low as she worked the buttons, the slight touch sending his breath whistling.

"Get into the water, Victoria." His voice was ragged. "You need to get warm."

She was tempted not to, to see if he'd take her right there. When she hesitated, he clasped her shoulders, turned her, and tapped her on the bottom to prod her forward. With shaking legs, she climbed the two steps leading up to the edge. As she sank into the water all the way up to her chest, she sighed in contentment even as she held her hand out to him.

He eased in, then drew her between his legs. She thought he would kiss her, but he moved her to put her back to his chest. He grasped a bar of soap and gently washed her hair, piling it atop her head so he could bathe her back and shoulders before moving to her upper chest. He scarcely touched her breasts. This was all business. He poured water over her hair and back, rinsing her clean.

"Your turn." She moved around in the basin to sit behind him. As he'd done, she washed him, massaging the tight muscles of his back, rinsing him off. To reach his chest, she leaned into his back, making sure he felt her breasts slipping across his skin. In an instant, he turned to her, kneeling, reaching out on each side of her to grasp the basin behind her. His whole body enclosed her.

He reached his head down to kiss and nip from her collarbone to her breast. She arched her back so he could taste her nipples. When he dragged his tongue over the first, his arms straightened and flexed around her. Her hands latched on to them, holding on as she raised herself to him. He licked and suckled mercilessly, and right when she thought she might reach her climax just from his mouth on her breasts, he groaned against one pebble-hard peak, "I can't take much more. I've wanted you too long."

"Then take me to bed," she murmured.

He sucked in a breath and stood, but she was slower, especially slow when his heavy shaft hung just before her face, commanding her attention. He reached down to lift her up, but she ignored his hand and grasped him. He groaned as if in pain, but she couldn't have let go if she desired to. So slick and hard, with water sluicing down the hollows and outcurves of rigid stomach muscles, running along the trail of hair to his engorged shaft.

"I missed this. . . ." Before he could stop her, she kissed

him lovingly, showing him how much. His flesh was hot against her lips and pulsed against her tongue, making her hungry to suck him into her mouth as he'd described all those nights ago.

With an inhuman growl, he buried his hands in her hair. She couldn't tell if he was pulling or pushing her away and thought he didn't know either. "You don't know what you do to me. Seeing your lips on me and knowing you *want* to pleasure me with your mouth. I've dreamed of this for so many nights."

"What else have you dreamed of?" she asked against the crown, right before she flicked the salty tip with her tongue.

"*My God.*" He threw his head back and she gazed upward over the straining muscles in his chest and arms. His body was a mass of power.

He didn't answer her question, but hauled her out of the basin, grabbed a towel, and roughly licked and dried every inch of her. She tried to do the same to him, but he pulled her to his chest, to look down at her eyes. "Did I frighten you the last time we made love? Did I hurt you?"

"No, never."

"Then let me show you what I've dreamed of." His words made shivers run up her spine.

He led her to the bed, pulling her to him when he sat, long legs stretched out, his back against the headboard. He was so strong he easily situated her where he wanted her, legs spread across him, straddling him as she had earlier in the night.

Would they make love like this? Her atop him? Before she could voice the question, he had his big hands on her bottom, pulling her sex forward toward his waiting mouth. When his tongue first found her, he groaned against her flesh, making her shudder. She felt herself grow wetter, knew he felt it when he growled, *"Sweet as honey."*

In total abandon, she twined her fingers in his hair, clasping him closer. At that, he groaned again and moved her down his body, placing her on his rod, guiding her down him. The movement was slow and torturing for her. For him as well, if she could tell by his squeezing and clutching, by the muscles straining in his neck and chest.

She let out a breath she hadn't known she held. Too intense . . . He went deeper than before, plunging far inside, and she still wasn't able to take all of him.

"I'm so near," she panted.

Immediately, he drew her from him, bringing her back to his hungry mouth as he casually sat devouring her.

"Oh, God," she cried, arching her back, pushing against his hot tongue rubbing inside her. Her peak loomed once more, but now it was sharper, near frightening.

When she placed her hands against the wall above him, preparing for the ecstasy about to take her, he again set her away, this time pounding her down on him, then surging his hips up.

She caught his gaze. He looked crazed, tortured, his control gone, and that took her over the edge. She cried out, convulsing around him, riding him, rolling her hips as he ground into her, making the pleasure too strong. . . . He watched her climax, his eyes dark and wild on her, fierce with want.

She was still squeezing around him when he wrenched her down against his chest, so rigid and wracked under her hands, until he yelled her name and his hot seed pumped into her.

Thirty-three

*D*iffused sunlight split the curtains in Victoria's room, waking Grant. When he looked down his chest, he was startled to see waves of blond hair covering him. Could he be so fortunate? Could he truly have spent the early hours of the morning making love to her and not just dreamed it again? Yes, last night had been real—incredibly, vividly real.

He was still alarmed by his want of her. Sometimes he felt craven with it. But now, with her sleeping form against his chest, his arms around her, he just wanted to squeeze her, to clasp her tight to him so she could know his feelings for her, how they confounded him in their strength. He'd never thought to have this and flinched to think how close he'd come to throwing it away.

He wanted to luxuriate in simply holding her, but knew he needed to ascertain the damage to the barn and get work under way, so with a weary exhalation, he rose and dressed. Careful not to wake her after the long night, he kissed her before leaving.

When he reached the valley, he saw that no part of the structure remained. In its place was a mound of smoking ash. Grant found Huckabee there and conferred with him, and they set the few who were there to work cleaning the old site.

Grant's first job was to find more workers. His second was to discover who'd dealt them this blow.

Stunned by the events of last night, Tori sat at her grandfather's desk, her emotions hurtling from elation that she and Grant had made love once more to devastation over the fire. When Grant strode through the doorway, she didn't even ask how bad it was. She could already tell from the tightness around his eyes.

He exhaled, then shook his head.

"Right before shearing and lambing," she said in a deadened tone. "Nothing could have hurt us worse."

When Grant raised his eyebrows, she realized she'd said "us." It didn't matter. He'd find out sooner or later that she wasn't letting him leave.

He sank down in the chair across from her and reviewed what he and Huckabee had decided for the rebuilding. "I hope I didn't overstep."

"No, I agree with everything you've said," Tori assured him. "I wouldn't have handled it differently."

He leaned forward and put his elbows on his knees. "Victoria, we need to talk about the actual fire. It was deliberately set."

"That's impossible—"

"I smelled kerosene. There was a puddle of water actually burning, and a section of sodden clay as well. As if someone had pitched the kerosene all around the ground."

She grabbed her forehead. "Why?"

"To send you a warning, I suspect. Or to make you vulnerable."

"Who? Who would—" She broke off as a suspicion arose. "I wrote a letter to the broker just a couple days ago. He'd been shorting us for years. He owes us a huge amount."

"McClure?"

At her nod, he said, "I want a list of all the creditors."

An hour later, after poring over contracts, Grant muttered, "*Son of a bitch.*"

"What?"

"This credit company—West London Financiers. That's the broker's company. M. McClure." He sat at the edge of the desk and slid the documents to her.

"That can't be. Wouldn't there be a conflict of interest?"

"Yes, but this company's as shady as they come. They offer favorable rates of interest, yet in all their contracts they reserve the right to escalate the rate. Just when the borrower has difficulties, McClure tightens the noose."

"How do you know all this?"

"Because several years ago, Ian was in to them for thousands of pounds. He had to borrow money just to pay off McClure's henchmen."

"Oh, my Lord."

"This man was lending the earl what was in essence his own money. He'd cheat Belmont and then extend the earl's credit. There can be no doubt that he wants this place."

She was silent for some time. "Now I know why you put such a high value on your honor." Her eyes were sad. "Because you've dealt with those who have none."

He said nothing.

"Grant, what should I do?" she asked. "Go to the sheriff? Bring the law into this?"

"It won't stop another attack."

Her eyes widened. "You think something like this will happen again?"

He regarded her with a grim expression. "No doubt of it."

She suddenly felt very tired. "What do you suggest?"

"I'd already made up my mind to confront McClure." His eyes narrowed. "Have the bastard beaten if necessary."

Tori was astonished. He looked dark and forbidding.

"If I have to, then I'll play his game to protect what's . . ." He trailed off.

"What's yours," she said quietly. "Like the estate."

He pulled her up to him and put his forehead to hers. "I wasn't speaking of the estate. I meant you."

"How should I know that?" she whispered.

"Because *you* are what I came back here to fight for."

She leaned back, shaking her head. "You don't have to say these things. You came back for the estate, and I understand why—"

"The deed is in your name."

"Wh-What?" she sputtered.

He stroked her cheek. "It has been since before I returned here."

"So why? . . ."

"I couldn't conceive of a better way to be around you."

"So you came back for me?" Her heart beat madly. *For me?*

He nodded solemnly.

"That was your plan?"

"It's always good to have a plan."

She gave him a wry grin. "How's it working out?"

The corners of his lips quirked up. "I am quite optimistic after last night."

"I can't believe you gave it up for me."

He turned from her and his face hardened. "It's not going to matter if McClure burns your home down around you. That's why I'm leaving today—"

"I'm going with you," she interrupted.

He smiled ruefully. "Why did I expect you to say that? I'd already planned to drop you at Whitestone."

She raised her eyebrows at him.

"It's not safe here, and you're not going to London."

"I most certainly am going with you. Or without you," she added ominously.

"This is dangerous. There's no way I'm risking you being hurt. You're going to Whitestone and that's final."

She tapped her cheek and assumed a thoughtful expression. "I hadn't thought your family the type to tie someone down or lock them in a bedchamber."

He looked nonplussed.

"That's the only way they'll keep me there."

"Forget it, Victoria. There's simply no way I'll allow it."

"I can't believe you're still grousing," Victoria said lightly as they walked arm in arm along a side street in London.

He scowled down at her, trying to ignore how excited—and beguiling—she looked with her bonnet ribbons flapping against her pink cheeks. He wanted to kiss her and draw her close. Instead, he grumbled, "I can't believe you manipulated me into taking you with me."

She smiled up at him, eyes adoring. When she looked at him like that, he could deny her nothing. Worse, he feared she'd concluded that as well.

"Grant, I just appealed to your logic. If you'd left me at

Whitestone, I'd have followed. Only then I wouldn't have been be under your watchful eye for protection. Imagine me"—she put her hand to her breast—"on the road to London, alone, afraid . . ."

His lips curled. She smiled back, then looked past him. "Wait, this is it."

He stopped her, placing her to face him. "I want you to say nothing. I'm going to handle this."

She rolled her eyes. "As you've told me twenty times already."

Grant made some growling noise at her and then opened the door for them. "We're here to see Mr. McClure," he said to the office attendant.

The young man looked confused but went to confer with his employer. Minutes later, he returned to show them into the office.

One look at the broker had Grant raising his eyebrows and Victoria dropping her jaw.

M. McClure was a woman.

Thirty-four

*T*ori inwardly groaned when the woman surveyed Grant appreciatively. She smoothed her shining, dark blond hair and sauntered up to him with a hand out. "Miranda McClure," she announced. He clasped her hand, but she thrust it into his palm so that they shook like men.

"Grant Sutherland," he answered in a discomfited voice. Young and alluring, Miranda was probably the last thing he'd expected.

Miranda's gaze flew to Tori, her ice-blue eyes narrowed into a censorious look. "You must be Lady Victoria. How strange, I didn't know you were connected with a Sutherland."

Grant moved closer to Tori. "She's my fiancée."

A pained smile of ruby lips. "How charming."

"Where's Mr. McClure?"

"My father passed away some months ago," she said

with a sigh, looking very aggrieved. "I'm handling his affairs now."

Tori was about to offer condolences, but Grant said, "Let's not waste each other's time. We know your father was bilking the earl out of a fortune and then lending it back to him at astronomical rates."

Tori gaped as the woman's look of sorrow disappeared as if never there. Miranda shrugged prettily. "I'm afraid that's the nature of business. And I believe those notes are due directly."

"Is that why you set the fire?"

"You don't expect me to walk into that one, do you?" She feigned a look of horror. "A fire? My goodness!" Her expression turned wooden. "If I were responsible, I'd never admit it."

"That's not a problem. I'll put this simply. You know that in London, money can mean justice, and I have more of it than you do."

"Oh, yes, those limitless Sutherland coffers. I've heard rumors that you make your own gold out in Surrey." She gave him a dazzling smile. "In fact, I was considering marrying you when you returned."

Tori stiffened. The look of disgust on Grant's face was the only reason Tori didn't slap her.

Miranda flashed Tori an amused glance. "Sheathe your claws, my darling. It's obvious you've got this one locked down."

"Enough of this," Grant said, his voice harsh. "I'd thought of trying to work out a settlement, but it's clear you belong in Newgate."

For the first time, her glowing skin paled and her eyes widened. "What do you think would happen to a woman like me in there?"

Tori answered, "I think you'd be corrupted." She snapped her fingers as though she'd just recalled something. "Oh, too late for that."

When she shot Tori a scathing look, Grant said, "I'd make preparations," then turned to escort Tori out.

"Wait!" Miranda grabbed Grant's other arm. "What if I paid back . . . half of what was owed?"

He gave her an incredulous look. "Too late. And we'll get the full amount from a settlement and still have the satisfaction of knowing you are rotting in a cell."

"What if I paid back everything?" When she saw them still unbending, she added in a sultry voice, "What if I had information? . . ."

"About what?"

"Where has dear cousin Ian gone off to?" She tapped her cheek. "It's not pretty, and I wager he's praying right now for someone to save him."

Grant grabbed her elbow. "Tell me."

She put on a strong front and managed to glare at his hand.

"Talk!"

"Deal?"

He released her. "How do I know you won't come after us again?"

"I would never have knowingly"—she shot a look at Tori—"come after a Sutherland." She put her hand on his lapel, but under his glacial look, she patted it and drew her hand away. "Miranda McClure knows better than to grab a tiger by the tail."

"I want the information now. And, of course, you'll accompany us to the bank."

She cringed at the word "bank." "Fine. But I want to continue being your broker."

"Are you mad? We'd spend our days making sure you didn't rob us again."

"Won't you do that anyway, wherever you go? I *know* I can't get away with it, but someone else might try."

"Forget it."

Tori tapped his shoulder. "Grant, let's hear her information first. She does have a twisted sort of point."

She flashed Tori a beatific smile. And Tori had the odd feeling that Miranda was making a mental note to pay her back the favor. Even more odd, Tori expected it.

"He's aboard a ship called the *Dominion*, based out of Liverpool."

Tori shivered. Even the ship's name sounded ominous.

Grant eyed Miranda suspiciously. "We tracked him to France."

"It last made port at St. Nazaire, then sailed for Foochow," she explained.

Tori shook her head. "Foochow, as in China?"

Grant nodded slowly. Of Miranda, he asked, "How would you know this?"

"I know just about everything underhanded that goes on in this city."

"Who did this to him?" Grant demanded.

"Again, *just about* everything . . . I don't know anything more than what I've told you." Miranda tsked at Grant's still rigid stance and grabbed her hat. "Now, as delightful as this visit has been, may I please go pay you a fortune and be done with you? For today," she added, emphasizing her expectation that they'd do business in the future.

When Miranda entered Cunliffe's Bank, the manager all but licked her boots, though he did seem distressed when she instructed him on the amount to be withdrawn. Tori gaped in open-mouthed astonishment when the woman tickled him under the chin and purred, "I'll come and plump it right back up for you, darling."

Tori looked over her shoulder as they left Cunliffe's. "Do you think we should have asked her more?"

Grant shook his head. "I think we got everything from her. If I'd pushed, she would have started fabricating. But when you were finalizing the settlement, I scratched off a note to our runners, detailing the new findings. They're to watch Miranda as well."

Tori nodded, unsure of what to say. It pained her to think of Ian out there alone, possibly hurt.

Grant slowed and faced her. "Victoria, listen to me. We will find Ian." His tone was without doubt.

She remembered Lady Stanhope describing Grant before he went off to search for Tori's family. He'd said to her, "If they're out there, I *will* return with them." Lady Stanhope had said she couldn't doubt it, though the odds were so against him. Now Tori knew what she meant. One look at Grant, so powerful and strong, his blue eyes clear, and worry lifted from her. They'd find Ian. Period.

"I believe you," she answered as they began walking once more. Yet even with her worry relieved, she found they were in a strange situation, as if they had just completed some grand chore as a team, but now would go their separate ways.

"She's a terror." Grant filled the silence.

"I agree," she said, glad to talk about anything, even McClure. "But as much as she is odd and ambiguous and complicated, I think she has a woman's heart buried underneath those layers of ice. In fact, when I saw her I was worried you might like her."

He stopped walking, looking affronted. "That is not my type."

She turned to him. "I'm sorry, then."

"No harm done."

The conversation was getting awkward. Where did they go from here? What was he thinking after their night together? She knew what she was thinking—that it would be the first of many nights *if they could just live through this conversation*. She plucked at her skirts; he rocked on his heels.

"You must be eager to spend some of that money."

"Oh, yes, especially after stinting—" She stopped. She didn't want to bring up any part of the last few weeks. That time was gone now, in the past. She whipped out a piece of paper from her skirt pocket and read. "I need to buy Cammy some fabric for new dresses—she's outgrown nearly everything—and Mrs. Huckabee a lighter bonnet." Tori shook her head and exhaled. "She'll simply expire this summer in that quilted winter thing she always wears. And Mr. Huckabee needs a walking stick. Huck needs boots." She turned the page over. "Oh, yes. I have his size here. And maybe a toy of some sort . . ."

She glanced up, aware that he was looking at her strangely. Her chin notched higher. "I can justify the expense—he works as hard as any of us and deserves a reward."

He grinned. "I think you should bring Huck a legion of toys if that makes you happy. That wasn't what I was thinking about."

She tilted her head and waited.

"So you've been taking note of what people need?"

"There was the possibility I could get a settlement. And someone once advised me on the importance of planning."

His grin widened. "He must have been a remarkably

intelligent man." She chuckled, but then his expression became intent. "Victoria, I've been planning myself. My entire family will be at the town house before noon, as will Camellia and the baron if they make it in time."

She frowned at him, at his . . . nervousness?

He began pacing. "I believe we can have a good life together. I want you to marry me. And rest assured that I will—"

"Yes, let's!"

"—keep asking till you say . . ." He trailed off. "What did you say?"

"I said yes."

His brows drew together. "But I thought you wouldn't marry without love."

She closed the distance between them and brushed her hands down his long arms. "Oh, you love me."

"Quite sure of yourself?"

She gave him a saucy grin. "Quite sure of you after last night."

He started to turn. "Then I suppose you don't need to hear it. . . ."

She launched herself at him, putting her arms around his neck and pulling herself up to his chest, heedless of the people milling around them. "I can *always* hear that."

He tenderly brushed a curl from her face. "I do love you. I think I love you more than is wholesome." His tone was low and very solemn.

She knew without a doubt that this was the first time he'd said the words. She felt instinctively that it was the first time he'd been in love at all.

That affected her so much. She could forgive the time it had taken for him to realize his love, since he *was* cutting a new trail.

When she gazed up at him and sighed, he said, "And you? Don't leave me out here—"

"Of course I love you—I adore you. I think I always have, even when I would've liked to toss you overboard." Then a thought fluttered through her mind. "Can we stay at the Court?"

"We can live wherever you wish."

"I mean stay and run the sheep farm."

"You need a sheep man. I'm your man." He smiled that heartbreaking smile.

"What about Peregrine Shipping?"

"Nicole and Derek have it running smoothly. And if they want to focus on Whitestone, hell, we'll let Ian run it when we find him."

She stared at him in amazement. Her sly grandfather had predicted this over a year ago and had counted on it when she'd returned. "You're ready for a life with me *and* a village of mostly octogenarians and more sheep than we can count—cheeky sheep at that—and a legion of red-headed Huckabees running about?"

"As long as you're there with me."

"Really?" she asked breathlessly.

"Anything," he said into her hair.

But she pushed him back, then stuck out her hand. "Partners?"

He took it.

Then she pulled him down, and rose on tiptoe to whisper in his ear. "After we get this marriage settled, we need to seal our partnership. Again and again . . ."

Thirty-five

Grant's whole family was indeed at the town home, and Camellia and the baron dashed in just before the minister arrived. Cammy drew Tori aside while Grant was slapped on the back and congratulated by his family and the baron.

Cammy asked, "Are you certain you want to do this?"

"Look at me," Tori said with a laugh. "I'm in love—I can't stop smiling!"

Cammy visibly relaxed. "Then I have to tell you, you're really going to enjoy married life." Cammy held up her hand to display an intricately wrought wedding band encircled with diamonds.

Tori's jaw dropped. "You're married?" Cammy bit her lip, clearly worried how she'd react, but Tori gave her a hug. "Oh, how wonderful! You'll be our neighbor!"

"I thought you might be upset that we did it so suddenly." She lowered her voice. "But the truth is, he wouldn't take me to bed again until I married him, that wretch. When I saw he wasn't jesting, I thought the sooner the better."

"I'm so happy for you!"

Lady Stanhope coughed delicately to get their attention. "Then let's make Cammy happy for you as well, shall we? The minister is waiting."

Grant took her gently by the hand and led her in front of the minister.

When asked for the ring, Grant patted his coat pockets. Everyone in the room seemed to get anxious. Derek groaned in the back and made some comment to Nicole about the beauty of eloping.

Finally, Grant pulled out a small box, covered with velvet. He took out the ring, ready to place it on her finger. Tori looked down; she couldn't help it. Any bride would want to know what she'd be wearing for the rest of her—

A small sob escaped her before she could yank her hand to her mouth.

I need that hand back, Grant thought with alarm. *Or at least that ring finger.* In a shaky voice, he said, "Victoria, I can get you another one."

"But y-you found my mother's ring."

His eyes widened and his gaze flew down. He cursed under his breath. "That was supposed to be for later."

A tear spilled down her cheek, and he could swear he felt her relief as his own. He brushed it away with his thumb.

"I can't believe you found it." She finally took her eyes off the ring and gazed up at him with such love, such raw emotion in her eyes, he was staggered by it.

He took a deep breath, aware that he'd begun speaking, unaware of what he was saying as he looked down into her eyes. "It was more difficult than the other things, but I knew how much it meant to you."

"The other things?" she asked absently.

Now he grinned. "Yes, I was running about the country trying to reacquire the Court's wrought iron, a score of very ancient paintings, one brass knocker, the horse I gave you"—he frowned down at her—"which I *know* was accidentally sold, and a collection of antique jewelry."

"My grandmother's jewelry?"

The way she was smiling up at him, as if he were a hero, made him pull at his collar. "In for a penny . . . ," he mumbled.

Derek cleared his throat. "Grant, give her the other damn ring." The minister eyed him sternly, and Nicole transferred a sleeping Geoff to her other arm so she could pop Derek in the stomach.

Grant patted more pockets and retrieved another small jewel box. He opened it for her, delighted with her reaction. Her mother's ring had made her cry with joy—the emerald made her gasp.

After their ceremony, everyone wished them well but cleared out soon after, the family wanting to give the newlyweds their privacy—or, in the case of Cammy and the baron, the other newlyweds wanting their own privacy.

Once Grant had shut the door on the last of them, he turned to his wife. His *wife*. He liked the sound of that. She was back to her confident self, beaming at him as if they'd just pulled off a coup. She'd let her hair fall from its conservative style and kicked off her shoes, running about in her stockings, and chattering happily. He was baffled that this remarkable woman had chosen him to marry, and humbled that she looked ecstatic about that fact.

Emotion threatened to swamp him. He intercepted her

and clasped her to his chest, putting a hand behind her head and holding her tight. When he bent down to kiss her, she took his hand and pulled him across the parlor. Stepping up on an ottoman so that she was eye level with him, she looped her arms around his neck and kissed and nuzzled his face.

"I love you, Victoria."

"Convince me," she murmured against his lips.

That night and into the next day, Grant and Victoria "sealed their partnership" so many times and in so many ways, Grant knew it could never be broken.

Thirty-six

Three months later . . .

The new sheep barn had been completed just weeks before the shearing crew was to arrive. Spring had exploded on the downs, and Tori and Grant hardly had time to take a breath before the wool was flying.

The shearing had ended just this day, and the village celebrated as it did each year at this time. This season, along with the ale, there were family members who'd heard of the Sutherland marriage and new co-ownership of the Court and had finally returned to their homes.

Tori and Grant joined everyone for the festivities, but after such a long day, they'd decided to return home.

Home. Such a lovely word. And the Court was becoming a lovely place, especially since Grant insisted on pouring money into it. If she smiled at something that was now repaired or beautified or installed, he redoubled his efforts. When she'd wished he wouldn't spend so much, he'd quipped, "We saved a bundle since we don't have to build a manor house for Camellia."

No, indeed. Camellia was living with the baron a few rises over on their own estate. The two were in no hurry to fill it with little ones, but instead enjoyed riding each day over the countryside.

Nearing the Court, Tori and Grant reached the final hilltop and paused to take in the vista before them. He held her in front of him as they gazed out over the valley. Lights twinkled in the distance, and they could still hear the revelry and music floating through the downlands. Contentment washed over her. After lambing, they were going to go to the seashore, where Grant had bought her a cottage right on the beach, near where his family had stayed when he was young. She couldn't wait to see it, and was beyond curious as to why everyone chuckled when she said the word *cottage* or wondered if it would be *cute*.

She sighed. Ian's disappearance was the only shadow on their happiness.

Reading her mind, Grant said, "This adventure has probably been good for him."

She snuggled closer against his chest. In fact, they had recently received word that not only had Ian escaped his captors, he'd started a mutiny and taken *their* ship, bound for somewhere unknown. There were rumors of a scarred, black-haired, and black-hearted devil pirating the South Seas, but Tori adamantly refused to believe that the dates of his marauding and Ian's escape were more than coincidental.

"Ian always lands on his feet, and since the runners have solid leads, we'll find him soon."

"I know," she sighed. "You found me."

Grant nuzzled her neck and smiled against her skin when she shivered in delight. "So don't fret, love." He gently laid his palm over her just rounding belly. "Worrying isn't good for the baby."

Lose yourself in the passion...
Lose yourself in the past...
Lose yourself in a Pocket Book!

The School for Heiresses ❧ Sabrina Jeffries

Experience unforgettable lessons in love for
daring young ladies in this anthology featuring
sizzling stories by Sabrina Jeffries, Liz Carlyle, Julia
London, and Renee Bernard.

Emma and the Outlaw ❧ Linda Lael Miller

Loving a man with a mysterious past can force you
to risk your heart...and your future.

His Boots Under Her Bed ❧ Ana Leigh

Will he be hers forever...or just for one night?

Relive the romance of days gone by
with Pocket Books!

Only a Duke Will Do ❧ Sabrina Jeffries
The School for Heiresses Series
A duke was the only man who could ever capture her heart—
and the only man who could ever break it.

Fairy Tale ❧ Jillian Hunter
To regain control of his castle, a Highlander must fight
the battle of his life...and surrender his heart.

A Woman Scorned ❧ Liz Carlyle
Forget fury—hell hath no passion like a woman scorned.

Lily and the Major ❧ Linda Lael Miller
In the major's arms she discovered how tender—
and how bold—true love could be.